Theodore Stanton, François J. Le Goff

The Life of Louis Adolphe Thiers

Theodore Stanton, François J. Le Goff

The Life of Louis Adolphe Thiers

ISBN/EAN: 9783337369804

Printed in Europe, USA, Canada, Australia, Japan

Cover: Foto ©Andreas Hilbeck / pixelio.de

More available books at **www.hansebooks.com**

L. R. Goodrich.

THE LIFE OF

LOUIS ADOLPHE THIERS

BY

FRANÇOIS LE GOFF

DOCTEUR-ÈS-LETTRES

TRANSLATED FROM THE UNPUBLISHED MANUSCRIPT

BY

THEODORE STANTON, A. M.

Patriam dilexit, veritatem coluit.

NEW YORK

G. P PUTNAM'S SONS

182 FIFTH AVENUE

1879

DEDICATION.

To M. J. BARTHÉLEMY ST. HILAIRE,
    Senator and Member of the Institute.

   In authorizing me to place your name at the head of this History of your illustrious friend, you give my work a most valued endorsement. I thank you for this in my own name and in that of my readers in the great American Republic. No testimony of confidence and esteem could honor me more, and my readers could not have a better guarantee of the spirit of justice and of truth, which has inspired the work now offered to them from across the ocean.

                                     F. LeG.

TRANSLATOR'S NOTE.

My own part in the preparation of this volume has been more than that of Translator. From the Author's large mass of manuscript, I have selected and arranged these three or four hundred pages. I have, either by clauses in the body of the page or by notes at the bottom, endeavored to explain references to French politics and customs, and to fairly identify the different characters mentioned; and I trust that I have, through the data thus given, succeeded in making the narrative sufficiently clear and complete. I have also, in a few instances, inserted an anecdote or letter, and added a paragraph or two that I thought would interest the American public. The opinions, however, expressed in this book belong to the Author.

The portrait of Thiers in this volume is engraved from an *eau-forte* of the celebrated painting of Bonnat. Thiers's Paris *hôtel* is from a photograph made for this work by M. Carjat, one of the best Parisian photographers. The *fac-simile* of Thiers's handwriting is from a photograph also by M. Carjat, taken, by the kind permission and under the obliging direction of Mme. Thiers, from the original manuscript of Thiers's famous posthumous letter to his constituents. I am indebted to Chief-Justice Geo. Shea, of the Marine Court, for the autograph of Thiers found under the portrait.

T. S.

Ithaca, N. Y.
December, 1878.

CONTENTS

AUTHOR'S PREFACE.

I do not think you have an exact idea in America of France. The Atlantic seems to hide her from you or lets you see her only through dense mists. The illusion often remains, even after the distance that separates you from her has been passed over. Afar off, you see little or you see badly; near by, the brilliant and agitated foreground alone attracts your gaze; you do not see the background, or rather the delicate blending of the colors, which is as important for an exact and complete understanding of a picture as the background itself. This phenomenon, however, is easily explained. An old society which aspires to a loftier life, to a new growth, which is struggling to throw off the narrow robe of the past, does not resemble a young society, full-grown, which cuts out for itself a generous garment from a tissue woven by its own hands. The same institutions do not breathe the same spirit there, nor have words the same signification, and, what appears not less strange, the same principles do not produce the same consequences. The best persons are liable, therefore, unless on their guard, to make mistakes concerning men as well as things, so that good intentions and impartial judgment are not always safe guides.

Perhaps there is not a more striking example of this facility of delusion concerning France, than the opinion of Thiers, expressed by Mr. John Bigelow in his book entitled *France and Hereditary Monarchy*, published in 1871. Party spirit has rarely brought against the illustrious statesman, even in his own country, so many and so grave accusations. Without limiting himself to those which might have their *raison d'être* in the events of the day, and which sprang, as it were, from the still smoking ruins of Paris, Mr. Bigelow has been pleased to go back to the earliest political life of the statesman whom he has taken to task, and he finds there almost all the germs of the misfortunes that have befallen France for more than twenty-five years. If the last of the Napoleons undertook that foolish and terrible war which overthrew his dynasty and mutilated his country, it is the fault of Thiers. If Louis Philippe fell from the throne in 1848, it is likewise the fault of Thiers. If the Empire arose in 1851 on the ruins of the Republic, it is again the fault of

Thiers, who, in reviving the Napoleonic legend, restored the adoration of Bonaparte and thus prepared a name and an instrument for despotism. Thiers, according to Mr. Bigelow, was not less hurtful during the latter part of his life than during this early period. As soon as he came upon the scene again, near the end of the second Empire, he is the auxiliary of the ultramontanes in their anti-gallican policy, and the enemy of all legislation favorable to the emancipation of the schools, opening them to the light of modern thought and popular influence; and, finally, placed at the head of the executive power by the Assembly at Bordeaux in 1871, Thiers was justly suspected of preparing the return of the Orleans Monarchy, (Mr. Bigelow's words are: "was merely warming the bed for some scion of the House of Bourbon;") of reviving the despotism he had combated, and of placing the government in an attitude of marked hostility towards the governed.*

---

* *France and Hereditary Monarchy*, pp. 9 and 10.

President White, of Cornell University, one of our best read students of French history, has about the same opinion as Mr. Bigelow concerning Thiers, if we may judge from the following extracts from a letter to the translator of this volume :

"Though Mr. Thiers' life has been very interesting, I have never admired him in the slightest degree, until the last days of his career, beginning with the close of the Franco-German struggle. Before that time, he seemed to me a curse to his country and to Europe , but then he became a sublimely energetic and patriotic public servant. * * * To him more than any other man in France is due a sort of Mephistophelian deification of Revolution on the one hand, and of Napoleonic despotism on the other. Yet, he did more to heal the wounds he had done so much to cause, than any other man could do."

If Mr. Bigelow were to draw up his act of accusation to-day, he would no doubt revise it in more than one of its articles. Recent events have thrown a light on certain points before obscured, which render all illusion of perspective impossible, and brings clearly before the most inattentive eyes the character of the man and the unity of his life. There cannot, I think, remain a doubt concerning the unity of the political life of Thiers after the perusal of this sketch. I have followed Thiers throughout almost all of his career with keen and constant interest, not to say regard; I have read all that he has written, all that he has spoken in the tribune; I have heard him deliver most of his great speeches for the last ten years; I knew him personally and I am acquainted with many of his friends. To this knowledge of my subject, I think I may add a fair share of impartiality.

In closing this preface, I would remark, that in spite of the great interest attached to the public life of a man who, occupied during more than a half century, so important a place in the history of his country, who played the first part under such different circumstances, and in such various situations, it is not so much Thiers whom I have in view in speaking of the former President of the French Republic, of the historian of the *Consulate and Empire*, of the Ex-minister of Louis Philippe, as the country and the epoch in which his long life was passed. It will be for me a sort of pretext, a means, the best perhaps, of penetrating into the intricacies of a society complicated of itself, rendered more perplexing by the agitations of its surface, and of seizing out the difficulties of the problems there being discussed, the passions and interests which there dispute for empire. All of these problems, passions and interests are grouped about Thiers, and form, as it were, his retinue. The light that he emits will flash upon them and will aid us to see clearly into this " visible darkness."

FRANÇOIS LEGOFF,

July 1878.   •   44 rue Monge, Paris.

LOUIS ADOLPH THIERS.

CHAPTER I.

EARLY LIFE.—1797–1829.

Thiers was born at Marseilles on the morning of April 15th, 1797, at ten minutes past two, in his grandmother's house, number 15 rue des Petits-Pères. The house to-day bears the number 40.* His mother's name was Marie Madeleine Amic: his father's, Pierre Louis Marie Thiers. He was baptized Marie Joseph Louis Adolphe, the first two names in honor of the poet Marie Joseph Chénier, who was his second cousin, Thiers's grandmother on his mother's side being the sister of the mother of the Chéniers.

The physician who was present at the birth of Thiers pronounced the child "turbulent and very viable,"† characteristics that were seen in the whole after life of the man, who was one of the most active spirits of his time, whose remarkable vitality carried him through four political revolutions, supported him in the midst of immense literary labors, and only failed him after he had passed the advanced age of four score years.

---

* See Appendix A for the Registry of Birth.

† See Appendix B for the curious note found in the diary of this physician.

On his mother's side, Thiers was of eastern origin, His grandfather was a merchant of Marseilles, but his grandmother, named Santi-Lomaïca,.was a Greek. They were as familiar with the Greek language as with the Provençal; were courageous, impressionable, quick to anger and not less prompt to reconciliation. They were strongly attached to royalty. The father of Thiers, on the contrary, was a friend of the Revolution and had even played a part in it as a member of the Committee of Public Safety at Marseilles. When the reaction against the Terrorists set in,* fearing for his safety, he was introduced into the Amic family by a common friend — an Italian lady, who lived at Château-Gombert, a little spot in the environs of Marseilles, — where he was sure his enemies would not follow him. Mlle. Amic fell in love with the guest of her father, touched by his misfortunes, dazzled, doubtless, also by the brilliancy of his mind, the distinction of his manners; and, in spite of his poverty, his widowhood, his family embarrassments — he had some children — in spite of his revolutionary opinions which she detested, Mlle. Amic decided to marry him. She was a beautiful girl, of a lively imagination of ready and highly-colored conversational powers, like all the children of Marseilles, and of an energetic and decided character.

It is customary to-day to endeavor to find in the gen-

---

* Robespierre, the soul of the Reign of Terror, was guillotined on July 27th, 1794,—the 9th Thermidor —and the Directory then came into power with milder measures.

ealogy of celebrated men the precursory signs, the psychologic seeds of their future growth and genius. Atavism has become one of the factors of history. Thiers was not repugnant to this doctrine, perhaps because he knew his own pedigree. What we have just said concerning his mother's family does not contradict the influence of origin, nor does that which is known and which he was accustomed to tell voluntarily concerning his father and his father's ancestors.

The paternal family of Thiers, which belonged to that ancient *bourgeoisie* of Marseilles that from 1560 to 1775 exercised in that city an almost absolute power, presents, in the course of three generations, some singular and not mediocre types. His great-grandfather, a rich merchant, talented, loving society and good eating, giving grand dinners, was finally ruined in speculations with the French colonies and died at the age of ninety-seven. His grandfather was appointed archivist of Marseilles by a decree of Louis XV, dated at Versailles, September 16th, 1770, in which, referring to the three candidates presented by the Municipal Council of Marseilles to fill the vacancy, the royal document reads: "His Majesty considers all three of them worthy, yet, being well informed of the fidelity and affection for his service of M. Charles Thiers, advocate at the Parliament of Aix, His Majesty designates him to exercise the functions of the office." He also wrote an able history of Provence, was a sturdy royalist, and died in his ninety-fifth year, pursued by the

wrath of his republican enemies. The father of Thiers
did not hold to the monarchical beliefs of his ancestors,
nor does he appear to have led as upright a life. His
father left him about ten thousand dollars — not a small
fortune in those days — which he quickly wasted in wild
speculations and in dissipations of the worst kind.* The
father of Thiers would be called in the parlance of to-day
a "fast" man. He was a wandering and original character, a great lover of novelties and adventures, a grand
builder of air-castles, by turns merchant, theatrical man-
ager, director of a gambling house, knowing everything,
talking about everything, never embarrassed by a question, sometimes rich, oftener poor, but never losing faith
in himself or despairing of the future. How many of
these characteristics he transmitted to his son! Good
sense, however, he seemed to lack, a quality that the
son, fortunately for his success, possessed in a large
degree.

Thiers's first years were spent either at Marseilles or in
short visits to little towns in the environs of the city. As
he advanced in years his physical development was slower than his mental. When he was seven years old he had
the stature and the features of a child of four or five. At
this period he was sent to a school where he acquired the
principles of the French and Latin languages, and at nine
he became a day scholar at the Marseilles Lycée.†

---

* *Adolphe Thiers*, by Achille Gastaldy, page 17.

† A Lycée in France is the State school that prepares for the University ;
it partakes of the nature both of our college and high school.

The school bills were paid by one of Thiers's aunts and by a cousin, the latter being the wife of a rich Marseilles merchant. Three years later, as the result of a competitive examination, he gained one of the scholarships at the Lycée. This was in 1809, at the age of twelve.

The delighted mother, too poor to educate her son and sensitive at his dependence on his relations, writes to the Mayor of Marseilles the following letter, which has recently been discovered among the archives of that city.

MR. MAYOR :

Accept my thanks for the attention you have shown me in informing me of the admission of my son to the Lycée of this city, by the letter with which you honored me, the fourth of this month ; he will try to make himself worthy of the favor, by his application and exactness, and thus merit in some degree the esteem of his superiors and of the head of the University ; yours also, sir, will be very flattering.

I have the honor to be, with respectful consideration, sir, your very humble servant,

THIERS *née* Amic.

His collegiate career did not fail to respond to the high hopes expressed in this letter. The young bursar was one of the most brilliant and studious scholars of the Lycée. The new University * while remaining classic, gave, in its curriculum, a large place to history, geogra-

---

* Napoleon I, by the decree of March, 17th 1808, established the University of France a great system of education by the State, embracing Primary and University instruction, which still exists in all essential particulars as marked out by its founder. "University," therefore, in France, means the whole system of public education.

phy and the mathematical sciences.   Thiers embraced all
with equal ardor and equal success.

Thiers says in one of the passages of his *Consulate and
Empire*, that there is but one miracle in the world, good
sense seconded by determined will.   He attributes all the
real success of individuals as well as peoples to the union
of these two powers.   This truth would not have been suggested to him by the study of history, if he had not
found it in his own mind and in the history of his own life.
There are few self-made men who have risen to prominence, in whom this trait is more distinctly seen, or who
grasped its meaning at an earlier hour.   Some one has remarked that Thiers was inspired by it even in his college
days, and that ever since it has accompanied him like a
familar spirit.

Two particular influences, besides the general influences
arising from study itself and a classical education, seem
to have acted strongly on Thiers's mind at the Lycée and
to have contributed a great deal towards giving it a certain direction—that of one of his professors, M. Maillet-
Lacoste, and that of the military spirit of the first Empire,
whose victorious bulletins, read aloud in the class-rooms,
in the dining hall and in the lecture rooms, then formed a
part of the University programme.

Maillet-Lacoste, a graduate of the Polytechnic school,
had had the misfortune to write against the Empire, for
which reason he was sent in disgrace by M. de Fontanes,
grand-master of the University, to teach in the Lycée of

Marseilles. He had aspired to be an engineer, but was
forced to be a college professor. A man of refinement
and lofty sentiments, he soon gained great influence over
his pupils. Thiers felt himself drawn towards him. The
young professor was struck by the intelligence of his
pupil. They frequently walked and conversed together.
History, politics, art, all topics were discussed on these
occasions and discussed on an elevated plain. Thiers
never forgot this early teacher and ever spoke of him
with respect.

The greater part of the students of the Lycécs of this
period, dazzled by the glories of the First Empire, had
their thoughts turned towards a military career. The
young bursar of Marseilles did not escape the fascination, and we can imagine the future historian of the *Consulate and Empire*, dreaming on the college benches of a
participation in that military glory which at a later day
he was to celebrate. In fact, Thiers always had a strong
taste for military affairs, and gave considerable thought
to questions of this nature. When the last bill concerning the reorganization of the French army was being
discussed in the Assembly a few years ago, a witty cari-
caturist drew a sketch of Thiers astride a drum, in the
uniform of an *enfant de troupe** of 1832, with the words
"Old Soldier" written under the picture. The artist's
fancy could have gone back farther into the past, and he
might have pictured the schoolboy, in the midst of his

---

* An *enfant de troupe* is a soldier's son brought up in the barracks at
the expense of the State.

games, dressed in the uniform of a *pupille de la garde,**
or dreaming in a corner of the study-room of the future
battles of Marengo or Austerlitz, and of the laurels that
awaited his prowess. But at the moment when these
dreams might have become realities, a new order of
things was instituted which opened another career to his
talents and offered other hopes to his ambition.

The Empire fell, and the Charter of Louis XVIII was
given France, and along with the Charter, enough liberty ·
to inspire the hope of being able to gain more. It was
1815. Thiers was eighteen. He had left the Lycée
covered with honors, to enter the law school at Aix.
An aunt and a friend of the family furnished the funds
that were needed. The young law student, with that
rapidity of glance and that prompt decision which are
not the least marked traits of his character, saw in a moment that politics was going to supplant arms, and that,
for him, the forum was to be more important than the
camp. His course was quickly chosen: politics henceforth became his chief occupation, and, for that matter,
the chief occupation of the college world. At Aix as
elsewhere—more than elsewhere perhaps—the new phase
into which the Revolution entered, now brought face to
face with its old enemies, was warmly welcomed, and the
struggle was more intense as the reaction was more
violent.

The *pupilles de la garde* were a body of youth attached to the guard of
Napoleon I.

The young Thiers, who was not, as can be imagined, the least ardent, was not slow in taking a prominent position among his fellow-students as an advocate of liberal principles. Independently of the earnest views which sprang in common from the closely united body of students, Thiers boldly assumed a more advanced position, and charmed his companions by his inexhaustible fund of information, by the piquancy of his language and by his eloquence, so brilliant, so full of feeling and so French. He had also, at this early date, what he never failed to have up to the day of his death, numerous friends and numerous enemies. It was, so to speak, the prelude of his after life. And he had intimate friends not only within the walls of the law school, but also in the city, where his name had caused not a little commotion. Among his college friends, Mignet, the distinguished historian, should be mentioned particularly, to whom he made the first proffer of friendship and with whom he was closely united throughout his whole life.

Aix opened to Thiers a freer, larger and more animated field than he had found at Marseilles, and circumstances seemed to conspire to bring into play the most striking and original qualities of his mind. Aix was a learned city. Besides its law school and its court of appeals, it possessed a nobility which contained a great number of distinguished men who had a keen relish for intellectual subjects. Thiers here found himself in his element. Mignet introduced his friend to the most hon-

orable and enlightened personages of the city. Thiers
was well received because of his vivacity and his already
inexhaustible conversational powers. Some aristocratic
and even Legitimist families* welcomed him to their
parlors. They called him the "little Jacobin," but he
did not hide his opinions. He never "put his flag in his
pocket," as he has been accused of doing. Royalism was
powerful at Aix; Liberalism was only the more ardent
for this very reason. It dominated on the benches of
the law school, and Thiers might be called its leader.
He had founded a club called the Cénacle—a sort of
debating society, where politics were tabooed. Thiers,
however, was the first to break over the rule. Politics
was his passion. He was preparing himself for the
future.

To this epoch belongs an episode with which the name
of M. d'Arlatan de Lauris, a judge of the court of appeals and a member of the academy of Aix, is connected.
Though found in all the biographical notices of Thiers,
it cannot be omitted here, for, besides its raciness of detail, it throws the first important light upon his character.
We refer to his *Eulogy on Vauvenargues.*†

The Academy of Aix had offered a prize for the best
eulogy on the young moralist, a friend of Voltaire. Vauvenargues's touching fate, his sturdy upright character, his

---

* The Legitimists are the adherents of the old monarchy, overthrown
first in 1793 and again in 1830.

† Vauvenargues. a French moralist born in 1715 at Aix, died in 1747,
after long suffering from diseases contracted in the army.

love of glory, that moderate system of philosophy which
was also Thiers's, in which thought and action combine and
balance, the fact, not unimportant to a youth, that he was
a native of the same province, so captivated his young
compatriot, that when M. de Lauris, who perceived
Thiers's abilities and divined his future, advised him to
compete for the prize, he was only too eager to do so.

His essay, written in a clear rapid style, where more attention was paid to the thoughts than to the language, and
animated by the fire of hopeful youth, was considered excellent ; but the name of the author had been divulged, and
it was not the time nor the country in which justice alone
was to decide upon merit even in the most harmless
things.   The royalists had a majority in the academy and
they determined to let the "little Jacobin," know it.
They did not, however, carry their partiality so far as to
award the prize to another, but contented themselves
with adjourning the contest to the next year, hoping to
have competitors more to their taste.   But Thiers, with
the obstinacy of youth, was resolved to have the prize
that belonged to him, and since the judges refused to
give it to him, he determined to snatch it from them.
He rewrote his eulogy on Vauvenargues and sent it once
more to the academy.   But this time, in order to put
them on the wrong scent and to outwit their partisan-
ship, he had the essay forwarded from Paris, through the
medium of a Parisian friend, whom he had let into the
secret.   He also took good care to hand in his former

essay without changing it in the slightest particular, except that of the handwriting. The academy fell into the trap, adjudged the prize to the essay sent from Paris, and made honorable mention of that dated from Aix. It is said that the academicians took their discomfiture with good grace, while Thiers, besides the joy of a double triumph, had also the pleasure of laughing at his judges, a pleasure without alloy since he had won his case.

This eulogy on Vauvenargues, by which Thiers made his *début* in letters, is of great importance to the student of his character, not simply on account of the little episode that it gave rise to, which, characteristic of the man, was not much more than a youthful frolic, but more particularly on account of the nature of the ideas and the way of looking at human destiny therein exposed. The youth traces the course he is to pursue in manhood, and points out clearly the aim he has in view. Action, according to Thiers, is the object and the province of life. "Since man is put on earth to work," he says, "the more he does, the more he fulfills his end." There is nothing extraordinary in this thought, the contrary being an absurdity. Its significance lies in the fact that as soon as the author sees his object, he disengages it from all the systems which might tend to enervate our activity by declaring the supreme reward of all our efforts to be found in an obscure and mysterious future. He does not deny the truth of these systems, whether religious or philosophical, but contents himself with not discussing them. He has to do with certain, visible, incontestable reality. He would ascertain the laws of our being which incite to action, and which are summed up in the exercise of our energies, and hence it is that he concludes that the aim and the reward, that work and pay, are the same thing. "Life is action," says Thiers, "and whatever the prize may be, the employment of our own powers is enough to satisfy us because it is the accomplishment of our nature." It is under the patronage of Vauvenargues that Thiers advances this thought, which is only, in fact, the formula of all the philosophy of the eighteenth century. Yet, at the same time, it is none the less his own, since this idea continually manifested itself during the whole course of his life, which was one long labor in a single cause, a continual exercise of the most elevated faculties, tending always towards some practical end, seeking no other recompense than that which emanated from the struggle, the effort and the result.

In France, politicians rarely rise to prominence in the provinces, where superior intellects are often outstripped by mediocre ones. Thiers knew this. He was graduated from the law school in 1820. In 1821, about the month of July, his friend Mignet left Aix for the capital, and in less than three months thereafter, Thiers joined him, armed with his diploma (of which he was to make no use), his courage and great confidence in himself and his future.

This latter sentiment, so powerful a factor in a suc-

cessful career, showed itself early in the life of Thiers.
He was accustomed to remark, in moments of friendly
communion with Mignet and in conversation with his
fellow-students, "When we are ministers———." He did
not hesitate to speak freely on this subject, even in public, and he does not appear to have been always over-
particular concerning the choice of his confidants. Thiers
was by nature careless and unreserved.

There stood at the gate of the law school of Aix, an
old apple-woman with whom Thiers frequently chatted.
The poor woman often complained of her lot, while
the young student, in order to reconcile her to the present, would talk to her of the future, especially of his
own, and would make fine promises, which, all in fun, he
would say he hoped might be fulfilled. "I know, my
good woman, that times are hard," he would remark,
"but be patient, they will change. When I am minister,
I will, of course, have a fine residence, and you will see
me some day coming in a coach to take you home.
That will be a gala day for us."

Thiers, notwithstanding his poverty, did not encounter
in his early efforts those sore trials which often check
the advance of the most talented minds. Dr. Johnson's
famous couplet,

> This mournful truth is everywhere confess'd,
> Slow rises worth by poverty depress'd,

is not true in Thiers's case. Thiers was, however, in
straightened circumstances for at least a year and a half

after coming to Paris.   He was at this time closely united
with the young literary circle that Abel Hugo, brother of
the poet, had brought together, and which, in summer, on
Thursdays, used to take dinner at Montrouge, on the
outskirts of the city, in the saloon kept by mother Saget,
as the landlady was called.   She did not then know what
a galaxy of future politicians and publicists were her
patrons.   One day in the year 1832, while looking over
her old account books, she was almost beside herself with
joy at finding that a *haricot de mouton* was still unpaid on
Thiers's bill, and Thiers was a minister!   The minor
journals of the time recounted the fact with merriment,
and the old dame all rigged out in her best, called on the
minister and the little debt was handsomely liquidated.

He had been recommended to Manuel, one of the
most popular leaders of the Liberal party, who opened
to him the doors of journalism.   He entered the
office of the *Constitutionnel.*   The views advocated
by this newspaper, the most credited of the opposition press, accorded with his own.   M. Étienne, a
man of wit and talent, the editor-in-chief of the *Constitutionnel,* had a disposition that exactly chimed in with
that of Thiers's, and they were soon on intimate terms.
The first article from Thiers's pen produced a favorable
impression on the managers of the paper, and those that
followed were eagerly seized and relished by the public.
One of them in particular, a review of the famous work

of M. de Montlosier on the French monarchy,* created a great sensation. His friends, and enemies, too, recognized in this production the hand of a polemic as well as the spirit of a historian and statesman. Thiers was not then twenty-five years old. He had arrived in Paris in September, 1821. His article on Montlosier appeared in the month of March following. In less than six months, he had won a reputation as a journalist, and had acquired a position in that Opposition of the Restoration, which, after the death of Louis XVIII, was to have such a powerful influence on public opinion, and to become so redoubtable an enemy of the monarchy. Thiers, though only in his first campaign, might have exclaimed with Cæsar, *veni, vidi, vici.*

This first campaign, furthermore, was marked by other successes gained in different fields of literary labor, which were not less flattering and brilliant than these journalistic and political triumphs. Thiers's intellect was as comprehensive as active. He liked to grasp different subjects and to range over several departments at one time. So, while by the superiority of his controversial powers, he boldly took possession of the editorial page of the *Constitutionnel,* he gave to the same journal remarkable articles on art criticism, and shortly afterwards an account of an excursion into the Pyrenees. At this same period, the busy journalist threw off a curious biographical sketch of Miss Bellamy, an actress who figured at Covent-Gar-

---

* *De la Monarchie française depuis son établissement jusqu'à nos jours.*

den at the close of the last century, and it is found preserved at the beginning of her memoirs.

The French politician, though distinguished as a journalist and orator, still lacks an important factor of success, if he is not an adept in the ways of the political
salons. In that society, so intelligent, so elegant in manners and education, the art of pleasing makes a part of
the art of governing, and it becomes necessary to conquer the men of the world as well as those of the market-
place. If this is true even to-day in Democratic France,
how much more so must it have been under the Restoration, when the body politic was made up of a select class
of electors. The *salons* were then as important politically as an American convention : there were made deputies,
ministers and even revolutions.*

Though impersonal journalism, by shielding the writer
and merging his individuality in that of the journal, has
its advantages, it has its objectionable features also, at
least for him, since his fame is confined to a narrow circle and does not consequently help in his advancement.
The *salons*, however, partially do away with this objection.
The invisible hand which strikes the blow is now recognized ; it can be grasped in the evening after the morning's combat ; the champions who had just pierced
through the shield of M. de Villèle † with a sharp-pointed
arrow, or who had thrown down the gauntlet to Prince

---

* It has often been said that the Revolution of 1830 started in the draw-
ing-room of M. Laffitte, the celebrated banker and statesman.
† Prime Minister from 1821 to 1827.

Polignac,* can now be seen face to face. The leaders are distinguished from the confused mass of followers; they leave the ranks and show themselves to the public.

Thiers aspired to be more than an editor, and he did not fail to play this card. At first he was received into the *salon* of M. Laffitte; and soon afterwards, M. de La Rochefoucauld-Liancourt, a distinguished member of one of the old aristocratic families of France, M. de Flahaut one of Napoleon's officers, Prince Talleyrand and others, were glad to welcome the vivacious journalist into their polite circles. He everywhere attracted attention by his brilliant animation, his wonderful conversational powers, so rich in facts and ideas, and by that precocious sagacity which enabled him to distinguish the true current of events and to divine their earliest tendencies. It was this latter faculty in particular that struck Talleyrand, who possessing it himself in a high degree, felt its importance, and knew that without it no one is worthy of the name of statesman. A witticism of Talleyrand, that has often been cited, shows in what esteem he held Thiers, and how well he read his character. It was in 1827, after the great success of Thiers's *History of the French Revolution*, that some one referring to the author, remarked rather contemptuously in the presence of the aged diplomatist, " Here's a self-made man." " No, he's a made man." † responded Talleyrand, indicating by this

---

* Last Prime Minister of Charles X.

† " Le voilà parvenu. '   " Non, il est arrivé."

mot, that Thiers belonged to that class of able minds which secure distinction without effort, and which properly form a part of that aristocracy of intellect to which all men may aspire.

The *History of the French Revolution* showed what the author was capable of, and at the same time, gave him great popularity. The work did not, however, reach the highest point of its success at its first appearance. The first two volumes, which comprise the history of the Constituent and Legislative Assemblies, appeared in 1823. Though spirited and filled with many happily inspired pages, they did not make the impression that was expected, and the historian fell short of the journalist. The work lacked strength. Though experienced beyond his years, Thiers did not possess the knowledge nor the maturity of judgment that such an undertaking demanded. He knew it, and began forthwith to prepare himself for the better execution of the remainder of the task. In spite of his extraordinary powers of application, he had been able only to skim over the special studies which the modern historian must be familiar with, in order to produce a great and lasting work. He resolved to master them, and with this end in view, determined to make use of the splendid opportunities that surrounded him. He learned finance from Baron Louis, Minister of the Finances under Louis XVIII, war from General Foy, who served under Napoleon, and from the celebrated military writer Jomini, and he consulted Talleyrand more than

once about foreign politics, and many other contemporaries concerning the events and actors of the great epoch
which he was to describe. Thiers's historical work is
faithfully done. He has neglected no source of information, recoiled before no fatigue, and has made every effort
to get at the truth. Though there are some grave errors
in the *History*, he did all he could to avoid them. There
are numerous proofs of his honesty and carefulness.*

The success responded to the effort. With the third
volume the nature of the work changes. It is more substantial, more vigorous and more spirited. There is more
color and force in the style. France could now claim
one more historical monument, which, though unequal
and even feeble in some of its parts, did not fall far
below the subject, nor the impression left by it in the
minds of men. The ten volumes of the original edition
of the work appeared during the period extending from
1823 to 1827, and were issued in parts. A successful sale
was assured after the publication of the third volume.
The first edition, however, was not remunerative, and it
was by the subsequent editions that the author received
his compensation.

Few books have made more noise or given rise to more
discussion than the *History of the French Revolution*. It
offended the royalists, who considered it an eloquent re-
habilitation of the memorable event, even the most honorable representatives of which, they daily stigmatized;

---

* See Appendix C.

it was a triumph and a hope for the Liberals, who saw revived, on a large and brilliant scale, great names which had been forgotten or never fully appreciated, and whose virtues were easily distinguished from the faults that marred them. Everybody considered it a bold act, a fearless and superb challenge. Even the historical method and the philosophical conception of the work were a stimulus to controversy, and a ground for hatred or sympathy for the author. He was accused of political skepticism, of historical fatalism, of partiality, of indifference, of adoration of force and success; as if it were sacrificing virtue to chance to point out how even the best men are liable to errors of judgment; as if it were to be without political honesty or deliberate and decided preferences to indicate the crimes of liberty or the allurements of glory. His friends easily repelled these attacks, and mitigated by increased esteem and sympathy the effects of the hatred and injury that his talent and courage had called down upon him.

This immense work, though laborious and absorbing, had not completely removed Thiers from militant journalism. In truth, it was only an isolated and victorious campaign, a sort of expedition to Egypt, in the great war undertaken against the menacing conduct of the old monarchy. He had not, for an instant, deserted his post on the *Constitutionnel.* He had even performed other tasks. In 1823 he was associated with Rémusat, the politician and writer, and Jouffroy, the well-known philosopher, on the *Tablettes Historiques*, a periodical publication. Thiers wrote the articles that appeared under the head of Political Bulletin. They were filled with the most caustic irony, tempered by exquisite French urbanity. A good critic of the period said that these articles were superior to anything that had appeared in the political press for a long time, and that he was certain that he recognized in them the stamp of a courtier of the old *régime*. He was astonished when told that they were written by a young man of twenty-five.

In 1824, together with Jouffroy and Mignet, he wrote for the *Globe* newspaper; in 1826, he contributed to the *Encyclopédie Progressive;* and in 1828 he published a book on John Law* and his system, in which he laid down the principles of credit and explained the functions of banks in his usual clear way, and with an ability which, considering the absence of special preparation, is remarkable.

But all this was not enough to satisfy Thiers's indefatigable activity and that desire for perpetual movement which is the foundation of his nature. After the *History of the French Revolution*, he wished to write a work on general history. He was contemplating a journey through Europe in order to collect data for this purpose, when it was announced that Laplace was preparing for his great voyage around the world. Curiosity immediately turned

---

* John Law, the Scotchman, who introduced into France, in the first quarter of the last century, a disastrous system of finance, based on paper money.

Thiers in this direction.   Besides the scientific interest
attached to such an enterprise, there was that about it
to tempt a sturdy, adventurous mind, eager for new impressions and discoveries which might tend to increase
his reputation.   He therefore took the steps necessary
to become a member of the expedition, and was ready
to embark when a political event, long foreseen, but
not considered imminent, abruptly changed his plans.

On August 8th, 1829, the Polignac ministry was formed.
The Martignac ministry, which it succeeded, had been
only a truce; open war was declared against the principles of the French Revolution.   It was no time to desert
the field of battle.   Thiers remained.   Long armed for
the final struggle, he determined to throw himself into
it, body and soul, and to wage an uncompromising warfare on this counter-revolution which the Restoration
had inaugurated.

But before entering upon an account of the new career
which the revolution of 1830 opened to him, we desire
to say a word concerning the man himself, and to discreetly unveil a portion of his private life.

It is difficult to imagine how a romance could insinuate itself into the busy youth of Thiers.   But Thiers
always had time for everything.   He had time for friendship, and he found leisure more than once for love.

His first passion dates from the law school of Aix, a
passion which, romantic in its beginning, came near being
tragic in its end.   The young lady who captivated Thiers

was beautiful and was endowed with all the moral qualities that could have been desired. He fell seriously in
love with her, and was soon engaged. But she was
poor; Thiers himself was far from being rich, and although he did not doubt of being so some day, still he
did not wish to inflict upon her all the trials and hazards
of a struggle for competence. It was agreed that the
marriage should be put off until better days began for
Thiers. He then left for Paris.

If a contemporary report can be believed, Thiers said,
one day, during the July monarchy, *à-propos* of the un-
successful efforts of the Duke of Orleans, eldest son of
Louis-Philippe, to obtain a wife from some one of the
royal families of Europe, "*Parvenus* ought to marry late."
Did this remark, so pointed in its application and which
would have come with better grace from Berryer,[*] eman-
ate from Thiers's recollection of his own conduct in this
matter of matrimony? Should we look for the cause of
the non-fulfillment of the vows of a young and inexperi-
enced lover, in his own belief in this ambitious and selfish
maxim? However this may be, the father and his
daughter having occasion to go to Paris after Thiers's
departure, saw him and demanded that the marriage be
consummated. Thiers was rising fast at the capital, as
has been seen, but he was not yet firmly established, and,

---

[*] M. Berryer, (1790-1869), the eloquent advocate and statesman, was the
leader of the friends of the Elder House of Bourbon in the Chamber of
Deputies, and was, consequently, opposed to the Younger Branch of which
Louis-Philippe was the head.

consequently was not in a condition to marry.   He asked
for a year's delay.   At the end of this time he requested
a second postponement.   But the father would not grant
it ; became angry; considered the excuses evasions; flew
into a passion ; and the interview was terminated by a
challenge to a duel.   The challenge was accepted.   The
father's second was Alphonse Rabbe, a well-known
journalist and author of the time, who afterwards related
the episode; Thiers's seconds were Mignet and Manuel.
The weapons were pistols.   The father being the injured
party, fired first.   He took good aim, and, if it had not
been for a slight sinking of his arm, occasioned by a false
movement of the body, his adversary would have been hit.
The ball, however, passed between Thiers's legs.   As for
the latter, he did not raise his weapon, for, on accepting
the challenge, he had decided in his own mind not to return the fire.   After having bravely sustained the first
shot, he said he was ready to receive the second, but the
duel ended here.   Several years later, however, after the
revolution of 1830, when Thiers had risen to power, and
was a minister, he is said to have provided good positions
in the Department of Finance, for the father and the
young lady's brother.*

---

* This same episode was related somewhat differently in an article published since Thiers's death in the Paris *Figaro*, from the pen of M. Aurélien
Scholl, an able journalist ; but the account given in the text can be depended upon for correctness.

CHAPTER II.

THE REVOLUTION OF JULY.

The Revolution of July, 1830, is an important date to us, because it marks a new era in Thiers's life. He is now arrived at maturity. The journalist, the writer, and the historian is about to enter a new field, to play a new part. One monarchy has fallen and another is raised on its ruins. Thiers, who contributed more than anybody else towards the overthrow of Charles X, on the advent of Louis-Philippe, passes from the Opposition to the party in power. Will he be worthy of his younger days in this new sphere of action? Will he be faithful to his early principles? Will he labor for the same cause? These important questions will be answered, we think, in the following rapid exposition of this period of his life, so rich in facts and in results that still endure. His individuality, however considerable, could be lost sight of without detracting interest from the events, in which France stands personified and which possess a grandeur of their own; but these events might be more clearly presented, if grouped around one of the principle actors in the drama, and if reflected in the part which he played.

Could the Charter of 1814, a compromise between the

dynasty of the Bourbons and the French Revolution, imposed upon France by victorious Europe, and upon the Bourbons by the nature of things, have long endured? This is a debatable question. But the fact was settled without peradventure by the revolution of 1830, that Charles X could not with impunity violate the compact. In setting at defiance, the principles of the French Revolution, the dynasty engaged in an unequal contest. The Revolution, the inevitable result of centuries of preparation, had put a period to an extinct society. The work had since been checked, thwarted and retarded. Bonaparte had done it by gaining battles, those who followed him, in a less degree, by prudence and ability. But to attempt it with a high hand, without popularity, without prestige, and with an army still cherishing the memories of triumphs with which the Bourbons had scarcely anything to do, was pure folly. Everybody saw this, so that when the feeble Charles X actually dared the Chamber of Deputies, the representatives of France, and made Prince Polignac Prime Minister, there was not a politician of so little foresight, as not to predict the approaching destruction of the dynasty. " Unfortunate France ! Unfortunate King ! " cried the * *Journal des*

---

* This journal—the *London Times* of Paris—which will be frequently quoted in the course of this book, is on the whole the best representative of French journalism. It traces its origin to the month of August, 1789. The celebrated French journalistic family, the Bertins, acquired possession of the journal in 1799, and under their management, which lasted for two generations, it took a high stand—which it has ever since retained—as a literary and political newspaper. Napoleon I himself wrote for its columns during the empire. Among its galaxy of distinguished writers, may be men-

Débats.   Talleyrand repeated to those who would listen to
him his celebrated prophecy, first uttered at the time of the
retreat from Moscow, " It is the beginning of the end."
Thiers did better ; he labored with renewed ardor, and
with an audacity which nothing but respect for the law
could arrest, to verify the prediction.

The enemies of Thiers, long before and since his death,
have been pleased to call him a politician who could not
be trusted, who had no principles, who would yield to
circumstances, and change with events, a sort of Machia-
velli, whose motto, formally applied to Talleyrand, should
have been the famous verse of Horace,

*Et mihi res, non me rebus subjungere conor.**

Such will not be the judgment of history.   Revolutions
have surged around Thiers, and in whirling him about in
their vortices, have often changed his position ; but he
has never been shaken in his principles and aims.   He
who does not see this, is determined not to look beneath
the surface, to confound the changing form of things with
the things themselves.   The adversaries of Thiers thus
sum up his history : He opposed the monarchy of the
Restoration, and that monarchy overturned, he raised up
and served another monarchy ; then, he combated this new
monarchy, helped to undermine it, and when it fell, de-

tioned, Chateaubriand, Nodier, de Sacy, Saint-Marc Girardin, and, at a
later date, Jules Janin, Rénan, and Michel Chévallier. Cuvillier-Fleury, (who
will be frequently referred to in these pages,) and John Lemoinne, both
members of the French Academy, contribute to-day to its columns. The
political policy of the *Débats* from its origin may be summed up in the words,
liberal conservatism. To-day it is conservative republican.

*Ep. I, 1, 19.   " ——the world's for me, not I for it."—CONINGTON.

clared war against the republic that followed it, until the
republic gave way to the empire; then, in fine, after a
long series of events, the republic having again appeared,
he welcomed it, served it, defended it, and was about to
continue to defend it, serve it, and perhaps even again to
preside over its destinies, when he was surprised by
death. And then, they cry, what inconsistency, what
vacillation, yea, what apostacy! But nothing is more
superficial, more puerile and more false than this summary
way of judging things. To properly understand the long
life of Thiers, it should be likened to the voyage of a ship
on the Atlantic, which must regard the currents that beset
it, the changing winds, the flow and ebb of the tides, and
the raging tempests, but which ever steers towards its
destined harbor; or, to use a comparison more suited to
Thiers's military turn of mind, his life was like a campaign
where the plan of battle is more than once modified to
meet the requirements of the action, to accomodate itself
to unforeseen contingencies and to the rules of strategy
and tactics. Thiers never served but one cause, the
French Revolution, and he served it only in a legal manner. Therein is seen the salient feature of his political
character. Whether acting with the party in power or
the party out of power, he defended the Revolution; he
attacked only its enemies, and he always found his means
of offence and defense within the pale of the law. When
he participated in a revolution or applauded others for
doing so, he never scouted the law, as was shown by his

conduct in the revolution of 1830, and in that of September 4th, 1870, when Napoleon III was dethroned. This made him many enemies even in the most opposite parties; for a political foe knows that moderation, which is rarely excused in politics, is the most powerful arm that the adversary can use; and friends too often take for weakness, what is in reality superiority of judgment and character.

On January 3d, 1830, when all France was in a state of political fermentation consequent upon the unpopularity of the Polignac ministry, and when the immediate future was threatening and uncertain, Thiers founded the *National.* He was well situated on the *Constitutionnel*, in which he was now pecuniarily interested and where his remarkable talent gave him immense influence. But his ideas of the demands of the hour, which seemed to him to call for the ardent and vigorous treatment breathed by public opinion and his own soul, alarmed his colleagues whose interests he did not wish to compromise. He desired also a personal organ in which to carry on the combat at his own risk and peril. Thiers liked responsibility; he took pleasure in it. This peculiarity of his nature will often appear in the course of his career. He knew that in this way talent secured the position belonging to it, especially in times of agitation and in free countries. He associated with him in this new enterprise, his friend Mignet, and afterwards Armand Carrel, one of the most distinguished and ablest intellects of the period—the *Junius* of the French press, as the critic Sainte-Beuve called him. Thus was started this liberal newspaper, which was destined to take an active part in producing two revolutions : one, that of 1830, with Thiers, the other, that of 1848, against Thiers, or at least against the Orleans monarchy, which he had helped to establish.

It has been said, in speaking of the political opinions of the *National*, that it desired the same thing as the *Globe*,* namely, a constitutional monarchy, but that the former sought it in a revolutionary manner. This is far from true. The principles of the *National*, no more differed from those of the *Globe* in their application than in their nature, the former were no more revolutionary than the latter. Both journals stood on the same foundation, the Charter ; they had to do with the same enemy ; they had the same object in view ; there was scarcely any difference even in their tactics and manœuvres. Thiers, however, was at the head of a division which was more alert and bold. " It is enough," he said, one day, " to drive the Bourbons into the Charter and shut the door on them ; they will jump out of the windows," and the whole political aim of the *National* was to shut up the Bourbons and to induce France to do the same thing, at the risk of forcing the King to break the panes and leap out of the window. Can this be called revolutionary ? Charles X was incorrigible ; he was, furthermore, in the hands of those who

* The *Globe* was founded in 1824, and for five years was devoted exclusively to philosophic and literary questions. Among its writers at this period was Jouffroy, the philosopher. In 1830 it entered the field of politics, as an advocate of liberal conservatism, but left politics after the revolution and soon disappeared.

do not let their prey escape, the Jesuits, who have so well
described themselves in the words of the democratic
poet, Béranger :

> Half fox, half wolf,
> Our order is a mystery.*

The Martignac ministry, so moderate and so devoted
to the old monarchy, had clearly shown by its fall that
the Bourbons were not to be depended upon. It had
settled down to a struggle between the old and the new
ideas. A *coup d'état* was evidently at hand, and it began
to be felt that the counter-action would be a revolution.
What was to be done? Should pacific protestations be
made and the throne be humbly requested to be wise and
reasonable? It would have been foolish and almost
criminal to try, after what had already been experienced,
to change the mind of the blinded King. The only thing
to be done was to press him into narrow legal limits where
he would be forced to capitulate—which seemed less
probable every day—or to make a disastrous sortie. This
is all the *National* of Thiers and Armand Carrel advocated.

The *National* marked out its line of conduct in the
earliest numbers of the paper. Thiers, in an article on
the Charter, stated its principles and pointed out the
liberties that it guaranteed. He demanded that these
liberties be respected, that the stipulations of the Char-

---

* Moitié renards, moitié loups,
Notre règle est un mystère.
Les Révérends Pères.

ter be carried out, and declared that herein lay the only
security for the present and the future. But it seemed
idle to him to limit his efforts to a declaration to which
the government would pay no attention. The government had thrown down the gauntlet to the nation, the
nation had picked it up, and it was now necessary that
the latter show the former what means of defense it had.
On January 5th, 1830, appeared an article which created a
great sensation. In it Thiers called the attention of the
deputies to the weapon with which the Constitution had
armed them, by according to the Chamber the right to vote
the budget, and then, going a step further, he explained the
difference between a refusal to vote taxes and a refusal to
vote appropriations. "The first," he said, "is a right
which pertains to the nation and which it alone can exercise; the other pertains to the Chamber." The ministry
was thus apprized that the most serious trouble might
result from the course it was pursuing.

To Charles X and the Jesuitical circle that ruled him
there seemed to be these alternatives: either royalty
must impose its will upon the country, or the country
would impose its will upon royalty. This was the pith
of the situation. Though simple, it was important to find
a watchword which all could understand, at which no one
would be alarmed, and which, at the same time, should be
firm and decisive. Thiers succeeded in meeting these requirements when he said, "the King reigns but does not
govern." The formula was admirable, bold but not revolu-

tionary. It was the theory of constitutional monarchy
epitomized. It showed on what conditions France would
accept royalty. The dynasty was not excluded, it was
only subordinated to the nation. True, the Bourbons
were driven into a corner and belittled by the maxim,
but it was because they would be absolute. Thiers could
not be blamed for this.

The whole policy of the *National* is embraced in this celebrated phrase, and its arguments are summed up in the
article in which the author develops it. Thiers would
establish two propositions : in the first place, that royalty, as conceived by himself and as intended by the Charter, is not to be despised ; and, secondly, that France so
earnestly desires to govern herself, that, if she cannot do
so with royalty, she will seek another form of government.

On the second point, he used these remarkable words :
" France wishes to govern herself because she is able to.
Will this be called a republican spirit? So much the
worse for those who like to get frightened at words. This
spirit, republican if you like, exists, crops out everywhere,
and cannot be repressed. There are two forms of government which will satisfy this spirit, the English and the
American. Here are the two ways of arriving at the
same end. Many bold and vigorous minds prefer the
second. But the body of the nation has a vague fear of
the agitation of a republic. We ought to rejoice at this
disposition which, unsteady and frequently attacked,
needs support. There is but one way to give it support,

and that is, to prove that the monarchical form of government offers sufficient liberty, and, that under it the country can realize its wish and govern itself.   In the present
agitated state of men's minds, if the people are not convinced of this, they will begin to look outside of monarchy for the consummation of their hopes, and will not
be satisfied even with what is found across the Atlantic."
On more than one occasion since the beginning of the
year 1830, Thiers's theory and his judgment concerning
the spirit and disposition of France, have been shown to
be correct.

The Chamber elected in June, 1830, was stronger in
Opposition members than the one that had been dissolved.
It is now a well established fact that Charles and his ministers had decided in May to have recourse to a *coup d'état*
if the elections went against them.   The celebrated ordinances* were consequently forthcoming.   On Sunday,
July 25th, 1830, on leaving the chapel of St. Cloud, where
he had been to hear mass, the King signed these repressive
decrees.   On the evening of the next day, they appeared
in the official *Moniteur*, and three days thereafter the
Restoration was at an end.

Thiers had expected the *coup d'état* and was prepared
for it. He had already decided upon the course he should
follow. As soon as he read the *Moniteur*, he called together his friends and the principal writers on the *National.*

---

* They were five in number, the first two being the most important, since
they suspended the liberty of the press and dissolved the Chamber elect.

The office of the journal became a headquarters of information and action. It was decided to resist, but there was difference of opinion concerning the means to be employed. The majority favored separate protests, in which each individual should express his own peculiar views on the question. Thiers thought this a bad plan, for it divided their forces instead of uniting them, as the gravity of the situation demanded. He spoke at length against the dominant opinion. M. de Rémusat, the liberal publicist, entered while Thiers was trying to bring his friends over to his way of thinking. "We must refuse to submit to the ordinances," he said, addressing his words to Rémusat; "but articles, however well written or however bold, will do no good. There must be a manifesto formally setting forth our refusal to obey. It should be an example for the people to imitate. It should be common to all and binding on all who wish to protest like ourselves." His opinion prevailed. A document was drawn up by Thiers. Some one having requested that it be given a collective or rather impersonal character, Thiers interposed again: "Names are necessary; we must risk our heads." And, then, with him, Mignet, and Carrel, of the *National*, representatives of the *Figaro*, *Temps*, *Globe*, *Constitutionnel*, etc., signed the protest. No less than eight members of the editorial staff of the *National*, more than twice as many as of any other journal, affixed their names.

The Charter, argues Thiers in this famous document,

calls upon Frenchmen to obey its articles, not regal ordinances.   The Crown itself has heretofore recognised the
authority of the articles.   Whenever a modification of the
existing laws has been desired, the Crown has had recourse
to the Chambers, not to ordinances.   The highest courts
of France have pronounced favorably upon the constitutionality of the Charter, and against the constitutionality
of ordinances.   Since, therefore, the government has
violated the law, Frenchman are not bound to obey the
government.   Legal authority is at an end, that of force
is begun.   As the writers of the press will be the first to
suffer, they should be the first to protest, and the first to
set an example of resistance to their fellow citizens.
They are determined, therefore, to attempt the publication of their journals without obtaining the permission
imposed by the ordinances.   In closing, the journalists
call upon the deputies elect, to stand by their rights.
The Charter gives the King the power to dissolve the
Chamber after it has convened, but, as the new Chamber
has not yet met, it cannot be dissolved, and it, therefore,
still exists, the legal representative of France and the
Charter. Such is the spirit of the protest of the journalists.

   The publication of the ordinances and of this protest
that they called forth, produced a profound sensation in
Paris, and throughout the whole of France. On Tuesday,
July 27th, the people of the capital began to show signs of
revolt, and it became evident that the contest was to be
decided in the streets in the form of an insurrection.

Nothing in Thiers's whole career reflects more credit upon him, than the attitude he assumed and the part he played, in these memorable events. It has often been said that Thiers, as soon as there was a resort to arms, retired to Montmorency, near Paris, where he remained during the three days of fighting, July 27th, 28th, and 29th, and that he did not again appear on the scene until the afternoon of the 29th, when the insurrection was known to have succeeded.* This is not true.

On the morning of the 27th, a large number of electors assembled at the office of the *National*, on the invitation of Thiers. The first topic discussed was the public expression of their opinion on the crisis, and the way to render such expression as impressive as possible. Thiers advised that the co-operation of the deputies then at Paris be made sure of, and that they be pressed to sign an energetic protest similar to that drawn up at the office of the *National*. The question of recourse to arms then came up. The opinion advanced by one of those present, that "all our enemies, both King and gendarmes," should be placed without the pale of the law, was not ill received by Thiers. A legitimate defence of their rights seemed to him perfectly proper. He hesitated, however, at the thought of the misery that would be occasioned by an unequal contest between an unarmed multitude and regular troops. But the insurrection once under way, and there being no longer any doubt of its

---

* See the *Pays* of September 5th, 1877.

assuming serious proportions, he did not shrink from putting himself in communication with its friends in order to do what he could to direct it. Another meeting for the consideration of this same subject, was held in the rue St. Honoré, at the house of M. Cadet-Gassicourt, who though a pharmacist by profession, was an active liberal politican. Firing was heard in the immediate neighborhood. A barricade had been thrown up near the Théâtre Français and cavalrymen with drawn sabres were charging upon the redoubt of the people. At this moment, Thiers left the house of meeting, and, placed between two fires, extricated himself from the danger with the greatest difficulty, though many passers-by were wounded. He immediately repaired to the office of the *National*, to perform the duties that circumstances should impose.

The night of the 27th was sinister. Paris was trembling. The streets were silent and the city seemed deserted. Thiers passed the night at the office of his journal, writing and supervising the publication of the next day's immense edition. Far from thinking of how to escape the peril of the situation, he printed in this number a call to arms, which, if the insurrection had failed, would have compromised him not only for the present but also for the future. But the revolt grew stronger every hour. During all the following day, the 28th, visitors poured into the office of the *National*, some seeking, others bringing news. Many were nervous, many alarmed. Thiers reassured all by the serenity of his

countenance and the firmness of his language and attitude. In the evening, about nine o'clock, apprised that
a warrant for his arrest had been issued, and prevailed
upon by his friends to avoid a danger which nothing
required him to encounter, and which, as the struggle
was still undecided, certainly existed, he left Paris
and passed the night at the house of a friend in the environs of Saint-Denis, a short distance from Paris. A
few hours afterwards, informed by a domestic who had
been left at the capital, that the insurrection was victorious, he immediately returned to the city, and at an early
hour on the 29th was found at the office of his newspaper, deliberating with his friends on the new situation.

The question that offered itself for solution was simple, but momentous. It is not less difficult to make
governments than to destroy them. Three ways out of
the difficulty lay open to the men who had brought
about the revolution of 1830:—1. To maintain the defeated monarchy on condition that henceforth it would
honestly accept the results of the French Revolution.
2. To establish a constitutional monarchy, by placing
on the throne Louis-Philippe, the head of the younger
branch of the Bourbons, who was known to hold liberal
opinions. 3. To proclaim the republic.

To understand the situation, and the reasons that influenced Thiers in favor of a constitutional monarchy
under the House of Orleans, it is necessary to enter into
the spirit of France at this epoch, to know the thoughts

of the people, to weigh the effect of the struggle in the streets of Paris on the imaginations of men and on the state of parties, and to discover how far it excited passions or alarmed interests.   This shall be done briefly.

The struggle had an immediate and powerful influence on the French mind. We need not speak of Auguste Barbier's *Iambes*,* nor of Casimir Delavigne's hymn of *La Parisienne*.† The spontaneity of the movement, the ardor of the combatants during the contest, the discretion of the victors, were subjects of admiration even among the Royalists.‡ From this same event dates Victor Hugo's renunciation of the belief of his childhood.   Though he had always accepted the spirit of the Revolution, which was as innate in him as his genius, but which youth and the social atmosphere that he breathed had smothered, he now first joined hands with the men of liberal principles, and entered heartily into the work which was to install and organize the Revolution.   The people, too, caught the fire that inflamed the minds of the intelligent. With the exception of portions of the west and south, the heart of all France beat with that of Paris.

The hatred of the Bourbons in France ante-dated the

---

* Auguste Barbier, the satiric poet, was born in 1815, and is still living, (1878).   In the *Iambes*,—a series of satires—the poet attacks both the political and social corruption of the epoch.

† Delavigne, (1793–1843), the poet and dramatist, was hand and glove with the Liberals of the Restoration. *La Parisienne*, which has been called the *Marseillaise* of the revolution of 1830, had but an ephemeral popularity.

‡ Chateaubriand, an earnest friend of the Bourbons, delivered an oration in the Chamber of Peers a few days after the conflict, in which he highly eulogized the conduct of the people of Paris.

revolution of 1830. It began in 1789; it was renewed in 1814, after the disasters with which their names were associated. Regard for the Revolution and national pride both conspired against them. The folly of the ordinances, the blood that had just been spilt widened the chasm. It was useless, therefore, to think of raising the fallen dynasty, even if the old King or his young heir* should have consented to become what has since been termed "the king of the Revolution." In the Liberal party, Royer-Collard, † Villemain ‡ and Casimir Périer himself—to whom we will have occasion to refer hereafter—regretted it deeply. But the necessity of conforming to the political belief, or rather the political belief imposed by necessity, was too powerful to admit of such a course.

There remain for consideration the alternatives of a constitutional monarchy under the House of Orleans or a republic. The Empire was not then a factor in French politics, since the heir of Napoleon was, with his mother, in the power of Austria.

The Republic was backed by an able body of talented men, such as Armand Carrel, Godefroy Cavaignac, § Ar-

---

* Charles X abdicated August 2nd, 1830, in favor of his grandson, the present Count de Chambord.

† Royer-Collard, (1763–1845), statesman, orator, professor of philosophy at the Sorbonne—the Paris university. He was the master of Cousin and Jouffroy. In politics he was a moderate liberal and founder of Doctrinarianism.

‡ Villemain, (1790–1867), famous critic and professor of French eloquence at the Sorbonne,

§ Godefroy Cavaignac, (1801–1835), politician and *littérateur*, was the oldest son of a member of the Convention, and brother of General Cavaignac, who took such a prominent part in the revolution of 1848.

mand Marrast, * Colonel Charras, † etc., who were afterwards reinforced by men like Ledru-Rollin, ‡ Michel de
Bourges, § Garnier-Pagès, ‖ etc. It had the prestige of the
principle of the sovereignty of the people, the shadow of
universal suffrage, logically associated with the doctrines
of 1789, the glorious souvenirs of the victories of the
Revolution, its conquests preserved by it but lost by the
Empire. It was, finally, the form of government preferred by the most virile part of the population of Paris
and of some of the other large cities, particularly Lyons.
But all this was outweighed by a thousand misconceptions,
by a thousand prejudices, by the bitter hatred of its enemies. The spectre of the Reign of Terror, kept alive by a
sort of idolatry,—if this word can be applied to animosity
—was ever opposed to the memory of great deeds, ever
invoked in the tribune, in the journals and even in the
pulpit, and, in the rural districts, it was a veritable bugbear.
Besides, the Republic implied, demanded universal suffrage, which, in the then state of the French mind, might
have been turned against republicanism, and even have

---

* Armand Marrast, (1801-1852), publicist and journalist ; imprisoned in
1834, because of his political opinions ; member of the Provisional Government in 1848; deputy and president of the Assembly at this same epoch, and
editor-in-chief of the *National.*

† Colonel Charras, (1810-1865), soldier, historian, and politician ; deputy
during the Republic of 1848, and exiled on the advent of the second Empire.

‡ Ledru-Rollin, (1807-1874), celebrated publicist, politician, and advocate ;
member of the Provisional Government of 1848, and deputy ; exiled by
Napoleon III ; deputy after the overthrow of the Empire.

§ Michel de Bourges, (1798-1853,) distinguished advocate and politician ;
deputy in 1837 and in 1849.

‖ Garnier-Pagès, (1803-1878), historian and politician ; deputy in 1842 ;
member of the Provisional Government and deputy in 1848 ; deputy in 1864.

delivered it over to its worst enemies, the clergy; for the cause of the clergy was wrapt up in that of the *régime* which had just been ended. The church sympathized and co-operated with the Bourbons, and it was the church which forced the court into its last fatal conflict. To neutralize the evils of universal suffrage in the rural districts, it would have been necessary for the whole body of the middle classes to be free from the prejudices that prevailed there. But unfortunately this was not the case. The middle classes were also divided in their opinions concerning the Republic. From another point of view, the Republic might again raise up a barrier between France and the other states of Europe. It would be looked upon as a revenge for the disasters of 1815, a renewal of revolutionary propagandism. The change from absolute monarchies to liberal monarchies which has since taken place, that whole transformation of Europe so well stated in Thiers's political testament,* had not then been brought about. The hostilities of the Holy Alliance — Russia, Austria and Prussia — were to be feared, as well as its prejudices. This prospect alienated from republicanism many in all classes of society.

The only possible government in the eyes of real statesmen was a Constitutional Monarchy under the House of Orleans. It was trusted by those who feared the Repub-

---

*This remarkable document—the last thing Thiers wrote—is given in Appendix D.

lic; and it satisfied the liberals, since the younger branch
could reign only by accepting the Charter, for the violation of which the elder branch had been expelled. If it
was opposed by the legitimists—the followers of the
elder branch, who could not forgive the Orleanists for
supplanting their own natural representative, and who
considered them disgraced by becoming the royalty of
the Revolution—it was supported, on the other hand, by
all the foes of legitimacy, that is to say, by the majority
of the nation. And finally, the republican party, although it would be an embarrassment, would not be
strong enough to materially check the government if it
were wise and remained faithful to its principles.

This was the way Thiers looked at the crisis, on which
he brought to bear that power of penetration, that sort
of political scent — his greatest gift, perhaps,— which enabled him to follow the course of public opinion as if it
were a trail, and to see clearly, in a given situation, what
ought to be done, and what could not be substituted for
it with impunity. Talleyrand took the same view of the
question as Thiers. Both worked, doubtless in concert,
to make a constitutional king by addressing themselves
to the only man possible for such a position at that time,
Louis-Philippe, Duke of Orleans. Talleyrand, as was his
way, kept himself hidden in his house at Paris, while, by
means of a confidential secretary, he carried on communications with Neuilly, just outside of the walls of Paris,

where the duke resided. Thiers, on the other hand, less prudent and less concerned about himself, acted in person. Both conducted themselves characteristically.

The partisans of the Orleans family said in 1871, when Thiers refused to aid in the restoration of the monarchy of 1830, that he showed himself ungrateful towards the King whom he had served. This was reversing the rôles in a singular manner. If, in affairs of this kind, there can be any such thing as gratitude or ingratitude, it was not Thiers who was the ungrateful party. No one did more than he to elevate the monarch who ruled in France from August, 1830, to February, 1848, for no one did more to remove the objections to him entertained by the two factions of the victors. On the one hand, he combated the views of those who favored a compromise with Charles X, and on the other hand, he opposed the efforts of those who would have the Republic forthwith.

On the return of Thiers from St. Denis, the *National* printed a short but clear article in favor of the Duke of Orleans. Worked off by the thousands, the paper was scattered all over Paris and produced a marked impression, which was generally favorable to the proposition. Already cries of "Long live the Duke of Orleans" were heard. In the evening, a large number of deputies, journalists and politicians met in the parlors of M. Laffitte.

Thiers was present. Two envoys from Charles X arrived, bearing proposals of accomodation. The assem-
blage seemed disposed to listen to them. Thiers opposed this with all his force in a vigorous speech, in
which he showed that it was out of the question to patch
up a compromise with Charles; that Europe did not expect it, that the people would not listen to it; that it
was their bounden duty to return answer to the deposed
monarch, that he must depart from French soil as quickly
as possible, and that not until it was known that he was
making sail for England, and that at least the breadth
of the Channel lay between him and France, could the
present leaders hope to be masters of the situation.
This sensible and fervent appeal carried the day, and
the advances of the King were repelled.

But it was not so easy to master the republicans who
held the streets, and who could not understand how so
important a question as the establishment of a new
government could be settled in a manner apparently so
thoughtless. To depose one king in order to set up
another, seemed to them very illogical. At their head
stood the venerable Lafayette, who, with his halo of 1789
—which Thiers had helped to preserve—still brilliant,
was all powerful. He ruled at the Hôtel de Ville, where
he sat surrounded by the most ardent leaders of the republican party. Thiers alone could bring him to a composition. Lafayette held in high esteem the author of

the *French Revolution*, who had spoken so well of him,
and would consequently listen to his advice.* Thiers
sent M. de Rémusat to the Hôtel de Ville, who did not
have much trouble in convincing Lafayette that the
Duke of Orleans was, for the present, "the best of re-
publics." When M. de Rémusat left the Hôtel de Ville,
the new monarchy was assured. There only remained
to remove the scruples of the duke himself. The prince
would not ask for the crown; at least, he did not wish
to appear to want it; he desired that it seem to be
forced upon him. However this may be, Thiers took it
upon himself to bring the duke to a decision.

Accompanied by some of the leaders of the movement, Thiers had an interview with the duke, who had
quitted his *château* at Neuilly and was installed in the
Palais-Royal at Paris. He was easily induced to take
the title of lieutenant-general of the kingdom. This provisional title had a magic influence. Conciliatory, apparently leaving everything to the free choice of the
nation, it was well received by everybody. The population of Paris was seduced and carried away by it. The
duke had accepted the tri-color of the Revolution, and
had declared in a proclamation that henceforth the Charter should be a reality. This was all that was needed
to respond to the two sentiments which filled all breasts,

---

* " Lafayette had not the passions and the genius which frequently lead to
the abuse of power; with an equable mind, a sound understanding and a
system of invariable disinterestedness, he was peculiarly fitted for the part
which circumstances had allotted to him — that of superintending the execution of the laws."—*Thiers's French Revolution*, Vol. I., p. 75, *et passim.*

patriotism, inspired by the tri-color cockade, which recalled so many glorious deeds, and love for the principles of the Revolution, which the Charter consecrated.
From that moment, the triumph of the new monarchy
was certain. It was not yet founded, but it was assured,
and with it, a new era was to open to the man who had
done so much to make it possible.

CHAPTER III.

EARLY YEARS OF THE JULY MONARCHY.—1830-40.

Mr. Sumner, the illustrious senator whose memory we honor, during his last visit to Paris, had a long conversation with M. Gambetta, on the state of France and its frequent and often terrible revolutions. The senator referred the origin of all these evils to the apostacy of Henry IV, to that political policy which sacrifices principles to circumstances, and which prompted the prince to express that famous sentiment, " Paris is well worth a mass." " No," said Mr. Sumner in a burst of eloquence, which forcibly struck M. Gambetta,* " however beautiful Paris may be, it is not worth a mass, if a mass is the abandonment of a belief or a principle. It is not by sinking to the level of circumstances, not by debasing one's self by capitulations of conscience, that principles are established which endure. The selfish abjuration of the friend of Sully has been a virus, which has not grown less noxious by age, a slow and deadly poison, which, penetrating into the whole social body, corrupted it, until the French Revolution came to infuse new blood into it. What a fatality proceeded from that original sin ! The last de-

---

* We have this anecdote from Gambetta himself.

scendant, the last representative of the father of the
Bourbons, may have been innocent; but the dynasty was
culpable; it was a just retribution that it perish in the
convulsions produced by the remedy which the crime of
its founder had rendered necessary. History is a Nemesis
without bowels, which punishes without pity."

That Mr. Sumner's opinion, the nobility of which—no
one at least would deny—is not irreproachable from a historical stand point, is doubtless true; but it is incontestable, that any political system whatever, is in great danger
if it do not proceed from a principle founded in the depths
of the national conscience, and if those, whose mission it
is to apply it, have not faith in it and subordinate it to
their personal views, to their own interests.

The reign of Louis-Philippe—to take an example that
can not be questioned—is a striking proof, not so much of
the necessity of a moral principle in the origin of a government which would hope to live and would pretend to
be something more than a mere expedient, but of the
vital importance of a harmony between the political system that is adopted and the vigorous application of that
system. Louis-Philippe, a descendant of the grandson of
Henry IV,—which fact he did not forget to proclaim at
the proper time—did not give up his faith in accepting
the crown of France; his dynasty was not born of infi-
delity to principle, the sin with which Mr. Sumner reproaches his great ancestor; though a prince and a Bourbon, he breathed the spirit of '89, which he had, so to

speak, sucked at the breast ; he was a son of the eighteenth century, and a great admirer of Voltaire. But he forgot, little by little, that under a constitutional monarchy " the King reigns but does not govern," and, if he did not enforce his will with a high hand as did Charles X, he pursued the same fatal course in a quiet way. Louis-Philippe was also too much absorbed in his own private interests and in the advancement of his family. On the one hand, he was too much of a king ; on the other, not enough of a king. So he fell, and along with him that system of government on which so many eminent Frenchmen, Talleyrand, Thiers, Cousin, Mignet, Rémusat, and a host of others, had founded their hopes for the future of France.

Thiers, some months before his death, had a long conversation with a friend concerning Louis-Philippe, the most interesting portions of which, furnished us by the lady herself,* we present below:

" The first time I saw the Duke of Orleans," said Thiers, " was on the evening of the day on which the fatal ordinances were signed. I was at St. Leu-Taverny, at the *château* of Mme. de Feuchères.† I had accompanied

---

* We refer to Mrs. Emily Crawford, the talented Paris correspondent of the London *News*, and now (1878, correspondent of the New York *Tribune*. Portions of this same conversation given in the text will be found, though in different language, in Mrs. Crawford's interesting article, *M. Thiers : a sketch from life by an English pencil*, published in *Macmillan's Magazine* for November, 1877. The account given in the text was written before Mrs. Crawford's article appeared.

† This is the woman who acted such a dark part in the tragedy attending the mysterious death of the Duke de Bourbon, " the last of the Condés," as graphically told in Chapter XII of Louis Blanc's *History of Ten Years*. The *château* of St. Leu, a village about ten miles north of Paris, was one of the legacies wormed out of the old duke by Mme. de Feuchères.

Mme. de Courtchamp, the friend of Mme. de Feuchères, at whose country seat not far distant, I sometimes spent Sunday.

"There were a great many people at the *château*. A comedy was being performed. During an intermission we found ourselves assembled in the *salon du théâtre*, a sort of neutral ground, a *foyer de l'opéra*, where grand dames, scrupulous of decorum and appearances, thought they might approach the mistress of the Duke de Bourbon without compromising themselves. Mme. de Feuchères, who was very intimate with Madame Adelaide, Louis-Philippe's sister, hoped, with the princess, to make the duke a king, if the folly of Charles X should render the throne vacant. Mme. de Courtchamp remarked to her, pointing to Louis-Philippe who was near by, 'Well, there is the king you need.' Mme. de Feuchères repeated the remark to the duke. It is but just to say that he paid little heed to her; he did not like adventures. Danton once predicted to him, as the witches did to Macbeth, that he would be king. But he scarcely desired it; it was not he who, in order to gain a crown, would have stained his hands with a drop of blood, which all great Neptune's ocean could not wash out. It was Madame Adelaide who eventually persuaded him to accept it.

"Louis-Philippe was a *bourgeois* in rather the derogatory sense that is sometimes applied to this word. Courageous, exposing himself to danger, with a just idea of his dignity, intelligent and spirited, both true heroism and lofty ambition were lacking in him. He was not attracted by glory, except the glory of money. It has been said, that one evening while playing billiards at the Tuileries, he dropped a franc, which, leaning over to pick up, but not finding immediately, he continued to look for, until one of the players, who was not by the way a millionaire, taking pity on him, pulled from his own purse a bank bill, which he lighted, in order to assist the King in his search, and, at the same time, to teach him a lesson. But this is a society calumny, a story gotten up by his enemies, though, to be sure, it is a counterfeit in which there is some truth. It is true that Louis-Philippe loved money too much, but it was not for himself that he wanted it, not to gratify costly tastes, since his were very simple. Nor was his passion that of an unfeeling miser. If he adored his family, it was for its sake, in order to establish it, to richly endow it, to make it the wealthiest in Europe, that he gave so much thought to the increment of his fortune, and so much care to protecting it from all danger. All the reproaches that this avarice brought down upon him, which fill the pamphlets of the period, were merited, if we except the inevitable exaggerations, and particularly the wicked calumnies of Cormenin.*

"Believe me, my dear madame, that, if I speak of all this, it is not out of any ill-will towards a prince whom I

---

* M. de Cormenin (1788-1868), also known under the *nom de plume* of "Timon," was a celebrated French pamphleteer, who, a republican during the reign of Louis-Philippe, finally went over to the Empire.

admired, and who returned my regard ; I am not given to posthumous slander. No, but it is because this characteristic which I have pointed out to you, has produced important consequences in our history; it is because these family preoccupations have played a very grievous part in our domestic and foreign politics, inasmuch as they often got complicated with the tendencies of personal government, and so affected the spirit of our institutions.

" If I were to write the history of this reign, I should divide it into two parts ; the first, from 1830 to 1840, the second, from 1840 to the revolution of 1848 : and I should say that the first period was characterized by the predominance of the protestant and liberal spirit ; that the second was marked by a catholic influence, and that —a result which necessarily followed—personal royalty now became more prominent, and there was a tendency to substitute the monarch's will for that of the country.

" This fact showed itself in the marriages of the family, or its attempts at marriages. In the first period, Louis-Philippe gave one of his daughters to a protestant prince, Leopold, who, after a revolution, became King of Belgium ; he married the heir presumptive, the Duke of Orleans, to a protestant princess, and he had great hopes of being able to win for his second son, the Duke de Nemours, the hand of the future queen of England, the Princess Victoria, to whom had been sent the prince's portrait, which she admired too much to please the old

King, William IV, whose preferences were for a Coburg. The match fell through because of the duke's unwilling-ness to change his religion.   This all occurred during the epoch of the protestant ministers, Guizot, Gasparin, * Humann † and others, not to speak of the free-thinkers. The Tuileries were then hermetically sealed to clerical influences.   This lasted so long as there were hopes of the consummation of the English marriage.   But when these fell to the ground, the royal father turned in an-other direction, and catholic princesses supplanted pro-testant princesses.   You know all about the grand affair of the Spanish marriages, ‡ into which Guizot entered eagerly, and from which he did not escape without tar-nishing his glory.   I have told you the consequences: Ultramontane influences entered the palace, the govern-ment had to compound with catholicism.   This was clearly evident in the question of non-sectarian educa-tion, in the venemous attacks made on the University, which was accused of all the crimes imaginable, but whose only fault was that of being a laical institution pervaded with the spirit of the Revolution.

"Another consequence still, which I have pointed out

* Gasparin, (1783–1862), famous agriculturist, politician, and soldier ; Peer of France, 1834 ; Minister of the Interior, 1836 ; of Agriculture, 1839 ; and member of the Academy of Sciences.

† Humann, (1780–1842), deputy under the Restoration ; Peer of France, 1837 ; and Minister of Finances from 1832 to 1836.

‡ Two of Louis-Philippe's sons the Duke d'Aumale and the Duke de Montpensier, were to marry Spanish princesses, the first, Queen Isabella, the second, the Infanta, Maria Louisa, the queen's younger sister.   The first marriage was given up through fear of provoking Europe, but the second was consummated on October 10th, 1846, much to the dislike of England.

to you. So long as the family considered its interests to lie on the protestant side, it was more liberal, more faithful to its origin; people governed themselves, and were allowed to govern themselves; but from the moment that catholicism got the upper hand, the Bourbon came to the surface; the Duke of Orleans was forgotten. They opposed the current so determinedly that it increased by resistance, until one fine day it became a torrent and swept us all into the abyss."

The whole secret of the conduct of Thiers under the government of July is thus divulged by Thiers himself; for the foregoing *résumé* of this historical conversation, however incomplete and tame it may be, exactly reproduces the thoughts of the illustrious statesman on the subject about which we are now speaking. . It seems to us that by reflecting on it, one can comprehend without trouble the whole rôle, apparently so contradictory, which he played in this drama of eighteen years' duration. It has been said by M. Cuvillier-Fleury * that combativeness entered largely into the cause of Thiers's "intermittent" opposition to Louis-Philippe. We can not entirely subscribe to that opinion. Man is not pure spirit; instincts are mingled with most of our acts, and Thiers, like all strong and active intellects, was moved at the same time by passion and reason. But it is not viewing him in his true light, to attribute in the slightest degree his

---

* M. Fleury is a member of the French Academy, a conservative republican, and a writer in the *Journal des Débats*. See the number for September 30th, 1877.

opposition to a passion or to an instinct. It arose from
a deeper and nobler cause, from devotion to the political
ideal that he had conceived, from belief in the maxims
that he had established for its realization. If we compare this ideal with Louis-Philippe's interpretation of
what a constitutional monarch should be, as just depicted
by Thiers, it is evident that antagonism must have arisen
between the King and him who had made the King.
Thiers was not the man to suffer even the shadow of personal government, and precisely for the reason that he
had more than any one else contributed to place the principles which were dear to him under the safe-guard of a
monarchy, he felt that it was his duty more than that of
any body to preserve them from every dishonor, from
every violation.

Thiers held a prominent position among the men
whom the revolution of July had put in power. He did
not figure, however, in the first ministry ; he was young,
but thirty-three years old ; he had to give way to his
elders, Guizot, Broglie,* Dupin,† Casimir Périer.‡ He
was, however, called into the Council of State, a
semi-political, semi-administrative body, and accepted

---

* The Duke de Broglie, (1785–1870), author and politician ; Minister of
Public Instruction, 1830 ; of Foreign Affairs, 1832 ; deputy in 1849 ; member of the French Academy, 1855 ; and father of the present Duke de Broglie, who is prominent in French politics.

† Dupin, known as Dupin aîné. (1783–1865), celebrated advocate ; member of the Provisional Government in 1830 : president of the Chamber of
Deputies, 1832-40 ; member of the Academy 1832 ; deputy 1848 ; senator
1857.

‡ Périer. (1777–1832), the celebrated orator, member of the Opposition
under the Restoration and Prime Minister under Louis-Philippe.

a position in the Treasury Department from the hands of Baron Louis.   But after the elections by which one-third of the Chamber was replaced, and while the Laffitte ministry was under consideration, the King, at the suggestion of Baron Louis,—who was high in praise of his ability,—offered Thiers a portfolio. He refused the proffered honor, for he did not consider himself perfectly prepared to accept it ; and he did not wish to retire from the Treasury Department, until he had made himself thoroughly acquainted with all the details of this important and complicated branch of the civil service.   The King—who desired to link Thiers more closely with his own fortunes—insisted in vain.   The young deputy—for the electors of Aix had sent him to the Chamber—would only take the post of Under-Secretary of the Treasury, under his friend M. Laffitte, who had succeeded Baron Louis and who was also Prime Minister.

The friends of the new monarchy differed from the first concerning the line of policy that should be followed. One party wished " to keep within the narrowest limits, the changes of dynasty or institutions," as Guizot said in November, 1830; the other, according to the words of Lafayette, desired a monarchy " surrounded with republican institutions."   Laffitte took ground with Lafayette. Thiers, too, seemed to hold the same views, but he had not yet committed himself in the tribune to either party. He had only occasionally, in coming to the aid of M. Laffitte, taken part in the discussions concerning the finances.

Thiers had many grave obstacles to conquer in acquiring the art of oratory. M. de Cormenin says of him at this period : " He has no figure, no stature, no grace. He resembles the little barbers of the south, who go about from door to door offering their services. In his prattle there is something of the *gamin*. His twang grates on the ear. The tribune comes up to his shoulders and hides him from his hearers. Physical disadvantages, distrust in his enemies and friends, all are against him." The portrait is exaggerated both physically and morally ; it borders upon caricature ; it is painted by the hand of an enemy. Thiers was small but not ridiculously so ; he had a harsh and piercing voice, but it was not nasal. It is true that he did not possess the external graces, which taken together make up what Buffon calls " the eloquence of the organs," and which have such a powerful effect on assemblages of men. His greatest fault, however, at his *début*, was the homage that he paid to the oratorical style then in vogue, a sort of academical or classical species of oratory, which was not suited to his talents, which ran counter to a nature that was full of animation, impulsive, formed of fire and flame like that of the Hippogriff of Ariosto. For this reason his oratorical powers did not immediately appear in their true light, and his enemies questioned whether he had any. " But it did not take him long," says M. Cuvillier-Fleury, " to learn the proper bearing and gestures of the tribune, to acquaint himself with the echoes of the Chamber, and to give the right modulation to his voice, which was always heard because always listened to. The speech that he delivered on December 9th, 1830,—his first set speech — displayed some of the best qualities of his oratory. This first production, this first effusion from a source which was to prove itself so rich, was marked by Thiers's characteristic clearness in treating of a multitude of details. There was a charm in its very length, in the varied development of the same idea, in the spirited insistence of the speaker, in the increased animation produced alike by accord or opposition, so that the greatest effects of eloquence were realized." *

This maiden speech of Thiers's concerned a question which set by the ears the different parties of the Chamber, the friends of the French Revolution against the counter-revolutionists, the new monarchy against that which it had supplanted. It was nominally a discussion about the further indemnity of the emigrants — the royalists who fled from France in the stormy era of 1789,—but in reality it concerned the legitimacy of the French Revolution; for to compensate its enemies for losses suffered by them while its friends were disregarded, was to condemn the Revolution by obliging it to disgorge. The great orator Berryer and the Count Alexis de Noailles† led the opposition. Thiers spoke several times in his capacity of an official of the Treasury Department, and, though he

* *Journal des Débats*, September 30th, 1877.
† The Count de Noailles, (1783–1835), statesmen and philanthropist ; deputy during the Restoration ; and a strong legitimist throughout his whole life.

had never as yet fallen below his subject, it was especially on this occasion that he attracted attention. He was in his element and felt himself equal to the emergency. He strongly held that the acts which had deprived the emigrants of their property were just; that indemnity was an iniquity; responded briefly but clearly to all the arguments of the other side; and closed by summing up the underlying principles of the new Government. It was a masterpiece of forensic oratory, if oratory consists in acting on men by responding to their feelings, and if it is measured by the effect produced. Thiers was the mouth-piece of the Chamber and the country, in their opinion of the emigration and the Revolution, as well as the organ of the Government; and, judging from the exclamations of approbation or disapprobation that are found in the official report of the speech, it evidently stirred up the passions of the Chamber. The public, too, eagerly commented upon the speech. It was a success,—perhaps not an astounding one,—but the first link of a chain which was to be so brilliant, and in which—as M. Barthélemy—St. Hilaire* once remarked—there was no break.

When Thiers gave himself up to a cause, he gave himself up entirely; when he marked out a course of action,

---

* Barthélemy. St. Hilaire, born in 1805, is well-known as philosopher, statesmen, and professor. He signed the protest of the journalists in 1830; was deputy under the Republic of 1848; was forced to resign his professorship in the Collége de France by Napoleon III; became the confidential friend of Thiers during the latter's presidency, and was deputy from 1871, until made life senator, which position he now (1878) holds.

he followed it to the end. It was not his nature to do things by halves, nor to abandon what he had undertaken. To him the July Monarchy was a step in advance in the onward progress of the French Revolution ; but it was not a disorderly or a too precipitous progression, which would expose itself to defeat or rout, as happened in 1848. Thiers's aim was to defend the new Government from its enemies, its friends and itself : from its enemies, the legitimists and the republicans, who were still very powerful, since the first were masters of the rural districts, the second, dominant in some of the great cities ; from its friends, who over-zealous, might cause a deviation from its principles ; and finally from itself, from the tendency of the executive to arrogate powers not belonging to him, and who not content to play his own part in the orchestra, (to borrow a favorite comparison of Louis-Philippe himself,) wished to be the leader, the composer, and the player of all the instruments, if such a thing were possible.*

From this point of view, the policy of Thiers in the different ministerial positions which he held from 1832 to 1840 is easily explained and cleared up, whether we regard him as Minister of the Interior or Minister of Foreign Affairs ; for his foreign policy was closely allied with the principles of the July Dynasty, as well as with the interests of the French Revolution, which to him were the glory of France.

---

* Louis-Philippe often expressed regret at not being able to defend his policy in the tribune of the Chamber.

After the death of Casimir Périer, in May 1832, Thiers became Minister of the Interior, then head of the Department of Public Works, and finally went back to the Interior again, where he remained until February 22nd, 1836, when his reputation had so increased that he was made Prime Minister with the portfolio of the Foreign office. In about six months the Molé ministry came into power —the first attempt at personal goverment—and Thiers was thrown into the Opposition. In March, 1840, he is again Prime Minister with the portfolio of Foreign Affairs. In all these changes he ever remains faithful to his plan, ever like himself.

The close of the Périer ministry was profoundly agitated by popular disturbances and external and internal political questions. Thiers took part in the discussions in the Chamber, where, to the astonishment of the public, he advocated among other measures not in accord with his former principles, the theory of an hereditary peerage, which he pronounced to be the best safeguard for the moderation and balance of power. But, though very aggressive and brilliant, he played only a secondary rôle at this time. After the death of Périer, however, he took a direct and responsible part in the councils of the government. He was now in a position to display his powers of intelligence, initiative and political energy, powers which have never since been surpassed.

This was the most troublesome and dramatic epoch of the July Monarchy, the most fitting for the play of that spirit of combativeness with which M. Cuvillier-Fleury thinks Thiers was so largely endowed. It was a period of desperate struggles and stormy skies, but nevertheless, the best, on the whole, of the reign, and that which did it the most honor.

Thiers, as Minister of the Interior, supported the brunt of the charge. The tempest assailed him on three sides: the legitimist insurrection in La Vendée which was smothered, however, in its germ, and which in its *dénoûement* bordered on the ridiculous, the revolts at Paris and at Lyons which were drowned in blood.

Thiers has always come to power in extremely critical moments. He is said to have remarked, " It must be that Providence has great confidence in me ; for, whenever I am called to the front, the most embarrassing affairs seem to await my treatment." It is certain at least, that at the moment when death carried off Casimir Périer, a weighty inheritance, a perilous and complicated situation, was left to his successors, and especially to Thiers. The legitimist party, champing its bit, was in a state of agitation in the western departments ; the republican party, more redoutable than the foregoing, though humbled at the funeral of General Lamarque, * had not disarmed ; while the Belgian expedition †—forced upon France

---

* General Lamarque (1770–1832), a distinguished officer of Napoleon I, and a liberal statesman, his funeral at Paris was seized upon by the republicans to make a demonstration against the July Government.

† Belgium rebelled against Holland soon after the Revolution of 1830 ; its independence was recognized by the great powers, and the crown was bestowed upon Prince Leopold, who had married the eldest daughter of Louis-

by circumstances—threatened to produce a European complication. Providence, therefore, had not spared the man in whom it had confidence. Thiers did not of course do everything, but he bore the heaviest load, for he was the Minister of the Interior, and it was there that lay the greatest difficulties, the greatest dangers.

The Vendean insurrection, undertaken against the wishes of the legitimist leaders, Chateaubriand, Berryer, and others, pertains as much to romance as to history. The Duchess of Berry, the mother of " Henry V," as the legitimists love to style their chief, the Count of Chambord, threw herself into the venture, not so much like Margaret of Anjou, as like Diana Vernon, or rather the Duchess of Longueville. But she had misjudged public opinion. The peasants of La Vendée were not in the least disposed to take up arms for their king; the nobles and the priests even in La Vendée and in Brittany, notwithstanding their hatred of the new Government, felt themselves powerless. A half dozen noblemen died bravely near Clisson, and this was all. The mass of the population, though on Vendean soil, did not move. Kindly welcome and ardent promises of devotion were about all the princess could obtain.

If the legitimists were to give the principle reason of the obstinate hátred with which they have pursued Thiers, and which has not passed away with him, it would

Philippe. The King of Holland refused to recognize the independence of Belgium, but England and France opposed him, and the latter sent an army against Antwerp in November 1832, which brought Holland to terms.

be, we think, his conduct as Minister of the Interior during the insurrection of La Vendée.   They could forgive
him a revolution which snatched from them the crown; but
they could not forgive him one measure or one act which
had for its object to expose to public malignity their
sovereign's mother, whose virtues they sang among the
faithful, nor the laying bare to the world the feebleness of
the woman whose heroism they had hoped to turn to the
profit of their cause.

One day Thiers received an anonymous letter.   The
writer offered for a sum of money to deliver up to him
the Duchess of Berry.   The rendezvous for the explanation of the conditions and means of execution was to be
the Allée des Veuves * in the Champs-Elysées.   Thiers
scented treason.   The means were not very honorable,
but he did not hesitate however, for it was a question of
public peace ; and what else but licensed deception is the
secret service, a regular weapon of government?

The minister went to the appointed rendezvous.   He
found there a Jew named Deutz, who was in the service
of the duchess and enjoyed her confidence.   The stipulations agreed upon, Deutz made known the retreat of the
duchess, at that moment at Nantes, and the more important fact that she was pregnant.   We need not speak
of her capture, of her imprisonment in the fortress at
Blaye, of her almost public *accouchement*, and of her consequent disgrace.   The woman had killed the heroine;

---

* To-day, Avenue Montaigne.

the July Monarchy had dealt a deadly blow at the legitimist cause.

The struggle with the republicans was more serious and more tragic. It demanded of the young minister the employment of more vigorous and more virile qualities.

The republican party came upon the scene armed from the first with three weapons, namely, the principle of popular sovereignty, which, though invoked by the revolution of July, was never formally established by it, but which was in 1848 to demand its logical consequence, universal suffrage; secondly, that sentiment of patriotism, which could not resign itself to the disasters of 1814 and 1815, and whose illusions and hopes, poetry, history and eloquence vied with each other to keep alive; and lastly, socialism, which existing in a latent state, was advanced only as a germ destined to develop. And these forces, so powerful by themselves, were organized and regulated by secret societies, which prepared in the dark a serious danger that political wisdom could perhaps avert, and which it was absolutely necessary to avert at any price, if the Government would not perish.

A great number of republican disturbances occurred in different cities of France during the first years of the July Monarchy. A strike among the silk weavers of Lyons in 1834, culminated in an insurrection on the sixth of April. This same day Thiers took up again the portfolio of the Interior Department which he had laid down for

that of Commerce and Public Works. In the first phase
of the Lyonnese troubles the Government had been leni-
ent, but Thiers, seeing how the republican agitation was
spreading from city to city, thought a different course
should be pursued, and wrote to the Préfect "to use energy if the sanctuary of justice is violated."   Energy was
indeed employed ; for five days Lyons was the theatre of
a violent and bloody struggle.

But the republicans were not discouraged. At Paris
some audacious and able leaders had organized an aggressive society.   Thiers, "with provident boldness,"—to use
the words of Guizot,—arrested the leaders of the Society of the Rights of Man, and seized the republican
organ, the *Tribune*. This did not, however, check the
threatened outbreak.   On April 13th, 1834—on the reception of the news of the defeat of the insurgents at Lyons—
barricades were raised at Paris in the most populous
quarters on both sides of the Seine. A terrible contest
ensued. Thiers, who had concerted the plan with General Bugeaud, wished to be present at its execution, for
he was possessed of rare personal courage. He left the
Hôtel de Ville in company with the general, and as they
were passing along what is now the rue du Temple, two
shots were fired at Thiers, who was easily recognised on account of his small stature. About a year later, when the
Corsican Fieschi exploded his infernal machine in the hopes
of killing Louis-Philippe, Thiers's diminutiveness stood
him in good stead, for the bullets that would have struck

him if he had been a few inches taller, passed over his head and killed Marshal Mortier, who was at his side.

The following episode, which occurred one night during this same insurrection, is given in the words of Guizot:

" M. Thiers, accompanied by General Bugeaud, wished to see for himself the extent of the combat and the danger. They marched along by the houses at the head of a little column, without any other light than that given by lamps in some of the windows, which fell upon the uniforms and arms. A shot from a cellar-grating killed one of the captains; another mortally wounded a young auditor of the state-council bearing a message to M. Thiers. As they advanced, new victims fell, and they looked in vain for the murderers. As soon as daylight came a general attack was made upon the insurgents. * * * By seven o'clock, A.M. the struggle had ceased, the insurrection was suppressed."*

The defeat of the republican party in these various revolts did not disarm its hatred of the Government, as was proven by the explosion of Fieschi's infernal machine. Peace, however, reigned in the streets of Paris, which until 1848 was only slightly disturbed by isolated affrays.

Was this unfortunate state of affairs the result of the energetic measures of repression that had been employed, or was it rather due to diverse acts, diverse laws that the ministry had had recourse to, as the law against associa-

---

* *Mémoires de Guizot*, T. III., p. 247.

tions, the refusal of amnesty, the famous enactments
known by the name of the " Laws of September," which
annulled all the liberal legislation concerning the press inaugurated by the revolution of 1830? However this
may be, Thiers felt that this policy of force had served
its time and that it was fitting to enter upon a new
era.

Public opinion pointed in this direction. The laws of
September had stirred up the whole press, and some of
the ablest leaders of the Chamber began to break with
the Government in its repressive policy. Royer-Collard,
the most considerable among them, protested against it
in the name of human dignity. He developed, with a
rare elevation of thought and language, the idea that the
evil which the Government pretended to remove by bitter
and cruel palliatives, was not an evil sprung from the
events of the day, but one connected with a series of
historical facts which France had experienced, the triumphs of force over right ; that the remedy—far from
being where the Government sought it—could only be
found in the moral sentiment of man, in respect for
human dignity, that is, in liberty.*

The strength of the liberal dynastic Opposition was
increased by the general discontent. The Government
was overstepping justifiable bounds. A party was being
formed, even in the majority in the Chamber, composed

---

*See the *Moniteur* of August 26th, 1835.

of strong men, like Dupin, Sauzet,* Passy,† Dufaure ‡ and others, whose numbers were increasing daily, and which was plainly leaning towards a change of policy. Thiers was not the man to overlook such warnings.

On February 22nd, 1836, Thiers became Premier with the portfolio of Foreign Affairs. If Guizot can be believed, this new cabinet resulted from considerations for the most part of a personal nature. Thiers was tired of the Interior and strongly desired the ministry of Foreign Affairs: he did not like the Duke de Broglie, who held this latter position ; he did not wish to appear too intimately united with the Doctrinaires: he was careful to stand forth independently of them. The proof of this, according to Guizot, lies in the fact that the new Cabinet continued the interior policy of its predecessor, " only it made a little more show about it." No, Guizot was a poor observer, or had a poor memory. And strangely enough he goes on to say: " There is in every great human enterprise a superior and governing idea which ought to be the fixed point, the guiding star of those who are called to play a part in it. This dominant idea, this great light of 1832, disappeared in 1836." Now,

---

* Sauzet, born in 1800, advocate, deputy in 1834 ; Minister of Justice from 1836 to 1847.

† Passy, was born in 1793, economist, politician, deputy in 1830 ; Minister of the Finances, and head of the Department of Commerce from 1834 to 1840 and from 1848 to 1849 ; Peer of France 1843 ; deputy in 1849.

‡ Dufaure, born in 1798, an advocate of distinction : deputy in 1834 ; a member of the Council of State during the Ministry of Thiers in 1836, and later minister of Public Works ; republican deputy and minister in 1848 ; Minister of Justice under Thiers's presidency ; life senator, and now (1878)' premier of France.

this great light which disappeared, was the idea of resistance. The change of ministry, therefore, brought about more than an apparent modification of the policy of the Government. Conciliation and compromise were substituted for antagonism and force. Able minds, and above all the quick brain of Talleyrand, saw that it was to the interest of the new royalty and to the welfare of the principles that it represented, that the course pursued up to this time be changed. The King himself had been struck by the power and progress of moderate ideas in the Chamber of Deputies. Thiers was too attentive to the various signs of the time not to see the change that had taken place in the public mind. It is puerile to search with Guizot for an explanation of facts which arise from a situation of public affairs, in secondary and simple personal considerations. It is true that the new Cabinet was not able to show what its domestic policy was to be, was not able to carry out its plans. Complications of foreign policy hindered it and cut it short in the midst of its career.

Louis-Philippe said one day to Guizot : " I have need of M. Thiers or you in the Chamber." He might rather have said : I lean first to one of you, then to the other, and I am sometimes embarrassed to chose between you. There is no doubt, in fact, that the King was, in the actual state of affairs, considerably embarrassed. He preferred Thiers's policy at home and Guizot's abroad, Thiers for interior affairs, Guizot for foreign affairs. The state of

things in Spain forced him to determine upon a choice.
The question of armed intervention in this country had
been considered in the last ministry, that of the 11th
of October, as it was called.   The King was opposed to
intervention.   " Let us aid Spain," he said one day, " but
let us not ourselves enter into their bark.   If we get in,
we must take the helm, and God only knows what will become of us!" The whole Cabinet, except M. de Montalivet,
Minister of the Interior, confidant and personal friend
of the King, favored intervention, and decided not upon
an indirect aid—the King was resigned to this—but upon
an immediate and effective assistance.   Liberal Spain
demanded it.   The treaty of the Quadruple Alliance,
which united the constitutional monarchies of England.
France, Spain, and Portugal, seemed to force France so
to act.   The King recoiled from the idea.   " The ice
must be broken," said Thiers ; " your majesty does not
wish for intervention ; we wish it ; I will resign."   And
he did resign.

Then was formed the Cabinet which was destined to
be, at a later day, the object of the Coalition.   Thiers resigned August 25th, 1836.   The Molé ministry was formed
September 6th.   Guizot was Minister of Public Instruction in the new Cabinet.

In the summer following his retirement, Thiers departed
for Italy. A history of Florence had occupied his mind for
some time, and he determined to take advantage of this
respite from political duties to collect on the spot data

for the book.   He visited Rome, having for *cicerone* the illustrious painter, M. Ingres, who was director of the Paris School of Painting in that city, and divided his admiration between the beautiful remains of antiquity and the masterpieces of the Renaissance.   Thence he went to Florence.   The approaching opening of the Chamber brought him back to Paris November 3d, 1838.
, The discussion of the Address * in response to the Speech from the Throne which followed the meeting of the Chamber, is worthy of attention, not only because it gave Thiers an opportunity to defend the foreign policy of his ministry and to explain its nature, but because it marks the beginning of his opposition to Louis-Philippe, and because it was the almost official revelation of the King's personal policy, a sort of public and solemn denunciation of the corruption of the true principles of government.

The two acts of Thiers's administration which were misunderstood were, first, the demand on Switzerland for the expulsion of a certain person named Conseil, who was represented as a dangerous refugee, but who was in reality an agent of the secret service of France, and secondly, the question of Spanish intervention.

On January 13th, 1837, the Conseil matter came up, and the next day the Spanish question.   Thiers spoke on both occasions.   Concerning the first affair, he recounted

---

* The " Address " was the response of the Chamber to the " Speech from the Throne."

the facts and said simply "that he acted honestly in demanding the expulsion of Conseil, for he supposed him
to be not a spy, but a refugee; that he had made the
criminative requisition on the representations of the Minister of the Interior;" and he added, addressing to his
opponents these words, which should be remembered:
"You have had recourse to a collective responsibility,
that of the president of the Council of ministers. One
has a right, you say, to turn to him for all the affairs of
the Cabinet. That is true; I was president of the Council, and I ought, therefore, to be responsible. Here is
my answer: Yes, as president, I ought to have known
everything, but I did not; I should have been told
everything, but I was not. Now it is yours to find on these
seats the person on whom rests the real responsibility."

Concerning the Spanish question, he spoke several
hours, giving with admirable clearness the whole history of the matter and ably justifying his policy. But
he did not stop here; he let it be known that the King
had a contrary policy which had put an end to the ministry, and which should be the real object of inquiry.

A graver statement could not have been made. Royalty found itself thus unceremoniously discovered. The
spectre of personal government reappeared again; its
return to the Tuileries was publicly denounced, and it
was done by one of the founders of the Constitutional
Monarchy, by the one of them perhaps the most powerful

The sensation was profound. The *Journal des Débats*

said the day before this speech was delivered : "We believe that M. Thiers belongs to the majority by indissol-
uble ties ; he has associated his future with that of the
majority by six years of glorious solidarity ; he has,
therefore, a marked position in the ranks of this majority, which is astonished to find him no longer at its head.
Will M. Thiers choose another position?" This sprang
from inquietude, but after the speech, inquietude gave
place to irritation. Thiers, by bringing the King in question, was accused of betraying the secrets of the council.
He did not try to defend his conduct on other ground
than that he had been driven to it by legitimate defense.

The rupture that the *Journal des Débats* feared was
therefore consummated ; but it was not only a rupture
with the majority, but, what was more grave, with royalty. Thiers felt that his principles required of him
such a course. It is certain that the King's secret inter-
meddling in politics, his pretension—which he carried into
effect—to a policy of his own, a personal action distinct
from that of his responsible ministers, by which he dis-
pensed with them—all this it was difficult to reconcile
with Thiers's vigorous maxim, "the King reigns, but
does not govern." Thiers's conduct is perhaps strengthened by the fact that Guizot, who was a member of this
same cabinet attacked by Thiers, was soon led (on April
15th, 1837,) to separate from it and take part, in the name
of the same principle, in the celebrated coalition formed
against M. Molé.

The period at which we have now arrived is full of
interest to the history of the parliamentary government
in France, and to the general history of the parties which
then disputed and still dispute for the control of the
country. It comprises Louis Napoleon's fiasco at Strasburg in 1836; the acquittal of his accomplices by the
jury; the changes in the Molé ministry, from which, as
we have just said, Guizot resigned, and which adopted
the conciliatory policy of its predecessor; the promise
made by Thiers to the King to come to the aid of the
Cabinet thus modified, into which, furthermore, his friends
of the Left-Centre * had entered ; a most brilliant oratorical struggle between Guizot and Thiers concerning the
secret service appropriations, on which occasion the antagonism between the statesmen burst forth in clear day;
and, in fine, certain events arising from the foreign policy of the country, which threw Thiers back into the Opposition again. But let us, for the present, pass over all
this and devote ourselves to the Coalition.

Royer-Collard said one day, in speaking of the Coalition,

---

* The terms generally employed to designate the parlimentary parties in
France, are the Right, (conservatives), the Centre, (liberals), and the Left,
(radicals.) Sub-divisions are made into Extreme Right, (ultra-conservatives),
Extreme Left, (ultra-radicals), Left-Centre, (advanced liberals), etc. The
political opinions of these groups change with the epoch of French history
under consideration. During the July Monarchy they might be thus designated : Right, (legitimists,) Centre, (constitutional monarchists), Left, (republicans and radical monarchists). To-day, however, we may say : Right,
(legitimists, Orleanists, and Bonapartists,) Centre, (liberal republicans), Left,
(radicals). It is difficult to be exact in these divisions, but a general rule
places the conservatives on the right, the radicals on the left, and between
these two extremes are ranged various groups whose political opinions often
merge one into another.

"I have seen better, I have seen worse, but I never saw anything like this." Royer-Collard would not have said this if he had troubled himself to look below the surface. Perhaps, too, he wished to point an epigram. The question, though less grave and of a different form, was nevertheless the same as that which had produced the liberal movement of 1828-9, and which had inspired and dictated the famous Address which the King, Charles X, had heard from the mouth of Royer-Collard himself. It was again a question of personal government or the government of the country by the country. Louis-Philippe never said, as has been pretended, " the government, it is I." But he had a policy of his own, and he took care that it should be known. He did not attack the prerogatives of representative government, but he perverted them. Guizot, in explaining his entry into the Coalition, has said that " the part that the Chamber took in the government was not large enough," that " the Cabinet of April 15th, (the second Molé ministry, gazetted in 1837,) was not able to establish between the Crown and the Chamber that cordial understanding and active harmony which, under a representative form of government, alone can guarantee the force and security of power, by centring in the ministers the whole responsibility of it." * There was enough ground here, to unite in one common action men divided on many other points, like Thiers, Guizot, Odillon Bar-

---

* *Mém. de Guizot*, T. I. p. 287.

rot,* Arago, the astronomer, and Michel de Bourges, and
to give some show of reason to the Coalition.   Personal
government has always been the bugbear of enlightened
Frenchmen; they have only been divided on the means
of combating it, and of finding the best form of government that will guard against it for the present and
the future.

Thiers directed the campaign, for he alone of the dis-
affected leaders combined in himself the antecedents, the
influence and the ability to secure the success of the enterprise.   He was the leader of the Left-Centre.   He had
in the Left and even in the majority men upon whom he
could count.   He had powerful supporters in the press,
and when they were wanting he knew how to create them.

The efforts of a political leader in France are exerted
in various directions, in the press, in the lobbies of the
Chamber, in the *salons*, in the tribune.   It may be said
that the press prepares the arms and the munitions of
war, that the talk in the lobbies and *salons* sounds the
disposition of the troops, animating some, sustaining
others, giving courage to the timid, hope to the ambitious,
assigning to the captains their parts and placing them at
their posts.   Then only is it, after all these preliminaries,
that the leader plants his flag in the tribune and deploys
before the enemy.

Thiers, who of course, excelled in this last decisive part

---

* Barrot, (1791——), advocate and liberal statesmen, belonged to the Left
under the July Monarchy ; to the Right under the Republic of 1848 ; and was
an enemy of the Empire.

of the action, was not less remarkable in the others. To a profound knowledge of men and of the means of influencing them, he added a peculiar talent for working upon the press and making it turn in his orbit.

One word on this last point. Thiers had promised the King to support the ministry of April 15th, whose domestic policy was a reflection of his own ; but the reflection soon became so dull that it was scarcely visible, and the foreign policy, on the other hand, had so changed by the abandonment of Ancona * that it was no longer possible for Thiers even to seem to stand by the ministry. The overthrow of M. Molé and the paving of the way for a new policy were to be the great questions of the new session of the Chamber that was about to open. Thiers, as we have said, left for Italy in the month of June, 1837. While studying there the wonders of art and the great battle-fields of Bonaparte, he was watching with an attentive eye the mistakes of M. Molé, the movements of public opinion, and was endeavoring, among other means of putting an end to a condemned policy, to influence the course of the newspapers which were open to him, both by instructions and advice, sketching out a plan for the campaign for this one, suggesting the manœuvres and evolutions that this other one should carry out.†

---

* The French took possession of Ancona, on February 22d, 1832, in order to protect Italy from the aggressions of the Pope through Austrian assistance. This popular measure of Casimir Périer was undone by Molé, who withdrew the French garrison in 1838, thus giving a triumph to Austria and the Pope, and, at the same time, increasing his own and the King's unpopularity.

† See, on this point, among Thiers's letters from Italy at this period, that dated, June 24th, 1838, written to M. Véron, editor-in-chief of the important newspaper of the epoch, the *Constitutionnel.*

The struggle began at the opening of the session in December, 1838. The committee of deputies appointed to draw up the customary Address to the King, pronounced for the policy of the Coalition. It criticised the whole foreign policy of M. Molé and the interior administration which showed too plainly the hand of the King. This last was the capital point of the Address. It recalled particularly the glorious origin of the monarchy in order to give the Tuileries to understand that this origin had not been forgotten. It laid especial stress on the insignificance of the ministry, in order to clearly point out the pretensions of the King to govern himself and to impose his personal policy. In closing, the committee said:

" We are convinced, Sire, that the intimate union of the public powers kept within their constitutional limits can alone effect the country's security and the strength of your government. A firm and able administration, resting on noble sentiments, causing your throne to be respected without and reminding it of its responsibility within, is the best guarantee of that co-operation which we heartily desire to lend you. Let us trust, Sire, in the virtue of our institutions. They guarantee, be assured, your rights and ours; for we consider it as an established fact, that the constitutional monarchy secures at the same time your rights and ours."

The reading of the Address created a great agitation in the Chamber, an agitation that can be easily explained, for the document that provoked it was a rupture not only with the ministry, but with the Crown, and the symptom of a division in the majority.

The discussion that it gave rise to proved this: M. Molé committed the fault of feeble men in weak positions. He forgot the noble words of Casimir Périer, addressed to his supporters: " In parliamentary struggles never seek to dishonor your opponents. It is debasing France herself." The ministry of April 15th, contrary to this high principle and patriotic sentiment, attempted to change the nature of the debate, to disfigure it, to contract it to the proportions of a personal fray, by representing Thiers and Guizot as ambitious men, who opposed the government because they had been ousted from power, and this opposition as a sort of parliamentary and constitutional Fronde. The *Journal des Débats*, developing this idea, and pretending to see no difference between the policy of the Cabinet and that which the two ex-ministers had followed, published, the very day the discussion began, one of the bitterest and most caustic articles that ever came from the pen of Saint-Marc Girardin.* Here is a portion of the article:

" We hear people ask concerning the Coalition, violent measures and the refusal of co-operation. What is the matter? M. Thiers and M. Guizot are not ministers. * * * What is different to-day? One thing, but one

---

* Girardin (1801–1873), celebrated professor, writer, journalist and politician ; became deputy in 1871. His articles in the *Débats* and in the *Revue des Deux Mondes* made him famous. This article, though not signed, is clearly the work of M. Girardin.

single thing: M. Guizot and M. Thiers are not ministers.
That's all there is of it. Antwerp, Poland, Switzerland,
the conversion of funds, the maxim: 'the King reigns
but does not govern,' the Coalition, the Address, all tend
towards this same end: M. Thiers and M. Guizot must
be ministers."

Guizot, who had perhaps just read the article of the
Journal des Débats before entering the tribune, took up
the accusation, and citing the words of Tacitus, *omnia
serviliter pro dominatione*, hurled back the taunt that had
been flung at him by giving M. Molé to understand that
in his case ambition was aggravated by servility. Thiers,
who spoke after M. Molé, thought fit to refer to the
article of the *Débats*, but his words were less bitter.
He limited his remarks to what everybody knew, namely,
that he had resigned of his own free will; that he
might have entered the new Cabinet if he had wished;
that he had been an opponent of the present policy
even in the councils of the Crown. But Thiers, to
speak only of him, did not stoop in this debate to irritat-
ing personalities, and immediately elevated the tone of
the discussion by placing it on its true ground, and keeping it there.

M. Doudan, the preceptor of the Duke de Broglie, one
of the most talented men of an epoch and a society
where talent was not lacking, called Thiers " the intestine
agitator of assemblies." Thiers possessed in a high degree the art of producing an agitation in an assembly,

of keeping it up, of throwing life into it ; but the agitations of his making were not aimless, not futile.   Thiers
never lost himself like Guizot, to use the expression of
Cousin concerning the latter, in sterility.   He always had
an object, an end in view.   The agitation that he created
was always associated with a clear, precise line of policy,
and he knew how to always keep it within fixed limits.

The situation, as developed by the Molé ministry, was
very simple ; the Cabinet had become the instrument of
the King's policy, and this policy, the character of which
was to yield too much abroad and to concede only with
bad grace at home, appeared to everybody—even to the
most enlightened friends of the Government itself—to be
fatal.   It was necessary, therefore, to change it, and to
substitute for it a policy which should be firmer and
more national abroad and at home more liberal, more in
conformity with the spirit of the revolution of 1830,
which was made against personal government ; more in
conformity, also, with the best interests of royalty, which
was weakened and compromised whenever it overstepped
its bounds.   The whole discussion concerning the policy
of the Molé ministry that occurred at this time in the
Chamber, which reëchoed with the eloquence of Thiers,
Guizot, Berryer, Lamartine, Odillon Barrot, Garnier-Pagès,
etc., was, in the numerous speeches made by Thiers, confined to this line of argument.   From his speech delivered on October 7th, 1839, we make a few extracts, which
show his independence in regard to the Crown and the

elevated reason for his resistance to the Crown when he was led to oppose it. His words should be remembered, for in them lies the secret of Thiers's opposition from 1840 to 1848.

"Gentlemen, it is not true that the hearts of these men (members of the Coalition) have been alienated; they are devoted, but in their own way. Yes, gentlemen, there are two ways of being devoted, two good examples of which are known to you. One way is to always serve the government, even when it is in the wrong; not to dare to tell it the truth, not to have the courage to break with it. There is another kind of devotion which is much better, a devotion which would always save governments, if it were always practiced. ◦ It consists in being independent of the government, in telling it the truth, in not following it when it errs. * * The mistake of all the governments which have preceded us lay in their not knowing how to stop, in their going too far. The Revolution, which came to reform the country, covered it with ruins. The Empire, which ought to have given us order and victory, left us despotism and defeat. The Restoration, which would reconcile the ancient monarchy with liberty, ended by the *coup d'état* and divine right. Our own Government does not seem to know where to stop."

The Coalition finally triumphed on March 1st, 1840, when the Molé ministry fell. The Chamber had dissolved and the electors had been consulted. The maxim "the King reigns, but does not govern," was again victorious. But the success of the Coalition did not put an end to the crisis. It called for a ministry composed of Guizot, Thiers and Odillon Barrot. But Guizot and Odillon Barrot were too widely separated. Thiers and Guizot could unite, but the Left and the Left-Centre would not listen to it, remembering Guizot's obstinacy in carrying out the policy of repression that the Coalition had done so much to crush. Furthermore, the King, though vanquished, did not like his conquerors, and he would not accept the radical Left. "God only knows whither the soldiers are leading their chiefs," he said one day to Guizot. In the midst of this political confusion, a republican insurrection broke out which created more excitement in a few hours than the parliamentary agitations had done in two months. The King tried to set up a compromise ministry but failed. He was forced by circumstances to call on Thiers, who seemed to be the only person who could bring order out of the parliamentary chaos which was growing worse. The King did not like Thiers, and it was a bitter necessity which drove him to the man who had done so much to make him a king. "I sign my humiliation to-morrow," Louis-Philippe remarked on February 28th, 1840. He had no thoughts of a *coup d'état*, no intentions of reisting openly the majority in the Chamber. He confined himself to manifestations of bad temper. Thiers being somewhat embarrassed to find a minister of finances, the King said, "He need not bother himself about that; let M. Thiers present to me one of the ministerial ushers; I give up." In the new ministry,— the ministry of March 1st, 1840—Thiers was made President of the Council, with the portfolio of Foreign Affairs.

Before leaving this period of Thiers's life, we wish to recall the most important acts of his two ministries, which we have had to pass by, in order to show more clearly the regular development of his dominant thought. Nor can we neglect to speak of his employment of the leisure moments that he was able to snatch from militant poli_tics, of the opinion that the public had of him, and of the noise that his name produced, for all this forms a part not only of his own history, but of the history of his time.

The political events of the early part of Louis-Philippe's reign had left commerce and industry in a lamentable con-dition. The great public works were interrupted. The highways, the canals, the light-houses along the coast, all demanded immediate attention. In Paris there was no work. At this crisis Thiers became Minister of Com-merce and Public Works. He forthwith called the at-tention of the Chamber to this crying condition of affairs, and obtained twenty millions of dollars to be applied to public improvements. Then it was that the Arc de Triomphe and the Madeleine were completed, that the column in the Place Vendôme was inaugurated. Yet many monuments remained unfinished. Paris demanded new embellishments. When Thiers became Premier in 1836, his first act was to ask for new appropriations to meet the necessary expenses. The Column of July and the principal adornments of the Place de la Concorde were the result of this demand.

Amid the many duties imposed by public life, amid the agitations, complications and struggles of this stormy epoch, Thiers seems to have found time, even in that terrible year of 1834, disturbed as it was by insurrections, to obtain admittance into the French Academy, and to deliver on that occasion a remarkable discourse; to visit England in 1833 for the purpose of studying industrial and commercial subjects; and to sketch the *History of the Consulate and Empire.*

On June 9th, 1839, the day after a great debate, in which Thiers took a prominent part, the newspapers made the following announcement:

" M. Thiers has just concluded with Paulin, the publisher, an arrangement for the publication of the *History of the Consulate and Empire*, a continuation of his *History of the French Revolution.* M. Paulin has secured a perpetual right to the MS. of M. Thiers by the payment of $100,000, $80,000 to be paid on the delivery of the MS., and $20,000 a year later." Talleyrand said, *à propos* of the *History of the French Revolution :* " Thiers would perhaps be still more happy if he should take up the Empire." Perhaps it was this remark of the illustrious diplomate that suggested to Thiers his great history.

Thiers, with antecedents such as were his, after his active and important rôle in politics for near twenty years after the prominent part that he took in the revolution of 1830, could not but occupy a great position in the eyes of the public. The legitimists were vanquished probably forever; the republicans were awed, though trembling less from fear than hope; royalty was advised to keep its proper place, if it would not compromise its mission and existence. Enemies would of necessity rise up against the man, who more than any other had contributed to such results. No one can escape destiny and human nature. Talleyrand said to Thiers on one occasion, "Would you be a man? Have lots of enemies." And Thiers followed his advice. Thiers said one evening in 1865—if we are not mistaken, in his parlor in the Place St. Georges, *à propos* of some impertinence of the courtiers of the time: "I am an old umbrella which has been subjected to many showers, and much misuse; you can't expect anything else in stormy times and civil war." Insults of all kinds were heaped upon Thiers, particularly during those periods when he was in power or opposed to the Government. It would require more than one folio to enumerate them. From the countless number we select but two, which are by no means the worst. A very radical journal said one day: "We have a kind of ogre among us called Louis-Philippe, and a sort of Tom Thumb, named Thiers." An extreme royalist sheet, attributing to Thiers an over-great love of the "almighty dollar," remarked : "We understand that M. Thiers is going to make a trip to Auvergne. Auvergnats, look out lest he carry off the Mont d'Or!"

CHAPTER IV.

THE RIVALRY OF THIERS AND GUIZOT—1840–1848.

Guizot wrote the following lines concerning Thiers, at the time of the formation in the Chamber of Deputies of what was called the *Thiers-parti*, which was made up of Liberals friendly to the dynasty:

"It is a characteristic of Thiers's nature, which, it seems to me, has betrayed him more than once, not to put enough confidence in his own powers, not to depend sufficiently on himself and himself alone, and to allow himself to be influenced too much by the desire of avoiding the criticism of the party which has been his political cradle. His judgment and his tastes mark him a statesman, which is rarely the case with individuals sprung from the ranks in which he has always lived. Hence it results, that between his station and his inclination, between the course of his life and the instincts of his mind, there is a discord which has often been to him a source of embarrassment and a cause of feebleness. If he had been more under the influence of a just pride, if he had more of a mind and will of his own, he would, I think, have better governed his own and his country's destiny; for he would have found in his independence much more strength than he could derive from the support of the revolutionary and fluctuating party with which he was associated."*

It is impossible to read these lines without profound astonishment. One believes himself dreaming to hear a man of such intellectual parts speaking in this wise. To represent Thiers as a man who lacks confidence in his own powers, above all, who does not rely sufficiently on himself, who has not a firm mind and will, is to produce the strangest paradox imaginable, and the most contrary to the truth. In order to explain such a mistaken appreciation, it is necessary to bear in mind the influence of the spirit of sect and system, the blindness of vanity and the bitterness of an old rivalry; it is especially important to remember—for Guizot was not an ordinary man— that he had an unlimited confidence in the value of his own theories, and that he believed in their infallibility, if not, which is uncertain, in his own. Now, there was an essential difference between Guizot's theories and Thiers's manner of looking at political questions, and this difference sufficed to ruffle the serenity of the judge's mind and cause him to give a biased opinion.

Let us consider this difference for a moment. With Guizot, everything was based on his theory of the middle classes and the *legal nation.*† The pre-

---

* *Mémoires de Guizot*, T. III., p. 290.

† To be an elector at this period it was necessary to pay taxes amounting to 200 francs, about $40.00. The whole body of electors, according to Guizot, made up the *legal nation* (*pays légal.*)

ponderance of power appertained to the *bourgeoisie*,
or middle classes. There was no political or legal
France outside of the electoral body. No one was
a legal Frenchman unless he paid a tax of 200 francs.
Guizot did not depart from this rule. He took up a
position in this theory as if in a fortress. From his
ramparts, from this belvedere, so to speak, he contem-
plated the outside world, judged society, and pretended
to govern it. To rule by means of the middle classes, to
satisfy their interests and wants, to give to the country
only the measure of liberty, air and light that this new
aristocracy demanded, and that its temperament was able
to support, to found a constitutional monarchy on this
unique base, narrow as it was, such was Guizot's object,
his dominant idea, the pivot of his policy. Thiers, without rejecting the principle, while also placing the axis of
government in the middle classes, in the *bourgeoisie*,
wished to strengthen the prop, to enlarge more and more
the base of the system by accepting the co-operation of
all those who sprang from the same principle, who had
the same origin, namely, the French Revolution. For he
was persuaded that the July Government would never be
in a condition to face its veritable enemies, the legitimists and the clergy, if it were also opposed by all the
ardent libérals and republicans.

There was still another difference between Thiers and
Guizot : the latter held firmly to a pacific policy, as did
the King ; the former, led by a desire to firmly establish

the new government and to support the dignity of France, did not draw back before the contingencies of war, even a great war, if it were rendered necessary by the country's honor and the interests of the Revolution of 1789.

Thiers, with these ideas, entered in 1840 into the councils of the Crown, with the intention of carrying them out. He exclaimed one day in one of those sallies which were common to him, " I am not liberal; I am national." This was true of him in the ministry of the 11th of October, 1833, but now he wished to be both, and if he was more one than the other, if the dominant character of the cabinet of the 1st of March, 1840, was national, it was due more to circumstances than to his own feelings in the matter.

The task that Thiers proposed to himself in assuming the direction of affairs, particularly when we consider the impulse and character that he wished to give to them, was difficult if not rash. He had to bring the King over to a foreign policy, which. Louis-Philippe always looked upon with trembling. He had to conquer a considerable part of the old majority which favored the King's policy, simply because it was the King's. Even the majority on which he counted, and which he had to have to govern, was neither compact nor sure, and a goodly number of his allies followed him less on account of himself than in order to check the Government. Accord was, however, possible among the different branches of government concerning domestic affairs.

No great domestic question at this moment divided public opinion. But this was not the case with foreign relations. On the occasion of a conflict between the Pasha of Egypt, Mehemet Ali, and the Sultan Mahmoud, the Eastern question was about to reappear, to bring face to face the peace policy of the King and the war policy of Thiers, and the Chamber was to be called upon to pronounce between them.

According to Thiers—and we would lay stress upon this point—the chief concern of France ought to be her foreign relations. The independence and honor of the country should never be lost sight of in the interest of domestic peace and the dynasty. Thiers saw everywhere the seeds of war: in the ambition of certain powers, in the nature of the governments, and in the agitations of the peoples, and he knew too well that, whatever question might be raised, France would be sooner or later drawn into it, either from necessity or duty. There re-resulted from this, these two things: first, that patriotism was a very important virtue for France, and that along with patriotism there should be foresight; and secondly, that it was the bounden duty of every government regardful of its mission, to always keep alive the military spirit—not the spirit of conquest—that France might be always ready for emergencies.

To understand Thiers and his ministry of 1840, and even the greater part of his writings, this fact should be born in mind. The *History of the Consulate and*

Empire is pervaded by this idea. To keep the patriotism
of France ever on the alert, to quicken this patriotism by
lessons from history, by the great examples of the past,
so that the country should always be equal to whatever
complications and necessities might arise, this, in Thiers's
mind, was one of the first duties of the statesman. Political, constitutional, material, moral questions should be
considered also, but afterwards. The soul of France
should be gotten ready before its armor, and put into a
condition to bear it. The situation of the hour argued
in favor of this line of policy, for, as we have said, the
irrepressible Eastern question was threatening the peace
of Europe.

Marshal Maison, one of the generals of the first Empire, died a few days before the formation of the ministry
of March 1st, 1840, of which Thiers was Prime Minister.
Invited to speak at the grave, Thiers delivered an eloquent
oration, which is an earnest expression of the ruling idea
that we have referred to. In one part of this speech he
exclaimed : " Of all the grandeur of the Revolutionary
period, what remains to us? Nothing of that national
grandeur which spread from the plains of Italy to those
of Holland; but the moral grandeur of its memories,
which lives imperishably in history, which will inflame
future generations, and make them worthy of the past ;
this grandeur has come down to us intact. Let us preserve it as the most precious heritage. It is the memory
of the lofty deeds of our warriors which should sustain

our young soldiers if their courage is put to the test. They should try to equal the soldiers of Kléber, of Massena, of Bonaparte!"

It was also with this same object in view, that he took the initiative in a measure which had been often agitated, the translation of the remains of Napoleon from Saint Helena to France. Of course international reconciliation was another motive that influenced Thiers. But the aims were not contradictory: the desire to efface past hatreds does not interdict care for the future, nor the duty of providing against their return. Yet at this very moment— and we mention the incident simply to show how much there is that is capricious and unforeseen in French political life—while the Prince de Joinville, the son of Louis-Philippe, with two French war vessels was traversing the ocean to bring home the dust of the great Emperor, the illegitimate* adventurer—"Napoleon the Little," as Victor Hugo happily terms him who afterwards became Napoleon III—made his absurd fiasco at Boulogne.

Those who like to believe that history is but a game of chance, and who are prone to descant upon the uncertainty of fate, can find here matter for the support of their skeptical philosophy. Here was a government which wished to pay homage to a national glory, and to draw therefrom new force and strength both for itself and the country;

---

* It is now an opinion widely held that Louis Napoleon was not a Bonaparte, but the son of a Dutch marine officer, Admiral Verhuell, one of the numerous lovers of Queen Hortense. See the posthumous article of Sainte-Beuve. *Cæsar and the Cæsars.*

and yet, at the same time, this country's heir, more or less legitimate, made use of this glory against the government which proclaimed it, converting it, so to speak, into a hostile banner, a machine of war.   And not less strange, perhaps, was the incident of France and England, seeking, in honoring a great name, to bury old grudges, and yet, at this precise moment, entering on a path which threatened to lead them to new wars.

But these coincidences, arising from chance, did not occupy in an equal degree public opinion or the thoughts o' Thiers.   The Eastern question gave rise to graver considerations than that of the abortive demonstration at Boulogne.   But, nevertheless, this episode can not be passed by in silence : the pretender had assigned Thiers a part in his projects and in his dreams ; and, further, was not this affair connected by an invisible link with events in which Thiers was to be found to act more than once an important part ?   Was not the second Empire conceived of these early *pronunciamientos ?*

The attempt at Boulogne had been preceded by that of Strasburg on October 30th, 1836.   The King's weakness had sheltered the pretender from justice and transported him to America.   Exile never reforms a person : Louis Napoleon soon left the United States and took refuge in England, where he meditated new enterprises.   Did he count on the unpopularity of the Government, which was, by the way, exaggerated ?   On the difficulties of its foreign policy ?   On the co-operation, foolishly presumed, or the connivance of the statesman who stood at the head of the Cabinet, and who, he knew, was a great admirer of his uncle? However this may be, on August 6th, 1840, he disembarked near Boulogne, accompanied by some devoted friends and servitors. Having entered the city about five o'clock in the morning, he presented himself at the barracks of the garrison, where he tempted the soldiers and officers with offers of money and promotions. There was at first, among the troops and in the city, a little confusion and disorder; but this lasted only a short time. The troops shrugged their shoulders, and the sub-prefect promptly arrested a majority of the companions of the prince. The audacious adventurer, however, had counted on success, and had prepared in advance a series of decrees, with the intention of organizing in a moment a new government. Among these curious papers there was one which named Thiers President of the Council of Ministers.

The pretender had deceived himself concerning Thiers and the country. Thiers saw in Napoleon I a great warrior and a powerful administrator, who was made for the time in which he arose, a sort of splendid and isolated meteor, at first useful, then fatal to others as well as to himself, and who could be followed through the heavens of history by the brilliant track he had left behind, but who had no successor, and who had nothing to do with an age of liberty. The Empire without the Emperor never appeared possible or desirable to Thiers. The immense majority of the

people at that time felt in the same way.   In certain districts, the interests of the nation were confounded with
those of the Empire, for its wild dreams had been forgotten and only its glories remembered.   But there was no
desire, however, on the part of these worshippers of the
first Napoleon, to lend themselves to the projects of a
young and ambitious upstart, and to stir up a revolution
on his account.   The *Journal des Débats* said in reference
to the Strasburg fiasco: "The first thing that strikes
one in the Strasburg affair, is the impertinent folly of
the enterprise, the incredible presumption of a young man
who, without any other title than his name, without other
means of affecting people's minds than by the aid of a coat
and hat ridiculously modeled after those of a great man,
presumes one morning to put on a crown and enthrone
himself Emperor and master of France."   Lamartine, in
a grand and magnificent oration delivered on January
7th, 1837, said, referring to the folly of this enterprise, that
"the Empire has left only a bronze column in a Paris
square."   And this was true.   The adventure found credit
only with some fanatics and a few corrupt and needy
officers.   The Boulogne enterprise was equally weak
and foolish.   Thiers was disturbed by it only in so far as it
was a symptom of the state of the public mind, of the
restlessness of the national spirit of the people which the
timid course of the King did not satisfy; it was one more
reason for strengthening the dynasty by some of that
military glory of which the first Empire was as prodigal

as the July Monarchy was parsimonious. He saw that his foreign policy might lead to war, but he also saw that if the war were successful or only nobly supported, it would exalt the cause of constitutional monarchy and give it a prestige that would stand all pretensions and all pretenders.

The Eastern question was of long standing. Thiers found the crisis in an already advanced state when he came into office. The victory of Nezib, in Northern Syria, June 24th, 1839, gained by Ibrahim Pasha, son of Mehemet Ali, Pasha of Egypt, over the troops of the Sultan, had in. creased the pretensions of the rebel vassal. He demanded, as the price of the victory, that he be made the hereditary ruler of Egypt and Syria. This was, in the opinion of England, prejudicial to the integrity of the Ottoman Empire; for France, on the other hand, it was the forti- fying of this empire, for she believed the real soul of the Turkish power to be, not at Constantinople, but at Alex- andria. France knew, also, that Mehemet Ali was not at all disposed to yield, and she feared that a prolon- gation of the struggle would give the finishing stroke to "the sick man"—as the Czar once called the Sultan — whom England and France, however, had an equal inter- est, an equal desire to save. Marshal Soult, who was President of the Council and Minister of Foreign Affairs before Thiers came into office, wrote, on February 19th, 1840, to Guizot, the ambassador of France at London: "The government of the King has held and holds still that, considering the position in which Mehemet Ali finds himself, to offer him less than the hereditary right to the thrones of Egypt and Syria would be to run the risk of a certain refusal on his part, which he would back, if necessary, by a desperate resistance, whose consequence would shake and perhaps overturn the Ottoman Empire." Another circumstance aggravated the already complicated question: a few days after the battle of Nezib, it was decided by a diplomatic note that the trouble should be settled by the great Powers acting in concert.

Thiers—become Premier—thus hemmed in, at first quietly strove against the situation, not wishing to sacrifice the Pasha nor to break with the Powers. He worked, in the first place, to avoid a conference where he was almost sure to have the others against him, and, in the second place, to bring about an understanding between the Sultan and Pasha. It was a difficult job. Thiers wrote Guizot at London, on July 16th, 1840, a letter which terminated with these words: "You and I have never got into a worse dilemma; but we could not do otherwise. In the beginning, we might have pursued a different course, but since the treaty of July 27th, 1839,* this is out of the question." He hoped, however, to get out of the dangerous dilemma, when he suddenly learned that the question had been settled without consulting

---

* This treaty, made between England, France, Austria and Russia, placed the defence and integrity of Turkey under the protection of these Powers.

France, on the overtures of Lord Palmerston, and that Mehemet Ali was to be forced to give up all claims to Syria; the treaty of July 15th, 1840, between Russia, England, Austria, and Prussia, had been signed.

France, thus excluded unceremoniously from the European concert, was keenly wounded. The blame was laid especially on England, who was looked upon as the ally of France. The old sores reopened. M. de Lavergne* wrote to Guizot at this moment, "The public mind is extremely bellicose." The band of the National Guard played the *Marseillaise* in the ears of the King at the Tuileries. At the opera, this refrain of a chorus in a new opera, *Charles VI*, was received with frantic applause:

> Non, non, jamais en France,
> Jamais l'Anglais ne régnera.†

This song was continually heard in the concerts and in the streets. All the organs of public opinion, with rare exceptions, were for war. The sons of the King leaned that way. Alfred de Musset, the poet, a frequenter of the Tuileries and a personal friend of the heir apparent, the Duke of Orleans, improvised, in a court soirée, it is said, a war song in response to a new song of Becker, the German poet, entitled *The German Rhine*.‡

---

* M. de Levergne, born in 1809, to-day life senator; friend of Guizot, member of the Academy of Moral and Political Sciences, an able writer on economic subjects, and in politics a strong conservative.

  † No, no, never in France,
  Never will the English reign.

‡ The German poet had said,
  "They shall not have it, our German Rhine."

Thiers was not less keenly affected. He was greatly irritated, above all, at Lord Palmerston. He called his proceeding a "deception." He wrote Guizot on July 21st, 1840: "France to-day has only to consider her own convenience," and he did not intend to suffer himself to be held in check. He thought he had been outraged. He sent to the Powers a very strong note, in which he protested against what had been accomplished. He was almost as greatly irritated at Austria as at England, finding no longer in its policy the wisdom of Metternich. The Austrian ambassador at Paris insisted that Syria was of little importance to France. "Yes, without doubt," responded Thiers, sharply; "of course we will for no consideration make a campaign in Syria; for Italy is better, and she is nearer!" This was a threat at Austrian influence in Italy. War, therefore, appeared to him an almost inevitable necessity, for which it was important that he should be prepared. The treaty of July 15th, 1840, however, was carried out. On September 11th, Beyrout, an important seaport of Syria, was bombarded by the united fleets of England and Austria, before the eyes of the sailors of the French fleet, unable to understand, said an officer, "why their cannon did not go off of themselves." On September 14th, 1840, Mehemet Ali was conquered. Thiers's ardor was not extinguished. He prepared to augment the army. Infantry, cavalry, artillery, all were increased.

De Musset replied proudly,
    " We have had it, your German Rhine."
Lamartine also answered Becker, in his *Marseillaise de la paix.*

Thiers proposed to raise the effective force to six hundred and thirty-five thousand men, and to mobilize three hundred thousand men of the National Guard. Thus prepared and decided, he wrote in a diplomatic note: "If you take Egypt from the Pasha, the cannon will decide between us."

In the meanwhile, the French fleet, anchored before Beyrout was ordered home. The enemies of Thiers called this feebleness, and the charge has often been reiterated. In truth, it was but an act of prudence. In the event of a war, the government wished to have all its strength at hand within its grasp. So earnest was Thiers, so far was he from doing an act of weakness, that he proposed · introducing the war question into the customary Speech from the Throne.

It was a solemn moment for the King and his dynasty. If Thiers's policy had prevailed in the councils of the Crown, the whole course of events which have happened since, the disastrous experiment of 1848, the twenty years of despotism that followed, with the terrible end whose consequences have not yet disappeared,—might not all this have been avoided? But it was fated that, at the supreme moment, the King should recoil. When the question came up before the cabinet, during the discussion concerning the Speech from the Throne, the diversity of opinion between the King and the minister showed itself. Thiers wished that the language of the King should energetically support the conduct of the ministry.   The King proposed a compromise.   Thiers, fatigued, and fearing that the Chamber would side with the King, handed in his resignation, as did all of his colleagues.   This was on October 29th, 1840.

It will be remembered* that in Thiers's earlier connection with the July Government, he was not unmindful of the internal improvements of the country, and during his short ministry of 1840, material as well as political questions received his closest attention.   The hesitation that he had formerly shown concerning the importance of railroads — a hesitation which malevolence has transformed into ignorance and old fogyism — had now long passed away, and he hastened to atone for his mistake. He caused a subsidy of about nine millions of dollars to be voted for the construction of several railroad lines. He encouraged steam navigation, and presented to the Chamber bills for the establishment of several great packet lines, three out of four of which were to be furnished with eighteen vessels constructed in the State ship-yards, and capable, if necessary, of carrying guns. The abolition of the monopoly of the manufacture of salt, the development of the trade in thermal waters, and several other matters of interest to commerce and industry were considered or carried out under Thiers's administration.

On the same day that Thiers resigned, Guizot was gazetted President of the Council of Ministers.   Here be-

---

* See Chapter III, page 88.

gins the strife between Thiers and Guizot, an ardent and bitter struggle, which was ended by the fall of the July Monarchy and the advent of the Republic of 1848.

Guizot's conduct, in accepting office at this time, has been severely criticised. He has been accused of having, while French Minister at London, deceived Thiers and then of having supplanted him. The keen remark of Royer-Collard is well known: "You called Guizot an austere intriguer?" somebody asked him. "Did I say *austere?*" responded the terrible old man. This remark, already in circulation, was now taken up and repeated everywhere. The words of the *Journal des Débats*, which were a commentary on it, were quoted again: "Our support you (Guizot) can have, our esteem, never." From this period dates the immense unpopularity which followed Guizot until the destruction of the monarchy, and which contributed not a little to precipitate it.

Is the reproach true that Guizot, while French Ambassador at London, acted in opposition to the instructions of his minister and the principles of parliamentary government, and obeyed the personal policy of the King? In this connection we will simply recall the fact that Thiers wrote to his ambassador on March 2nd, 1840, the day after he became President of the Council, "on leaving Paris you declared to me in the *Salle des Conférences* that your foreign policy was mine;" that Guizot admitted that he occupied, while Minister at London,

"as regards the war, a decisive position;"* that Lord
Palmerston, however badly disposed towards France he
might be, could be arrested by the Tory party, whose
principle personage, Lord Wellington, said, "nothing can
be done without France, war is at hand, we desire
peace; therefore, it is necessary to be on good terms with
France." † "It is also certain"— it is Guizot himself who
says so—"that Austria and Prussia did not hold to the
policy of war;" ‡ and that Lord Palmerston would have
shown less obstinacy if he had believed that France
would go to extremities.

It is at least inexcusable in Guizot, that he did not see
the impropriety of his being the successor of a man
whose policy he was supposed to have favored, and of
forthwith adopting a policy of an exactly contrary nature.
Guizot did not like Thiers, and—not to speak of feelings
of jealousy and rivalry—he often imputed to Thiers intentions and sentiments which had no foundation in fact.
Guizot, while Minister at London, wrote to one of his
friends *à propos* of the translation of Napoleon's remains :
"I notice without surprise the art with which the ministerial organs or those of the Left have avoided speaking
of me in this affair. This will continue, though I have
been written to that,' if we succeed in this affair, we will give
you all the honor of it.'"§ To suppose that Thiers would

---

* *Mémoires de Guizot*, T. V. p. 20.
† Id. p. 370.
‡ Id. p. 364.
§ Id. p. 118.

descend to such petty acts can not be excused on the
ground that the injuries of the one atone for the injuries
of the other.   The ambassador ought to have dominated
over the man.   The simplest sentiment of decorum would
have counseled him to follow his chief into retirement
and to check his ambition for a time.   But there were
many audacious actions and many defects of conscience
hidden under the Puritanical gravity of Guizot.

M. Odillon Barrot, the brilliant orator of the Left, in a
scathing speech, characterizes Guizot's conduct in this
affair after this manner: "Henceforth, men will say,' who
will feel safe in the direction of the Government, when a
minister, having chosen a foreign representative from the
Chamber and having confided to him not only official
documents but his most private thoughts, suddenly sees
this representative rat, mount this tribune to lay bare before this country and the world the unfortunate spectacle
of such an antagonism, and even take advantage of documents wherein are disclosed the confidential opinions of
the minister?' Do you ask my opinion? You, the ambassador of this policy, the intimate confidant of the author
of this policy, you are the last man to replace the minister who was carrying it out."

Thiers, throughout the discussion of the Address which
followed the change of ministry and in which Guizot was
so roughly handled by the Opposition, defended his policy
with his customary vigor and frankness.   But the most
important feature of this apology, which had much more

to do with his acts than with his relations with his ambassador, was the direct attack which he made on the Crown. For, according to Thiers, more serious than the question of external politics, was the sacredness of the Constitution, which had been violated, if not in its letter, at least in its spirit. Personal government had reappeared: the fall of the ministry of March 1st, 1840, was caused by a new and graver act than any that had preceded it, was due to a single will. Called upon by the attacks of the partisans of the war to explain the inaction of the last days of his ministry, he made this declaration which pointed right to the King: "If the 29th of October* replaced the 1st of March, it was because the 1st of March was not able to obtain the measures that it judged necessary."

This was a Parthian arrow. Thiers went on to bury it deeper in the side of royalty, but not with the design of killing royalty. Thiers never had but one enemy—personal government, because he never had but one idol—the French Revolution, to which personal government is more than the antithesis. But this enemy he pursued, whatever form it assumed, by whatever good intentions disguised. In denouncing its presence in the working of the Constitution, he desired to defend and strengthen the Constitution. There is nothing less revolutionary in France than respect for the Revolution.

Thus Thiers found himself again at the head of the

---

* The Ministry of Guizot, which lasted until the revolution of 1848.

dynastic Opposition, forced by the very nature of this principle to form a new coalition which should be more ardent, more impassioned than the old. It was also to have a slower growth and another and more redoubtable result. Thirty years were to pass before its chief was to return to power, to reappear in the tribune and speak in the name of a government!

Some of the measures of his ministry were not entirely accomplished when he retired. The solemn reception of the remains of Napoleon did not take place until December 15th, 1840, and the appropriation for the construction of the fortifications of Paris were not voted until the month following.

This latter project gave rise to a great and memorable debate in which the principal orators of the day participated. The enemies of the Government and the Cabinet held that the scheme had for its object not so much the protection of the capital as its intimidation. Lamartine considered the plan useless, Garnier-Pagès, dangerous. Thiers defended his project in an able and powerful speech. " Fortify the capital," he said, "and you greatly modify war and politics ; you render wars of invasion, that is to say, wars for principles, impracticable. * * * Suppose Paris defended by permanent works, by walls; the conditions of war change immediately; it is no longer a battle, it is a siege. But, an army, however large it may be, cannot carry on a siege with its ordinary resources. Special materials are necessary. Siege-guns, which cannot be carried into the field, which are transported with difficulty in one's own country, and which are conveyed with great labor in an enemy's country, even after several successful campaigns have rendered one absolute master of it,—great siege-guns must be had.   Again, an army must sit down before a fortified town for a number of days, which it cannot do for lack of victuals, munitions, and resources of every kind.   *   *   * ' But, for what purpose,' some ask, ' would you expose a million souls to the terrors of a siege, to the horrors of a bombardment, to the misery of starvation?   How, in such extremities, can you govern them and restrain them ? How can you grasp in a sort of vice great capitals in which beats the heart of the country—the government, the chambers, the principal organs of the public ?   What ! all this blockaded at one time !   Subjected to the severities of military rule !   The mind is frightened and recoils in horror at the thought of it.'   These are phantoms which vanish as soon as approached.   The moment that you render the capital capable of sustaining a siege, at that moment you deliver it from all the dangers of a siege.

The walls of Paris,* therefore, stand as a monument of Thiers's rule of six months, a monument, which, if it has not fulfilled all his hopes, is none the less a part of his glory.   It was a grand and patriotic conception, and the

---

* The walls are about twenty-two miles in circumference, thirty-two feet high, and have an average thickness of about twelve feet.   A ditch fifty feet wide, which can be flooded with water, surrounds the walls on the outside, while a broad macadamized military road follows the course of the fortifications on the inside.   It took three years to complete this immense work.

recent events which have contradicted Thiers's theories, surpassed all human forethought in 1840. There is a sort of insanity in statesmen and in peoples which escapes all the powers of clairvoyance. The Krupp guns and the means of rapidly concentrating and victualing an army, which played so prominent a part in the war of 1870–71, might perhaps have been foreseen in 1840, but no one could have supposed that France would ever give herself up, bound hand and foot, to an adventurer, to be led into a suicidal war.

Thiers, finding himself out of office, and convinced that he would not soon return to power, bent himself once more to literary pursuits. He had already collected considerable material for the *History of the Consulate and Empire.* With the curiosity and indefatigable industry of a man who, rising at six o'clock in the morning, terminates his most laborious days in society, he had reaped all the harvest that Paris could afford, and already a large part of his task, in so far as it concerned France, was done before it was commenced. But the scope of the work which he had outlined in his mind, did not embrace France alone : it included all Europe. He, therefore, visited Europe, studied the archives, questioned illustrious survivors of the great epoch which he was describing, examined the celebrated battle-fields and the cities which had sustained memorable sieges, all the places famous in connection with the gigantic struggles that he would portray. It is for this that he is seen by turns in Italy, Germany, Spain and England from 1841 to 1845. At length, he was able to publish, during this last year, the first two volumes of the work, which embrace the Consular period.

The success of the work was immense. The critics were not weary of praising it. Royer-Collard who, confining himself to the ancients, no longer *read* but simply *re-read*, as he liked to say, devoured Thiers's two new volumes. One day the latter, calling on him, found the old gentleman in his study. Pointing out to Thiers a volume of the *Consulate and Empire* lying on his table beside a volume of Plato and Tacitus, he said, "You see you are not in bad company." Thiers replied that he trembled at his situation. "Don't fear," was the response; "you can hold your ground against everybody." "The remark is charming," says Sainte-Beuve, who recounts the anecdote, "and furthermore it is just, and of great weight from the mouth of a man who seldom paid compliments." Talleyrand had been a good prophet: the historian of the Revolution had in truth succeeded still better in dealing with the Empire.

Neither literary work nor success, however, turned Thiers's attention from political affairs, which every day became more worthy of the attention of the friends of the Revolution.

Guizot continued in his course, abandoning himself more and more to the policy of resistance at home and peace at any price abroad. "The spirit of the Emigra-

tion and the Church," as the *Journal des Débats* said one
day, "killed the Restoration, and the July Revolution
sprang from opposition to this very spirit." Yet Louis-
Philippe seemed to have entirely forgotten this. In a
word, as Thiers has said,* Catholic influence supplanted
Protestant influence, and he entered upon this inauspi-
cious period, having for standard-bearer and trumpeter
an orthodox Protestant who was almost a Puritan. For it
is Guizot who opened the door to ultramontane influence,
and was to try to use it as an instrument of government,
for a *régime* sprung from a liberal and patriotic revolution, under the pretext of securing by its means good
order, conciliation, pacification and the elevation of
mankind !

Contradictions destroy themselves : the Government
could not disregard the spirit of liberalism, its prime
source of birth, without also disregarding that patriotic
fermentation which was its secondary origin. Guizot and
the King thought to become monarchial by favoring the
religious spirit, to enter into the family of legitimate
sovereigns, into the Holy Alliance, by pursuing a peace
policy. The King carried his love of peace even to a
degree of weakness. The English alliance, looked upon
as the palladium of peace, was to be maintained at any
price. Hence it was that France, against every principle, gave England the Right of Search, where French
vessels were supposed to be slavers. The flag was al-

---

* See Chapter III., p. 55 *et seq.*

lowed to be insulted under color of philanthropy.   Hence
it was that the right of the United States to annex Texas
was called into question in the name of a fanciful American equilibrium, analogous to the famous theory of the
Latin races, invented at a later period by the complaisant
Napoleon III, in order to give plausibility to the foolish
Mexican expedition.   It was also this system of peace
at any price that led the Government, on more than one
occasion during the latter years of Louis-Philippe's reign,
to suffer England to influence its action both in European
and extra-European affairs, occasions that we are only too
glad to pass over in silence.   And it should also be borne
in mind in this connection, that this senile policy did not
even possess the merit of always being consistent.   For,
after having made for so long a time concessions to
England, the Government, on a sudden, falls out with her
à propos of the Spanish marriages and thus loses all the
benefits of its sacrifices.   It is true that there were two
interests combined against the English interest : the
Catholic, which was kept restrained, and the family, the
all-important interest, which controlled everything.

Thiers, with that firmness of spirit and conviction,
which we have recognized in him, could not—all interest
of ambition and popularity aside—remain impassive in
the presence of such a policy, or even appear to compound with it in the slightest way.   However, from 1840
to 1844 he rarely appeared in the tribune to combat it.
But towards the end of 1844, the faults of the adminis-

tration increased in such an alarming manner, the system
began to display itself in a series of acts in which the
spirit of the Revolution and the interests of patriotism
were so manifestly disregarded, that Thiers thought it
his duty to assume a firmer, more aggressive and more
systematic attitude of opposition.   He protested with all
his force against the Right of Search, and combated the
policy of the English alliance with its few advantages, its
inconveniences and its humiliations.   On laying before
the Chamber a bill concerning secondary education,* he
called attention to the rights of the State in matters of
education, which he declared to be those of the new era,
the modern spirit, and pointed out the dangers, in the
form of Jesuitical pretensions, which lurked under the
mantle of liberty.   The next year, carrying on the same
fight, he remarked on the encroachments of the church,
favored by the Minister of Justice, M. Martin (du Nord),
and M. de Salvandy, Minister of Public Instruction, and
did not hesitate to remind his hearers of the laws abol-
ishing the Jesuits, and demanded their enforcement.†
Furthermore he attacked the Jesuits before the public at
large in his newspaper, the *Constitutionnel*, which pub-

* The system of education in France may be divided into 1. Primary,
2. High School, (*instruction secondaire*,) 3. University.

† *A propos* of these two personages, we can not refrain from recounting
some recollections which seemed to be signs of the times.   M. Martin, the
protector of the Jesuits, was accustomed to indulge in the lowest habits.
This was brought up against the society.   Denounced by the police, he was
surprised in a low resort and escaped by suicide from public dishonor.   M.
de Salvandy, a very worthy man, had a very different character.   Though
friendly to the Jesuits, he did not believe in the morality of their education,
if we can judge from what he said at an official dinner which we attended

lished as a *feuilleton*, Eugène Sue's famous romance of
the *Wandering Jew*.*

It would be very interesting to enter into details, and
to examine closely the incidents of the struggle which
we well remember, in which Guizot and Thiers deployed
all the resources of their talent, but we are forced to
choose and concentrate our attention on some of the
more important portions.

The discussion in the Chamber of the Address of 1846
took place in the midst of a great fermentation of public
opinion. People were grieved and humiliated more and
more by the foreign policy of the Ministry, and above all
by its unmanly attitude towards England. They were
irritated by its opposition to the simplest and most
popular liberal reforms, and by its ever-growing concessions to the clergy. The friends of royalty were
afflicted by the increasing unpopularity of the Ministry,
which reflected back on the King. His enemies were
delighted at this. Among these latter were the legitimists, to whom, however, many advances and concessions had been made. They had been hastily admitted

---

in 1846. At this time the trial of Beauvallon, who was, by the way, one of
the Broglie Prefects in 1877, was attracting a great deal of attention. Beauvallon had killed in a duel Dujarrier, a journalist and a lover of the famous
Lola Montez, who finished her curious career at New York in 1861. " I
have had the curiosity," said M. de Salvandy, "to look up the antecedents
of these different persons, and it is a fact that all of them were educated at
religious establishments. I wish to draw no conclusions, but yet this does
not prove much in favor of the claim which is advanced by the Jesuits, that
they make virtuous men and women of their scholars."

* The *Wandering Jew* is from beginning to end an attack on the spirit of
covetousness, monopoly and ambition of the Society of Jesus.

into the highest public offices, for no other reason than because of their nobility or family relations, and they now began to grow bolder in their opposition, turning against the new monarchy the arms it had used to over-throw the old. The legitimists argued in this wise: The revolution of July was an uprising against personal government, but personal government remains. It was to bring about better order at home, but it has not done so. It was to give greater liberty within, and to elevate the prestige of France abroad. It has failed to do both.

As for the republicans, the *National* appeared too moderate. A new newspaper, the *Réforme*, stronger and more ardent in its opposition, was founded, and appeared in the political arena under the auspices of Ledru-Rollin. Then there was the Socialistic party, with Louis Blanc, Proudhon * and others at its head, inimical to the present order of things. And lastly, the clerical party, for which the dynasty had done ·so much, but which attacked it all the more bitterly for this very reason. The *Univers*, then as now the clerical organ, complained daily that the Church was in a state of servitude, because it had not the right to enslave everybody and everything.

Thiers, who followed with an attentive eye this work of decomposition, where the good and the bad were mingled, where the most laudable aspirations were not the less dangerous, saw that, in order to control the situation and rule the political parties or at least to check them, the

---

* Proudhon, (1809-1865), the noted publicist and radical speculator on social and political subjects.

Government ought now more than ever before to change its policy, to satisfy generously the liberal and patriotic demands of the people, and to accept frankly and honestly as in 1831 and 1832 the representative *régime*.   He expressed these opinions frequently in the whole discussion of the Address and throughout the whole session of 1846, where, among other speeches, he delivered two remarkable ones, that of January 20th, dealing with the policy of the Cabinet, and that of March 17th, treating particularly of home politics and parliamentary reform.

We will only cite that portion of his speech of January 20th, 1846, where he speaks of Guizot's policy in relation to the Texas question.   Few Frenchmen have spoken with more truth and sympathy of the American Republic than did Thiers on this occasion.   It sounds like an oration of the centennial year, though pronounced thirty years before that date.

"If one notices what has occurred in America during the last sixty years, he must needs be surprised.   When he remembers that the day we went to the succor of the United States, they scarcely occupied the shores of the Atlantic, that in sixty years they have crossed the Alleghanies, filled the immense valley of the Mississippi with their intrepid settlers, bordered the five lakes, attained the Rocky Mountains, reached the Gulf of Mexico through Louisiana, which we gave up to them, taken Florida, and that to-day they dispute Oregon and the coasts of the Pacific with England ; when one thinks of this, who can help experiencing a feeling of surprise? They had but three millions of inhabitants, and to-day they have from eighteen to twenty millions; they were only thirteen States and now they are twenty-six or twenty-seven; they had no marine and to-day they have vessels and frigates. But this is a poor estimate of their powers. They have an immense maritime population. They have not a great army, it is true, but they have among their farmers fearless riflemen who have checked the English army, trained in our great wars. They possess in addition, the tremendous pride of Democracy. I think that in the presence of such grandeur, one may indeed stand surprised.

"But, I address myself to all of you; look into your hearts, consult your most secret instincts, go back to the traditions of our country for the last quarter of a century, and tell me, are you uneasy and to what degree? Is there anyone here who thinks that this picture gives the slightest ground for fears of rivalry, that it is a source of danger to France? If, gentlemen, there be any that the most piercing eye can discover, I declare myself either a poor Frenchman or an ignorant one, for I can see none; and I am sure that the unfortunate Louis XVI, when he founded the United States, that Napoleon I, when he increased their territory by giving up willingly, voluntarily, Louisiana, did not set up rivals of France.

"If I were an Englishman,—a very great honor I assure you — I should feel anxiety, displeasure, discontent. I am a very decided, a very firm, a very resolute partisan of the union with England; but I cannot identify myself with the hopes, with the fears, with the sentiments of England, so as to believe that America can be either a rival or an enemy of France. No, I feel no anxiety whatsoever when I contemplate the grandeur of America.

"I know what national jealousies are as well as another. I wish well to all peoples; but of grandeur, I desire it only for our own. And, I declare, that America is perhaps the only nation of the world, after France, which I desire to see great."

The speech of March 17th, 1846, touched the delicate and sensitive spot of the political situation, parliamentary reform. Thiers pointed out the corruption sustained and favored by the presence of public functionaries in the Chamber—lobbyists, to use an American term; he dwelt upon the state of dependence in which a great number of deputies was placed, the inevitable result of which was to pervert, to cast discredit upon the representative system, and to leave the way open to personal government.

In this question of personal government, Thiers had clearly the advantage over his adversary; for had not Guizot said in his letter to his constituents, February 6th, 1839, at the epoch of the Coalition, that "the King did not accept frankly enough the influence of the country;" that the policy of the Molé Ministry had been "unpatriotic;" that the authority of France had

grown weaker in Italy, Switzerland, Belgium and Spain ? *
But, however great the temptation was to be personal
in the debate, Thiers did not take advantage of these contradictions, of these numerous changes of his rival, which
Berryer stigmatized later when he spoke of "the au-
daciousness of the apostacies." He wished to aim
straight at Royalty. The King was his objective point
when he indicated the deviations from the representative system that were increasing daily; for he was
sincerely grieved and indignant to see, as he said at the
beginning of his speech, "the government sprung from
the Revolution become more than the accomplice, the
dupe of the counter-revolution at home and abroad."

More than one of the traits of Thiers's character are
seen in this speech. The loftiness and vivacity of his
sentiments show themselves in a striking form in that
passage, for example, where he defends himself from the
charge of being prompted in his attacks on Royalty by
personal reasons: " I will admit it, from the bottom of
my heart, that I am almost ashamed to come here and
recall to you all the reasons I have for confidence in this
Royalty, and, I say this, gentlemen, in all honesty. If
Royalty has been deceived, if it has been made to doubt
my devotion, my wounded dignity asserts itself and I
would not try to undeceive it. I shall never try to make
those believe in my devotion who doubt me." But we
wish simply to point out the object that the orator had in

---

* *Mémoires,* T. IV. pp. 454-5.

view in waging so fierce a war on this Royalty that he
admired. This object was, as we have said, the destruction of personal government.

The defenders of Guizot's course hold, that as he had
a majority in the Chamber and governed with this majority, the essential conditions of representative government were fulfilled and that all the attacks made upon
the Government and Royalty were indefensible. Thiers
argued, on the other hand, that unless Royalty was kept
in the background and set aside, the representative *régime*
was a mere fiction, not a reality. He cited England,
where is never heard "'the queen wishes this, or the
queen wishes that,'" and he added, "this is the true
model of representative government. For myself, I have
sought it since my youth. I desired it under the Restoration; I wished nothing else. I wrote in 1829 this
watchword, which has become celebrated: *The King
reigns but does not govern.* I wrote this in 1829. Do you
think what I wrote in 1829 I do not hold to in 1846?
No, this is my opinion still. But there are able minds
that will say to me, 'You overlook the differences that
exist between France and England,' Whatever may be
said, I cannot see that there are such differences between
France and England that one is destined to have only the
fiction of representative government while the other has
the reality. But if this were true, what then? Representative government would be impossible in France!
Ah, we should have been told so in 1830! * * * We

are often informed," he said in closing, " that this will all
come in due time. Very good. I am reminded of the
noble language of a German writer who, referring to
opinions which triumph late, said, ' I will place my vessel on the highest promontory of the coast and will wait
until the sea is high enough to float it off.' It is true
that in supporting this opinion I place my vessel high, but
I do not think I have put it on an inaccessible position."

This speech produced a profound sensation both within and without the Chamber. A recess of twenty
minutes followed its close. The Court was keenly
wounded. "As leader of the Opposition," said the
Journal des Débats,—" for this is the title he has given to
himself, the crown he has proudly placed on his own
head with his own hands,—a brilliant and successful career
still lies open to M. Thiers; but as minister, after the
engagements he has entered into, he would only cause
his own ruin and that of France. This speech of M.
Thiers is his *compte rendu*."*

The newspapers of the Opposition, on the other hand,
were high in praise of Thiers's boldness and eloquence.
Armand Marrast wrote in the *National*, the organ of the
moderate Republicans : " We will not try to weaken the
powerful impression that M. Thiers made to-day on all
who heard him. Though M. Thiers is an enemy of our
ideas, and though we will never accept his, still this will
not hinder us from doing justice to the talent that he

An allusion to the *compte rendu* of Necker, which occasioned the rupture
between him and Louis XVI, and his dismissal in 1789.

has shown, and the success that he has attained. We have never seen him so full of energy, so brilliant, so happy. At times he rose to the loftiest inspirations. His style, sometimes wandering, beating about the bush, scintillant, was rapid, direct, steady in its blaze. He moved right on, fearless of all obstacles, and, it must be said, if that obstacle was the Throne, it did not arrest him."

In 1847 Thiers's opposition to Guizot, or rather to personal government in favor of the " strictly veritable representative government," had arrived at its last period. Public opinion was growing more and more excited. It had in vain asked for parliamentary reform; it now demanded electoral reform.* That the right of suffrage be given to those citizens who had taken the degree of *licencé*.† Lamartine has just launched a fire brand of war in his *History of the Girondists*, where the Republic appeared radiant in the light of an apotheosis, and the author, breaking away from his former opinions against Democracy, exclaimed that he was working to found " democratic fraternity." Ledru-Rollin's newspaper, the *Réforme*, daily waged war on the Ministry and asserting the sacredness of the right of public meeting, propagated the reform agitation of the *banquets* where were delivered after-dinner speeches of a political nature, against the Government.

---

* The system then in vogue sometimes presented astonishing situations. A newspaper of the period reported that at the royal college of Caen, there was but one vote in the whole *personnel*—the doorkeeper ! Jules Simon, who has since been Prime Minister of France, was then professor of philosophy at Caen !

† The *licencé* is the intervening degree between the baccalaureate and the doctorate.

Thiers, always watchful of public opinion, redoubled his attention that he might seize its import and his energy, that he might direct it. He was leaning more and more to the Left, where he exerted an influence by means of the *National.* He had other newspapers, especially the *Constitutionnel,** more particularly devoted to him and his policy. Thiers felt that something decisive was at hand ; and, persuaded that Guizot, entangled in his unpopularity, would destroy Royalty, he determined to force him to retire, without recourse however to a revolution, and yet without being frightened at the chance of one.

The persistence of the Government in its policy of resistance to all the demands of public opinion, determined the attitude of the champions of the Opposition in the discussion of the Address of 1848. Thiers took the most active part in this great and solemn tourney. In the whole debate the orator only repeated what he had said often before. The reason of this was simple : at a distance of eighteen years, under different forms and circumstances it is true, the Revolution and the counter-revolution still stood face to face. It was a discussion concerning the grandeur or the abasement of France that was listened to by the Chamber and the public. Thiers, therefore, found himself forced to reproduce the same

---

*Though Thiers was the founder of the *National,* (see page 30,) he severed his connections with it soon after the establishment of the July Monarchy, and at the period mentioned in the text he was political director of the *Constitutionnel,* on which newspaper, it will remembered, (see page 15), he gained his first journalistic experience.

arguments, to harp on the old theme. But with what brilliant variations, with what loftiness of mind and warmth of soul, with what versatile talent he acquitted himself of the task, those can tell who heard him. It is certain that nowhere has he been so completely himself, nowhere more liberal, nowhere more national. The debate shows him to us in his entirety. He echoed the patriotism of the nation when he exclaimed, referring to the treaties of 1815, "They must be observed, but detested." Thiers's political character is depicted in its completeness in the following words: "I am not radical; but mark it well, I belong to the party of the Revolution in Europe. I favor only the principles of the Revolution in the hands of the moderate. I shall do all I can to keep it in their hands; but if it pass into hands that are not moderate, I shall not, therefore, desert the cause of the Revolution. I shall always stand by the party of the Revolution."

The struggle was drawing to a close. It was about to pass from the parliamentary arena to the streets. In every conflict that sets parties and governments at enmity, there is a distinct and immediate cause. In the revolution of 1848 it was the denial of the right of holding public meetings. The banquets organized in the autumn of 1848 by the Opposition in the Departments, laid the train which the prohibited banquet of February 22nd, 1848, at Paris ignited. A revolution was the result.

After a long debate in the Chamber concerning the

right of holding public meetings, the Opposition, weary of abstractions and desirous of actually testing the question, appointed a committee to consult with the electors of Paris concerning a banquet in that city, which should be "a protest against arbitrary pretensions."

Did Thiers foresee that the contest, if carried on in this way, if transferred to the streets, would have a conclusion other than that desired by him and the majority of the Opposition? That he at least feared it can be surmised from a remark attributed to him: " Duvergier de Hauranne"* he said, "thinks he will go to the banquet in yellow gloves!" Furthermore, did Thiers want things pushed to extremes? He caused to be published in the *Constitutionnel*: " The Opposition, in assembling, desires only to bring the question of the right of holding public meetings before the courts for their decision." This was written on February 18th, and the banquet was set down for the 22nd. On the 20th the Chief of Police prohibited the banquet. M. Odilon Barrot, in accord with Thiers, immediately called the Opposition together at his house, and it was decided not to go to the banquet, while, at the same time, the meeting expressed the hope " that good citizens will abstain from all gatherings and illegal demonstrations." But it was too late. The dispute was to be

---

* Prosper Duvergier de Hauranne, born in 1798 and still living (1878), is a historian, publicist and statesman; a Doctrinaire ; deputy from 1831 to 1847, and a consecutive deputy under the Republic of 1848 ; imprisoned and exiled by the Empire ; member of the French Academy in 1870 ; and father of M. Ernest Duvergier de Hauranne, who has written much on America, in the *Revue des Deux Mondes*.

decided not by the courts but by force, or, as M. Baroche
(one of the republican agitators of 1848, who afterwards became a minister of Napoleon III,) said, by "the
justice of the people." The excitement spread all over
Paris.

The Opposition, nevertheless, hoped still to direct the
movement to a legal issue. On the 22nd a demand for
the arraignment of the Ministry on the ground of its
anti-liberal and anti-national policy, was signed by fifty-
two of the Opposition deputies, among whom are found,
side by side with such notorious republicans as Carnot,*
Marie,† and Garnier-Pagès, these friends of Thiers, Odilon
Barrot, the Count de Maleville,‡ the Count de Lasteyrie,§
Georges de Lafayette,‖ etc. But, though the banquet was
adjourned, the *Marseillaise* was sung in the faubourgs,
and everywhere resounded the cries of "Down with
Guizot!" "Long live Reform!" The King now saw
that it was necessary to yield to the storm and sacrifice
Guizot. But, in his despair, he called upon M. Molé, in-

---

* Carnot, born in 1801 and still living (1878), son of the celebrated Carnot
of the Revolution ; historian, publicist and statesmen ; deputy from 1839 to
1848 ; Minister of Public Instruction and deputy under the Republic of
1848 ; member of the Corps Législatif of the Empire ; and life senator
under the present Republic.

† Marie, (1797——), advocate and politician ; deputy under the July Monarchy ; member of the Provisional Government of 1848 : Minister of Public
Works and President of the Assembly under the Republic of 1848 ; and a
member of the Corps Législatif in 1863.

‡ Léon de Maleville, (1803——), deputy in 1834 and in 1848 ; retired to
private life during the Empire ; and made life senator by the present Repulic.

§ Lasteyrie, (1810——). archæologist and politician ; deputy in 1842 and
under the Republic of 1848 , member of the Academy of Inscriptions, 1860 ;
and cousin of the Marquis de Lasteyrie ; and made life senator under the
present Republic.

‖ Georges Washington Lafayette. (1779–1849,) son of the great Lafayette,
played a secondary part in the political events of the July Monarchy.

stead of having immediate recourse to a strong and possible remedy—Thiers ; so that when he sent for Thiers
on the night of the 23d–24th, after the refusal of M. Molé
to accept the responsibility, all was lost or at least very
nearly so.

At half past ten on the morning of the 24th, Thiers
addressed his first proclamation to the people, in which
he announced that the troops were ordered to cease firing.
At two o'clock a second proclamation made known " the
abdication of the King, amnesty, dissolution, an appeal to
the country." But the work was already achieved. The
troops had begun to fraternize with the people. M. Dupin had tried in vain to proclaim the regency of the
Duchess of Orleans, mother of the Count of Paris, in
whose favor the King had abdicated. A Provisional
Government was soon established at the Hôtel de Ville,
of which Thiers was not a member. The revolution of
1848 was accomplished.

At the close of this new and long trial of representative monarchy, which, like the first—that of the Restoration—ended in a revolution, an inevitable question presents itself concerning the man who acted so considerable
a rôle in the diverse phases of both trials: What part of
the responsibility belongs to Thiers for the fall of the
July Monarchy, a fall which he did not ask for, and
which, without any doubt, he more than once regretted?

M. Cuvillier-Fleury has said : " One can trace throughout M. Thiers's whole political history this principle of

'the King reigning but not governing,' which he not only created but boldly carried out. It was his armor: now a lance for attack, now a shield for defence. A man cannot carry such an arm without being sometimes transported by the intoxication of the battle. With this principle of defensive and offensive warfare, which had become a part of his very being, M. Thiers began in 1830 with a legal revolution. With this same principle carried to extremes, he contributed, without intending it, towards a second and very different revolution, that of 1848, thus leaving the monarchy, which he preferred, for the republic, which he had not yet learned to like."

Thiers, then, had carried too far, to that degree of exaggeration which in a statesman would be a very grave fault, the application of a legitimate principle, which is in fact the political soul of the French Revolution, and thus thoughtlessly brought on the revolution of February! It would be Guizot then who would stand justified before history at the expense of his rival. We cannot agree with M. Cuvillier-Fleury on this point. Though deploring, doubtless with him, the turn that events took later, we cannot admit that Thiers was wrong in opposing the introduction and perpetuation of personal government under the mask that it had assumed; in attacking Royalty, which would shape the policy of the country to its own liking, subjecting it to the bed of Procrustes, which would resort to electoral corruption to carry its measures, which would allow the influence of Jesuitism

to penetrate everywhere, and to extinguish at the very
hearth-stone all great and generous inspirations.   There
are principles to which it is impossible to subscribe
and remain true to one's self.   Lafayette has said : " Suppose that a man say that two and two make four, and
that a second hold that two and two make eight.   What
would you think of a third who, to avoid the extremes,
should modestly insinuate that it is necessary to take a
middle term, and declare that two and two make six ? "
In judging between Thiers and Guizot, Lafayette's remark should be kept in mind.   Guizot, to please the
King, had adopted a policy which consisted in saying
that two and two make six.   Thiers did not think that,
in order to get the credit of a false wisdom, or to gratify
the longings of ambition, he ought to deny point blank
the axioms of political arithmetic and the primary truths
of his intellect and conscience.

We are of those who applauded the revolution of
1848, and who have since regretted it, on seeing the long
chain of misfortunes that resulted therefrom :—a people
armed with a right which it did not yet know how to
use, which it turned against itself, which it comprehended
only after the most cruel trials ;—a republic ignorantly
thrown into the hands of an adventurer without honor or
genius ;—a petted *bourgeoisie*, brought by groundless fears
under the yoke of antiquated and long-execrated doctrines
—Jesuitism ;—eighteen years of a reign which corrupted
public morality and enervated all institutions, and which,

wrecking itself, wrecked France also, and lost to her two
beautiful provinces;—a new republic called upon to repair the evils of the fallen *régime*, condemned to see
reborn, under other names, the same pretensions of personal government, of arbitrariness, of retrogression towards
the deleterious doctrines of the past.   But our regrets, all
this past of ruin and of tears—of which we personally
have had more than our share—will not render us unjust
to Thiers.   He did what he ought to have done, and all
this desolate retrospect had been bright—it is our honest
conviction—if his policy had prevailed against Guizot's.

There are often singular coincidences in contemporary
impressions and conclusions.   Thiers has been more than
once condemned by judges actuated by entirely different
sentiments and opinions.

On September 4th, 1870, at the moment when Thiers's
motion concerning the vacancy of the throne and the
nomination of a provisional governmental commission was
adopted in the Corps Législatif, Bégère, who afterwards
was a member of the Paris Commune, penetrated into
the lobby of the Chamber.   A group of deputies surrounded Thiers, to whom the adoption of his motion
was announced.   Bégère broke into the conversation,
and said to the circle, as he pulled out his watch : " The
people gave the Chamber two hours to make a government ; it is a quarter past three now ; it is too late ! "
And when Thiers protested, Bégère, placing his hand on
his arm, said :   " Come, come, M. Thiers, don't get angry ;

you are well versed in overturning governments, you,
who have overturned two or three." On Thiers denying
this, the unsparing Bégère answered: "Well, all right,
you overturned one and you suffered the others to be
overturned."

There was more justice in M. Bégère's opinion than
in that of M. Cuvillier-Fleury. Thiers overturned but
one government, that of the Restoration. The others
were overturned without his aid, sometimes in spite of
him. To speak only of the July Monarchy, the responsibility for this catastrophe should be laid at the door of the
King, a man of ability, full of good intentions, a friend
of the Revolution, Voltairian and skeptic, but often.
through feebleness and regard for family, yielding to the
influences of the old *régime*, and, in a word, unfaithful to
the two great moral forces which had placed him in
power, the spirit of liberty and of nationalism.

M. Saint-Marc Girardin, in his *Souvenirs and Political
Reflections*, says that Louis-Philippe was in the habit of
looking upon the National Guard of Paris, "as the acknowledged armed interpreter of public opinion," and that
when he learned that some of its battalions appeared to
be pronouncing against him, he considered, (too soon in
the opinion of M. Girardin), that all was lost. Then it was
that he made this remark to those who advised him to
use force: "What, would you have me fire on my electors?"

The King was right; but in thus giving the true state

of the situation, he condemned himself; he condemned that policy which ended by alienating from him his old friends, his electors, to use his own words, because he would substitute his own ideas for theirs, because he tried no longer to comprehend them, because he turned against himself, the sentiments and principles to which he owed the Crown; and, in condemning himself, he justified Thiers as well against M. Cuvillier-Fleury as M. Bégère.   Governments stand only by being logical, by being faithful to their principles and their origin. And, if we may again refer to Senator Sumner's remark:* "Paris is not worth a mass," for nothing is worth so much as principles.   But if to get possession of Paris, it is essential to go to mass, and if going to mass does not demand the sacrifice of principle, then it is necessary to continue attending mass or give up the city.   Apostasies, even sincere ones, in the long run accomplish nothing in politics.

---

*See the beginning of Chapter III, page 50.

CHAPTER V.

REPUBLIC OF 1848.—1848–1852.

Thiers did not wish for the Revolution of 1848; but it is not true that he accepted the Republic unwillingly, and with mental reservations of a monarchical nature. Neither his past nor his principles absolutely separated him from a republic. He had celebrated its heroes in his *History of the French Revolution* with as much enthusiasm, if not with as much pomp and poetry, as had Lamartine in his *Girondists*. He regretted its fall under the hand of Bonaparte November 9th, 1799, in spite of the fascination that the genius of the destructor exercised over his young imagination. It was implicitly contained in his celebrated formula: "The King reigns but does not govern." He had attacked the Old Monarchy as if by way of reprisal, and it was not his fault if the New Monarchy, to which he was warmly attached, did not understand the meaning of his assault, if the threat was accomplished at its expense. If he was provoked at the unexpected revolution of 1848, and alarmed at the tremendous uncertainty that it threw about the future of the country, he had too much patriotism to allow the accomplished fact to pursue without him the new career so brusquely opened, a career that might be a bloody arena ; and he had too great an intellect to be incensed or sulky over it. After the first moment of stupor had passed away, he came forward to the support of the Republic. On March 8th, 1848, he addressed the following letter of acceptance to the electors of the department of the Bouches-du-Rhône :

* * " I am ready to resist tyranny in every shape, but I shall never resist the force of circumstances unequivocally manifested. I, therefore, acquiesce in the Republic without any reservations, but I do not intend to disavow any part of my life. I have concluded, therefore, to accept the nomination from feelings of duty, devotion and honor, not that I may work in the future National Assembly for a disguised Restoration, but that I may work there' openly to establish the new Republic on a durable and solid foundation."

This declaration, as lofty as sincere, was not equal to the suspicions and imputations then rife concerning Thiers's conversion to republicanism : he was defeated. This injustice was, however, soon requited. In the complemental elections of June 8th, 1848, he was chosen in the four departments of the Seine, Mayenne, Orne and Seine-Inférieure. He decided to represent the Seine.

Events succeeded each other with that giddy rapidity

characteristic of sudden revolutions. The Days of June[*]
had mortally wounded the new Republic, because the insurrection had maddened the multitude and furnished the
enemy pretexts for opposing it. The election of December 10th, 1848, had introduced that enemy into power,
by confiding the destinies of France to the inheritor of the
name of him whom Thiers called, in a letter to Guizot,
"the greatest of men." Neither threats nor popular enthusiasm caused Thiers to lose sight of his principles, or
of the promise which he had given to support the
form of government which represented them at this
moment.

On February 15th, 1850, when the Empire was being
prepared, he pronounced these words, so often repeated
since: "The Republic has this advantage in my eyes: of
all governments it divides us the least." Nor did he
forget that it had another claim, that of being the child
of the Revolution. A short time before the *coup d'état*,
when Napoleon, in order to accomplish his ends, did
not blush to make use of the enemies of the Revolution
to smother it, while at the same time he pretended
to be its continuator and inheritor, Thiers spoke in the
tribune of the Legislative Assembly in this manner:

---

[*] The Assembly, by the decree of June 22nd, 1848, ordered a number of
workmen of the National workshops to enroll themselves in the army. In
case of refusal, they were to be discharged from the workshops. A terrible
insurrection, lasting from June 22nd to June 28th, was the result. Paris
was declared in a state of seige, and General Cavaignac was made Dictator
by the Government. Eleven generals were killed or wounded, the Archbishop
of Paris lost his life, and thousands of people and soldiers were slain before
order was restored.

" Yes, we are Jacobins, and we would not be anything else ; yes, we are of the people's party, Jacobins, together with Mirabeau, Sieyès and Barnave. On our side are also found the Jacobins who suffered and died like Lafayette. The Jacobins, in our eyes, are all those men who since 1789 have uttered a prayer for liberty ; yes, we are glad to be members of this Jacobin party. It would be base to desert the cause of the Revolution, to which we are indebted for all that we are. Our adversaries themselves, who defame and calumniate the Revolution, owe a new existence to it, a new nobility, liquidated debts, the freedom which they employ against it, all, even the very bread that they eat."

This language not only attests Thiers's constancy to his principles, but it was also a political act which published to the world his attitude in regard to the new order of things. At the same time, he struck a blow at the enemies of the French Revolution, at the legitimists and the clericals, and at all those who, while pretending to restore the Revolution, shut out liberty, its very essence : he arraigned, in fact, the abettors of socialism and Cæsarism. To both he distinctly said that they would have to reckon with him. It was with socialism that events first brought him face to face.

On January 4th, 1839, Lamartine, in a great speech, in the course of which, while referring to the July Monarchy as a government of transition, and revealing a leaning towards a Republic, he thought it his duty to defend the prerogatives of the Crown against the attacks of the Coalition, was interrupted by Arago, the astronomer, who, called out to him from his seat : " And the socialistic party?" " The socialistic party?" responded Lamartine; I am asked what the socialistic party is? Gentlemen, it is not yet a party; it is an idea."*

Lamartine was right. The socialistic party was then only an idea. He would have been more correct, if he had said that it will always be an idea; and he would have come still nearer the truth, if he had said that the socialistic party is found everywhere, and at all times, pertaining to all parties, since they all, through politics, strive after a certain type of society which is the force and *raison d'être* of each of them. We have, however, recalled this incident because it displays two tendencies, and shows the republican party thus early divided into two factions, in one of which, political questions dominate, in the other, social matters; the one, taking civil society as produced by the upheaval of 1789, sees in a republic only a means of ameliorating it; the other, bolder and less patient, would bring about an immediate reform, not hesitating sometimes to employ dictatorial measures in order to set up its ideals. Arago, Marrast, General Cavaignac, Crémieux,† Garnier-Pagès, Michel de

---

* Mém. de Guizot, T. IV., p. 290.

† Crémieux, born in 1796 and still living, (1878), is a distinguished advocate and politician ; a radical deputy in 1842 ; Minister of Justice in the Provisional Government of 1848 ; deputy under the Republic of 1848, and again in 1869; Minister of Justice in the Provisional Government of 1870 ; deputy in 1872, and now life senator. As president of the Universal Israelite Alliance of Paris he has done much for the Jewish race all over the world.

Bourges, Ledru-Rollin and Lamartine himself belonged
to the first of these divisions; Louis Blanc, Pierre Leroux,* Proudhon and Considérant,† though differing profoundly, may be classed under the second division.
Thiers, when he came over to the Republic, could, of
course, associate himself only with the first.

We already know Thiers well enough to be sure that
if he took up arms against socialism, he would not hesitate to aim his weapons at its most dangerous representative, and, in his desire to destroy the system, would not
recoil from charging the very centre of the armed square.

Socialism, to take the vague and elastic word that has
prevailed, had affected many forms and many systems, and
under the various names of Icarianism, ‡ Phalansterianism,§ the Rights of Labor, Babœuvism,‖ Communism, etc.
had offered many panaceas to the public.   Some laughed,
seeing in the Utopias of this intellectual movement only
the natural product of a great and agitated society,
the play of the imagination, or innocent inspirations

---

* Pierre Leroux, (1798–1871,) was one of the early socialists, becoming an
ardent advocate of Saint Simonianism in 1831 ; Deputy in 1848 ; left France
after the *coup d'état* of 1851 and did not return until 1869.

†Considérant, (1808 ——) was the chief advocate of the social system
named after its founder, Fourierism ; deputy in 1848 ; founded a colony
called Reunion, near San Antonio, Texas ; returned to France in 1869.

‡ Etienne Cabet,(1788–1856,) a French socialist and radical democrat, published in 1842 a romantic socialistic book entitled *Travels in Icaria*, which
enjoyed great popularity among the working classes of Paris.   He established
several communistic colonies in this country.

§ Phalansterianism is derived from *phalanstery*, a large building intended
to be the common dwelling of all the members of a social organization established upon the plan of the French socialist, Charles Fourier.

‖ So called from Babœuf, who, a French socialist of the last century, assumed the name of "Caius Gracchus." He advocated equality and community
of property.

analogous to those of the Sermon on the Mount ; others excused the movement, considering these idealities, the fermentations, and necessary stimulants of social activity, like the mirage of the desert, which keeps up the strength of the traveler, by holding out to him an oasis ; but the more thoughtful, without yielding to needless alarm, recognized in socialism warnings for a selfish society too forgetful of the destitute. But when socialism along with the February Republic entered the Hôtel de Ville, backed by a population exalted by a revolution, deep apprehensions were awakened, and as socialism, whether it wish it or not, is always looked upon by the great mass of people as an attack upon property, property was alarmed. Reflection easily proves, that in a nation which numbers more than seven millions of property holders, whose soil already so worked, can still produce more than five times what it now produces, whose personal property is continually increasing, whose manifold and immense activity finds so many outlets,—in such a nation, it is evident that property is impregnable, and need fear no danger. But reflection counts for little in times of revolution. This solicitude, though it had no foundation in fact, was none the less real; and the anti-republicans, furthermore, vied with each other in turning it against the Republic and the Revolution.

Hence it was that Thiers did his utmost to calm the fears of those who thought property in danger, and, on the other hand, to show the socialists, that, if it were true,

that they wished to found a society which should exclude
property and its essential consequences, the family and
transmissions by inheritance, they were pursuing a
chimæra. He, therefore, attacked Proudhon, him, who
surpassing in his boldness all the other innovators more
or less threatening to property, had dared to cast at
society his audacious paradox : *Property is robbery.**

Thiers's book deserves to be known, and we shall consequently analyze it at some length. It is not a book
written for the moment. The author, it is true, threw it
off in three months in the country, to which he had retired, and where,—as he remarked in the preface of the
book with a little choler—he enjoyed" the repose which the
voters of his native province had procured for him." But
the ideas had been revolving in his mind for three years,
and he had a right to hope the book would survive the
time which saw it produced.

The work is divided into four parts. In the first Thiers
shows how the right of ownership in property has been
questioned in our century, and then goes on to say,
that the study of human nature is the only method to be
employed in settling what are the rights of man in society. Man possesses in his personal faculties a primary
and incontestable property, which is the cause and origin
of all the others ; a secondary property, property, strictly
speaking, the result of labor, and held sacred by society
in the interest of all, is but the consequence of the ex-

---

* La propriété, c'est le vol.

ercise of the human faculties themselves. This principle
established, he easily proves that inequality of riches arises
necessarily from inequality of abilities. Passing on to
the transmission of property, he undertakes to show that
without this essential condition, the right of property is
incomplete and almost useless. Finally, the author ex-
amines the different modes of transmission, the accumu-
lation of wealth and its functions in society, and closes
by showing that the universe, far from being devastated
by the growing extension of property, is, on the contrary
rendered more fit for the wants of man, more capable of
development, in a word, that property civilizes the world
instead of usurping it.

The second part is given up to communism. In the
author's opinion, communism gives rise to community
of possessions and goods, extinguishes all ardor for work,
denies absolutely human liberty, destroys the family in
destroying property, its *sine qua non*, and, consequently,
extinguishes the noblest sentiments of human nature.
In fine, it is but a poor imitation, a sort of counterfeit of
monasticism, which only aggravates the contradictions
that render this latter plan of life impossible.

The third book brings us face to face with socialism
properly so-called. After showing how the adversaries of
property, not always daring to throw it absolutely aside,
have ended, in their efforts to correct what they consider
to be an evil, by adopting different systems, as co-operative association, community of possessions and goods,

and labor rights, he endeavors to find out what are the
real social evils that ought to be remedied. In his eyes,
co-operation is applicable only in certain agglomerated
populations, among the working classes of the cities ;
there only can it hope to succeed. As to the capital
of the co-operative association, if it be furnished by the
State, it is unjustly taken from the pockets of the mass
of the taxpayers, and, if it be deducted from the wages of
the workmen, it is an imprudent investment of their
savings.   Good business management under the co-
operative system is impossible, and tends to substitute
for the principle of personal interest, which is alone suit-
able to private industry, the principle of general interest,
which is applicable only in the government of states.
By the abolition of competition, piece-work is destroyed,
and the workman is thus prevented from participating in
the benefits of capital.   Competition is the source of all
amelioration of the condition of the poorer classes, and,
competition removed, there remains a monopoly to the
profit of the co-operative workmen, at the expense of
those who are not so fortunate as to be associated with
them.   Cheapness cannot be brought about by legislation, and specie could not be safely replaced by paper,
unless this paper is as difficult to obtain as the coin itself.
The obligation imposed upon society to furnish work to
those who want it, cannot constitute a right. Socialists
attack property none the less than communists, and it is
noticeable that they are concerned about but one part of
the people, those agglomerated in cities.

The fourth division of the book treats of taxes. According to Thiers, it is not true, as some pretend, that governments have had as their chief object, during all these centuries, to unburden one class of citizens at the expense of the others, to take money where it was the easiest to find it. Taxes should be levied on all kinds of revenues, whether arising from property or toil. They should be proportional not progressional. He thinks taxes are tending towards infinite diversification : they will be equally and universally distributed, will become confounded with the price of things, in such a way that each person will support his share of the impost, not by reason of what he pays to the State, but by reason of what he consumes. The modifications in the system of taxation, which will do the most good to the laboring classes, are not those most commonly proposed.

M. Louis Veuillot, who is the authorized mouth-piece of the Papacy in France, in speaking of Thiers's attack on socialism, wrote the following lines : " M. Thiers has experienced the fearful shudder that socialism gave him, when it finally appeared, coming forth from the depths of the revolutionary dogmas. Before this monster he found himself helpless. The absolute weakness of his book against Proudhon is remembered. To answer Proudhon it was necessary to have recourse to the Catechism, to Catholicism. M. Thiers never imagined that the Catechism contained arguments against Proudhon, and Donoso Cortés * could not convince him of it, so incapable was his dull intellect of grasping the point, so completely did his famous good sense abandon him at this moment. A Pagan cannot be an able statesman at fifty : he has too much vanity to study the Catechism and learn its lessons. Then, Thiers sought Louis Napoleon and began to recover ground slowly, until Louis Napoleon threw him off, thinking that he had no need of him, and believing that he could stand alone. Thiers and Louis Napoleon closely resembled each other, though Thiers was no dreamer. Both were vain. In his spite, Thiers passed judgment on Napoleon in this wise : ' I like the kitchen, but not the cook.' This witticism reflected more severely on himself than on Napoleon."†

M. Louis Veuillot has seldom more maladroitly tortured common sense and dressed up history, than in these lines, written almost the day after Thiers's death. How could Thiers think of arming himself with the Catechism against the " red spectre," in a society which no longer believed in the Catechism, and where even those who professed to believe in it, scarcely did more than to mumble over its precepts with their lips ? He thought to do better, by addressing himself to men's reason and interests, by pointing to the experience of history, the

---

* Donoso Cortés, (1809–1853), was a Spanish author and diplomate ; conservative in politics and a vigorous defender of Catholicism. His *Essay on Catholicism, Liberalism, and Socialism*, written in 1851, is referred to in the text.

† *L' Univers*, September 16th, 1877. This is the chief Catholic organ in France, and M. Veuillot is its editor.

sentiments and beliefs of all ages and places, which passion might violate in moments of trouble, but whose truths could never be completely extinguished. He had not to do with men of the Middle Ages, but with the descendants of Voltaire, who, on account of the June insurrection, began to lose faith in the philosopher, and with the disciples of Rousseau, led astray by sophisms or a desire to better the world. As regards M. Veuillot's comparison of Louis Napoleon and Thiers, nothing more absurd can be imagined.

Contemporary history does not present two more dissimilar persons, two more opposite opinions concerning the ways and the needs of France. Never was there a man more positive than Thiers, more regardful of rights and law; never was there a man more chimerical than Napoleon, more selfish, and more disposed, in order to accomplish his object, to trample on the rights and laws of his country. Furthermore, there was nothing in Napoleon III to attract Thiers. He knew his origin: he was well aware that the future Cæsar, who was about to avail himself of the true Cæsar's name, had not probably a drop of the true Cæsar's blood in his veins. He saw that Louis Napoleon threatened all that he loved, all that he had worked for, that he was both a mediocre and a dreamer, and, consequently, to be doubly feared, on account of his pretensions and incapacity. It would have been the height of folly, for a man like Thiers, to think one instant of attaching himself to the fortunes

of Louis Napoleon. And yet, after the Days of June,
when Louis Napoleon offered himself as a candidate for
the presidency of the Republic, in opposition to General
Cavaignac, Thiers voted against the general, whom he
esteemed, in favor of the prince, whom he despised.*
Here is an apparent contradiction which has often been
thrown up at Thiers. It must be explained.

Thiers always sought order and liberty, always labored
for their alliance ; and in contests where they were found
to clash, he always ranged himself on the side of the one
he thought the most threatened. After the sanguinary
Days of June, which had agitated the whole of France
and terrified the conservatives, order seemed to be in the
greatest peril. Now, the party of order had but two candidates, General Cavaignac and Prince Louis Napoleon. The general since his June victory had lost much
of his popularity in the republican party, which, opposing
him with Ledru-Rollin and Raspail† was thus divided.
The whole order party rallied around the prince, either
on account of fear or hatred of the Republic, filled with
the secret hope of seeing it soon fall under the weight of
difficulties, which it was not thought capable of supporting. Thiers could not be influenced solely by such
sentiments : it was " the force of circumstances unequiva-

---

* It was held at the time, that he said that " the election of Louis Napoleon would be a disgrace to France." Thiers denied it emphatically in
the Chamber. M. Bixio, a deputy, cried out : " I heard it." Thiers at
the end of the sitting, sent seconds to M. Bixio, and a duel was fought
immediately in the gardens of the palace of the Assembly.

. † Raspail, (1794–1878), the famous radical agitator, who fought in the
streets in 1830 and 1848, and was connected with the Commune in 1870–71.

cally manifested," as he said in his letter of acceptance
to the electors of the Bouches-du-Rhône, that weighed
with him. He hesitated a long time, before he yielded
to the pressure.

To use the words of M. Louis Veuillot, would the
kitchen, that was about to be gotten ready, meet with his
favor? No, no more than the *cook*. Thiers did not like
Cæsarism any more than he did socialism. The Republic
still existed though Louis Napoleon was its president,
and Thiers will be found·defending this Republic against
Cæsarism as he had defended it against socialism. He
bowed before the force of circumstances, but not to the
point of sacrificing the principles and convictions of his
life.

It is but just to say of the old liberal party, of the old
dynastic Opposition, vanquished in February, with the
Dynasty itself, and even of a great part of the majority
which followed Guizot, that it remained true, in spite of
the part that it took in the election of Louis Napoleon
to the presidency, to the great principle of self-govern-
ment. The *Journal des Débats* said on March 11th, 1848,
almost the day after the February revolution: "The discussions of the constitutional monarchy have perished with
that monarchy. Political questions no longer exist; social
questions supersede all others. * * * The question is
whether the industrial, commercial and scientific fabric,
which has existed in France for the last thirty years, will
weather the storm through which it is now passing."

The moderate liberal party, which the *Journal des Débats* represented, had not suddenly deserted its former principles: social questions and political questions are really inseparable, and while it still preferred a constitutional monarchy, it wisely supported the Republic, the government *de facto* and the only rampart against Cæsarism resolved, it is true, to get possession of it, to keep it out of the hands of the extreme republicans who were in the minority in the country, and to monarchize it, so to speak, as much as possible, by giving it the character known at a later period under the name of " Conservative Republic." Thiers found himself in a strong and important party in the Legislative Assembly, and, backed by his friends Odilon Barrot, Dufaure, de Tocqueville * and Léon Faucher, † who had become minister, he strove not to help on the Empire, but, on the contrary, to retard it ; to protect the liberties threatened by an hypocritical and unscrupulous ambition.

To secure this end two things had to be done : 1. To rally round the Constitution as large a conservative party as possible, by drawing off from Napoleon those who followed him because of fear of republicanism,—the timid conservatives before whose eyes the "red spectre" was ever rising ; 2. To consolidate the republicans, by pledging the party to respect the Constitution and defend it from any at-

---

* Alexis de Tocqueville, (1805–1859), the celebrated author of *Democracy in America.*
* Faucher, (1803–1854), economist, journalist and liberal statesmen ; deputy in 1846 ; deputy and minister under the republic of 1848 ; and retired from public life on the advent of the Empire.

tempt at a monarchical or Napoleonic *coup d'état.* These were the two things that Thiers did or tried to do, and herein lies the explanation of his conduct up to the day when the destinies of France were abandoned to force.

Current events are never thoroughly understood ; hence arises the difficulty of writing contemporary history. This policy—which we have just pointed out—Thiers publicly advocated in the Chamber and in the press, and yet, of all the acts of his long and intricate political life, perhaps none has been so misunderstood and so distorted. Many errors persistently survive even at this late day. Thiers is accused of not having preserved an equal balance between the two forces with which he wished to fight the common foe. On the one hand, according to the republicans, he sacrificed too much to the Order party, in voting for the expedition to Rome,* in speaking in favor of the law of March 15th, 1850, which, while rendering primary education unsectarian, left the country districts to the mercy of the Jesuits, and in voting for the law of May 31st, 1850, which mutilated universal suffrage ; on the other hand, he did not give hearty enough support to the friends of the Republic, and on some occasions even caused them inquietude. For our part, we think the republicans mistaken, and we say so the more willingly, since we were

---

* The spirit of the revolution of 1848 spread into Italy, and at Rome a republic was set up by Mazzini and Garibaldi. The Pope called upon France for aid, and Louis Napoleon, who had been recently elected president, sent an expedition to Rome, in April, 1849, which drove out the republicans and reinstated the Pope.

then of their opinion. Thiers could not have done less for the conservative party without dividing it, without throwing the largest portion of it into the arms of the simulating savior who opened them to receive it; he could not have done more for the republicans than he did, by his reiterated declaration of support of the Republic, and of co-operation in defense of the threatened constitution. And Thiers's co-operation was substantial, for all that he did for the conservative party smote Napoleon: the law of May 31st, 1850, just referred to, lost Cæsarism more votes than liberty. This is an important point in Thiers's political life, and the following extract from one of his speeches, shows the sincerity of his sentiments at this period concerning Cæsarism and the Republic.

It was at the beginning of the year 1851. The war that Louis Napoleon was making upon the constitution, which he had sworn to support, was becoming every day more alarming. General Changarnier,* who stood guard as it were to protect the National Assembly, had just been dismissed. A debate immediately began on this bold and significant act. Thiers was among the first to denounce the conspiracy. On January 17th, 1851, in a reply to those who would appeal to the prerogatives of the executive power, and who maliciously foreboded a con-

---

* Changarnier, (1793-1877,) served with distinction in Algeria during the July Monarchy ; was a deputy and commander of the Paris national guard during the Republic of 1848 ; exiled after the *coup d'état* ; fought on the side of France, in the Franco-German war ; and was a conservative life-senator under the present republic.

flict between the President and the Assembly, he said in closing his speech :

"Gentlemen, there are times when we should feel uneasy about the Executive. We are beginning to arrive at a period when we should demand new assurances concerning the power, the pledges and the intentions of the Executive. By this means the Executive would be led to make some useful reflections, which I do not think would humble him before the nation. But if the Assembly give way, permit me to point out the following result : When two powers, brought face to face, have encroached one upon the other, if the one that has infringed be obliged to draw back, an unpleasantness results, it is true, in the very nature of things ; but if the one that has been encroached upon gives way, its feebleness is so evident that it is lost. There are but two powers to-day in the State : the executive power and the legislative power. If the Assembly yield, there will remain but one, and when this is accomplished, the form of government is changed. The Empire will soon follow, but when, is immaterial to me. What you say you do not wish, you will have this very day, if the Assembly yield, for there will be but one power. The order will be given at a fitting time : *the Empire is made !* "

Thiers, on descending from the tribune, was received with tremendous applause, and with the hearty congratulations of a large number of his colleagues, and the sitting came to an end amidst the greatest excitement.

The veil was torn away, and the approaching *coup d'état* revealed. The Empire was established. Thiers no longer doubted it, for he knew the forces that were working for it: a secret ambition, prejudices and the Napoleonic idolatry, which he had unthinkingly done so much to perpetuate. This latter fact only spurred him on to greater resistance. From this moment he is found marching with the Left, supporting every proposition protective of the Assembly. Some advanced republicans, led by a continued distrust of Thiers and over-confidence in the people—"the unseen sentinel," as Michel de Bourges once said—separated from their friends. A still larger body, made up of moderate men from the Right, had also seceded. But Thiers, nevertheless, stood firm, neglecting nothing by which he might hope to check the coming inglorious Brumaire. When on July 19th, 1851, M. de Molé and M. de Broglie, out of dislike for the Republic, supported a project that had for its object a revision of the constitution, so that the President might be re-eligible, he voted against the measure, and advocated with all his strength the Baze resolution,* whose aim was to protect the Assembly from any illegal act on the part of the Executive. The Assembly, unfortunately, was mad and ungovernable. The reactionary party was divided between fear of the Empire and the

---

* M. Baze proposed that the Chamber assign " to the Questors the power of summoning directly the armed force to protect the National Assembly." A questor in a French Assembly is a deputy who performs the duties of a treasurer. M. Baze, who resembles Thiers a little, holds a similar position in the present French Senate, of which he is a member.

Republic; the clerical party leaned towards Napoleon,
who seemed to promise them a flattering future; and the
republicans, one-half defying the future master, and the
other half confiding in the strong attachment of the
Parisians for the Republic, were heedless or divided.
The danger which Thiers had hoped to avert could no
longer be warded off: about two weeks after the presentation of the Baze proposition, the *coup d'état* was accomplished.   Thiers was arrested together with the *élite* of
the Orleanist, legitimist and republican deputies.

If M. Granier de Cassagnac * can be believed, the very
thought of arresting Thiers filled the conspirators with
joy.   After handing over to an emissary a bundle of
papers, on which was written the word *Rubicon*, and
which contained all the decrees that were to be posted
up the next day throughout Paris, Louis Napoleon and
Mocquard, † his secretary, began to laugh " at the figure
that the two littlest men in the Legislative Assembly
— Thiers and Baze — would make, when they would
find themselves prisoners in their night gowns."   However this may be, the following is the way the order was
carried out in so far as concerns Thiers :—

On the night of December 2nd, 1851, Thiers's residence

---

* Adolphe Granier de Cassagnac, born in 1808, and father of Paul Granier
de Cassagnac, the notorious political duelist, is like his son a strong Impe-
rialist, and has held an important place in French journalism and politics
since 1832, when he became one of the editors of the *Journal des Débats*.
Both father and son are now (1878) members of the Chamber of Deputies.

† Mocquard, (1791–1864,) confidant and friend of Napoleon III, became
attached to the Prince and his cause in the early days of the July Monarchy,
and was made a senator in 1863.

in the Place Saint-Georges was buried in sleep. A
commissary of police got in without any noise with
several of his men. He had gone through the mu-
seum, the library, and then into the bedroom, when
Thiers awoke. The officers pulled back the curtains
of the bed, when Thiers, rubbing his eyes, exclaimed:
"What is wanted of me?" "We have come," was
the reply, "to search your house." "You, therefore,
ignore the fact that I am a deputy?" "No," was the
response; "but my orders must be executed." "It is a
coup d'état then?" "I cannot answer your questions;
get up, if you please, and follow me."

One of the apologists for the *coup d' état*, M. Belouino,*
has written these words: "The commissary paid no
attention to the attitude of the ex-minister, and did not
listen to the pleasantries that he took the liberty to indulge in."

Thiers had the right and he used it, of treating with
disdain and of piercing with his irony the clumsy imita-
tors of the great crimes of that history which he knew
too well, not to be struck with the grotesqueness of the
contrast between this of to-day, and those of the past.
In the cab that bore him to the prison of Mazas,† he saw
fit to continue his indignant protestations, "as if," says
M. Granier de Cassagnac, "he would by all sorts of com-

---

*M. Belouino, a writer, who published in 1852 a book entitled: *The History
of a Coup d'état*, from which the citation in the text is made.

† This prison is on the Boulevard Mazas, very near the Lyons depot, at
Paris.

minatory arguments turn the officers from their duty."
It was not in Thiers's nature to be impassible and to conceal his feelings. He knew how to be resigned, not how
to bow the head in humility.

His conduct in the prison was what it should have
been. He felt in a moment that the blow that had struck
him would wound France still more than him. He was
not transferred to Ham, as were the greater part of his
colleagues. Louis Napoleon, perhaps, remembered that
he had made Thiers President of the Council in his
" Provisional Government," at Boulogne in 1840.* He
was permitted to gain the frontier. Mignet came to the
prison and escorted his old friend to the Strasburg depot
at Paris. From Strasburg Thiers went to Frankfort by
the way of Kehl.

His exile did not last long: a decree of August, 1852,
permitted a certain number of the proscribed to return
to France. Thiers was included among the favored ones
without having requested it. On arriving at Paris, he
resumed his historical studies. He had profited by his
exile to visit Belgium, England, Switzerland and Italy,
and to make new researches in the interest of his great
work, the *Consulate and Empire.*

---

* See page 99.

CHAPTER VI.

THIERS AND THE EMPIRE.—1852–1870.

The *coup d'état* of December 2nd, 1851, and the new constitution of January 14th, 1852, paved the way for the second Empire, which was proclaimed on December 2nd, 1852, without a convulsion.

Thiers, though permitted to return to France, as we have just seen, retired from public life, determined to occupy himself with literature so long as the Empire pursued the dictatorial *régime* instituted by the new constitution; for, under such a government, nothing was to be done for the principle of order, which was now being carried to excess, and nothing could be done for the principle of liberty, which was banished from the political arena: nothing to do for the two principles which were the two poles of Thiers's policy. But the decrees of November 24th, 1860, and February and December 1861, having loosened a little the grip of the constitution and given some liberty to the tribune, Thiers felt that he ought to accept the Empire as *de facto* and enter the political lists once more. A step in advance had been made towards parliamentary government; public opinion began to awaken; and a policy, patiently and wisely pursued, might bring about new concessions. Thiers, therefore, decided to revive again the war against all-powerful Cæsarism, and to renew the struggle that he had before maintained to prevent it imposing itself upon France. He had just written in his history that "the country should never be surrendered to one man, no matter who the man is, no matter what the circumstances are." * Would he not have been wanting to himself, if he had kept silent, instead of repeating in a louder voice and in such a way that it would have been better understood, this grand truth so often forgotten in France?

There was a stir at the Tuileries when it was known that Thiers intended to return to public life, and that he was to offer himself as a candidate for the Corps Législatif in the second *arrondissement* † of Paris : the general elections of 1863 were at hand. Louis Napoleon received the news calmly. But M. de Morny ‡ frowned. The Empress was angry, and M. de Persigny, § the spokesman of

---

* *History of the Consulate and Empire*, Vol. X, p. 796.

† France is divided into departments, the departments into *arrondissements*, the arrondissements into cantons, and the cantons into communes. In a political sense, an arrondissement resembles our congressional district.

‡ The Duke de Morny, (1811–1865), generally believed to be a son of Queen Hortense, mother of Napoleon III, began life as a soldier ; then turned business man ; entered politics in 1842 as a conservative deputy ; was a monarchial deputy under the Republic of 1848 ; one of the leaders in the *coup d'état*; for short time minister ; and deputy and President of the Corps Législatif under the Empire.

§ The Duke de Persigny, (1808–1872), became a staunch Bonapartist soon after the July Revolution ; participated in the Strasburg affair and also that of Boulogne ; a Bonapartist deputy under the government of 1848 ; one of the principle actors in the *coup d'état*; a minister and senator under the Empire ; and one of the Emperor's confidants. His letters on public affairs, published from time to time, were supposed to be inspired by Napoleon himself.

the Tuileries, attacked the redoubtable candidate in an impertinent letter, filled with thread-bare criticisms, whose
import can be judged from this sentence : " In the face of
this France, which has attained its present glorious and pros-
perous condition since M. Thiers and his followers retired
from power, universal suffrage will not support against the
Government, which snatched the country from the abyss,
those who allowed it to fall in." M. de Persigny deceived
himself in believing that the electors would take his accusations for serious. It is doubtful if it was the same
with M. de Morny and Napoleon III, who, in spite of
the delusive atmosphere in which he moved, began to see
that Paris was falling away from him on all sides. But,
however this may be, Thiers was elected deputy.

Thiers had already marked out the course he should
pursue: he would second the awakening of political life
of the country, profit by the liberal concessions made by
the Government to force others from it, and bring it back
if possible to the *régime* which it had supplanted; he
would endeavor to throw light upon the condition of the
finances, around which an administration, not over-scrupu-
lous and without any real restraint, had cast a thick veil ;
and, lastly, he would watch closely the foreign relations,
which, since the Italian expedition, filled him with dis-
quietude. His convictions, his past, his patriotism could
not dictate to him another course.

The whole of Thiers's home policy is found summed
up in his great and memorable speech on the " Necessary

Liberties," which he delivered a few days after his entry
into the Corps Législatif, on January 11th, 1864, and in another speech, on the same subject, delivered on March
28th, 1865. These two speeches are monuments of political
science and eloquence, and are applicable to all countries.
The exordium of the first speech reads like a page of
autobiography.

" I know that great assemblies have other things to do
than to occupy themselves about individuals. But when
I ask permission to speak to you for an instant concerning myself, an instant only, it is a duty that I think I owe
my constituents who have asked of me no pledges, and
all my colleagues whose confidence I desire to possess.

" It is now thirty-four years, gentlemen, since I entered
for the first time within this precinct. I was a member
of the first Chamber of the July Monarchy, and of all the
Chambers that succeeded each other from 1830 to 1848;
then, under the Republic, I sat on the benches of the Constituent and Legislative Assemblies; and now, here am I
among you in the Corps Législatif of the Empire.

" Throughout this long period of time, I have seen pass
away, men, institutions, opinions and even the affections,
and, in the midst of the torrent which seemed as if it would
sweep away everything before it, principles have alone
stood firm—the social and political principles on which
modern society rests. Even these were at times in imminent danger: we have seen moments when society was
in such disorder, that it was a question whether it would

ever be restored. Later it was the idea of liberty which seemed effaced from the human mind. Yet order is re-established and liberty is about to reappear. These grand principles are like those orbs which give us light: they are some times enveloped with clouds, only to burst forth again more brilliant than ever.

*   *   *   *   *   *

" There are three principles which I think every worthy man should observe: the principle of national sovereignty, the principle of order and the principle of liberty.

" I was born and I have lived in that school of '89, which believes that France has the right to dispose of its destinies, and to choose the government which it likes. I think that it ought to make use of this sovereignty but rarely, I even think that it would have been better if France had never had recourse to this power, if that were possible ; but, when it has spoken, its word should be law. It seems to me wanting in justice and good sense to strive to substitute individual views for the clearly expressed will of the nation.

" But, when we have submitted to the legal government of our country, we have always the right to demand two things of it : order and liberty. * * * On this ground, even in the midst of the greatest confusion, I have always taken my stand. When in 1848 the Republic was pro-claimed in France, I submitted, although it was not the government of my past efforts, and I joined with the courageous men who, even here, defended order in an

Assembly which, though large and passionate, was honest and brave, and knew how to listen to truths which were displeasing.

"Order, gentlemen, was preserved, and France soon returned to monarchical principles. I again submitted, out of respect for the national will, but I forthwith retired from public life, for a very simple reason, because there was nothing to do for the principle of order which was preserved, and nothing to do for the principle of liberty which was deferred.

"In my retirement, permit me to say, everybody knows what I did: I wrote with sincerity the history of my country. I would have contentedly passed the rest of my life there, if it had not been for the decrees of November 24th, 1860, and of February and December, 1861. You know what changes these decrees made in our institutions. You could formerly come together only in silence in order to receive the bills laid before you by the Councillors of State, which you might discuss with them, but almost without any power to amend. Then came the budget, which was voted department by department, in the lump, and as regards supplementary credits, you could only find out about them through the auditors, that is to say, when it was too late to exercise a useful control.

"The Emperor has changed all this; he has restored political life by allowing you to discuss the Address. He has done more; he has brought you face to face with his Government, by introducing here the Ministers without

portfolios,* and even a Minister with a portfolio, the
Minister of State; he has made your sittings public;
given you the right to vote the budget not department
by department, but by sections; and, as regards the
supplementary credits, if he has not suppressed them, as
was at first expected, he has diminished the time between
the epoch of their discussion and the epoch of their employment, and has thus given you an incontestable influence over these credits.

" Gentlemen, you will never find me either detracting
or flattering.   I do not say that these decrees contain all
the liberties that we desire, but they do contain a considerable part of them, and they are the pledge of the rest.
As for myself, I thank the Emperor for them.   Ingratitude is a bad feeling and a bad return.

" When these decrees were promulgated, I said to all
those who held the same convictions as myself, that I
thought, as they could now discuss here freely the country's affairs, and as they could now co-operate for the re-
establishment of the public liberties, abstention on their
part, would be no longer wise, worthy or patriotic.   I advised them to take the oath of allegiance to the Emperor,
and to participate in the elections either as electors or
candidates.

" I will admit to you, gentlemen, that after having given

---

* Under the second Empire, there was a body of ardent friends of the
Government, who, though neither heads of the different departments nor
deputies, had the right to speak in the Chamber.   They were called " Ministers without portfolios."

this advice, I would have liked to be excused from following it ; for having found in my retirement, study, exemp-
tion from party troubles, and fair play, it was hard to
return into the midst of the storms of public life. But
the inconsistency would have been too great, to give' advice and then not follow it myself.

"Furthermore, this last consideration influenced me
decisively : in coming among you, no one could accuse
me of ambition. At my age, after the posts that I have
held in the State, I could only have one desire now : that
of offering you the modest tribute of an experience dearly
acquired, of discussing with you State affairs, with the
country's interest at heart, not as a partisan, but filled with
the hope of being able sometimes to offer you at least a
trifling aid in your deliberations, and of not letting the
last years of my life be entirely useless to my country."

This preamble of such simple grandeur, the personal
part of which is excused by the speaker's position, was
followed by a complete and luminous exposition of the
principles which are the essence of every free government, whether it bear the name of Republic or Monarchy,
and without which governments, whatever may be their
pretentions, are but dictatorships and despotisms.

Napoleon had promised to give the country very nearly
the same form of government that Thiers had rapidly
sketched in his speech ; but he was slow in fulfilling
his promises, to carry out—to use an expression which has
become famous—"the crowning of the edifice." His

promises were really only lures. He feared liberty; it
was to him a Banquo's ghost.   Many of his friends urged
him not only to stop short in the new path upon which
he had entered, but to retrace the steps he had already
taken in the way of reform. His newspapers, and his
most devoted orators heaped up sophism upon sophism
in the hopes of bringing him back to his first and natural
policy.   Thiers was determined not to let his uncertain
adversary escape him.   In his speech of March 28th, 1865,
he refuted all the objections that had been brought up
against liberalizing the Empire, and showed that new
France, the France of the Revolution, was not destitute
of the conditions necessary for the enjoyment of true
liberty.   On April 2nd, 1869, during the debate on the
budget, having presented the exact state of the political
institutions at that moment, in order to see what progress
had been made since 1863, at which date the Empire
began to introduce liberal reforms, and when Thiers re-
entered the chamber,—and having explained what further
progress was possible, he summed up his theory of the
" necessary liberties " in this wise:

" In order that a nation be free, the citizen must enjoy
absolute personal security, no matter what may be his
opinions: this is individual liberty.   He must receive instruction from an untrammeled press not only concerning
theories and doctrines, but also concerning all questions
that interest the country: this is a free press.   He must
be independent in the choice of his representatives, not

exposed to menaces and bribes: this is a free ballot. The representatives must know all the affairs of the country, and the will of the majority must be obeyed: this is legislative freedom. In fine, the national representatives must co-operate with a government that is ready to carry out the expressed wishes of the nation."

This speech made a great impression, especially the peroration, in which the orator revindicated the right of the country to declare war or peace. But this was not due simply to the expression of this opinion, which was but a corollary of the theory of the " necessary liberties," but because it was a warning, a symptom of the situation and the hidden designs of the Government. " That tremendous act," said Thiers, referring to the right to declare war, " to whom belongs its initiative? To France alone. She should not be exposed to the danger of seeing, on awaking some morning, her children ordered to the frontier!"

A despotism is by its nature not economical of the public funds. Montesquieu's comparison of a despotism to the "savage who cuts down the tree to have its fruits," is always more or less true. In civilized societies corruption is palliated, and hidden, but it always exists in a greater or less degree, according to the age, the country and the people.

The Empire had almost doubled the budget of the July Monarchy and the February Republic. The field of the unproductive expenses was greatly enlarged. The

Government endeavored to hide this from the public by illusive complications and subterfuges.

Thiers—who understood thoroughly the secrets of the science of finance, and who knew all the artifices employed since 1852 to deceive the country—had entered the Chamber with the firm resolve to give to the examination of the budget the most scrupulous attention. His first speech, (December 24th, 1863,) was on the finances. He took up the floating debt and pointed out its enormous proportions, the obscurity which surrounded it, and dwelt upon the evil effects of this on trade, and upon the good name of the country. On another occasion, he attacked the financial follies of the city of Paris, where the tax-payers did not know what was done with their money, and which state of things occasioned all sorts of suspicions of malversation and peculation.

The Empire—forced at any price to keep the public mind engaged, by continually offering it some new subject for discussion—bethought itself of the free trade question. M. Rouher*—Minister of State during the latter half of the Empire—was easily persuaded into accepting the theories and arguments of Bright and Cobden.

Free trade has incontestable advantages in great productive countries not dependent on foreign nations for

---

* Rouher (1814——) advocate; conservative deputy and minister of Justice under the February Republic : senator and minister under the Empire ; and Bonapartist deputy since 1876. He negotiated free trade treaties with England in 1860, with Belgium in 1861, and with Italy in 1863. His duty as Minister of State, was to support the policy of the Government in the Corps Législatif.

those things which are essential to national defense, as iron, for example. England is such a country. Was France in a state to accept the new theories born of England? This is a difficult question to answer, since certain parts of France favor free trade, while others are opposed to it.

However this may be, Thiers took up the side of protection and advocated it in the tribune, with the abundance and variety of argument of a man profoundly versed in the subject. The discussion which ensued resulted, however, only in the appointment of a parliamentary committee to enquire into the commercial condition of France. Thiers, though offered a position on the committee, declined the honor.

The year 1870 had arrived : the foreign relations of the Empire were becoming complicated, and were daily growing more and more disquieting to the patriot. The Empire, on account of its home policy, on account of its origin, which was not forgotten, and on account of the opposition encountered in all the great cities of France, which all its democratic pretensions did not disarm, was compelled to seek abroad an outlet for the country's restlessness, and was forced to agitate the world. The prime cause of the Crimean war * was to divert the public mind and to please the army. The Italian war † had been undertaken through fear of the dagger. ‡ The Mexican

---

* 1854–56. † 1859.

‡ Towards the end of the year 1858, Napoleon III received every morning a letter from Italy or Paris, which reminded him of his former promises to

war†—suggested by the little circle that surrounded
the Emperor, and having in view very ignoble aims—was
magnified little by little into a grandiose conception,
which Napoleon loved to dilate upon, without perhaps
believing in it himself, and which he was accustomed to
pronounce the grand idea of the reign.   But, whatever
were the real or pretended objects of these enterprises,
they produced only keen anxiety in the minds of all sensible men who knew the then state of Europe.

✕ Thiers's mistrust of Napoleon III was of long standing.
Though captivated for a moment by the Crimean war—in
which, however, he clearly distinguished the dynastic interests—he had no faith in the narrow and chimerical
spirit of the chief.   The Italian and Mexican wars more
alarmed than astonished him.   From the moment of his
re-entering Parliament, his greatest care was to watch
and combat the foreign policy of the Empire.   It was at
that moment a thankless and painful task for a patriot

---

free Italy from the Austrian yoke, and which threatened him with death if he
forgot them.   One day, when Cardinal Gousset, Archbishop of Reims, came
to beseech him not to begin the war which he had threatened—a war that
would result in the destruction of the temporal power of the Papacy—Napoleon's sole response, was going to a drawer in his secretary and taking therefrom a bundle of papers which he laid before the Cardinal.   They were the
letters of the friends of Orsini, the Italian revolutionist, who attempted to
assassinate Napoleon in January, 1858.   We have this from a former secretary of M. de Falloux, the distinguished ultramontane political and literary
leader.

† It is very probable that Guizot had something to do with this expedition.
Napoleon III often consulted him.   This reminds us of a witty and rather
prophetic remark of M. Paul Bethmont, the deputy.   Jules Simon said to
him one day before us, as we were passing the Tuileries, (we believe it was
in 1868) that Guizot sometimes advised the Emperor.   " My heavens," said
M. Bethmont, "if he wants to know how to fall, he can't find a better
master."   This war lasted from 1862 to 1863, but the French troops were
not entirely withdrawn till 1867.

and statesman like Thiers: he could point out the evil,
but he could not apply the remedy. Napoleon III had
not the breadth of mind to comprehend the extravagance
of the system which he had built up, nor enough modesty
to take advice from a superior and more experienced
mind. The great legislative bodies of the State—the
Senate and the Corps Législatif—moulded after the
master, thought as he did even when they condemned his
thought. Every road towards reform was, therefore,
closed. This, however, made Thiers only the more determined in his attack. The Italian and Mexican wars
were accomplished facts when he re-entered Parliament
in 1863, but their consequences remained, pregnant of
issues still more dangerous. He stubbornly maintained that the first resulted from previous mistakes,
and declared that the latter would be fatal if the system
were not changed.

In 1864, the folly of the Mexican policy of the Empire—
though it had not yet produced all its fruits—was too
evident to require long or frequent speeches to convince
the public of it. The impossibility of success on one
hand, and the danger of a rupture with the United States
on the other, struck everybody. Thiers did not dwell
upon this view of the question, in the debates concerning
the Mexican expedition, that took place in the Chamber,
but he repeatedly called attention to the effect that such
a distant and expensive undertaking would have on the
financial and military strength of France, in need of all

its force to meet the enemies which the adventurous policy of the Empire had made in Europe, and to defend itself against the results of the Italian war, which, though finished five years before, still hung suspended over the continent like a cloud charged with electricity, ready to flash forth at any moment.

A lady, who knew Napoleon III very intimately, being asked one day in London by Louis Blanc, what she thought of her former friend, replied: " He always had on me the effect of a woman," meaning by this, that he had only the appearance of vigor, and that his mind was as wavering and variable as it was chimerical. This opinion—whose justice Louis Blanc does not question—is at least confirmed by the whole sequel of the Italian war. Everything is indecisive and incoherent. It is given out, that war is to be carried into Italy for the sake of an idea, and this idea is scarcely born, before it is deprived of life. " Italy must be free from the Alps to the Adriatic," said Napoleon in one of his proclamations, and the army stops short before the Quadrilateral,* as if the existence of such a barrier were unknown, as if it had suddenly sprung up from the soil. After the victory of Solferino, June 24th, 1859, it began to be seen that Prussia made a part of Europe, and, in order to steer clear of this danger, a hasty treaty is made with Austria, at Villafranca, on July

---

* A Quadrilateral, in military language, denotes a combination of four fortresses, not of necessity connected, but mutually supporting each other. The Austrian Quadrilateral referred to, comprised the four strong forts of Mantua, Verona, Peschiera, and Legnago, in Northern Italy.

11th, 1859. Italy does not realize her hopes and champs her bit. The Papacy—seeing its temporal power threatened—complains loudly. In order to get out of the difficulty, the Italian Confederation is formed, the Presidency of which is given to the Pope, who looks with disdain upon an artificial conception hastily improvised. Italy is thrown into commotion, and Sicily and the Kingdom of Naples fall before Garibaldi. Piedmont joins the patriotic movement which is irresistible. The Papacy is about to be swept away by the torrent. Intervention saves it, and the short-sighted convention of September 15th, 1864 * is entered into, which was of necessity one day to bring Piedmont to Rome, and to add the ruins of St. Peter to that of so many other Italian thrones. Never did a government try harder to do something grand and so utterly fail in the attempt.

It was at the session of 1865, of the Corps Législatif, on the occasion of a debate concerning the convention of September 15th, that Thiers was led to speak of the Italian question. He had no difficulty in showing that the conciliation aimed at by the convention was impossible, that neither of the interests concerned would capitulate, neither the Italian nor the Catholic, that one of the two would be necessarily sacrificed, and that all the chances

---

* " Let me sum up this convention in two words : we are to evacuate Rome in 18 months from to-day, two years from last September. On the other side, the Italians will change their capital and carefully respect the Papal territory. Such is the material form of the engagements entered into."— Speech of Thiers on April 15th, 1865. Napoleon and Victor Emanuel were the parties to this convention.

were against the Catholic interest.   And he added with a prescience that later events justified, that not only the Papacy would not be saved, as was apparently desired, but that Italy, by opposing its dearest wish, would be alienated from France, and that this wish would be realized in spite of France, perhaps even against France ; that Italian unity, not abetted by France, would be accomplished by the aid of Prussia.   The inconsistency and hypocrisy of the French policy in Italy was rendered transparent by Thiers's speech.   The course of events was to show its blindness.

Mistakes are born of mistakes by a sort of fatal descent, and, as it is in the nature of things that some one turn up just in the nick of time to reap advantage from the mistakes of others, Bismarck appeared, who, taking in at the first glance the insufficiency of Napoleon, the incoherency of his mind and designs, put himself in the way to turn this to his benefit.   In a letter written after his second visit to Napoleon III, Bismarck, in order to express his idea of the Emperor, cited the following well-known verse of La Fontaine :

*De loin, c'est quelque chose ; et de près, ce n'est rien.**

Napoleon, in the midst of his dreams, always had his eye fixed on the Rhine.   He imagined that by bustling about and keeping Europe in a state of agitation, he could in the end secure to France, forcibly or peacefully, her

---

* Afar, it is something, but near by, nothing. *Fables*, Book IV, Fable X.

old frontier. After the Italian campaign, towards 1862, he began to hope that he might bring this about pacifically, simply through the magic influence of his "principle of nationalities." One day, while on a visit to a former colonel of engineers, mayor of a city in the neighborhood of the camp at Chalons, where the Emperor frequently went, the old soldier expressing a regret that France did not have its frontiers on the Rhine, the Emperor remarked: "Don't despair of the Rhine, colonel; what would you say if we should get it back without firing a gun?"

On that day the secret thoughts of the "Taciturn," so well characterized by Lord Cowley, at one time English Minister to France, when he said that "he always lies though he never speaks,"—on that occasion, Napoleon divulged his real intentions. The Rhenish frontier was the temptation that lured him on, the deceitful mirage with which Bismarck charmed him. It is the secret of his whole policy from 1863 to 1866. It explains the abandonment of Denmark to be preyed upon by Prussia in 1864,* by which act England and all the small states were alienated from France. It was the source of the odd conception of an European Congress, † for the remodeling of the map of Europe, where the Emperor

---

* Denmark was forced by Prussia and Austria to cede its southern province of Schleswig-Holstein in 1864, Austria occupying Holstein and Prussia Schleswig, but after the war with Austria, in 1866, Prussia became the possessor of both.

† On November 4th, 1863, Napoleon III, without any forewarning, suddenly addressed autographic circulars to the sovereigns of Europe, inviting them to meet in Paris for a general consideration of European affairs. But the project fell through.

should play the part of arbiter and doubtless also that of "pedagogue," to use the expression of Bismarck.*

It is the reason of his denunciation of the treaty of 1815 in a speech delivered at Auxerre, in which were expressed sentiments that he dared not utter officially. It was the main spring of his ambition to arrange Europe according to the laws of a new sort of transcendental æsthetics, which was to give to Prussia, "badly bounded," as was said, a form more in conformity to its mission. In a word, it was the cause of all those fancies of a poorly balanced head, of all those phantoms of a mind intoxicated by its dreams, so brutally dissipated by the cannon of Sadowa.†

Thiers's fears concerning the result of this policy increased daily. In 1866, a few days before the defeat of Austria, he mounted the tribune and tried to make the Chamber feel the gravity of the German conflict, and the importance of the intervention of France, which, by a simple demonstration, could arrest all. He called attention to the danger to France of Italian unity and German unity, the hypocritical complicity of France, and the old equilibrium of Europe destroyed by the probable victory of Prussia.

Prussia was victorious as Thiers had predicted, and the North German Confederation, the first step towards the German Empire, was founded. Bismarck did not show

---

* Bismarck said in a speech delivered on February 19th 1869 : "I do not think that we are bound to follow in the steps of Napoleon and affect the rôle of arbiter or that of *pedagogue* of Europe."

† The battle of Sadowa occurred on July 3d, 1866.

himself in the least disposed to pay his confederate, become his dupe, the price which, if not promised, he had at least allowed him to expect.

Every thing was not lost, however. A wise, pacific, but firm policy could still, with the resources remaining to France, and backed by the apprehensions of Europe, have kept the evil from spreading, if it could not have repaired what was already lost. But a new madness had replaced the old. Having allowed himself to be duped when he was strong, the Emperor was possessed with the idea to have revenge, now that he was feeble. Weakened by the consequences of the Mexican expedition and debased before European public opinion, Napoleon III was eager to punish Prussia.

At the session of 1867, Thiers made a new effort to bring France back to the old policy, and developed with his customary warmth and clearness, the reasons which called for this change, if new disasters were not be added to those which an opposite policy had brought down upon the country. Thiers was only the interpreter of public opinion in demanding this change. All far-seeing men thought with him. The press, the *salons*, the workshops held the same sentiments concerning the perils that the foreign policy of the Government was in danger of encountering.

As proof of this, if we turn to the private correspondence of a man of the world of the period, we will find him saying in his letters, just what Thiers spoke in a loud

voice from the tribune of the Corps Législatif. M. Doudan, whom M. Fleury called "a free-thinker in high
society,"* and whom we have already referred to, as the
friend and former preceptor of the Duke de Broglie,†
had—if we except a few moments of optimism before the
coup d'état—like Thiers, an early presentiment of the
baneful destiny of Louis Napoleon, and of the disasters
that he was likely to inflict upon his country. All of his
correspondence is full of traits showing the keen observer
and witty writer. But it is above all, in 1859, and concerning the foreign policy of the Empire, that his judgments are valuable to those who are curious to know the
effect produced on the enlightened minds of the period,
by the series of theatrical performances which made up
the history of the foreign policy of the Empire.

He wrote in February 1859, a few weeks after the Emperor's words addressed on New-year's-day to Baron
Hübner, the Austrian ambassador, which showed that he
meant to begin the threatened Italian war: "Nothing is
more like a lottery, than the decision of one single man,
left, without counsel and without control, to the most
complicated and contradictory influences. Perhaps he
sees every thing in equilibrium, but a breath, a sensible
or a foolish word, changes all. This is an important side
of the philosophy of history.' He then points out the
folly of the Emperor's course: "If he had resolved
upon war, the simplest prudence would have suggested

---

* In the *Revue des Deux Mondes.*   † See page 84.

to him that he let everybody sleep in ignorance of it, in order that he might not be disturbed in his preparations, that public opinion might not be excited, or the foreign press aroused, and that the defensive operations of the enemy might be retarded." As early as 1862, M. Doudan considered the fall of the Empire probable. Three years later—foreseeing the fatal consequences of the Mexican war—he longed for a Cato who might cry daily at the Government: "Shun Mexico!" The day after Sadowa, he predicted the inevitable encounter of France and Prussia in the near future, and called the German Empire by its true name: "The Prussian Empire." "Teach your little boy the use of the breech-loading needle-gun," he wrote to a friend. On July 3d, 1866, the date of Sadowa, he wrote: "Sooner or later, lots of breech-loaders will be necessary to repair the evil that has been allowed to happen this day. Can you understand the mania that has taken possession of every body, of setting up against himself neighbors more powerful than he is?" On April 12th, 1867, referring to the speech of Thiers of which we have just spoken, M. Doudan wrote: "You must have read very inattentively the battle between M. Rouher and M. Thiers, to hesitate which side to take between these two combatants. I only wish that M. Thiers were a thousand times wrong in his exposition of our foreign affairs; we don't know where we are in this matter. Since Prussia, encouraged by us, has extended her frontiers, and become the most powerful empire of the continent, we are not at all at ease when war with her is spoken of." And lastly, in 1868, *à-propos* of the taking of pictures from the Louvre to decorate the houses of the dignitaries of the Empire, he remarked : " These gentlemen remind you of Thermopylæ, for they say : ' Passers-by, go tell to whomsoever you will, that we are here to violate the laws, to mock at morality, and to laugh at the battle of Sadowa, and at those who are depressed by the inordinate greatness of Prussia. After us the deluge: we will have had a gay time.' "

To cite one more example of prognostication of the approaching ruin, we quote these prophetic words of Prévost-Paradol* written in 1868 : " France will have to expiate, in one way or another, with the blood of her children, if she succeed, with the loss of her grandeur, perhaps of her very existence, if she fail, the series of faults committed in her name by the Government, since the day when Denmark was dismembered before her eyes, and a policy of general disorder was adopted in the hope of profiting by it."

France was far from a Thermopylæ, but the deluge was approaching. Many persons hoped for a moment, after the general elections of 1869, that the change of public opinion, which had considerably strengthened the repub-

---

* Prévost-Paradol (1829-1870), professor, journalist and author, was throughout his life the champion of constitutional monarchy, and consequently, a bitter opponent of the Empire. He was French minister to this country, when, upon hearing of the declaration of war between France and Prussia, he shot himself.

lican and liberal Opposition, would impose upon the Government a more national policy both at home and abroad. The ministry formed on January 2nd, 1869, with M. Ollivier * at its head, was expected to inaugurate a new era. Thiers hoped so for a moment, for he had friends in the new ministry. "My ideas find representation there," he said one day in the Corps Législatif, pointing to the ministerial benches. But the *plebiscitum* † of May suddenly appeared and re-awakened all his former apprehensions. War appeared to him almost inevitable. The Opposition, which partook of his fears, but which wished to show to Europe that France did not want war, and which hoped, at the same time, to exercise some influence on the mind of the Emperor, proposed a reduction of the army of 10,000 on the quota of 1871. The Government, in order to hide its intentions, assented to this measure. Thiers, better informed, broke this time with the Opposition, persuaded that it was of prime importance to be in a condition to make war. His motto was: *Si vis pacem, para bellum.*‡ He believed that too much attention could not be given to this subject. He was thoroughly

---

* Ollivier (1825——), advocate, deputy, and minister, was at first a strong opponent of the Empire, and when he became Napoleon's Prime Minister, and presided over the cabinet that declared war against Prussia, he was looked upon as a political renegade. He was elected a member of the French Academy in 1870, and has since disappeared from public view.

† A *plebiscitum* (French, *plébiscite*), was a Napoleonic dodge, resorted to by both the first and the second Emperor, to legitimize, by a specious recourse to universal suffrage, illegal acts or pretended reforms. The vote of May 8th, 1870, stood thus : for the *plebiscitum*, 7,336,434, against it, only 1,560,709.

‡ If you want peace, prepare for war.

acquainted with the state of Europe; he saw the increased power of Prussia, which, since Sadowa, instead of nineteen millions of souls as formerly, now had forty millions. "In consideration of this new force," he said, "we need a new and stronger military organization. * * * We should not be deceived. I abjure each one of you to think on the gravity of the situation, and I supplicate you to do your duty as patriots and worthy Frenchmen." And he uttered in a reply to Jules Favre,* who supported the reduction, these prophetic words: "Why did Sadowa take the world by surprise? Because Vienna was not prepared and Berlin was. Thus perish Empires!" Thus, indeed, was to perish the Empire of Napoleon III.

The candidacy of a prince of the Prussian royal family to the Spanish throne, put forward by Bismarck with the consent doubtless of General Prim, the temporary ruler of Spain, who, if certain reports are to be believed, was bought over by German thalers, was the prime cause of the dreadful conflict. On July 5th, 1870, M. Cochery,† deputy from the Loiret, called upon the Government for an explanation of this candidacy, which was only contingent, and, the next day, the Duke de Gramont, minister

---

* Jules Favre (1809———), famous advocate and liberal statesmen; deputy and minister under the February Republic; opposed Napoleon from the days of the *coup d'état* to his fall; ably defended Orsini, the would-be assassin of the Emperor, in 1858; deputy under the Empire; elected to the French Academy in 1868; one of the prime movers in the establishment of the present republic, and to-day (1878) a senator.

† Cochery (1820———), Opposition deputy under the Empire, moderate republican since 1871, and ardent supporter of Thiers during the latter's presidency.

of foreign affairs, declared that France would not suffer a foreign power, by placing one of its princes on the throne of Charles V, to endanger the equilibrium of Europe and imperil the interests and honor of France.

Such a statement was equivalent to a declaration of war. There was, however, an interval of hope for the friends of peace. Prince Leopold of Hohenzollern withdrew his candidacy. The war party wanted more. On July 12th, the Emperor left St. Cloud for the Tuileries to preside at the Council, and it was then decided, that they should demand of the King of Prussia a promise, that would interdict for all time the throne of Spain to any member whatsoever of his family. This was carrying things to extremes, and the King of Prussia could not do otherwise than repel this haughty demand.

A most terrible war was about to be begun over a question of etiquette, a point of honor, a shade of meaning. When Emile Ollivier came before the Corps Législatif for the last time with the question and asked for a vote of confidence, Thiers tried to show the futility of the reasons alleged by the Government to justify a move so full of peril, and which set at naught the opinion of Europe. We were present at that memorable sitting of the Corps Législatif, at that struggle of enlightened patriotism against the delirium of a blind majority. We can never forget the scene, one of the most dramatic in the parliamentary history of France, a day whose consequences mark a date in the history of Europe.

The President, M Schneider, at the moment Thiers
rose to speak, saw fit to remark that the solemnity of the
question in debate called for unanimity of sentiment and
a forgetfulness of all petty differences. Thiers repelled
this insinuation in this wise : " When war is declared, no
one will be more eager than I, to render the efforts of the
Government victorious. My patriotism is equal to anybody's here. * * * But the question before us is a
declaration of war." The orator then went bravely on—
interrupted every moment by questions, by cries of opposition or cheers of approbation—attacking the proposed
declaration. " Every one here," he exclaimed, " has only
to take upon himself the responsibility that belongs to
him. As for me, I am concerned about my memory, and
I decline all responsibility in this affair." Further on he
remarked : " I regard this war as very imprudent." A
Bonapartist interrupted him and said : " You are the
trumpet of the disasters of France. Go to Coblentz ! " *
Thiers coolly replied : " I repeat, in spite of your cries,
that you have choosen poorly the occasion for obtaining
the satisfaction that I desire as well as you." M. Jérome
David,† of the Right, who favored the war, accused him
of using language that was harmful to the country.
Thiers, who had left the tribune, remounted and answered with redoubled energy : " It is not I who have

---

* During the French Revolution, the nobility who fled from France, (the
émigrés), made their head-quarters at this city.

† Baron David (1823——), the ultra-Bonapartist, was a member of the Corps
Législatif throughout the Empire, and has been a deputy under the present
republic since 1876.

hurt France.   I have never harmed her; it is those who
would not listen to my warnings, when I spoke here of
Sadowa and Mexico, who have wounded her.   *   *   *
You wish to check Prussia; so do I.   Taunt me with being a friend of Prussia; the country will judge between
you and me.   But I leave the tribune worn out by your un-
willingness to listen to me."

This debate was Thiers's Waterloo: his oratory was
never grander nor ever less effective.   The last folly of
the Empire was neither arrested nor averted.   Destiny
had spoken and the penalty was pronounced: France
was to suffer a series of unprecedented disasters and the
Empire a profound and final fall.

CHAPTER VII.

THE REVOLUTION OF SEPTEMBER 4TH.

There have been many revolutions in France which have had a character of legitimacy, or which, at least, have laid claim to a theory or political doctrine. The revolution of 1789 was made in the name of two great principles, the sovereignty of the people and the sovereignty of reason. The revolution of 1830 was a protest against the violation of the *Social Contract*.* The revolution of 1848 was a vindication of political rights disregarded or usurped by a privileged class, or at least by a class which was looked upon as privileged. These grand events were not accomplished, however, without coming into collision with not only private and collective interests, but also with doctrines and principles ready to protest and even combat. The revolution of September 4th, 1871, is the only one of all the political revolutions, so numerous in France, which was accomplished without resistance, simply, easily, naturally, inevitably. The reason of this was because the Empire never had had the veritable characteristics of a real government, because when threatened it could not

---

* Rousseau's political work, the *Social Contract*, (*Contrat social*), is the catechism of the French Revolution, and is used as synonymous with the principles of the Revolution.

call to its aid a principle that it had not itself denied or
violated, because it had against it at this moment its
origin and its conduct. Usurper of the sovereignty and
powerless to protect the country, it had for enemies those
who believed in liberty and those who believed in independence. When the storm burst, its partisans and
servitors were as if paralyzed. It appeared perfectly
natural that the Empire should perish in the tempest that
it had excited, but which it could not master. Its authority having emanated from force, from the moment
that it had ceased to be strong, it had no *raison d'être.*
This truth was so evident to all, that from the moment
of the news of the first disasters of the war of 1870-'71,
the deputies of the Corps Législatif were convinced that
it was useless to try to prop up the Empire, and their
only concern was to smooth its fall, by giving to the revolution the appearance of legality. But no one spoke of
the legitimacy of the existing Government or of its right
to govern. If it was allowed to stand, it was in virtue
of the wisdom of the old saying, that one should never
change horses while crossing the stream. Not only the
enemies of the Empire, but its friends too, looked at the
situation in this light. The deputies who were elected
as official candidates—if we except perhaps the "Mamelukes," * who clung to the dynasty through personal or
interested motives—held the same views on this point

* The Mamelukes—meaning in Arabic, *purchased slaves*—were formerly
a class of Egyptian bondmen. This name was happily applied by the anti-
Bonapartists to the blind and servile friends of the Empire.

as Thiers, Kératry,* Picard † and Cochery.   They would
tolerate the Government, though they would not sustain
it.   If they could have changed or transferred the supreme
authority without danger and without confusion, if they
had had at hand a monarchy or a dynasty all ready
formed, or even a general endowed with the necessary
qualities or enjoying the prestige demanded by the occasion, they would not have hesitated an instant to clear
the Tuileries.‡

Consequently, as they could do no better, they took
upon themselves the direction of affairs and the sovereignty.   The whole aim of the Corps Législatif from
August 20th to September 4th, 1870, was to discover a
political combination which could preserve, in the midst
of the ruins of the artificial edifice which had fallen,
public order, and to build up in the Corps Législatif an
authority which should meet the demands of the hour.
The revolution was so thoroughly the result of public
opinion and the circumstances of the moment, that it
forced itself upon those who feared it the most.   The
usurpation by the people came after that by the Corps
Législatif.   It is one of the characteristics of the revolution of September 4th, that it was made a long time be-

---

* Count de Kératry (1832——), began life as a soldier, became an Opposition deputy in 1869, but has not participated in public life since 1870.

† Ernest Picard (1821-1877), journalist and advocate ; Opposition deputy
under the Empire ; member of the Government of National Defense in
1870 ; minister under Thiers ; and deputy and life-senator under the present
republic.

‡ Thiers's testimony before the Committee of Inquiry on the Revolution
of September 4th, (*Commission d'Enquête du 4 Septembre.*)

fore it broke out; it was the last term of a series of usurpations, the crowning of a succession of illegalities. There are those in France to-day who think it to their interest to protest against this revolution; but they forget that they did not wait for the disaster at Sedan to change the government. The Corps Législatif, the very day of its convocation—not content with casting aside the miserable ministry which had so thoughtlessly declared the war—arraigned the head of the State himself, who was not, however, responsible to it, and, going still further, deprived him of the command of the army,* thereby violating one of the most essential principles of the Constitution, and exposing itself to the danger of seeing turned against itself, the army whose chief it had struck down.

The imperial Constitution, tearing itself to pieces by its own hands, and offering itself of its own accord to the castigation of awakened justice, presents a curious and instructive lesson to the world. All the parts of this dictatorial instrument made with so much care, suddenly get out of order and clash one with the other. The moment the hour of reverse sounded, France, which had sacrificed so much to secure a strong government, found itself in a day brought face to face with a government, which not only could no longer govern, but which could no longer stand. The executive power, which was to be every thing, was now nothing, and the Corps Législatif,

---

* Bazaine was named Commander-in-chief in the place of Napoleon.

which, according to the spirit of the Constitution, was to be nothing, was now everything. The Senate, a moderative and conservative body, the keystone and the crown of the edifice, was forgotten in its palace by the public in the midst of its impotent majesty. The Corps Législatif alone, the elect of the nation, by virtue of the principle that animated it, which still lived in spite of its long corruption, the Corps Législatif alone survived the universal shipwreck. Such was the confusion of opinions and ideas, or rather such was the power of the elective principle, represented by the Corps Législatif, that all force irresistibly gravitated towards it, and obliged it involuntarily to declare the revolution and found the Republic.

The Corps Législatif could not have done otherwise. After the first disaster of the campaign, it was under the influence of the same fatality which swayed the population after the last catastrophe ; it obeyed the same sentiment, that superior instinct of preservation, which in great crises dominates and directs assemblies in the same way that it does individuals and peoples. The Corps Législatif, doubtless, would have preferred to resist this impulse and preserve its normal and legal position, and thus remain a subordinate power. It tried to do so. Thus, after the fall of the Ollivier ministry, it suffered an act of sovereignty on the part of the Government which formed a new ministry. And yet, at this very moment, the seat of power was transferred; the minister was much more the ser-

vitor of the Corps Législatif than of the Emperor. It was
the Corps Législatif which took or suggested all the measures demanded by the situation.   It was the Corps Législatif which imposed the immediate arming of the country, a
step that the Government declined to take on account of a
selfish fear of the results, a desire to preserve the Dynasty.
If the Corps Législatif did not appoint the military com-
manders, it designated them, and its designation was law.
It even happened on one occasion, that a decree issued by
the Government—that naming Thiers a member of the
Committee of Defense—appeared an usurpation to the
Corps Législatif which had not countersigned it, and, on
the motion of a deputy, the Government came near seeing its decree destroyed and made over again by this body.

It is not less significant and shows the profoundness of
the revolution of September, that this assumption of the
real sovereignty by the Corps Législatif, redounded to
the advantage of those deputies who owed their seats to
the liberal element of the country, who were the furthest
separated from the Empire, and that those who opposed
this assumption—the official candidates—were in the end
the worst enemies of the Empire.   The paralysis which
had seized the Government, had also attacked its supporters in the Corps Législatif.   There was no life, movement, initiative, except on the benches of the Opposition.
It was Thiers, Jules Favre, Gambetta, Jules Simon,*

* Simon, (1814 ——), professor, author, and republican statesman ; Opposition deputy under the Empire ; member of the Government of National
Defence in 1870 ; minister under Thiers's presidency, 1871–73 ; Prime Min-

Ferry,* Picard and their friends, who ruled and directed. If they did not hold the helm, they commanded frightened and inert pilots who feared to direct the vessel. The republicans governed before the revolution.

The last night of the Empire was, so to speak, a wake. The session of the Corps Législatif from the 3d to the 4th of September, was simply a consecration of a fact already accomplished. The Empire had surrendered before the Emperor gave up his sword to the King of Prussia. The resolutions that killed it—the marked features of this famous session—were only different formulas of an imposed situation. This fact strikingly demonstrates the weakness of this Government, a few weeks before apparently so strong, and shows what a slight hold it had on public opinion. Jules Favre's resolution dethroning Louis Napoleon and his dynasty, though postponed until the next day, gave rise to no objection; the proposition of the Cabinet—presented by General Palkao†—vague, timid, and equivocal, concealed the same thought; and Thiers's resolution which had the same tendency—since, though calling upon the country for an expression of its wish, it left the convocation of the new Assembly to an undeter-

ister in 1877; member of the French Academy, and to-day, (1878) lifesenator.

   * Ferry, (1832 ——), advocate, journalist, and republican politician; Opposition deputy in 1869; member of the Government of National Defence in 1870; and republican deputy since 1871.

   † Count de Palikao, (1796–1878), after long service in the army, became a general in 1851; made senator and count by Napoleon III for military successes in China, in 1860; and succeeded Ollivier as premier and Minister of War, in August, 1870.

mined future—was backed by forty-seven deputies, belonging to all the factions of the Corps Législatif and counting among its friends even Bonapartists.

Finally, when Gambetta, rising after Thiers, demanded—in order to arrive at a more rapid conclusion—that all these propositions be considered "urgent," not a voice was heard to exclaim that the Corps Législatif was usurping power and was making a revolution. The Revolution was so inherent in the actual state of public affairs and had so taken possession of the public mind, that when Thiers's bill was carried before the different standing committees it was accepted unanimously.*

When the people came upon the scene the next day, they only followed the example set by the deputies. If Paris was guilty of overturning the Empire, the Corps Législatif was equally guilty, and, furthermore, Paris did not take the first step in this direction. The declarations of dethronement, though put off and modified, were no more normal than the bursting of the people into the hall and lobbies of the Palais-Bourbon,† or the setting up of a new government at the Hôtel de Ville. ‡ The appearance of

---

* *Souvenirs of September* 4th, by Jules Simon.

† The palace of the Corps Législatif across the river from the Place de la Concorde at Paris.

‡ When the news of the disaster of Sedan reached Paris, on September 4th, 1870, the extreme republicans deserted the Corps Législatif, which was dispersed by the populace, and set up at the Hôtel de Ville a provisional Government of National Defence, which conducted the affairs of France until February 13th, 1871, when it transferred its power to the National Assembly, elected an February 8th, 1871. Among the members of this government were Gambetta, Jules Simon, Jules Favre, Garnier-Pagès, Rochefort, Ferry, and Crémieux.

legality was, at that moment, an act of prudence and
policy, but it was nothing more than an appearance.
Usurpation was abroad because peril was on every hand,
because everybody felt that the Empire—which had just
lost everything—was incapable of saving anything. In a
crisis where existence itself is in jeopardy, every one has
the right to seek safety where he hopes to find it. At
such a time, the ideal line that separates right and legality is lost sight of. The official candidates of the Empire
had forgotten it; how could it have held back an ardent,
trembling, indignant people?

The revolution of September 4th, was, therefore, necessary and is justified by the conduct even of those who
have since denounced it. Without speaking of the force
of public opinion that the Empire had raised up against
itself for a long time back, of the feebleness with which
it had been afflicted from its very origin, of the weight
of its old faults and especially those of the moment which
bore down upon it; without considering the general conviction that the Empire was too weak to repair the evil,
those who made this revolution might say with much
show of reason, that the only difference between themselves and the deputies was, that they were forced to become revolutionists, that they acted in self-defence, because the deputies—letting precious time slip by, when
there was not a moment to lose—were indecisive and
vacillating, at an hour when—as Thiers said at a later
day—"the cry of necessity was entreating them to act."*

---

* Thiers's testimony before the Committee of Inquiry.

The Empire fell under the blows of this necessity, and it was evident that the Republic alone could replace it. There was the same unanimity of opinion on this point as on that of the destruction of the Empire. The proclamation of the Government of National Defense from the Hôtel de Ville, was the natural consequence of all that had preceded it, of the compounding conduct of the Corps Législatif, of the impatience of a nation at bay. Some persons may regret that it did not spring from a more legal source, and that Thiers's proposition—which left the form of government to the convocation of a Constituent Assembly—was not assented to ; but if this bill had been adopted, a provisional government would have been necessary until such an assembly could be convened, and this government—as much an usurper as that which sprang from the ruins of the Empire—would have been like it, a government of public safety and republican in form, for this very simple reason, that no monarchy was possible and no one of the claimants would have been so foolish as to put forward his title in the then state of politics.

Thiers did not, however, wish to enter the new Government. He felt that it was necessary and consequently legitimate, but he did not believe that his place was in it. The course that public opinion imposed upon the Government of National Defense did not meet his approbation. He favored peace, but the nation wanted war. He thought the nation in the wrong. He believed that the best thing to do was to treat. Several of the more influential members of the Government of the Hôtel de Ville entertained the same opinion.   They, therefore, offered Thiers the mission of laying before the courts of Europe, the real interests of Europe at that moment, and of instilling into victorious Prussia the spirit of moderation.   This was the only way of arriving at a peace, for France, and especially Paris and the great cities, would, at this hour, listen to no other terms than those expressed by Jules Favre when he exclaimed : " Not an inch of our territory, not a stone of our fort-, resses !"

Jules Favre has related the interview that he had with Thiers, when he offered him this important mission.   It was on September 9th, 1870.   Favre went to Thiers's house in the Place St. Georges, and "pressed him to accept the mission.   He was confined to his bed, suffering from a severe cold and fever.   ' You perplex me infinite-ly,' said M. Thiers, ' in making so unexpected a proposi-tion.   You know my sentiments; they are not hostile to the Government of National Defense.   I hope it may suc-ceed, but I would prefer not to be associated with it. You see, I am in no condition to act as its messenger. But this, however, is the least important obstacle.   The principal trouble is the hard-heartedness of the European cabinets.   It would be unpleasant for me to be treated by them with indifference, and, yet, I have the presenti-ment that such would be the result of the mission you offer me.   Nevertheless, our disasters make me so unhappy, that it pains me that I am not seconding the men who are trying to repair them. Allow me to reflect on this proposition for a few hours. I will give you my answer to-morrow.'

" The next day he came to see me. He was active and well; the thought of giving his country a new proof of his indefatigable devotion had cured him. In fact, this is one of the characteristics of his privileged nature, where are found inexhaustible physical and moral resources, and an elasticity which confounds those who are not acquainted with its wonderful richness. While listening to him explaining to me the motives that had led him to accept the mission, I could not but admire the simplicity and the vigor with which—in spite of so many excellent reasons for sparing himself the fatigues, the perils, and the mortifications of so thankless an enterprise—a man of his age, who had so many times paid his debt to his country, readily gave this new proof of his patriotism, without apparently imagining that there was any merit in not refusing it. I had asked him to go to London; he also offered to go to St. Petersburg and Vienna, where he hoped to have a favorable reception.* I thanked him with all my heart."

Thiers, in accepting the mission that was offered him, undertook a struggle with the impossible. He knew this himself. He has expressed this feeling in a way that makes it easy to comprehend his meaning.† In London,

---

* Thiers visited also Florence, then the capital of Italy.

† Thiers before the Committee of Inquiry.

where he was received with merited attentions, he found the Cabinet possessed of an irremovable inertia. The most he could hope for, was that England would put herself at the head of the neutral Powers, " to exert an influence on Prussia at the moment when peace negotiations should be begun."

Bismarck had shut up all the channels by which diplomacy might have penetrated into the Courts and Cabinets. Austria was as much restrained as England was inert. Russia was perhaps an accomplice. Thiers found her polite, but that was all. Italy sympathized with France; but the folly of the Empire, as Prince Napoleon has shown,* had paralyzed her. No armed aid was to be expected from Europe. There was little ground for hoping that even a moral influence would be exerted at the overtures of peace. Thiers, therefore, found himself necessarily forced to turn towards Bismarck.

But this was going from one impossibility to another, falling from Scylla into Charybdis. Bismarck had his own perfected plan, and Paris another, just the contrary. Bismarck wished Alsace and Lorraine, and the government of the Hôtel de Ville, following in the wake of Paris, could not yet bring itself to pass under the Caudine yoke. Between these diametrically opposite situations there was no compromise possible, and every attempt to find a middle term, to reconcile them, failed utterly.

Thiers, from the very beginning of the war, saw clearly

---

* *Revue des Deux Mondes*, for April 1st, 1878.

what the result would be. He knew the insufficient preparations on the French side, and the incapacity of the men
who were to direct the French armies.   This was the principal reason why he so earnestly opposed the war before it
began.   After the disasters which he had predicted—greater, however, than he had foretold—a peace policy became
all the stronger with him. To bring this about, he undertook
that futile mission to the Courts of Europe, and defeated
there, he still continued his opposition to the war, and,
consequently, to the policy of the Government, which, at
Tours and Bordeaux, favored the plan of Jules Favre, to
fight to the last.   But soon Paris capitulated and France
imitated the capital.   An armistice was concluded ; the
electors were summoned to choose a new Assembly which
should decide upon war or peace.   Thiers, elected by
twenty-six departments, was made Chief of the Executive
Power, and was to act, "under the control and the authority of the National Assembly, and with the co-operation of Ministers chosen and presided over by himself." *

Thus, the misfortunes of his country opened to Thiers
a new career, and were to impose upon him a task, which
was heavier and more glorious perhaps than all those with
which changing events had up to that time loaded his
long and active life.

---

* Decree of the National Assembly, February 11th, 1871.

CHAPTER VIII.

THIERS'S PRESIDENCY.—1871–1873.

We have come to the last period of the history of Thiers, the most memorable and the most meritorious, which is the crowning of his long life, and which will remain marked in the annals of France, as the greatest effort yet accomplished to give it a government in conformity with its genius.

France, at the moment when Thiers took the reins of power, after the elections of February 8th, 1871, was in the most critical and grevious condition. The Germans in possession of its territory as far as the river Loire, its armies in part prisoners, its treasury empty, its credit gone, its administration disorganized; the political parties alive and ready to come to blows; an Assembly that was monarchical and clerical; the great cities of the South, Lyons, Marseilles, Bordeaux and Toulouse, conspiring against the Assembly; the Paris National Guard chafing under the humiliation of defeat, and controlled by a factious spirit ready to turn to advantage its irritated patriotism, —such was the picture. Furthermore, there was no government, and, in the multiplicity of parties, their divisions and their subdivisions, with an Assembly considered as the expression of a transitory sentiment, of a panic, not the manifestation of the permanent wants and sober reflection of the country, and where all was confusion and clashing, there was ground for fear that it was as equally impossible to found a monarchy as a republic. There seemed no end to, nor issue from, the chaos.

Thiers felt deeply this lamentable situation. As a citizen he deplored it, and as a statesman he was profoundly troubled by it. His attention was, above all, engrossed by the opinions and parties of the Assembly. Though depressed by the misfortunes arising from the war, and recognizing the necessity of repairing them so soon as possible, he was too well acquainted with the resources of the country, to be alarmed at the difficulties that the work of reparation would impose upon him. But how was a government to be formed from the intellectual and moral anarchy which surrounded him, one single will to rule so many divergent minds, a fixed policy to be shaped out of so many parties, which wished, the one a monarchy, the others a republic, and which, whether monarchists or republicans, were divided even among themselves?

There was the difficulty, there was the rub, which—though lost sight of for the moment in the all-absorbing question that the new Assembly was elected to decide, namely, war or peace with the victorious Prussians—was sure to come forward again as the most vital and dangerous subject for consideration. It presented embarrassments on every side: to attempt to resolve it immediately, was to receive a certain check; to leave it undecided, was to keep alive the hopes of the ambitious, and to inflict on the country all the evils of an unsettled government. If a middle course were adopted, if the powers of the Assembly were limited to the pressing question of peace, and that of the form of government were given over to a new Assembly—a Constituent—elected by the people, the difficulty was not disposed of, for there was no ground for believing that the Assembly would consent to abdicate so promptly, or that the new elections would materially change the state of affairs. Furthermore, if the Assembly would dissolve, it would only be increasing the perplexity of the work of reparation by a still more delicate and more laborious task, that of imposing upon a nation already fatigued, and in need of perfect rest, the toil and excitement of a passionate and hotly-contested election.

Thiers—after examining the question in all its aspects —rejected the idea of an immediate solution of the difficulty, and adopted the plan known under the name of the *Truce of the Parties*, or the *Pact of Bordeaux*, which imposed upon him—to employ his own words, pronounced a few hours before he fell from office—" an immediate task, that of making peace, re-organizing the country, and removing the enemy from the soil of France; and a subsequent task, one of foresight, that of directing the Assembly towards a durable form of govern-

ment." * But—and this point must be insisted upon—
though he postponed the question of a permanent government, he was not undecided in regard to its solution. He
said one day,† that skepticism did not enter into his nature,
his mind, or his character, and he spoke the truth. It is
equally true that he understood at the same time both
parts of his task. He had entered office with a conviction
and a resolution: with the conviction that a monarchy
was impossible, and with the resolution to work for the
foundation of the Republic.

M. Cuvillier-Fleury—a former partisan of constitutional
monarchy, and like Thiers, a convert to the Republic—
seems to think that it is to the circumstances in which
Thiers was invested with the executive power, that is
due his conversion to the Republic. ‡ M. Cuvillier-
Fleury is mistaken. This conversion was of earlier date.
His long-standing preferences for constitutional monarchy had given way before the spectacle of our revolutions, as M. Grévy § remarked at his tomb. He said so
himself more than once, long before he had any thought
of being called upon to found the Republic, ‖ and he did
not hesitate to show that he meant what he said when

---

* Speech of May 24th, 1873. † Speech of May 24th, 1873.
‡ M. Cuvillier-Fleury in the *Journal des Débats*, September 29th, 1877.
§ Jules Grévy, (1813 ——), advocate and republican statesman ; partici-
pated actively in the three days' fight of the July Revolution ; deputy under
the February Republic and the Empire ; and deputy and President of the
Chamber of Deputies under the present Republic.
‖ This important point would be vouched for by M. Barthélemy-St.-
Hilaire, his intimate friend ; M. Laboulaye, M. Madier de Montjau, the
deputy, and even the Duke de Broglie, his implacable enemy.

at the close of his life, the course of events gave him the opportunity.

Thiers could not, in the month of February, 1871, say all he thought ; for, by so doing, he would have contradicted his official policy. His language, nevertheless, in spite of some necessary reserves, but more especially his acts, was very significant, as can be easily proven by even a cursory glance at the varied events of the day. As late as November, 1872, for example, Thiers said in the Assembly : " If I am applauded, it is not because I am unfaithful to the beliefs of my life, not because I hold the opinions of the honorable deputies who sit on these benches (pointing to the Left), not that I hold the opinions of the most radical or the most conservative among them. No ! They know that on most social, political and economic questions, I do not hold their opinions. They know it. I have always told them so. No, neither concerning taxation, nor the army, nor the social organization, nor the organization of the Republic, do I think with them." *

This is but an apparent contradiction. The peculiar situation in which Thiers was placed, the condition of the country, the mind of the people, the voice of Europe, all these were conflicting elements that a statesman of Thiers's practical nature had to consider and carefully observe. This point will be more fully developed in the course of this chapter, and in the one which follows, wherein we shall show, we think, that, as a whole, the

---

* *Journal Officiel*, November, 1872, page 7409.

conduct of Thiers, throughout his presidency, was favorable to the Republic.

Named by the National Assembly Chief Executive, on February 17th, 1871, he declared, on making known the names of his ministers, that he had chosen them for no other reason, than because of the esteem universally accorded by the public to their character and their ability; that he had selected them " not from one of the parties that divided the Assembly, but from all, as the country had done in electing its deputies, in presenting often in the same deputation very different names, men apparently of diametrically opposite opinions, united only by patriotism, intelligence and good intentions."* This was true, for out of the seven ministers whom he had chosen, three were republicans of an early date, Jules Favre, Jules Simon and Picard, while Dufaure, Lambrecht,† Admiral Pothuau, ‡ General Le Flô § and even Baron de Larcy, ‖ a legitimist, were convinced of the necessity of the Republic.

No wonder a Republican newspaper, the *Avenir Na-*

---

* Speech at Arcachon in 1875.

† Lambrecht, (1819–1871), engineer by profession ; Opposition deputy in 1863 ; deputy in 1871 and Minister of Commerce under Thiers.

‡ Pothuau, (1815 ——), in active naval service for many years ; liberal deputy in 1871 ; Minister of the Marine under Thiers ; and now (1878) life-senator and Minister of the Marine and Colonies.

§ Le Flô, (1804 ——), distinguished himself in Africa during the July Monarchy ; deputy under the February Republic ; exiled by Napoleon ; deputy after the September Revolution ; Minister of War under Thiers ; and now (1878) ambassador of France at St. Petersburg.

‖ Baron de Larcy, (1805 ——), advocate, statesman and publicist ; deputy under the July Monarchy and the republic of 1848 ; retired to private life after the *coup d'état* ; deputy in 1871 and Minister of Public Works under Thiers.

tional, wrote, after his nomination as Chief Executive, recalling the fact that he had been suggested to the Assembly by Dufaure and Grévy: "In a new situation M. Thiers wishes to be a new man, and the little we know of what has been going on at Bordeaux since February 13th, seems to indicate that M. Thiers is in reality turning his face not towards the past but towards the future."

All the republicans were not so penetrating. Thiers continued to be distrusted not only by the survivors of 1848, those whom he had combated during the foundation period of the July Government, but also by the new generation, and not always by the least intelligent of those who represented it. His past alienated the first, his conduct during the recent war gave the second ground for suspicion. His impartial and neutral policy was looked upon by many as a sort of seesaw which hid his personal aims, and which, according to circumstances, could tip towards monarchy or republicanism. And yet his real opinion escaped him even in the tribune. On March 10th, 1871, repeating his declarations of neutrality, recalling the necessity of "postponing numerous differences and questions relating to the constitution," in order that he might give his undivided attention to the reconstruction of the country, he was asked in what form this reconstruction would come about. He replied: "In the form of the Republic and in its favor."

This opinion was brought out more clearly by the

course events took. It is seen in Thiers's speech, delivered on March 27th, 1871, in the midst of the insurrection of the Commune. He could not have gone further without breaking in pieces the Pact of Bordeaux, which would have produced an insurrection within an insurrection. The same thing is true of his speech delivered a little later, on June 14th, 1871, after the defeat of the Commune, concerning the amnesty of the Orleans princes,* and their admission into the Assembly to which they had been elected. This proposition had stirred up the whole country. The Government was troubled by it, and would have liked to expel the princes from the Assembly. Thiers, though at first opposed to their admission, finally favored it, on condition that the terms of the Pact of Bordeaux were rigorously observed. He explained once more what this Pact was, and did not hesitate to unequivocally declare that he was not working for the Monarchy; "that he would not govern ill to please it, though his government should aid the cause of the Republic." "You have accepted this Pact," he went on to say; "it was a sensible Pact, and so far we have succeeded with it, because we have been faithful to it. I trust that we will still remain faithful to it. But what did I join to this statement? I added these words, which I remember displeased some of you when I pronounced them: ' Under this Government

---

* The Prince de Joinville and the Duke d'Aumale, sons of Louis-Philippe.

that belongs to everybody, which for the first time for
many years is not the Government of a party, but that
of all parties, under this Government, called the Republic, if we do well, it is the Republic that will profit
by it.' Yes, gentlemen, although I have said that the
future form of government is postponed at the risk of
helping the Republic, I shall go on governing as best I
know how. Nothing is more respectable than to believe
in monarchy, and to yearn for it. But it is also respectable to believe in the Republic, and to long for it. Gentlemen, I entered into an engagement with honest intentions, and this engagement I shall never break. It is
the Republic that has been placed in my hands, that I
accept in trust. I shall not betray the Republic."

This language does not accord with that which Mr.
Bigelow uses in his opinion of Thiers, when he says that
he was working for the Orleans princes at Bordeaux.*

It is not necessary to push the point further. Thiers
was thoroughly in favor of the Republic. His only care
was to prepare its foundation, a hard task, the more
difficult of the two that he had undertaken, as will soon
be seen; a task that will always receive the particular
attention of the historian of this epoch. For there is no
spectacle more interesting to men, than that of a superior
mind struggling to establish a government, especially
when the struggle is long, obstinate, full of vicissitudes,
and crowned, after the greatest difficulties, with success.

---

* See Author's Preface, p. ix.

Since Thiers saw the necessity of the Republic and honestly wished for its establishment, certain republican statesmen, at the moment of the elections of February 8th, 1871, thought that it would be well to profit by the occasion and submit the form of government to the votes of the people. M. Emile de Girardin,* on February 7th, the very night before the elections, wrote to Thiers suggesting that he restore the republican constitution of November 4th, 1848, and call upon the electors, according to the requirements of that constitution, to choose a president, after having previously submitted to their votes the question of peace or war.

" Reflect on this, my dear and illustrious colleague," wrote M. de Girardin, " as carefully as I have, in my closet, and you will be, I am certain, of my opinion. And if you accept it, you will reap this double advantage : You will escape the heavy responsibility of making peace on exorbitant terms ; and you will secure for your name in history, a glory equal to that which has made immortal the names of Washington and Jefferson."

After the elections, M. de Girardin returned to the charge. Thiers repeatedly repelled his propositions, though he agreed with his former colleague on the real question. He was not opposed to the constitution of 1848 in itself. It was simply a matter of dignity with him, of form, of conduct. It was the business of the re-

---

* Emile de Girardin, (1806 ———), the distinguished journalist and publicist, and husband of Delphine Gay, the poetess, novelist and dramatist.

publican party, and not his, to take the initiative in the
question.

Thiers acted wisely. France was not in the same situation as the United States in the time of Washington
and Jefferson. Other means were to be employed to
reach the same end. Monarchy was no more possible at
this moment in France, than it was in America in the
time of these great men; but a majority of the people—
and among them, many worthy men—had not yet shown
themselves favorable to the republican idea, and such a
demonstration was necessary, in order not to jeopardize
the plan of bestowing upon France an enduring government.

Thiers's whole effort was to awaken republican feeling.
At first he wished to thoroughly convince public opinion,
that no other government than the Republic was any longer
possible in France; and to work upon the anti-republican
Assembly for the same purpose, by pointing out to it the
variance between its own views and those of the country,
by bringing to bear upon it the whole weight of public
opinion, and by demonstrating to the sensible and honest
conservatives, that the Republic was not only a necessary
government, but that it was also a good government,
capable of performing great and even most difficult acts.
For, in his mind—and he has many times stated this
opinion in his writings—it is not enough to improvise a
government—even though it be given a most legitimate
character—in order to secure its permanence. Whether

it spring from a revolution or from a *coup d'état*, whether it afterwards pursue a worthy course with greater or less honestly and earnestness, every government must always submit to the trial of experience, which will be more or less favorable to it, according to its wisdom or folly, its useful-ness or inefficiency. The Republic—supposing the popular vote, directly or indirectly consulted, had intrusted its fortune to the hands of Thiers—could not have escaped the necessity of this trial, which would have been the more decisive as the difficulty of governing would have been greater, since the Assembly was not republican. But why not postpone this inevitable trial? This was Thiers's original idea. When the Republic should have accomplished useful and difficult tasks, impartial men, that is to say, the mass of the nation, would be quick to do it justice. Its legal conservation would necessarily follow in one way or another ; and all the arguments against re-publicanism, drawn from the past and employed by its ene-mies, would vanish like thin smoke. As there is no better way to prove motion than to move, so there is no better way to show the excellence of a government than to govern well.

Thiers hoped that this indispensable condition of suc-cess would not fail him. He had great confidence in himself ; and he was sufficiently well acquainted with the resources of France, to be sure that they would be equal to the magnitude of the first part of the task, and with its good sense, to know that its support would never be

withdrawn from those who governed according to the instincts and interests of the country. He hoped also that,
without missing his object, and, at the same time, without
concealing it, he might quietly bring the Assembly around
to his own way of thinking. He thought that necessity
would prove stronger than its bad temper, that it would
follow him though provoked, and would continue to submit to him so long as the necessity lasted, and that
when this necessity no longer existed, the services rendered by the Republic would be sufficient to secure the
respect of France.

The insurrection which broke out on March 18th,
1871,—the Paris Commune—which might have compromised everything, and which did, in effect, by
accumulating new difficulties, greatly complicate Thiers's
undertaking — was the first term in the demonstration. It had this good effect at least, that it proved
that the Republic, even in its provisional and tentative
form, was able to endure a most trying and exhaustive
strain. For this reason, as well as for the important
place that it holds in the history of Thiers's Government
and in the public mind, and on account of its tragic
nature we must devote a few pages, not to a complete
consideration of all its phases, but to point out the
causes and the character of the struggle, and the policy
of the Versailles Government in regard to it.

After the elections of February 8th, 1871, which named
the Assembly that brought about peace, the National

Guard of Paris was divided between two feelings: it would not pardon the Government of National Defense the capitulation made necessary by what it considered a weak resistance; and it feared that the Assembly wished to destroy the Republic. The entrance of the Prussians within the walls of Paris, and the first acts of the Assembly, such as the numerous incidents attending the establishment of the powers of the various branches of the Government; especially the scandalous discussion concerning the election of Garibaldi, whom a deputy dared to call a " supernumerary of a melodrama ; " * the resignation of Victor Hugo, made in a burst of proud and patriotic indignation; † the removal of the seat of government from Paris to Versailles, thus offending the municipal government of the capital, left to the power of a Bonapartist general, Vinoy,‡ suspected of meditating a *coup d'état*; the measures taken by this general, which gave ground for these suspicions; the fact that the capital was under martial law; the abrupt suspension of the liberty of the press and the right of holding public meetings; an unfortunate law concerning credit, which ruined business and estranged the *bourgeoisie*; the prospect of a long stoppage of work for the workmen, succeeding the cruel sufferings of the siege; the sudden discontinuance of the pay of the National Guard—all

---

* Garibaldi was elected deputy in 1871 as an acknowledgment of his services on the French side in the war of 1870–71, but he did not take his seat.

† Victor Hugo resigned because the Chamber *had refused to listen to him*, as he said.

‡ General Vinoy is now (1878) Grand Chancellor of the Legion of Honor.

these various and important acts had increased daily in
every class the feeling of discontent. At the moment
when the Assembly left Bordeaux for Versailles, where
it was to convene on March 20th, 1871, the insurrection
appeared certain to many minds. M. Louis Blanc, in a
remarkably eloquent speech, had predicted it at Bordeaux. All the materials had been brought together,
and the slightest incident might produce the explosion.
What has been called the *cannon question* was the first
spark.

The day before the Prussians entered Paris, the National
Guard seized a certain number of cannon, made during
the siege by private industry, with funds derived from
private subscriptions. These pieces had been carried
into different quarters of the city, and the National
Guard was ordered to protect them. The Government
demanded them in vain. Influential members of the republican party, among others M. Clémenceau,* interfered
in order to bring about a pacific solution of the difficulty.
They even hoped at one time to succeed in this effort, for
the Government had solemnly promised them to make
concessions. But, on a sudden, in the morning of March
18th, 1871, an attempt was made to sieze the cannon by
main force. The attack, which was poorly carried out,
failed at all points. The troops, at the first contact with
the people, surrounded by women and children, raised

---

*Clémenceau, (1841 ——), physician by profession ; and radical deputy
since 1871.

the butts of their muskets in the air. Blood was shed in
the Montmartre quarter of Paris: Generals Lecomte
and Clément Thomas, seized by an infuriated band, were
killed on the spot.

It appears to be admitted that the check is attributable
to the measures taken. It might have been repaired the
very same day, if the military authorities had acted with
some vigor. Unfortunately, after as before the defiance
of the troops, slackness, sluggishness and indecision
marked the conduct of the affair. The conquerors, during
the first two days, appeared very much embarrassed by
their victory. The largest number of the battalions of
the National Guard did not wish to go as far as a revolution. It is not certain that the Central Committee* itself, to which has been attributed the initiation of the
movement, had a fixed plan. A bold attempt to unite
the battalions of the aristocratic quarters, might have dis-
concerted the plan, held its partisans in check, and at
least have given public opinion time to make itself felt.

This was never thought of or was not desired. The
conduct of the responsible authorities seems to point towards a premeditated design, in the interest of a party, to
leave the way open to an insurrection. The measures
taken the next day presented the same character as those
of the previous day. There was no more good sense
shown in the retreat than in the attack. Although Thiers

* The Central Committee was composed of certain unknown names said
to be affiliated with the International Association.

had forseen the necessity of leaving Paris, nothing was done to meet the emergency. The departure of the Government resembled a rout. General Vinoy left behind him troops, as well as the public coffers.

The insurrection, therefore, does not appear to have been one of those inevitable events, which seem to be fated in the course of history. M. Vautrain, formerly a deputy and mayor of Paris, said one day in the Chamber, that if the Assembly had been at Paris, the insurrection would not have taken place. " From the 15th of March," he said, " the outbreak was obvious. More than one man foretold the movement and felt it. But.the Minister of the Interior * had a terrible responsibility : he might have suffered a check, he might have succeeded if the proper vigor had been employed.—But he could not act, *because you were not there.*"

There was some hope, however, even after the triumph of the insurrection. The mayors of the different quarters of Paris and the deputies of the capital, endeavored to effect an understanding. A conciliatory resolution offered by M. Arnaud de l'Ariége † in the name of his colleagues, would have greatly embarrassed the Central Committee, if it had been adopted by the Assembly; for it would have divided the National Guard, and separated the moderate from those who wished to carry things to

---

* Ernest Picard.

† Arnaud de l'Ariége, (1819–1878), advocate, publicist and republican politician ; deputy under the republic of 1848 ; deputy in 1871 ; and, at the time of his death, senator.

extremes. But it did not enter into the policy of the Majority to accept an accommodation. It hoped that, as in 1848, after the excesses of the month of June,* terrified society would long for a protector, and monarchy would be considered the only issue from the danger. It conceived, at this early day, the idea of putting the Prince de Joinville—son of Louis-Philippe—in Thiers's place. In one of the sessions of the Assembly at this time, the suggestion was actually introduced in the course of debate, but the Government, rightly thinking that the remedy would only aggravate the evil, secured an adjournment, and all idea of conciliation was thenceforth abandoned. M. Jules Simon has well said in his recent work on Thiers's Government, that " there were two militant governments standing face to face," two blind powers, the Central Committee and the legislative majority. Thiers, placed between the two, could only bow before that which had legality on its side.

The mayors and deputies of Paris, in their ardor for pacification, hoping against all hope, made another attempt to bring about an accommodation. Thinking that an authority emanating from the suffrage of Paris, would be more acceptable to the Assembly than the revolutionary Central Committee, they took measures to bring about the appointment of a representative body by a municipal election.

The Commune sprang from these elections. Though

---

* See page 140.

the new power had a more clearly defined plan than the
Central Committee, though it was rather political than
social, it was as bitter in its feelings towards the Versailles Government as its predecessor, and, though it was
more strongly republican, still, as before, the same interval
separated the two camps, which now could not approach
each other except in battle array.

Two unfortunate circumstances, two accidents, as
always happens in crises too prolonged, precipitated the
struggle. An army surgeon was killed by the National
Guard, and, almost at the same time, three members of
the National Guard, surprised at Chatou, a little town a
few miles west of Paris, were shot on the spot. From
this moment all the passions of civil war were let loose.
It was no longer adversaries that one had before him : the
National Guard were now only " the villains of the
Commune," and the regular soldiers only " the Versailles
assassins."

There is sometimes in human events a fatal succession
of calamities. From the infatuation of the crowd for
the name of a warrior, sprang the second Empire ; from
the senseless ambition of Napoleon III came the Prussian invasion ; from the invasion, the insurrection ;
from the insurrection, civil war ; and, as the last resulted
from tremendous wrongs, it was naturally guilty of awful
excesses.

The entry of the troops into Paris at the end of the
month of May, 1871, which marked the fall of the Com-

mune, is one of the most tragic episodes of history. An ambassador, a man of wit, who was asked what he did during the Commune, replied that he spent his time going from Bicêtre to Charenton and from Charenton to Bicêtre,* that is to say, from Paris to Versailles, and *vice versâ*, meaning by this witticism, that the same folly ruled in both camps. The contest was in fact a long series of insane acts, whose final paroxysm lasted a whole week. The summary execution of the Commune prisoners commenced from the moment of the entry of the troops at Auteuil, the most westerly suburb of Paris. The order had been given—it is Marshal MacMahon who says so in his testimony before the Committee of Inquiry—to shoot down every member of the National Guard taken with arms in his hands. Paris replied to the Versailles executions by conflagrations † and the murder of the hostages. It has been estimated that there were twenty thousand summary executions and two hundred assassinations in the prisons. Bismarck was not mistaken when he said to M. Jules Favre : " You will see again the horrors of the siege of Jerusalem."

What part of the responsibility of these tragic events belonged to Thiers? When the insurrection is considered in its first causes and the civil war in its principal acts, we remark first the vote of the Assembly

---

* Towns in the environs of Paris, famous for their insane asylums.

† We ought to state that the idea of incendiarism was thought of a long time before this. We heard it very often developed, in the Club of the Medical School, by Armand Lévy, an old Bonapartist.

which decapitated Paris, the conduct of the military authorities, both before and after the episode of the cannon, the attempts at pacification made on the part of the mayors and the deputies of Paris, and, lastly, the summary executions. Now, the first of these acts was done against the wishes of Thiers, and by the will of the royalist majority in the Assembly. It was also the Assembly which checked the negotiations that looked towards an accommodation. It was the military authorities alone who ordered the executions. Thiers is responsible only for having chosen for the post of Governor of Paris, a person who did not know how to take such provident and vigorous measures, as would prevent or disarm the insurrection ; and, for having placed confidence in a general,* who did not possess enough authority to impose upon his troops respect for victory and for the laws of humanity observed by civilized nations.

Mr. Bigelow, as we have seen,† presents Thiers to us, as suspected of having systematically wished to place the Government in an attitude of marked hostility towards the governed. The real truth is precisely the contrary. The whole history of Thiers's political life proves that his constant care was to adapt his own views to those of the nation, and to seek the aid of public opinion whenever he was forced to resist the ruling powers. And it is a curious fact, that never was this more clearly seen, than in this very crisis of the Commune, which suggested the

---

* Marshal MacMahon.   † See Author's Preface, p. ix.

accusation, although the perils and the passions of the hour were of the very nature to invite the worst temptations. Two things were evident: In the first place, the character of the insurrection, which, if we except the eccentric frenzy of the leaders, was purely republican, and which would never have occurred if it had not been for the fear of seeing a monarchy issue from the palace of Versailles; and, secondly, the sentiment of the country outside of Paris, particularly the great cities, which, without approving of the insurrection, coincided with it in the fear of a monarchical restoration. Thiers, who was not ignorant of this, was so little tempted to place his Government in an attitude of hostility toward the governed, that his republican declarations were never more explicit, in spite of the neutrality imposed by the Pact of Bordeaux.

The day after the affair of the cannon, the Minister of the Interior, M. Picard, had posted throughout Paris a proclamation in which he said that " the Government of the Republic did not have and could not have any other aim than the welfare of the Republic." Thiers himself, in spite of the imperative necessity that he was under of propitiating the Majority, which he needed in order to be able to govern, repelled with the greatest vehemence the accusation of hostility towards the Republic. On March 27th, 1871, he said in the Assembly : " There are enemies of good order who say that we wish to overturn the Republic. I deny this flatly. I found the Republic established when you confided to me the executive power, and

I shall no more betray it than I have betrayed any other government. They lie, they lie a hundred times, who say the contrary."

Though Thiers treated the insurgents as enemies, which was his right as the head of the Government, he sided with them in so far as he could, without wanting in his duty, by his fidelity to the Republic, a fidelity that he could not render more significant without absolutely breaking the party truce, and adding, as we have said, another insurrection to the insurrection.

The Majority was not ashamed of its attitude, and marked its resentment by incessant attacks, at the risk of augmenting the difficulties of the situation and annoying the Government. One day, a legitimist deputy proposed to return to legitimacy, " to crown our provisional edifice," as he said. On another occasion, it was the Government of September 4th, that was brought into the debate, in order to stir up the republicans against Thiers. Finally, on May 11th, near the end of the struggle, a direct attack was made. M. Mortimer Ternaux,* a fiery reactionary, laid before the Assembly a document, purporting to give a report of a conversation of Thiers with the members of the municipality of Bordeaux on the subject of the Commune, and he called upon Thiers to defend himself against the indulgent sentiments attributed to him in this document. Thiers could no longer contain himself, and he

---

* Ternaux, (1808 ——,) author, and Opposition deputy under the July Monarchy and February Republic ; retired to private life after the *coup d'état* and deputy in 1871.

qualified in merited terms the contemptible policy, based on passion, prejudice and folly, which had no regard for the public welfare.

Thiers rarely employed to such advantage, as on this occasion, that eloquent indignation which characterized his temperament. Scarcely had the reactionary orator finished his remarks, when Thiers rushed to the tribune. He was pale and indigant. Emotion choked his voice. " I refuse," he cried, "to give the explanations asked of me." And then, instead of being the accused, he turned judge, and reproached the Assembly for its spirit of distrust, for its annoyances and ingratitude. "I cannot govern any longer," he continued; "tell me if you are weary of me. We must understand each other clearly on this point. There must be nothing equivocal here. There are those among us who are imprudent, who are in too much of a hurry. Wait a week longer and at the end of that week we will have Paris. Then all danger will be past. Whether the task be difficult, will depend upon your courage and capacity."

The majority yielded. Thiers asked for a vote of confidence and obtained it. The majority, by its question, showed what Thiers's political position was, and what his dignity was, by its vote. It had furthermore, been very unfortunate in its choice of the time to accuse Thiers of quasi-complicity with the insurrection, for at this same moment the Commune had decreed the destruction of his Hôtel of the Place Saint-Georges, and at the same hour that it disregarded his services, he signed the treaty of peace with Germany.

The defeat of the Commune, the attitude of the majority, which was feeble and timid throughout the course of the whole struggle, and the firm and vigorous conduct of Thiers, had strengthened his authority in the country, and so advanced the interests of the Republic. But he was aware that this very thing only increased the hostility of the majority towards him, and he thought it wise to take precautions against it.

There was a danger, however, that political prudence was called upon to guard against. Thiers's confidence did not arise from the illusions of optimism. It did not shut out from his calculations opposing chances. But this belief in the necessity of accepting the Republic, on which he counted, might fail and be destroyed by the violent passions which pervaded the Assembly. The Assembly was sovereign and held to this power the more firmly as it was called in question. The chief that it had chosen in spite of itself—Thiers was fully conscious of this—might be wrecked by a sudden tempest before his work was finished, before he had presented the country —as a sign of the happy advent of republicanism—the retirement of the German soldiery from the soil of France, one of the main objects of his solicitude, which, he believed, would be the crowning of the republican movement. Thiers was in fact at the mercy of a careless vote, of a dissent that might not even be of a political nature.

He might fall from some parliamentary mistake. People feared this. Under such conditions, how was he to carry out his plans of satisfying the universal longing for peace, of re-establishing credit, of re-assuring public opinion and Europe? How was he to govern with this "temporary power, revocable by a vote at any moment," as Thiers defined his authority? It was not only "striking a bargain with the fickle public," as Thiers wrote M. de Girardin, but it was running the chance of being cheated, attempting to walk a rope in fetters, of performing an act of fruitless and puerile devotion. Thiers saw his dangerous situation from the first day. Events that followed only increased his desire to protect himself from the agitations and passions of the Majority, until his work was accomplished.

Political passions are like other passions: they consider that alone good which serves them. Thiers had shown that he was equal to the emergency by the masterly performance of the first part of his task, that of healing the wounds made by the war; and he thus demonstrated the fact that the Republic, even under a provisional form, was capable of doing good work when it was loyally supported. He had brought order out of a most formidable insurrection—the Commune; he had re-established credit, since the loan of five hundred millions of dollars for the payment of the first two installments of the Prussian indemnity had produced not this sum, but a sum almost double that asked for; he had re-assured the public mind and won its sympathies, for the supplementary elections of July, 1871,* which had gone strongly republican, were more or less approbative of his policy and condemnatory of that of the monarchists. But all these services, though great, for this very reason, rendered the situation of him who had done them, all the more dangerous. Thiers saw this. The Majority showed its feelings by repeated unfriendly acts. For example, the repealing of the laws concerning exile, which opened the gates of France to the Orleans princes ; the law which conferred on a committee of the Assembly and not on the Executive, the pardoning power; and still other similar laws and resolutions forming a list too long to enumerate. It was prudent to find a check for this unrestrained resentment, to strengthen the Government by having its powers more clearly defined than had been done at Bordeaux, and assuring it a personal existence, independent of the often thoughtless wishes of the Assembly. This it was that produced the Rivet† resolution which gave Thiers the right to exercise the executive power as long as the Assembly lasted.

Sensible men—even those who were the least in favor of the Republic—accepted this proposition. " M. Thiers

---

* At these elections,which occurred on July 2d and 9th, 1871, 122 deputies were elected, of whom forty-six were radicals, and only thirteen belonged to the monarchical parties. Gambetta was chosen by three different districts. Laboulaye was also returned at this time.

† Rivet, (1800 ——), an Opposition Deputy under the July Monarchy ; voted with the Right during the February Republic ; opposed the *coup a'état* ; and deputy in 1871.

and the Assembly," said M. de Mazade,* in August, 1871, "are the two real forces of the situation in which France is placed; and a common wisdom, the only law, the only rule, that binds these two forces, characterizes the present *régime*. It has been proposed more than once already to regulate and render more precise these relations, by assuring them at least a fixed duration, and by removing them from the danger of daily changes.   *   *   * Nothing, assuredly, is more natural than to wish to give certain stability to the necessary conditions of government, nothing is more statesman-like than to try to keep in power, wisdom and ability, when they are fortunately found united in a man who is an honor to his country."

M. de Mazade forgot to say that the two powers thus associated—the Executive and the Legislative—were forced to the union by necessity; that one of them at least had nothing more at heart than to disembarrass itself of the other, for, the proper moment arrived, it did not hesitate to do what it might have attempted earlier; and that it was one more reason why the other power— the Executive—should be on its guard. But M. de Mazade was not expected to say everything or to know everything. The important fact to be understood—and there is nothing to contradict the belief that M. de Mazade comprehended it—is that Thiers looked for guarantees

---

* Ch. de Mazade, (1871 ——), the voluminous contributor to the *Revue des Deux Mondes*, on literary, historical, and political topics, has edited, with but an occasional break, since 1852, and still edits, the able political *Chronique*, found at the end of this periodical. The citation in the text is from the *Chronique* of the number for August 1st, 1871.

of stability for himself outside of the good sense of his*
associate, the Assembly.

This was not an easy thing to do. The proposition
of M. Rivet gave rise to a sharp discussion. It was carried, it is true, by a large majority—by a vote of 480 to
93; but, in order to obtain this result, Thiers was forced
to threaten to resign.

This law—called the *Rivet Constitution*, after the name
of the deputy who introduced it—marked out clearly the
course to be followed by the two powers. It set up a
sort of "principality"—to use the word of a talented
publicist—for Thiers; but this principality, this consulate
of unlimited duration, though of necessity ever approaching its end, was not a stepping-stone to a monarchy; it
was the beginning of the Republic. M. Weiss,* the writer
to whom we refer, said one day, at about this time,
among some friends, that Thiers more than anybody else
was laboring to found the Republic; and he added, when
asked the reasons of his opinion: "My reasons? I have
two, both of which are excellent, but which you will
excuse me from developing. In the first place, M. Thiers
detests the Orleans princes; in the next place, he does
not wish to be second in Paris." M. Weiss was unjust to
Thiers in the vulgar interpretation that he placed upon
his intentions, but the opinion was at bottom correct.
Thiers was, indeed, resolved to found the Republic. This

---

* J. J Weiss,(1827 ——), professor, journalist and publicist; at one time
editor of the *Journal des Débats*, and founder of the *Journal de Paris*.

principality, which M. Weiss, in his newspaper, loved to shoot at with the arrows of his irony, had been established for this very purpose, namely, that it might eventuate in the Republic. Thiers's opponents in the Assembly—more bitter than M. Weiss—saw this as clearly as did the latter. The title of " President of the Republic," conferred by the Assembly on the Chief Executive, proved this conclusively. The title of the book, so to speak, showed what was to be written. Its enemies thought, however, to render illusory the law that circumstances had forced them to pass. In the meanwhile, they strove to hinder the march of the Government by bringing up all sorts of troublesome and trifling questions, as, for example, the proposition of M. Dahirel,* a legitimist deputy, who wished to prohibit Thiers from mounting the tribune ; and a multitude of inquiries threatening to external peace, as, for instance, the question put the Government by another legitimist deputy, concerning a favorable consideration of the temporal power of the Pope. The Assembly was thus ushering in a state of affairs, which, at a later day, became known as *the policy of conflicts.†*

The passage of the Rivet law was followed by a prorogation. The Assembly adjourned on September 18th, 1871, leaving behind, in conformity to Article 32 of the Constitution of 1848, a permanent commission of twenty-

---

* Dahirel (1804–1875), advocate ; legitimist deputy in 1848 ; protested against the *coup d'état* and retired from public life ; and became a deputy in 1871.   † *La politique des conflits.*

five members, and did not re-assemble until December 4th
of the same year. There was, therefore, a sort of lull
in the political storm. The Government had ground to
hope that the partisans of monarchy, brought into inter-
course with their constituents, would see that the state
of public opinion was favorable to its policy and to the
Republic. But nothing of the kind happened. The
parties returned as they had separated. The monarchists came back with all their old hopes and illusions,
and with the intention of checking as before every project that Thiers should advance. The Left and the Left-
Centre, on the other hand, were more than ever in favor
of establishing an out-and-out Republic.

Thiers had hoped that the minds of reasonable Orleanists would be changed by contact with their electors ;
that some of them, seated on the extremity of the Left-
Centre, might be detatched from their group, and that
there would thus be brought together in the united Centres, a compact mass of liberal conservatives favorable
to the Republic, who would form the pivot of his policy.
It was this idea that inspired the political portion of
Thiers's message of December 7th, 1871. Thiers appears
to speak in this document with premeditated complais-
ance of the sovereign rights of the Assembly, to leave
to its discretion the choice of the hour when it would be
pleased to constitute his powers, to diminish himself to
the point of becoming a "simple delegated administrator," and, in a word, to seem to forget and reduce to a

zero the Rivet Constitution. Was this done for policy, or was it, as has been held, an act of capitulation? It is certain that if Thiers was ready to surrender, it was only for a moment. Before and after the supplementary elections of January 7th, 1872,* he took a firm step in advance. His ministers, his friends, and Thiers himself, employed a language which could but re-assure republicans. M. Barthélemy-St. Hilaire, the President's secretary and confidential friend, who was rightly reputed to know all his secrets, wrote a letter which was made public, and in which he urged the candidacy of a radical, M. Testelin, † in the department of the North. On December 22d, 1871, M. Casimir Périer,‡ Minister of the Interior, in a letter to the prefects of the departments, concerning their conduct in the approaching supplementary elections of January 7th, 1872, spoke out clearly of the government of the Republic. M. Dufaure refused to prosecute M. Ranc § for having been for a short time connected with the government of the Commune, though the question was pressed by a member of the Assembly. A few days later, December 26th, 1871, Thiers himself, in a great speech on the budget,

---

* These were the first parliamentary elections that occurred after those of July, 1871. Eight deputies were chosen, of whom three were monarchial. Among the five republican deputies, two were radicals.

† Testelin, (1814 ——), physician and republican politician ; deputy of the Left in 1848 ; exiled at the *coup d'état* ; deputy since 1871 ; and now (1878) life-senator.

‡Casimir Périer, (1811–1875,) son of the celebrated minister of Louis-Philippe, (see page 58,) economist, diplomatist, and liberal politician ; deputy from 1846 to 1848 ; deputy under the February Republic ; member of the Academy of Moral Sciences in 1867 ; and senator at the time of his death.

§M. Ranc—elected deputy on May 11th, 1873—was, however, condemned to death, through contumacy, on November 13th, of this same year.

said, amidst the applause of the Left, that he intended to give the Republic a fair trial, and that he did not mean to conceal himself under a mask.

" This trial should be made seriously and sincerely," he said ; " and I see every day by your sensible votes, that you are all of my opinion. No, we are not comedians, but sincere men. We want it to be an honest trial. Gentlemen, I wish to unite you, not divide you ; and when I speak of sincerity and honesty, I do not divide you, on the contrary, I unite you. I am speaking to those who wish that this trial be successful, and I address myself to this whole Assembly. But I am speaking more especially to those who are thoroughly friendly to the Republic, and I am of that number. I call upon them in the name of the secret and profound wishes of their hearts, in the name of universal justice, to stand by the Republic."

M. Ernest Picard, holding the same opinions as Thiers, proposed, a few days after the elections of January 7th, 1872, in a caucus of the Left Center, that an end be put to the provisional Republic, and that a definite and permanent Republic be proclaimed, that two Chambers be created, and that the Assembly be elected by thirds.

This step in advance was singularly aided, we are forced to admit, by the mistakes of the enemies of the Republic, by their divisions and by the ever-increasing difference that existed between their own views and those of the country, as revealed in every supplementary election.* The

---

* There were six supplementary elections during Thiers's presidency, at which 157 deputies were chosen. Out of this number, only twenty-one were

applause which Thiers and his government received from France and Europe, also helped on the new movement.

One of Thiers's ministers remarked to us one day, on leaving the Assembly Chamber at Versailles: " When you leave that hall, you really feel like getting out of a lunatic asylum." M. Edgar Quinet * used the same language, and repeated what he had said of another Assembly: " They were a body of children crying on the edge of an abyss: Republic or Monarchy! Life or death! Head or tail! On coming nearer I saw that these children were old men. They bore the wrinkles of several centuries; their hearts had not beaten in their breasts for years out of mind; and they discussed questions that concerned the blood and tears of the world." These judgments were not far from right; for, if it be the part of a fool and a child to set at naught the spirit of the age and of his country, no Assembly—not even that of which M. Quinet spoke—better deserved the charge of puerility and folly, than that by which Thiers was harassed. But it is not so much an absence of good sense and a disregard of public opinion, as a lack of dignity and continuity, that strikes one most forcibly in observing the conduct of this Assembly.

When we yield to necessity it should be done with

---

monarchists, and of the remainder, no less than fifty-eight were radical republicans.

   * Quinet, (1803–1875,) author and radical ; deputy in 1848 ; an exile during the Empire ; deputy from 1871 to 1875 ; voluminous contributor to the *Revue des Deux Mondes*, and author of various historical, political and critical works.

firmness. This is as true in politics as in anything else. Thiers so acted under the Empire, and the republican party did the same, opposing the Government only in the name of a self-evident right and of imprescriptible principles. Nothing of this kind is seen in the attitude of the leaders of the majority under this "principality," which, they had accepted, and which was not forced upon them as the Empire had been upon Thiers and the republican leaders. At every instant the majority brought up questions which it dared not resolve, and raised objections which it was well aware it could not defend. It knew not how to patiently champ its bit, nor to carry out its audacious machinations. Such a course redounded to the detriment of the Majority. The motion concerning the temporal power of the Pope—which has already been referred to—was an act sufficiently insane to destroy a party in a country enjoying free speech and a free press; and M. Dahirel, by trying to shut the tribune against Thiers, only attested the power of his words.

The opposition shown to Thiers's personal views concerning this or that question, demonstrated more forcibly than ever the necessity of his remaining at the head of affairs; for, having forced him into a corner, the reactionists would, in their success, fall to fighting among themselves. All this irritated and sometimes roused the indignation of Thiers. But, upon the whole, he profited by it, as did the Republic also. The nation was the more impressed with the importance of keeping him in power,

and he himself was the more determined to preserve
France from falling into such hands.

The claimants to the throne of France, on their side,
seemed carried away by the prevailing spirit of madness,
and either fell into disrepute or abdicated. The Orleans
princes—the Duke d'Aumale and the Prince de Joinville
—named deputies, having promised Thiers, in the interest
of public peace, not to take their seats, broke their word,
and were admitted to the Chamber on a motion made by a
clerical legitimist. The Count de Chambord, the legitimist heir, issued manifesto after manifesto, and declared
in each one that he would never be the king of the French
Revolution! As for the son of Napoleon III, he guarded
a profound silence, and seemed to be buried in oblivion.

But what aided the Government much more than the
faults and follies of princes and parties, what strengthened it in its determination to proceed from a provisional
to a definitive form, was its own wisdom, and its rapid progress in reconstructing the country. For all the difficulties thrown in its way, all the agitations of parliamentary
life, did not turn the Government for one single instant
from its task of building up shattered France.

In order to form an idea of the activity employed by
Thiers in governing, in reconstructing the country, in re-
establishing the finances, in remodeling the army, in presenting a good front to Europe and the world, we must
read the budget for 1873 prepared by Thiers, and the
speeches that he made in support of it. So also should be

studied the picture that he painted on March 30th, 1872, of the condition of the Government and the country, of the progress of good order, of the *esprit de corps* of the army, " which considers itself to-day," he said, "not the army of this or that faction, but the army of the law," and of the spirit of the European governments and their feelings towards France. The impression that one receives in looking on this picture—but a few outlines of which we have given—is something like that produced on the soul by a calm after a violent tempest, or a sudden and powerful regeneration of a broken and ruined mass.

Republican sentiment, therefore, was growing among the people. It was not necessary to proclaim the Republic in order that it might exist. It was welcomed for its works. But a last act was about to increase this favorable impression, an act that struck the public mind as a victory, and thus gave another decisive advance to the republican cause. For Thiers had not neglected the second part of his task—that of establishing the Republic—any more than he had the first part—that of regenerating the country. It would be puerile, however, to say that he governed only for the purpose of founding the Republic; but it is unquestionable, that his design was to turn the successful acts of the Government to the profit of the Republic and its definitive establishment.

After the defeat of the Commune, Thiers had recourse to national credit in order to satisfy the more pressing demands of the situation. In order to efface the last traces of the war and the insurrection, in order to restore France to herself, he made a great effort, and secured Bismarck's consent to a convention, which hastened the evacuation of French soil by the German army by nearly two years, France to anticipate the payments of the war indemnities agreed upon between the two Powers. On July 2nd, 1872, M. de Rémusat,* Minister of Foreign Affairs, laid the convention before the Assembly, and asked for a loan of seven hundred millions of dollars. The Majority, hostile to the Government, saw the blow that would be dealt it by this successful measure, and it did not possess enough *sang-froid* or dignity to conceal its wrath. In the first place, the convention was attacked in the committees by such leaders of the Opposition as the Duke de Broglie, Buffet,† Daru,‡ Rouher, etc. They soon changed their minds, however, when they saw that public opinion was rising against them, and the Duke de Broglie, the chairman of the committee to which the convention was referred, reported favorably upon it, and it was ratified on July 6th, 1872. The Minister of the Finances was thus authorized to negotiate the loan, which was announced on July 21st, 1872, in the *Journal Officiel*, and two weeks thereafter the Government obtained not

---

* Count de Rémusat, (1797–1875), friend of Thiers in the July Revolution (see pp. 36 and 48); liberal statesman, philosopher, and member of the French Academy. His son, M. Paul de Rémusat, is now (1878) a deputy.

† M. Buffet, (1818 ——), has held since 1871 the position of deputy, President of the Chamber of Deputies, Premier, and is now (1878) a life-senator.

‡ Count Daru, (1807 ——), son of the well-known Count Daru of the first Empire ; Peer of France in 1832 ; deputy in 1848 ; and Minister of Foreign Affairs for a short time under Ollivier in 1870.

only the seven hundred millions of dollars that it had asked for, but over seven thousand millions in addition!

The effect of such a result was tremendous. It was not only amazing, but most profoundly touching. The country, from all sides sent to the President its tokens of grateful acknowledgement. It was also remarked, that the only opponents of the Government in this project, were found among the monarchists. Thus the Republic was again benefited by Thiers's ability and the faults of its enemies.

The moment was therefore arrived to take up the second task, that of giving the country a permanent form of government. The capability of the Republic as a government was no longer doubtful. The desire of the country was evident; all the elections, municipal, departmental and national, gave majorities for the republican candidates. The end of the provisional government was called for on every hand. The country was tired of the prevailing incertitude. The people longed for security after so many trials, and they hoped to find it in the organization of a definitive government.

The Pact of Bordeaux, furthermore, clearly demanded this, for it had in view two objects: the reconstruction of the country, first in the matter of order, and secondly by the establishment of a government. The first of these aims was attained. The second remained to be accomplished. But did this second task appertain to the present Assembly, or to a new one to be elected? On this

point, however, the Majority and the Government were
agreed, though the republicans as a body demanded the
dissolution of the Assembly and the election of a new one.
Thiers had already recognized the constituent power of
the Assembly, and he had no idea of asking it to re-
nounce this right. He even preferred perhaps to work
with this Assembly, than to run the risk of having to do
with a younger and bolder body, in which he might encounter greater opposition, not only to the government
that he wished to found, but to his personal views, and to
the plan of a constitution which he had in mind. But
as regards the question of the necessity of establishing a
government, his stand was irrevocably taken, and, on November 13th, 1872, in a message, he formally demanded
of the Assembly that it pass from the provisional to the
definitive, that it put a period to that critical state of
affairs which Gambetta termed, "the incertitude of the
morrow." *

The success of the venture was very uncertain. Thiers
had calculated all the chances. He had against him the
legitimists, the clericals, the Bonapartists, under the
leadership of the veteran Rouher, and the intriguing
spirit and ambition which the friends of the Orleans
princes employed, with the expectation of realizing their
long delayed hopes. But he had for him, the enlightened opinion of the country and of Europe, and the
whole republican party, which, though nettled by his

* Speech in the Assembly at the sitting of December 14th, 1872.

opposition to a dissolution of the Chamber, was ready to back him on this question.   In the Majority there was a faction of the Right-Centre, made up of old liberals favorable to the constitutional monarchy, who saw that circumstances demanded the Republic.   Here perhaps lay the balance of power.   There were, therefore, grounds for hoping that reason would prevail.   Thiers, consequently, thought himself able to meet the attack.   He began the struggle by the message just referred to, a document, which—to use the words of Gambetta—" made to leap the heart of France," * a page of history which can be placed side by side with the best Thiers ever wrote.

---

* Speech of December 14th, 1872.

CHAPTER IX.

THE FALL OF THIERS.—MAY 24th, 1873.

Thiers says in the *History of the Consulate and Empire* : * " There are in all parties two divisions: one large and sincere, that can be gained by carrying out the wishes of the people; the other small, inflexible and factious, which is provoked by carrying out these wishes, and is vexed because its pretexts for existence have been removed."

Thiers was about to prove, by his own experience, the truth of this assertion. The greater division, spread through the nation, had been easily brought over to the Republic, because, even under its provisional form, the Republic had responded to the desires of the country; but the other division, secreted in the Assembly, the inflexible and factious division, angry because the existence of the phantoms that it called upon daily was in danger—(for Thiers's message had shown the groundlessness of the feigned or real fears of the conservatives) — furious because the longings of the country were to be gratified, determined to punish Thiers for having pierced the bubble of their pretensions.

* Vol. II., page 172.

It was the conservative spirit that the message breathed, the title of "Conservative Republic" on which Thiers had based his work, as on a rock, that troubled them the most. For, if the proposed Republic satisfied the conservative spirit, what would become of the party which pretended to alone represent this spirit? The very ground on which it stood was taken from under it. The bond, which united the heterogeneous elements of which it was composed, was broken at a blow before the eyes of the world.

The struggle that followed is one of the most curious, and one of the saddest that the history of French parties presents. The means, the acts, the passions brought into play, are marked by a character that is *sui generis*, which recalls at the same time the spirit of the Lower Empire and of China. The enterprise was not only senseless and wicked, senseless because monarchy was impossible, wicked because it prolonged the anxieties of the country and abandoned it to the unknown future; but what was done to carry out the undertaking, reveals a spirit of knavery and scepticism, that grieves and makes blush the patriot.

Duke Victor de Broglie, father of the present Duke Albert de Broglie, has written in his book, entitled *Views on the Government of France*, that the friends of constitutional monarchy, ought, if circumstances establish the Republic, to accept it honestly, and wait patiently until the course of events, so changeable in France, produces a man or finds a prince capable of founding a monarchy.*

This idea—though entirely perverted—was the pivot on which turned the policy of the Right under the leadership of the Duke Albert de Broglie. In the mind of the father, it implied an honest treatment of the Republic, not a Machiavelian opposition to whomsoever wished to try republicanism. To the son it had become a system of government. The father held that the situation of affairs, whence was to issue a constitutional monarchy, must be quietly awaited. The son, believed that it should be forced forward, that it should be sought by every possible means, that violence should be employed if events did not naturally so shape themselves, as to favor the realization of the preconceived idea.

The whole policy of the Duke de Broglie, from February 8th, 1871, up to the day of Thiers's overthrow, is explained on this ground. For a moment Thiers had been looked to for the realization of the conception of the old duke. But he had refused the rôle. When pressed by the Orleans princes—Joinville and Aumale—to restore the July Monarchy, he politely declined in their presence, and remarked to Madame Thiers after their departure: " These young fellows, I know them, do I not? Always for themselves; themselves first; the country afterwards. When I served their father, I did not serve his fortune—I served France. I greatly respect the memory of the king, but his children's affairs are not those of the country. They

---

* *Vues sur le Gouvernement de la France*, pp. 226-7.

have too often confounded the two; but I do not confound them.   These princes wish me to become Orleanist
again; but I desire to act for the good of my country."*

Thiers, therefore, had to be gotten rid of, and
government plunged into confusion.   For might not a
more pliant man thus be found, a tractable agent, who,
if he would not bring about a constitutional monarchy in
a day would pave the way for it, until time, amid its infinite vicissitudes, should smile upon the realization of
the paternal conception?   Thiers, however, was not to
be easily broken down, though he was not, at the same
time, inpregnable.   Though the Rivet Constitution gave
him the right to hold office as long as the Assembly
lasted, he could voluntarily resign, and his inclination so
to do could be easily increased.   He was weary, and he
had the highest respect for the law of majorities, which
had been the ruling principle of his whole political life.
To drive him from power, it was only necessary to continually harass him, and to force him into a situation,
where he would have to choose between this life-long
principle and the Rivet Constitution.   Such a situation,
consequently, was to be brought about, and a majority—
decisive for the moment—was to be found.   This was
the plan of the Duke de Broglie, the final success of
which the remainder of this chapter will show.

It is only necessary to follow attentively the debate on
the message, to discover at every turn the plan of attack

---

* Mrs. Emily Crawford in *Macmillan's Magazine*, November, 1877, p. 24.

that we have just indicated. The struggle began by a
manœuvre which was not wanting in cleverness. As the
Republic could only stand by a union of all the factions
of the republican party in the Assembly, an attempt
was made to embroil Thiers with Gambetta, who represented the advanced portion of the republican party,
baptized under the name of the radical party, and, at
the same time, to frighten the moderate Left-Centre by
visions of the " red spectre." The attempt failed, at least
for the moment. Though Thiers did not approve of
many of Gambetta's more radical utterances, he was
very careful not to break with the strong party that
Gambetta represented, and, on the other hand, he did
all he could to dispel the real or pretended fears, that
these speeches gave rise to among the more moderate
republicans.

Thiers, in the course of the debate, defied the monarchists to found a monarchy. The Duke de Broglie responded
to this challenge by trying to make Thiers himself a constitutional monarch. He caused the committee, to which
had been referred the message of November 13th, to
propose a law concerning ministerial responsibility. This
was equivalent to putting the Government in the hands of
the Majority, that is to say, the Monarchy, and giving
full scope to the intriguers who were working for it.
Thiers replied by substituting for the measure that would
bind him hand and foot, the following proposition: " A
Committee of Thirty shall be appointed by the various

parties, to draw up a law to be presented to the Assembly, fixing the powers of the different branches of government, and the conditions of ministerial responsibility."

This was the question so dreaded by the Majority, which, by a skillful move, the Government thus brought forward and forced upon its deliberations. Instead of an under-handed thrust, Thiers gave a direct and open blow, that conformed to the demands of the situation and to the dignity of his Government. The Duke de Broglie's motion affected Thiers and his ministers alone; Thiers's proposition would regulate the powers of the Assembly, as well as the powers of the President and his ministers, would, in short, establish a permanent government, the very thing the monarchists did not want. So the committee sustained the measure of the duke.

It was November 28th, 1872, and public opinion was at a high pitch of excitement. The enlightened and impartial portion of the country demanded what Thiers also wished, a permanent government. Ministerial responsibility, in the eyes of the country as in the eyes of Thiers, was only one of the elements of the great problem The people longed to put a period to this state of affairs. In order to meet this demand, M. Dufaure, the Minister of Justice, brought forward the above-mentioned proposition of the Government, and on November 29th, 1872, he began the debate Thiers came to his support with his usual talent, and again baffled the calculations of his enemies. He had no difficulty in showing that the proposition of the Majority—offered under a parliamentary mask—was simply a stealthy personal attack. M. Dufaure's proposition, which, as we have said, had for its object the establishment of a permanent government, and which devoted to the question of ministerial responsibility, in the general problem, only as much attention as properly belonged to it, was adopted and referred to the proposed Committee of Thirty.

In spite of this new check, the monarchists did not consider themselves lost. The bill was carried by only thirty-seven majority. These thirty-seven deputies could be influenced. There are in all parties timid, changeable and corruptible consciences. The reference of the bill to the Committee of Thirty gave them time to be worked upon.

It would be too long to enter into the details of the vast intrigue, whose threads end in the Committee of Thirty, and whose object was the overthrow of Thiers. We can only touch upon its principal phases. Thiers, planting himself on his message, presented a bold front to the committee.

The committee was appointed on December 5th, 1872. Thiers appeared before it on December 16th, spoke for a long time with much good sense and ability, and concluded by saying, "that the best thing to do is to consolidate what exists." On his second appearance before the committee, on January 14th, 1873, he limited his remarks to some general observations concerning a counter-

project of a conciliatory nature, offered by M. Tallon.*
Finally, on February 5th, 1873, in an examination of this
whole project of M. Tallon, in which his critics were
not spared, he devoted his attention more especially to
the inconvenience and absurdity of the article, which
regulated the conditions and the forms to be observed
in the communications of the President with the Assembly. The article required that the President communi-
cate with the Assembly by messages; that he be heard
when he thinks it proper, and after the presentation of a
necessary message; that debate be suspended when he
speaks on a question; that he be heard again on the
next day, unless a special vote give him permission to
speak on the same day; that there be an adjournment
after his speech; that debate be resumed only at a subsequent sitting; that the debate take place out of his
presence, etc.

"All this is very complicated," said Thiers. "Permit
me to say that in following it, we shall resemble the Chinese, who, on solemn occasions make polite salutations,
which those thus honored return as they show them out.
Then the latter come back, and the same politeness is
repeated. Surely this proposition is not put forward in
earnest."

No, in truth it was not in earnest, but the following
remark of M. Dufaure, made on February 7th, 1873, before
the committee, was really in earnest. The article relating

---

* Tallon, (1828 ——), republican politician and journalist; became a
deputy in 1871, and is still (1878) a member of the Chamber.

to the establishment of two Chambers and the revision of the electoral laws, was being discussed. M. Dufaure read an amendment which had been drawn up by the ministers, in which it was urged that "without delay" special laws be passed, concerning the composition and manner of electing a new Assembly in place of the one then in existence, concerning the organization of the executive power, etc. The words "without delay" fell on the ears of the Majority like a funeral knell, as was remarked by one of its members. The legitimists and Orleanists of the Majority knew very well that they would not be returned, if a new election were to occur, and they did not wish to disappear from the political arena. The Government had regard for this weakness, effaced the objectionable words, and a sort of accord was established. On February 19th, 1873, the committee adopted, with slight modifications, M. Dufaure's amendment, by a vote of nineteen to seven, and the question of a constitution was finally brought before the Chamber.

Thiers said one day in a circle of friends: "I assure you that a majority — what is called a majority in parliamentary language—I never had for one minute in the Assembly elected on February 8th, 1871—an incongruous body composed of monarchical factions. I made successive majorities for every important and necessary question. You have blamed me for not having established the Republic quickly enough. I took up the most important thing first: I made haste to free French soil from foreign troops before I should be overthrown, and so be too late."

Thiers here refers to the time which preceded the laying before the Chamber of the question of a constitution. Then it was that these majorities, the product of chance and necessity, began to fail him. It was a fatal situation. The Committee on the Constitution—the Committee of Thirty—did not resist Thiers very stoutly to his face, satisfied to make up behind his back and by increased hostility in the Chamber, for the concessions made through timidity, decorum or calculation. But even if a majority of the committee had been sincere in the concessions made in private, could the Orleanist leaders—when the question came up for discussion before the Assembly—have been induced, by argument or patriotism, to recognize the necessity of establishing the Republic, when they saw that they would not be followed by the legitimists, or even by their own rank and file?   In order that these men—and we are speaking of the more intelligent portion of the Orleanist party—might grasp the actual state of affairs, it was necessary that they see with their own eyes the check of the monarchical fusion—the legitimist, Orleanist and Bonapartist combination, the failure of the *Septennat* * to bring about a monarchial restoration as they had hoped, the impotence of their ministerial chiefs against growing

---

* In November, 1873, the National Assembly prolonged MacMahon's term of office to seven years.

republicanism, and, in a word, that the cycle of their misconceptions, which began after the fall of Thiers, on May
24th, 1873, be completed. All these lessons were taught
them by the events which followed the downfall of Thiers.

The reception of the report of the Committee of
Thirty by the Assembly proved, that even if the committee had been honest in its concessions, the Chamber
would not have backed it. The Duke de Broglie as
chairman, presented the report on February 21st, 1873.
He was only applauded by the Right-Centre, composed
of the more liberal monarchists. And the duke himself,
he who had devised the intrigue, who had conducted all
its operations, and who, from the beginning, had endeavored to veil its real purposes, was not able, throughout
the whole debate, to hold the ground he had decided to
stand upon. On February 28th, 1873, in answer to a
speech of Gambetta against the report, he could not restrain himself from saying: " We will not rally around
the Republic, but around the Commonwealth."*

The debate continued fifteen days, from February 27th
to March 13th, 1873. Thiers was placed in a very false
situation. The Committee of Thirty had yielded only in
appearance. A part of the Left was opposed to the idea
of two Chambers, which he had favored in concert with the
committee, and was not willing that the existing Assembly decide upon a constitution for the country. The Left

---

* Nous nous rallierons non pas à la République, mais à la chose pub-
lique.

held that this Assembly had been elected in 1871 to choose
between war or peace with Prussia; that it did not represent the opinions of France in 1873, and so was not fitted
to determine what the government of the country should
be. To get out of the difficulty, and accomplish the
liberation of the country from the German occupation,
Thiers had recourse to the Pact of Bordeaux, on the
one hand, thus satisfying the Right, which wished to pro-
long the provisional state of the government; and, on
the other hand, he declared, in order to please the Left,
which desired to put an end to this provisional government, but by another Assembly, that dissolution should
forthwith follow the liberation of the territory, thus giving
all parties to understand that the constituent power of the
Assembly, however incontestable it might be, should not
be exercised. It was only by these concessions, which
neutralized each other, and which were only justified in
his eyes by a patriotic anxiety for the deliverance of
French soil, that he succeeded in securing a majority.
The bill reported by the committee was adopted March
13th, 1873, by a vote of 407 to 225.

It was another victory, apparently very great, but in
reality very small. Nobody was deceived by it. The
Duke de Broglie was working secretly to pervert the law,
which he had proposed, from the Republic to " the Commonwealth," constructing in his mind out of this preten-
tious and puerile conceit a machine of war, to be used first
against Thiers, and then to undermine the essay at a re-

public, which Thiers wished to make a success. By this means the duke hoped to pave the way for a monarchy, or for something resembling a monarchy. This was not a difficult task; for, to accomplish it, there was only needed a firm and decisive majority, which would not be frightened at the uncertainty always occasioned in timid minds by the thought of the absence of executive power. The interval of the recess—from April to the beginning of May—was employed in getting together this majority, and in finding a man fitted by ambition or intelligence to lend himself to the scheme, and to dare to take the place of the deposed "sinister old man," as Thiers's enemies at this epoch designated him.

At this moment an event happened which, it would seem, ought to have arrested the movement, but which in fact only precipitated it. On March 16th, 1873, the *Journal Officiel* published a note which announced that French soil would be entirely free by September 5th, that is to say, nearly two years before the stipulated time. The effect of this news was immense throughout all France. In the Assembly, M. Christophle,[*] of the Left-Centre, moved that a vote of thanks be offered Thiers by acclamation. The Majority refused to thank him by acclamation, seeing what increased authority this great stroke of policy was to give the President, and what a decisive check it might prove to the monarchical hopes of

---

[*] Christophle, (1830 ——), jurisconsult and republican politician ; Minister of Public Works in 1876 ; and deputy since 1871.

the Chamber.   Under the influence of such unworthy feelings, the Majority higgled over a recognition of its acknowledgement, and claimed a part in the work, thus doing a
double wrong, for—as Gambetta himself once admitted
to us—nobody but Thiers could have obtained such a
result, and the Assembly had assisted him only in so far
as it was forced to.   This action was also unfortunate, because, since it increased Thiers's reputation and diminished
the number of his enemies, the intriguers saw that they
must make haste to destroy him, or that the time would
come when they would not be able to do it.   The country
fully recognized the merit of the great work, and in proportion as it admired Thiers, it hated a selfish Assembly,
which, to its other faults, now added that of ingratitude.
This feeling showed itself in the supplementary elections,
which were frequent, and which would soon give the
party that favored a dissolution a majority in the Assembly, and thus put a period to the monarchical plots.   It
was, therefore, decided that Thiers should be overturned
at any price, and so soon as possible.

An unforseen incident—doubtless pre-arranged by the
Duke de Broglie's followers—gave new strength and
encouragement to the intriguers.   M. Grévy, President
of the Assembly, wounded by an appeal from a decision
of the chair, concerning a call to order which had been
justly inflicted on a member of the Right, handed in his
resignation, which, though not accepted by the deputies, he insisted upon, because he did not think the

vote large enough. It was a grave symptom of the state
of mind in the Assembly, not only among the members
of the Majority, but also among the supporters of
the Government. The audacity of the attacking party increased, while the defense became weaker. M. Buffet,
one of the chiefs of the intrigue, replaced M. Grévy as
President of the Assembly. The intrigue was sure of
the floating group placed between the two Centres, afterwards known under the name of the Target* Group, and
also of the connivance of Marshal MacMahon. Everything was prepared for the decisive day.

We have spoken elsewhere of Thiers's Waterloo.† His
real Waterloo was that of May 24th, 1873. The resem-
blance is perfect, even in its treason. Thiers came upon
the battle field resolved to fight to the bitter end. He
was not ignorant of the design of his enemies, since they
had urged him the night before, to aid them in a monarchical restoration. He also knew their plan of battle:
their newspapers had declared that it was a question of
protecting conservative interests. In order to destroy
the force of this argument, not in the minds of those
who had invented it—this was of course impossible—but
in the minds of the people, he selected a ministry whose
conservative spirit it was impossible to deny. The pre-
ceding ministry was dissolved on the occasion of a speech

---

* M. Target was a liberal monarchist who figured in the first Assembly of
the present Republic.

† See page 188.

at the Sorbonne * by M. Jules Simon, who, referring to the liberation of France from the Prussian soldiers, attributed the honor to Thiers alone. It was replaced May 18th, 1873, by a ministry selected from the Left-Centre, in which Casimir Périer, Waddington,† and Bérenger ‡ had portfolios.

The names, the antecedents, and the social position of the new ministers would have satisfied the most timid members of the Right, had they not been determined to be frightened. Some of them, however, were possessed of an honest fear. A deputy of the Majority, to whom, on this very 24th of May, we expressed the regret that they did not wait at least until the Prussians had gone, before beginning the struggle, said to us naïvely and seriously: " We have other things to think of than the Prussians; we have worse enemies than they." But such was the feverish state of the minds of the deputies, that, on the very day of the re-assembling of the Chamber after the Easter holidays, May 19th, 1873, M. Buffet, President of the Assembly, presented a communication—an " interpellation "—drawn up by the Right in these terms: " The

---

* The Sorbonne is the historic centre of Paris university learning. Here are the faculties of science, letters and theology, and here also occur the great university ceremonies.

† Waddington, (1826 ——), a naturalized Frenchman, born at Paris of English parents and educated at Cambridge : made a member of the Academy of Inscriptions and Belles-lettres in 1869, on account of his profound study of numismatics ; entered politcs in 1871 as a republican deputy ; Minister of Public Instruction in 1873 ; elected senator in 1876 ; and to-day (1878) Minister of Foreign Affairs.

‡ Bérenger, (1830 ——), advocate and conservative republican ; deputy and minister under the present republic ; and now (1878) life-senator.

undersigned, convinced that the gravity of the situation demands at the head of public affairs a cabinet whose firmness will assure the country, desire to question the ministry concerning the modifications made in its opinions, and to demand that the Government pursue a policy that is resolutely conservative."

Hostilities thus begun, the signers of this interpellation, impatient of a success, which they considered as certain, wished to precipitate the battle immediately. M. Dufaure said that the Government was taken by surprise, and asked time to deliberate. He then laid before the Chamber the bills concerning the organization of the different branches of the Government and the creation of a second Chamber. The Right and the Right-Centre refused to allow the bills to be read, and a sitting and standing vote—both equally doubtful—were decided in their favor. Thiers was now certain of his fate. All that remained, was to fall with honor.

The Extreme-Left has been accused of fanning the flames by a resolution of M. Peyrat,* which would force the Assembly, after a delay of fifteen days, to vote its dissolution. We do not think the accusation very grave. This movement could not have had any influence on the Right, which was well aware that if it were vanquished, a dissolution would follow in the natural course of events. Its plan was distinctly marked out, and was irrevocable.

---

* Peyrat (1812 ——), publicist and radical politician ; deputy since 1871 ; and now (1878) senator.

Its majority was sure. This was seen by the re-election of M. Buffet to the presidency of the Assembly, for he gained fifty-five votes over the first election. The Orleanists and the legitimists were united for the work of destruction in the name of conservative principles, and nothing, at this moment, could tighten or loosen the knots that bound this coalition together.

The same day, M. Dufaure announced that the Government would reply on Friday, May 23d, to the questions asked by the Majority. Though the public longed for an end to the struggle, it did not see the crisis draw near without anxiety. All Paris was in a state of solicitude. At an early hour of the 23d, Versailles began to show signs of more than usual animation. The Assembly Chamber was filled. Thiers's family occupied the presidential box. Marshal Mac-Mahon, in civilian dress, was present, as mute and unmoved as a sphinx. A group of officers in uniform surrounded him. The whole diplomatic corps was there. Thiers was seated on the government bench, anxious not for himself, but for the country, which his fall might afflict with new troubles. At the beginning of the sitting, M. Dufaure informed the Assembly that the President intended to exercise his right of speaking. Then the Duke de Broglie took the tribune, in order to develop the questions addressed to the Government. The speeches of M. Dufaure and the Duke de Broglie filled up the whole sitting of May 23d. The latter was one long harangue, a labored and passionate

development of one single accusation presented under a
multitude of different forms, namely, that Thiers had too
much regard for the radical party, and that his alliance with
this party disturbed the conservatives; the former—the
speech of M. Dufaure—was a rapid and energetic refuta-
tion of the accusation, sharpened with irony, which closed
with the declaration, that the power of the radical party—
about which the Majority made such great ado—was one
of the very reasons why he and his friends wished a fixed
government, and had presented to the consideration of
the Assembly constitutional laws that would bring this
about. "We presented them in all honesty," he said.
"We were ready to declare to you that, if you did not
grant what we demanded, namely, the recognition of the
republican government, we would not feel ourselves any
longer responsible for order in the country."

Social danger was only used as a pretext by the Duke
de Broglie, as Thiers the next day clearly showed, while
he brought the question back to its true ground, that of
politics. Thiers's speech—one of the most remarkable
he ever made—was at the same time a comprehensive re-
trospective review of the two years of his presidency so full
of grand efforts, a vigorous apology for his policy which was
ever sincere in its declarations, loyal in its acts, conservative in the loftiest sense, unmerciful to the disorderly,
moderate, impartial, with no other aim than the sacred
performance of the engagements entered into by the
President in accepting office. Then, in closing, he

turned upon the Duke de Broglie and pierced him through and through with the arrows of his fine and mordant irony.

The Duke de Broglie—in a passage of his speech not happily inspired—not content with blaming Thiers for his admiration of the radical party, went so far as to predict for him a disastrous end. Thiers replied by a more appropriate prophecy, which was realized two years later, on the day when the Duke de Broglie was named senator by his department.* "We have been told," said Thiers, "with a tenderness that has touched me deeply, that our fate is to be pitied, that we are going to become *protégés*. Whose *protégés?* The *protégés* of radicalism! A sad end has been predicted for me. I have, with eyes open, run this risk more than once in doing my duty, and I am not sure that I have done it for the last time. * * * I thank the orator for his compassionate sentiments, and hope he will permit me to return the compliment, and to tell him that I pity him too. He will no longer have a majority any more than we; and he, too, will be a *protégé*; he is to have a protector whom the old Duke de Broglie would have spurned with disgust; he will be the *protégé* of the Empire!"

Great and prolonged excitement followed this speech. It made an immense impression. Many republicans began to count on victory, which could not have been doubtful, if it had been given to the side that had dis-

---

* The duke owed his election to Bonapartist votes.

played the greatest good sense and eloquence. But all
was pre-arranged. The Right had in the morning favored
an order of the day, requesting the President to change
his policy and ministry, and thus surrender to the Duke
de Broglie, and put himself at the mercy of the Majority.

According to the terms of the law of the Committee of
Thirty, the morning session was brought to a close immediately after Thiers had finished his speech, and the
continuation of the debate was postponed to the next
session, which was fixed for two o'clock P.M., of the same
day.

M. Casimir Périer, Minister of the Interior, spoke for
the new cabinet, and replied in proper and sometimes
bitter terms to the ambiguous attacks of the coalition.
" He (the Duke de Broglie), has declared that we are not
to be trusted, saying that he cares nothing for our words,
but only for our acts. And yet we have not done a thing,
nor said a word!" There was no reply to the argument.
The Majority did not think of the ministers. It was
Thiers and the foundation of the Republic that was
aimed at.

The debate was closed, and an order of the day, submitted by a legitimist deputy, was expressed in these terms:
" The National Assembly, considering that the form of
government is not being discussed; that the Assembly is
occupied with constitutional laws—presented by virtue of
one of its decisions—which it ought to examine, regrets
that the recent ministerial changes have not given con-

servative interests the satisfaction that they had the right
to expect, and passes to the order of the day."

The Majority dared not express its honest opinion. It
was afraid to come boldly out from its equivocal position.
Everything had been arranged to inveigle the timid, to
aid and cover up ratting. Under the pretext of giving
the vote an entirely unambiguous meaning, M. Target, a
member of the Right-Centre, declared that in voting for
the order of the day, a certain number of his colleagues
and himself were resolved to accept the republican solution, as furnished by the constitutional laws presented by
the Government. Over a dozen deputies, former adherents of the Left-Centre and of the policy * of M. Casimir
Périer, were thus able to pass over to the enemy without
blushing. They were to work in the name of the Republic, for the establishment of the Monarchy.

We hasten over the incidents that followed. The
order of the day was carried by a majority of sixteen.
Thiers handed in his resignation in the form of a message, which was read at the opening of the evening session, at about nine o'clock. Less than three hours
thereafter, M. Buffet, President of the Assembly, announced that after an earnest resistance Marshal Mac-
Mahon had been prevailed upon to accept the presidency
of the Republic.

Thus Thiers was overthrown; but his ideas still dom-

---

* M. Périer was a conservative republican who advocated the establishment of the conservative republic.

inated the situation, which was so strong, so imperious, that his enemies did not dare, in striking him down, to touch the Government *de facto* which he had set up. Indeed his ideas were so exactly the expression of the situation, that his vanquishers were forced to follow his plans of republican reconstruction, thus adding to the spectacle of their weakness that of their inconsistency, and in some cases even of apostacy. The situation presented the curious "spectacle of an Assembly profoundly royal and clerical, finishing, without knowing it and without wishing it, by establishing, with its own hands, the Republic!" *

Thiers helped greatly to bring about this result. For, out of power as in power, he always kept his object in view. In his parlor, in the lobbies of the Assembly, in his travels, by his speeches, he never ceased to repeat, that the only government possible in France at that moment was the Republic, and that all good citizens should work for that end. He bent all the force of his incomparable mind to this task.

After the Republic had been established and provided with all its organs,† he did not repose. Before the general elections of February 20th, 1876, when the Republic was no longer merely a legal fact but a constitutional right, he labored to give his friends good advice. This ad-

---

* John Lemoinne, of the French Academy, in the *Journal des Débats* of May 28th, 1877.

† The present constitution of France was adopted by the National Assembly, on February 25th, and July 16th, 1875.

vice was simple but necessary in the face of a power that was "uncertain, unfixed, enigmatic, in which you cannot find the idea that directs it," and he conjured them, "to work for a government that will be sincerely republican and for a Chamber that will be sincerely republican." *

This enigmatic nature of the Government, so happily named by Thiers, showed itself in plain day on May 16th, 1877, when Jules Simon, the Prime Minister, was dismissed, Marshal MacMahon gained over and the Duke de Broglie once more got possession of the helm of state. Then was the Government, which Thiers had worked so long and earnestly to found, in a most critical condition. But he came to its assistance, and, though the hour of his death was drawing near, with the spirit of youth, he made a rampart for it of his popularity, of his talent and of his name. He fought for it from his very coffin, so to speak, for when he was surprised by death, on the eve of the elections of October 14th, 1877, he was giving the last touches to that famous letter to his constituents, which was published a few days afterwards by his executors, and which had such an immense influence on public opinion.†

Thiers, therefore, may be looked upon as the founder of the Republic in France.‡ Individuals, whoever they

---

* Speech delivered at Arcachon (Gironde) in October, 1875.

† See Appendix D for this document.

‡ Henri Martin, the celebrated French historian, touches upon this point in the following interesting comparison between Thiers and Washington. "With a different character and under different circumstances, M. Thiers is the principal founder of the durable republic in France, as is Washington in America. Neither of them, however, was born a republican. Washington was — using the word in its best sense — an aristocrat. Under other cir-

may be, can not do every thing, whether it be a work of construction or destruction: but there would be no history without powerful individuals.   The French Republic would not have fallen on the 18th Brumaire,* if it had not been for Bonaparte; it would not have risen so rapidly in the crisis of 1871, if it had not been for Thiers. It is to this that he owes the maledictions of the royalists and the gratitude of their adversaries.   Thiers—as is well known and as we are to show in the next chapter—was not only a politician; he was a historian, an orator, a superior polemic, a writer of rare spirit, and an incomparable talker.   Like Voltaire, he was endowed with a universality of acquirements and aptitudes, and possessed also this great philosopher's activity.†   All this will give him a distinctive place in the history of France, but, without any doubt, the greatest part of his glory and his most incontrovertible title to the remembrance of posterity, will ever be his having contributed more than anybody towards giving to the French Revolution the form of government that conformed most to its spirit.

---

cumstances, he would have favored a constitutional monarchy like that of England, though in reality he is the founder of the first truly democratic republic that the world has seen. He did not so act through sentiment of coercion, but through reflective reason, which leads to resolutions which are never changed.   This too, is the history of M. Thiers, with a slight difference of course. M. Thiers had behind him the precedents of the Revolution; he was the child of the Revolution; he wished to be so, and never disowned his mother, even when he was entirely at variance with the advanced parties who wished to continue and complete the Revolution." Speech at Laon, August 27th, 1878. *Journal des Débats,* August 30th, 1878.

  * November 9th, 1799.

  † "Like Voltaire, Thiers occupied himself with everything, was interested in everything, studied everything, vulgarized everything. The last time we saw him, was at the sea-shore, and while promenading, he gave us a fine lecture on astronomy, which we listened to with big eyes and ears." John Lemoinne in the *Journal des Débats,* May 29th, 1878.

CHAPTER X.

THE HÔTEL OF THE PLACE SAINT-GEORGES.

Cousin, the philosopher, returning from dinner at Thiers's in October, 1847, said : "What does Thiers lack ; that incomparable ivy whom we have just left ? An oak to which to attach himself. So long as he has not this oak, every wind will agitate him."

This *mot*—which has often been repeated, and more than once distorted—would be a calumny, if Cousin had wished to convey the idea, that Thiers lacked firm fixed principles in politics or in his life. We have seen what he was in politics. In his life he was—with scarcely a contradiction, even in the ardent years of his youth— governed by a deep feeling of personal dignity, and ruled by a lofty philosophic belief, that the inconsistencies, weakness and even apostasies* of his masters could not shake. Who doubts to-day—to speak only of the political side of Thiers—that the oak, which Cousin could not see on leaving the dinner table in the dazzle and confusion of conversation, where his argumentative talent had perhaps suffered defeat,—who doubts that it was the spirit of modern France, the spirit of the French Revolution?

* Cousin was a liberal under the Restoration and the July Monarchy, but went over to the Empire.

Twenty years later, another friend of Thiers, but of a different generation, was much better inspired, when, on also leaving the *hôtel* of the Place Saint-Georges, he exclaimed: "Thiers, he is living France!" M. Prévost-Paradol had discovered the oak that sustained the incomparable ivy.

This *mot* of Prévost-Paradol suggests to us so important a view of the character of Thiers, that we must stop a moment to consider it. Called forth by the admiration of a young friendship, by the warmth of an honest conviction—as often happens in youth—it will be accepted and preserved by history. France does not possess among her illustrious contemporaries, a personality in which she is more clearly reflected with her virtues and her faults, when the faults are but the excesses of her virtues. By his aspirations and his ruling passions, by his intellectual activity and his practical sense, by his universal curiosity, by his hardihood, at one time spontaneous, at another profoundly considered, Thiers is beyond contradiction the most perfect representation of the epoch in which he lived. Prévost-Paradol, when he passed the judgment that we have recalled, was not thinking simply of the politician, but of the man. We will soon see, by penetrating into the *hôtel* of the Place Saint-Georges, that he was not mistaken, and that, as in politics, so in everything else, Thiers was indeed "the living France" that the world recognizes. We do not intend, however, to enter into any argument on this point, but allow the thought

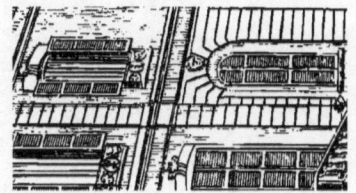

of Prévost-Paradol to find its illustration in the following loosely connected impressions and souvenirs.

We have referred elsewhere to the note of the physician who was present at the *accouchement* of Thiers.* The "turbulent" baby, full of vitality at the hour of his birth, became one of the most prodigiously active men of his century, among those who participated in public life. His childhood was full of the usual pranks of boys, and his youth was not exempt from the customary frivolous distractions of that period of life. He had a taste for sporting, in art he was an amateur, and withal he was a man of the world. This all sprang from the exuberance of the forces of a rich nature, which had need of many and varied outlets, and which did not detract from the serious occupations of life nor from its necessary work. If we take Thiers at any point of his long life, we shall not find one single day voluntarily unoccupied. In his portrait of Talleyrand, to whom he denies the gift " of directing, as chief, the affairs of a great state," he bases his judgment on the fact that "in order to direct, a will, convictions and industry are necessary, but he had none of these things." †

The contrary is true of Thiers. Though his opponents might deny that he had any convictions, they could not refuse him a strong will and indefatigable industry. If we consider Thiers in the latter years of his life, when

---

* See page 1, and Appendix B.
† *Consulate and Empire*, Vol. VI, p. 118.

his physical forces began to desert him, we will see that nothing could arrest the activity that his iron will imposed upon his vigorous constitution. His body was governed by his mind.

Every morning he arose between four and five o'clock, though, during the night, he had wakened his domestic, Louis, more than once, in order to secure paper and pencil with which to jot down an idea. "It is good that I am sixty," Louis used to say; "it is the saving of me. If *monsieur* were served by a young man, the young man would not last long." As soon as dressed, seating himself at his writing-desk, on a light ebony chair, before that small white or light green English paper, which has carried his autograph to the four corners of the world, armed with a big stubby goose-quill, its broad point plunged into a thick ink, always very black,—the illustrious author would meditate an instant, and then, slowly write a whole page without an erasure and without stopping. When the bottom of the page was reached—while waiting for the large firm characters, with their thick ovals and chunky tails, to get dry—he would look over the sheet and complete the punctuation. Then the next page was filled without a halt, dried and punctuated, and so on to the end. This done, Thiers generally had by heart what he had just written, and did not review the whole. He once said: "Be assured that it is very difficult to write only what you want to say; and also that very few words are necessary to express a fine thought."

By seven or eight o'clock in the morning, the important literary work of the day was finished, for he let no
day pass without writing something. *Nulla dies sine linea.*
The rest of the time was given up to his beloved studies,
as he said, to his correspondence, to researches which he
made, pen in hand, with his secretaries, Messrs. Faure
and Aude. Then he might be seen for entire hours
surrounded by immense maps or collections of foreign
books, heaped upon two little tables between which he
worked, and filled with book-marks and large double sheets
replete with pencil and ink notes.

These were doubtless the happiest hours of the day,
even at the period of his supreme power, especially, per-
chance, when public affairs permitted him to enjoy them.
Public life was disagreeable to him only in so far as it
disarranged him. After his fall from power, on May 24th,
1873, the reconstruction of his *hôtel* in the Place Saint-
Georges not being completed,* and the *hôtel* Bagration,
which he entered soon afterwards, not having been found,
he took possession of the second floor—the *entre-sol*—of
the house on the Boulevard Malesherbes, on the corner
next to the Church of St. Augustine, where he was
troubled by the sun, the dust and the noise. He was
dissatisfied with the situation. " How does the President find his new quarters?" said a visitor one day.
"Very good, except that the heat and the clatter of the

---

* Thiers's *hôtel* was destroyed by the Commune and rebuilt by the Government.

street hinders him from working as he would like to," was the reply of a member of the family. This displeased him more than the loss of the presidency. He regretted in the palace of the Elysée only what he did not find in his *entre-sol.* Happily for him, he soon moved and took possession of the *hôtel* Bagration. There, the same visitor, a week later, found him in a room encumbered with herbs, plants, lignites, etc., which he had classified, and labeled as a Jussieu might have done. The next day perhaps the indefatigable old man would go to the Observatory to contemplate the heavens with Le Verrier.*

Thiers was accustomed to shave himself about eight o'clock. It was his first recreation, a souvenir of the recess which at the same hour he had enjoyed when a boy at the Lycée of Marseilles! He was fortunate who could enter at this moment, for Thiers was now to be found loquacious, witty and affable. Mounted on a little stool before the glass near the window, he would pass the razor over his chin by short systematic movements, stopping from time to time to listen to the recital of this or that piece of city gossip. Each story called forth some pointed comments, which were accompanied and enlivened by little expressive gestures, whose effect was increased by the lathered face. In a short time business claimed its rights and the recreation was at an

---

* Le Verrier—who was a great friend of Thiers—followed him in three weeks to the tomb, dying on September 23d, 1877.

end. Dressed from head to foot at the hour when even
the soberest people have not yet laid off their *robe de
chambre*, Thiers was pacing his garden in a broad-brimmed
hat, sack coat, patent-leather pumps and black over-
gaiters, all ready to receive morning visitors or to go out
if business called him.

We have forgotten the frugal morning meal of eggs,
cold meat and stewed fruit, which scarcely interrupted
the work in progress, and, at noon, the breakfast—the
déjeuner de famille — copious but simple, when Thiers
found at the table Mme. Thiers, her sister, Mlle. Dosne,
and from time to time some visitors.

Thiers's way of sleeping has often been spoken of. A
little hair mattress, as hard as the famous bed of the
Emperor Nicholas ; a pillow not much larger than the
two hands ; a comforter of red, quilted silk ; over his
feet, a fur robe. His afternoon nap—very rarely forgotten—was taken on the same bed. When he began to feel
sleepy, he would close the window blinds, spread out a
handkerchief for his head, and continue to chat with the
visitor who happened to be present. He would listen to
the conversation, and answer questions, until regular
respirations showed that he was asleep, when he was left
alone until he called. But he always gave orders to enter
and waken him, if anything of pressing importance demanded his attention.

Thiers fully appreciated the value of time. In his old
age he was annoyed less by infirmities themselves than by

the derangements that they made in his hours of work. These infirmities, however, had respected the essential parts of his nature. In spite of age, Thiers's eyes were excellent, his hearing quite delicate, his brain active and its productive powers still remarkable. But sometimes he had slight troubles with his lungs, which occasioned some pain and anxiety.

After the crisis of May 16th, 1877, Thiers was afflicted with bleeding at the nose and with faintness. Doctor Barthe feared the return of the troubles. Thiers discussed with him the remedies that he should take, which, in fact, were not so much medicines as the observance of a few simple hygienic laws, a course, by the way, which he followed throughout his whole life. " How do you stand so much work?" he was asked one day. " Because I am sober," was the reply.

But we must leave these details, however interesting they may appear to those who—not without reason perhaps—believe that nothing is immaterial in the life of illustrious men. Thiers's day is not finished. We have not yet arrived at his dinner hour, when he almost always had some guests; we have not followed him to the Chamber, to the Council. But we must make selections from this mass of illustrative data. We hasten to view him in a position where we have not yet seen him, and where his personality shines in most brilliant colors, at every period of his life—in his *salon*, in the midst of his friends and visitors.

Lamartine, in his *Souvenirs and Portraits* has related his first interview with Thiers, which took place, a few months before the Revolution of July, in a parlor of the *restaurateur* Véry of the Palais-Royal, and he has there given the portrait of his guest, who was then already celebrated. Certain traits have a fidelity of touch not often found in the imaginative style of the historian of the Girondists, and it will not be out of place to recall a few of them.

After having painted the external man, and spoken of his face with its "intellectual beauty triumphing over its lineaments, and forcing a rebellious body to express mental grandeur," he adds: "His mind was, like his body, upright, robust and active. Perhaps, being a man of the south, he over-estimated a little his powers. Modesty is a northern virtue, or a fruit of refined education. He spoke first, he spoke last, he paid little attention to replies; but he spoke with a correctness, with a boldness and with a wealth of ideas which caused the volubility of his lips to be excused. It was plain that he had been accustomed from an early age to be listened to by his companions. But his conversation—perfectly familiar and fitted for the time and place—was neither labored nor eloquent. It was the mind and the heart that flowed forth."

Then—passing on to a later period, when his young and new friend had become one of the masters of the tribune—in a rapid review, where he attempts to charac-

terize, by a few expressive words, the contemporary orators, Royer-Collard, Dupin, Odilon Barrot, etc., arrived
at Thiers, he can find no other word to paint him but
that of "prodigy." "Yes, the prodigy," cries Lamartine, "for it is a prodigy that has endowed him with
everything, even his voice and gestures, or rather he dis-
penses with voice and gesture through the mere force of
talent. For whole hours at a time, and hours that do
not drag, he will pour out his thoughts, common sense
and sometimes sophisms, without ever exhausting the interest of his audience or his own resources. He does not
strike great blows, but he strikes a multitude of little
ones, with which he breaks ministries, majorities and
thrones. He has not the might of soul of Mirabeau,
but he has his power in detail; he takes Mirabeau's club
into the tribune and makes arrows of it. He shoots
them into Assemblies to the right and to the left. On
one is written argument, on another sarcasm; on this
one grace, on that one passion. It is a shower from
which there is no escape. As for myself, who often opposed his policy, it was impossible for me not to admire
the pre-eminent artist."

These last traits of Thiers's nature must be borne in
mind, if we would form a correct idea of Thiers in a
salon, especially in his earlier and the first part of his
maturer years. It was indeed a shower, as Lamartine
has well said; a brilliant shower of ideas, colored with
all the magic tints of the rainbow, delicately shaded,

changing with the topic, the surroundings, the moment. On this point there is abundant testimony.

We are in the year 1840, or thereabouts. Mme. de Girardin in her *Parisian Letters** did not spare the minister whom she disliked. It seems that Thiers had called her in a *salon* a blue-stocking full of holes. "M. Thiers," she said, "is badly brought up, badly made, and lowly born." "Badly made," responded Thiers quickly; "how does she know it?"

In this same sprightly series of letters, Mme. de Girardin tells, good naturedly, at least one anecdote of Thiers worth quoting. It shows the quickness and humor of his mind. "He met the other day," says Mme. de Girardin, "an Academician who, though not old, was nevertheless somewhat advanced in years. 'How young you look,' said Thiers; 'what's this for?' 'Why, nothing.' 'None of that: we never rejuvenate without an object.'"†

He possessed the art, as we have just seen, of making repartees, which sometimes, it must be admitted, were rather cruel. Doctor Véron, ‡ in 1840, had placed the columns of the *Constitutionnel* at the disposal of the

---

* Mme. de Girardin, (1804–1855), had made a literary reputation as Delphine Gay, before her marriage with the well-known journalist, M. Emile Girardin, who still (1878) follows his profession, being editor-in-chief of *La Liberté*. Mme. de Girardin wrote the celebrated *Parisian Letters* under the *nom de plume* of the *Vicomte de Launay*.

† *Lettres Parisiennes*, Vol. IV, p. 26.

‡ Véron, (1798–1867), a famous journalist during the July Monarchy and February Republic, though not very highly respected. See the last foot note on page 81.

minister, and asked that in return he be provided with a good office which would give him "respectability." "An office that will give you respectability?" said Thiers. "Why, my dear sir, you ask me to do an impossibility."

Thiers's family, as we have before remarked, was in a lowly condition at the time of his birth. One day some one was talking before him about the old nobility and the vanity of the inheritors of a great name. "I do not think that it is wrong to turn up one's nose at the old nobility," he said, with a sly look, "though I am myself sprung from the old commonalty, and I am none the prouder for that."

Thiers was always ready to resent any slur cast at the middle classes—the *bourgeoisie*—from which he sprang.

Théophile Silvestre, the art critic and *littérateur*, though not an admirer of Thiers as a politician or writer, was very desirous of seeing his curiosities and objects of art. The opportunity was given him, and on leaving Thiers's *hôtel*, he expressed himself dissatisfied at finding so fine a collection marred by what he considered several inferior objects of art. "Nest of a *bourgeois*," he said on daparting, "I must refuse you the laurel wreath, but I will award you a lot of old women's nightcaps."* The *mot* was repeated to Thiers. "After all," he said, "M. Théophile Silvestre is right. *Bourgeois* I was born, *bourgeois* I will live, and *bourgeois* I wish to die.' And then, assum-

---

* "Nid d'un bourgeois. Je lui refuse la branch de laurier, mais je lui décernerai cent bonnets de coton."

ing the oratorical air of the tribune, he continued:
"What have the poets and critics of to-day against the
bourgeoisie ? What would become of the modern world
without them ? As early as the time of Louis XIV they
excelled the nobility. Molière, Bossuet, Corneille, La
Fontaine, Boileau, were *bourgeois.* So was Lebrun,
Eustache Lesueur, Poussin, Puget, Voltaire, Diderot,
Vanloo, Watteau and Rousseau. And from what class
to-day does France draw her orators, her engineers,
her artists, her generals, and her masters in everything?
From the *bourgeoisie.* And what is it that the reformers
and Utopists wish to make of the people? Princes?
No. Nobles? No. *Bourgeois?* Yes, and even that is
now found a very difficult thing."

The Faubourg Saint-Germain, formerly the most aristocratic portion of Paris, was long the pitiless enemy of
Thiers, because of his low birth. From 1830 to 1840 the
press of the legitimist party delighted to twit Thiers for
his plebian origin and rustic manners. The *Mode* had heard
that Thiers at table had cut bread with a knife instead of
breaking it, and this little fault was quickly seized upon
and cast up in the face of the new statesman. Some
great ladies sent him a red morocco case containing six
little wooden-handled knives worth two or three cents a
piece, with this inscription printed in gilt letters on the
lid of the case: "To M. Thiers for his state dinners." *

---

* At a later date—when Thiers had won a European reputation—this little
case of knives figured in a charity lottery, gotten up by the late Countess
Duchâtel, the noble philanthropist.

The following estimate of Thiers—made at about this same period by an Englishman—is of a piece—in so far as it touches upon personal qualities—with the opinions held concerning him by the French aristocracy :

> "*September* 10*th*, 1833.—Dined on Friday with Talleyrand, a great dinner to M. Thiers, the French Minister of Commerce, a little man, about as tall as Shiel,* and as mean and vulgar-looking, wearing spectacles, and with a squeaking voice. He was editor of the *National* ; an able writer, and one of the principal instigators of the Revolution of July. It is said that he is a man of great ability and a good speaker, more in the familiar English than the bombastical French style. Talleyrand has a high opinion of him. He wrote a history of the Revolution, which he now regrets ; it is well done, but the doctrine of fatalism he puts forth in it he thinks calculated to injure his reputation as a statesman.†

Thiers often indulged in punning. M. E. Pascal, whom he had made Prefect at Nantes, at Lyons, and afterwards Councilor of State, abandoned him after his fall on May 24th, 1873, and became one of the most zealous of his enemies. Such desertions sometimes occur in politics. M. Pascal had been a mediocre journalist ; he was ambitious, and vainer than he was ambitious. Thiers one day in private, laughing at M. Pascal's bragging spirit, compared his talents to those of the village charlatan, who, to attract attention, sticks feathers in his hat. " He never knew how to use his quill," said Thiers, " and now he has wound up by using it for a feather." ‡

His puns were sometimes very pointed in their mean-

---

* Right Hon. Richard Llalor Shiel, (1793–1851), lawyer, dramatist and eloquent Irish agitator ; entered the House of Commons in 1829; and was British minister at Florence at the time of his death.

† *Greville Memoirs*, Vol. II, p. 196, (Am. Edition). Greville—whose memoirs are only published in part—was Clerk of the Council for about forty years. He died in January, 1865.

‡ "Il n' a jamais su se servir de sa *plume*, et il a fini par en faire un *plumet*."

ing. Though they occasioned a laugh they also awakened a thought. He more than once by their aid, impressed upon the public a fact that it was important the public should know. For example, during the sittings of the Committee of Thirty,* Thiers—after his fall, disgusted at the petty vexations and the base double dealing of its members—wished to express his real feelings without creating an explosion. He had recourse to a *lapsus linguæ*. " I was shut up," he said to the committee, " in the depths of the Palace of Penitence—of the Presidence I mean to say."† The *mot* was taken up in the evening by all the newspapers, and the desired effect was produced.

On another occasion, it was a gay sally bursting out in a most original and unexpected form. In 1850, Thiers went to visit Louis-Philippe at Claremont. After the interview, while walking along the terrace of the *château*, he noticed the old parrot of Madame Adelaide, Louis-Philippe's sister, the same one that hung formerly in the windows of the princess at Neuilly, near enough to the council chamber to be heard by Thiers when he was minister. " Ah, there you are my poor poll," he said on perceiving the parrot, " there you are again. Unlike us you still have your say. You remember, we were ministers together?" And he laughed at this souvenir of a past that he then however had many reasons to regret.

Thiers was the author of many delicate sentiments that

---

* See Chapter IX.
† " J'étais enfermé dans les profondeurs du palais de la Pénitence—de la Présidence veux-je dire."

sank deep into the human heart. His mind produced wise maxims as well as witty sallies. Count Enzenberg, who at one time represented Hesse at Paris, and who was an indefatigable collector of autographs, gave his album to Prince Bismarck one day, with the request that he write therein a sentiment. Bismarck consented after some hesitation. The page on which he was to write, already held two sentiments. The first, by Guizot, was as follows:

"In my long life I have learnt two wise rules: the first, to pardon much; the second, to never forget."

Thiers had written under this:

"A little forgetfulness will not hurt the sincerity of the pardon."

Bismarck added:

"For my part, I have learnt to forget much and to ask to be pardoned much."

Thiers's sentiment is at the same time a thrust at Guizot, and a moral maxim which not politicians alone might do well to heed.

The following charming and characteristic witticism deserves to be mentioned. While President, Thiers visited one day the War Department. Noticing a pair of spectacles on the floor he picked them up, saying: "Let us see if they are as good as the ones I use." A letter was handed him—apparently on purpose—which contained a pompous eulogy of his Government. Thiers, hastily throwing down the spectacles, said: "They are no better than my own; they magnify objects too much."

Some times his allusions were very caustic. He was undoubtedly thinking of MacMahon, his successor, when he said one day: "Don't despise small things nor small men. A mite is a wonder of the lowest degree of organic beings." And he added with a smile: "An ant, providing for winter, might teach a marshal of France a lesson, who is not ready on the day of battle." MacMahon was not prepared at the battle of Wörth in the war of 1870–71, and consequently suffered defeat.

In private he was more direct in his allusions to the Marshal-President, though it should be said that his arrows were shot without premeditation. His words were suggested by the occasion.

Thiers had a great liking for physical sports, and often talked about his skill as a hunter and an equestrian. A short time before his death, during the crisis of May 16th, 1877, somebody spoke to him of MacMahon. "I knew his brother very well," he said; "we have hunted together. He was killed by falling from his horse." And he added laughingly: "You see, my dear fellow, in horsemanship as in politics, it is necessary to sit well in the saddle and to hold a good rein." These words are a keen criticism of the scheme of May 16th. The Duke de Broglie was not well seated in his saddle, and of course did not hold a good rein: a fall was, therefore, inevitable.

The *salon* of the Place Saint-Georges, which comprised

several rooms, a study and a library, suggested the idea of a man of the nineteenth century, of a civilization rich, elegant and perfect.

In the antechamber of the study, in the middle of the room, rose the bronze statue of the *Perseus* of Benvenuto Cellini, a reduction, but nevertheless superb, which was made at Florence, by M. Manéglia, to replace another reduction which had perished in the flames of the Tuileries during the Commune. Not far from the *Perseus* was the *Apollo, the Lizard-killer*, and the *Satyr playing on a flute*, which Thiers called one day, before M. Charles Blanc,* "the standard of beauty." And scattered about the room, were other pieces of art that we must pass over in silence because of their number. The door of his study was guarded by two antiques, marble reductions: an *Apollo* and the *Satyr* of Praxiteles, executed by Mercié.

In the large room, over the mantelpiece, was a fresco of The *Last Judgment* of Michel Angelo, copied in water colors by Numa Boucoyran, and scattered about were other exquisite copies of the principal masterpieces, that charmed the distinguished amateur in his travels. The *Sistine Madonna*, for which he made the journey to Dresden ; the *Assumption* of Titian, from the Academy of Venice ; the *St. Cecilia* of Bologna, the *Communion of St. Jerome*, praised by Nicolas Poussin as one of the three most beautiful pictures of Rome ; the frescoes of Raphael from the Vatican : the *Dispute of the Holy Sacrament*, the *School of Athens*, the *Parnassus*, the *Transfiguration*, the *Sibyls*, etc. To the right and left of the *Last Judgment* rose on pedestals the *Farnese Hercules* and the *Slave* of Michel Angelo, and, on either side of these, in the corners, were the sculptures from the tomb of the Medicis, *Day* and *Night*, *Dawn* and *Dusk*. "Those four figures," says Charles Blanc, "so proud and so sad, so beautiful and so formidable in their stern elegance, which wear an anxious look on the mausoleums, as if the troubles of life, lasting even in death, were still agitating, from the depths of the tomb, the heroes buried there."

There were also precious bronzes, nearly all of the Renaissance, and of exceptional beauty. In the study were an antique *Mime*, an equestrian statue, modeled perhaps by Leonardo da Vinci himself, a bust of Lorenzo Ghiberti, a *Florentine Venus*, a little *Satyr* scratching his leg and holding a cow-herd's horn, an antique bust of Anacreon, a child and a serpent, a child and a goose, the *Marine Venus*, in high relief and a delicious bronze of the *Mercury* of Buda, worthy the great masters. There stood in the middle of the room on a pedestal the equestrian statue of Colleone—the only exact copy—which Thiers was permitted to have made on the spot at Venice.

It was in the midst of these wonders of art—of which we have here presented but an epitome—that Thiers was accustomed to receive his friends, his visitors, his guests, and, in a conversation by turns courteous, light and earnest, which riveted attention, to give vent, in a continuous and dazzling flow, to the spontaneous inspirations of his rare mind.

Thiers, before his marriage with Mlle. Dosne, in the earlier years of the July Monarchy, was a great frequenter of the *salons* and Paris society, particularly in those circles where politics and the *esprit français* predominated. When he became lord of the *hôtel* of the Place Saint-Georges, and to the prestige of his popularity added that of great fortune and influence, he loved to receive the intellectual *élite* of his own and foreign countries. None were excluded of those who occupied a place in the world of letters, of art, of science, of politics, of war, of industry, of commerce. Young talent, those even who as yet inspired only hopes, was brought face to face with names already celebrated. Sometimes the most obscure journalists were here able to stand on the same footing with the distinguished ambassadors and ministers of Europe, the Granvilles, the Clarendons, the Gladstones, the Bismarcks, and the Gortchakoffs, all those who, from 1833 to 1877, were famous in France in the course of three generations.

Sainte-Beuve has written an extremely interesting work, entitled *Chateaubriand and his Group*, in which he has arranged about the principal figure, the friends and familiars of the illustrious author. A similar work for Thiers, if composed by as able a hand, would be of superior

interest of itself and valuable for the history of the *esprit
français* in the nineteenth century.

The first place in the group that we have imagined,
would belong to the friends of his youth and the companions of his early political career. There would be seen,
in the first place, Mignet,the eminent historian,and a writer
remarkable for the eloquent vigor and elegant purity of
his style ; Charles de Rémusat, a man of parts and of a
mental acuteness that has not been surpassed ; Cousin,
not a sound philosopher, but a writer of the first order,
an incomparable talker, sometimes unjust in his estimates,
often paradoxical, but always brilliant ; Barthélemy-Saint-
Hilaire, a real philosopher in respect to science, firmness
of principles and elevation of character ; Dufaure, the
statesman, distinguished for the logic and flexibility of his
mind ; and others like M. Calmon,* and Casimir Périer, son
of the former Premier under Louis-Philippe, who form,
as it were, the connecting link between the first and the
second generation, which begins about 1840, and which,
preserving a few survivors of the first, still lingers to-day.

In this new group should be placed Grévy, Henri Martin, the accomplished historian, Jules Favre, Jules Simon,
Arago, the astronomer, separated a little from Thiers
politically, but always united by the common tie of cul-
ture and intellectual sympathy ; Le Verrier, the famous

---

* Calmon,(1815—), advocate, and liberal politician ; deputy in 1846 ; retired
from public life on the advent of the Empire, and devoted himself to literature ; member of the Academy of Moral and Political Sciences, in 1872 ;
deputy in 1874 ; and now (1878) life-senator.

astronomer, an intractable character, whom Thiers seems to have conquered; Laboulaye, the friend of America, and director of the College of France; Bersot of the *Journal des Débats;* and, at a little later period, Prévost-Paradol, Caro of the French Academy and Professor of Philosophy at the Sorbonne, Janet of the Sorbonne, and About, the voluminous writer, all men of distinguished talents; and that galaxy, more or less brilliant, of journalists, novelists and of young historians, who have not yet reached their zenith.

It is indeed difficult to imagine the topics of discussion, and the interest of the conversation among such men. All the faculties of the mind appeared on this intellectual theatre, enriched with so many wonders of art, where everything suggested thought and excited effort. As Thiers, according to Prévost-Paradol, was living France, so his *salon* was a brilliant reflection of that France. In it was a continual exchange of ideas, souvenirs, anecdotes, stories, where ruled incontestably the spirit of the France of the nineteenth century; that spirit, free from prejudices, tolerant, recognizing no other sovereign, no other royalty than that of the mind, exalting only reason, offspring of Descartes and Voltaire, loving truth and liberty, like Thiers himself, more or less sincerely according to the varying characteristics of persons, but, like him, accepting no other rule of life than that imposed by truth and liberty.

It can excite envy in nobody's breast, if we endeavor

to give an idea of the conversational lustre of Thiers's *salon*, and point out the large share of wit and learning that emanated there from the distinguished host himself. The *mots* and anecdotes that we have already recounted, present the less important side of the picture. They are only the small coin that tells of the immense treasures within. To grasp the whole intellectual grandeur of the spirit that pervaded Thiers's *salon*, to pierce beneath the petty details of daily talk, which, if we except the form, is about the same everywhere, in the Faubourg Saint-Germain as in the Faubourg Saint-Honoré, at New York as at Paris,—to see into the depths of the soul of the *hôtel* of the Place Saint-Georges, we have only to read a few chosen pages from the writings of the historian, the journalist and the art critic. Thiers, by his *abandon*, his unstudied ease of manner, by his naturalness, by the freedom of his style, carried sometimes even to carelessness, —is very often, with his pen in his hand, just as he was when standing in his parlors in the midst of an attentive circle, or seated at a *tête-à-tête* with some official or privileged personage. It is only necessary to add the accent, the gesture and the play of the features. And the picture may be rendered still more realistic, by reading the fragments of the conversations scattered here and there, and published by some of his auditors whose reports can be depended upon, for Thiers was one of those whose thought once spoken, especially in private, was engraved on the memory in lines that are never effaced.

We wish, in order to give more completeness to the sketch, to present a few of the opinions emanating from the *salon* of the Place Saint-Georges and inspired in the host by the objects that surrounded him, and with which he was, so to speak, penetrated; for it was amid his art treasures that Thiers thought and wrote. We will thus view Thiers in a light in which he is not generally regarded, but in which he must be seen to be thoroughly comprehended. Thiers was an art critic as well as an amateur of the first order, and his judgments, like his preferences, have a value.

M. Charles Blanc, who frequented the *salon* of the Place Saint-Georges, gives a very exact idea of its character by recalling some of Thiers's printed criticisms, and some of the conversations had with him. He cites the following description of David's picture of the *Death of Socrates*, and of Delacroix's *Dante and Virgil in Hell*, criticisms written in Thiers's younger days for the *Constitutionnel:*

"Socrates in his prison, seated on a bed, points to the heavens, which indicates the nature of his conversation; he receives the cup, which recalls his condemnation; he moves to drink off its contents, which announces his philosophic absorption and his sublime indifference to death. The epic poet chooses what aids his narration, the tragic poet what pertains to the drama, the painter what can become visible."

In speaking of Delacroix, he said:

"No picture, it seems to us, reveals more clearly the future of a great painter, than that of M. Delacroix representing *Dante and Virgil in Hell.* It displays great talent and is full of promise. Here is found the selfishness and despair of hell. In this subject, bordering in fact upon exaggeration, there is, however, a severity of taste and a local fitness that exalt the design, which some stern but poor judges might reproach with a lack of nobility. The pencil is large and firm; the color vigorous, though a little harsh. The author sketches his figures, groups them and bends them at his will, with the boldness of Michel Angelo and the fertility of Rubens. I know not what souvenirs of great artists seize me when I look on this picture. I find there that wild, burning but natural power which produces enthusiasm without effort."

The critic is found to hold the same opinions, expressed with the same vivacity, more than fifty years afterwards. Michel Angelo was Thiers's great admiration. One day, when on the point of departing for Athens, M. Charles Blanc went to bid Thiers good-by, and receive his commissions, the latter said to him, as if responding to a remark which M. Blanc was about to utter: "Yes, without doubt, yes, the Pantheon has the first prize, of course; but let us talk about the second prize and the honorable mention." He thus characterized his personal preference, and the independence of his admiration. On another occasion, when the same person said to Thiers that he had a decided preference for the Renaissance, which was indeed true, Thiers interrupted him abruptly to show him the *Apollo, the Lizard-killer*, and the *Satyr playing on a flute*. "There is the standard of the beautiful," he said ; " it should always be within sight. Believe me, that I have not ventured on this ocean of innumerable varieties of human art, without knowing the safe spots to cast anchor."

At another time, M. Blanc and Thiers were looking at one of those lacquered boxes, bright with aventurine, and filled with satin neck-handkerchiefs, Chinese crape, furs of Thibetan goats, and Liliputian slippers, when M. Blanc brought a smile to Thiers's face by remarking: " May we not believe that a Mongol Jupiter, wishing to seduce the Danaës of Nankin, caused this rain of gold to fall into their wardrobes?" " The god of the arts," replied Thiers, "has not disinherited any part of the world. Each people has attained in its way a perfection that the others have not reached. This one has a genius for form, that one for color and decoration. Some share the greatness of conceptions, others the beauty of materials. In those latitudes where humanity, left to itself, could not have created for itself the enjoyments and the consolations of art, nature has kindly come to the aid of man by furnishing him wonderful substances, splendid colors, materials which await and provoke the genius of the workman."

" So speaking," says M. Blanc, " M. Thiers unrolled before us some of those very long silk strips, on which the Chinese artists had represented fantastic designs in the richest colors, and, at every instant, the most piquant and serious reflections were suggested to the mind of the illustrious amateur, which showed that art was for him what it really is, the splendid form of the idea, and that he was better qualified than anybody else to inter- pret it."

Among the drawings in Thiers's collection is one of extreme beauty from the pen of Leonardo da Vinci, where are delineated with incomparable skill and vigor, the figures of a number of knights on horseback, fighting with live skeletons on foot.　The latter have the best of the contest ; they unhorse the knights, strike horror into them, and kill them with their lances.　This very precious sketch, is supposed to have been a study made by Leo- nardo for the celebrated cartoon, which he was going to paint in competition with Michel Angelo, for the ducal palace at Florence.　Thiers saw in it the embodiment of a thought of Macchiavelli, that infantry would in the end supersede cavalry, that is to say, that nobility would be one day vanquished by the people.　"They are strug- gling, those starved wretches," said Thiers, "to infuse a little divine justice into human institutions."

To those who are familiar with art questions in France, it is very easy to see, by the nature of these various opinions, that Thiers was of no party.　He has been ac- cused of being classic.　He was indeed classic, by his style and by his preference for the language of the seventeenth and eighteenth centuries. He it was who wrote, *à-propos* of M. de Fontanes's * *Eulogy on Washington*, prepared at the request of the first Consul: "M. de Fontanes, a pure and brilliant writer, the last who has employed that French language, formerly so perfect, but buried to-day with the eighteenth century in the abyss of the past."† This preference did not arise wholly from what he called his " fanaticism for simplicity," but because the language that he regretted, and which, by the way, is not completely lost, was more lively, more limpid, and stronger than that which, under the influence of Chateaubriand and his school, had replaced it. But the independence of his judgments was not fettered by his preferences. For him, the classic idea was never confined within the narrow limits, where a certain school of the time of his youth endeavored to imprison it. Thiers had a profound liking for the poetry of Lamartine. His predilection in art was in general for original minds, proud and independent geniuses, as is shown by his passion for Michel Angelo and his bold opinion of Delacroix. In this respect also Thiers was with his time.

Along with this independent spirit, which he carried not only into art—as we have already seen in his political history—he was furthermore possessed of that feeling so

---

* Marquis de Fontanes, (1757–1821), the French poet and orator ; member of the Academy ; deputy and senator under the first Empire ; Grand-Master of the University of France ; and member of the Chamber of Peers under the Restoration.

† *Consulate and Empire*, Vol. I., p. 218.

powerful in the society of to-day, ambition, the desire to rise. Thiers's mother early discovered this characteristic in her son. She said to Mignet when he was very young: "Adolphe will never go afoot. He will catch on behind the wagon, then he will work forward on to the seat, throw out the driver, and seize the reins himself." Thiers's after life did indeed realize the prediction in so far as it concerned his ambitious spirit. His *History of the French Revolution* was the first and grandest result of an honest and noble ambition. But he did not mount upon the seat for the sole purpose of rising and seizing the reins of power. He guided honorably the chariot of state through more than one danger, struggled more than once to keep it on the broad highway, and finally raised it up again after its fall.

All Thiers's gifts, whether of mind or character, were ever kept most actively employed, as we have already seen, through the great value that their possessor placed on time, and because of his insatiable curiosity. He had traversed all the paths of human activity, and the entire circle of knowledge. And he was not satisfied with a general glance: in everything he had a passion for details. "How did you know all about the battle of Wagram?" an old officer of Napoleon said to him one day. "I was there, but I saw nothing of all this." If many errors are found in his history, it is because authors are human. His enemies, a long time ago, pictured him as "impressing everybody into his service, demanding of everybody information for his *History of the French Revolution,* for, in all his works, this is his way of proceeding, by forced conversations and by the aid of other people's memories. He is more the mendicant friar, than the Benedictine monk of history." Another said very wittily, but not more unjustly: "He will go right up to Soult and tell him boldly, that he did not leave Genoa by the Gate of France but by that of Italy; and if Soult were wounded at the battle of Salamanca, he will sustain, amidst the applause of the Chamber, that it was in the left leg and not in the right, as Soult had always supposed, and he will prove it to him so clearly, that the old general, to satisfy himself, will involuntarily put his finger in the cavity of the wound."

The criticism here proves the fact that is questioned. The passion for details which is necessary in history and in life, in public as in private life, and which may also be regarded as a measure of activity, was found developed to the highest degree in Thiers.

Old age did not change him in this particular; his curiosity and his activity remained the same. We have seen him in his study. It even seemed as if time had only increased his forces. His mental power, kept ceaselessly on the alert, had given him a robust old age, and, which is rarely the case, a fruitful old age. It was during the last years of his life that he put forth the greatest activity, and that his efforts were the most useful. During the whole term of his busy presidency, his eye and hand were everywhere. Throughout the insurrection of the Commune, all the plans of attack were discussed in the Council and placed under his eyes. The great financial operations were studied by him in all their parts, and even to the smallest items. At every instant he was besieged by important, inevitable visits, and he was always ready. The tribune and the committees also required a large portion of his time, and they never found him remiss. He even gained leisure to read the reception orations delivered before the French Academy; and, when the newly elected members came to pay him, as President of the Republic, the customary visit, after their public reception by the Academy, with their neatly bound orations in their hands, he liked to let them see that he had carefully read their efforts, by the solid and piquant observations that he expressed. "I will never forget," says M. Cuvillier-Fleury, "the spirited and unexpected estimate of the *Commentaries* of Cæsar, that he pronounced in our presence, on the day when I had the pleasure of presenting to him the author * of the *Siege of Alesia*, the historian of the Condés,† recently elected to the Academy. He admired the vanquisher of Vercingetorix, and recognized, in the successful rival of Pompey, the powerful genius who had momentarily suspended, in

---

* The Duke d'Aumale, son of Louis-Philippe. On April 3d, 1873, Thiers appeared at the Academy as the introducer of the Duke d'Aumale, who, in a burst of gratitude, praised him in these words: "The brave and able pilot who has steered the ship in her distress."

† *History of the Princes of Condé* is the title of the duke's work.

the Roman world, the scourge of civil war. His admiration stopped there. In the same way had he celebrated and glorified the French Cæsar. He was a judicious and earnest admirer of the genius of the man, but never the accomplice or dupe of the dictator."*

When he wished to accomplish an immediate and imperious duty, then it was that his powers of work and application, that his contempt of toil, showed themselves, and he gave himself up mind and body to the performance of the task. His journey during the severe winter of 1870 to London, Vienna and St. Petersburg will be remembered in this connection.

At this point belongs a very characteristic anecdote. It occurred at Versailles during the armistice, at the end of February, 1871. Thiers, accompanied by the delegates of the Assembly of Bordeaux, was discussing the conditions of peace with Bismarck and Moltke. After the preliminaries, they arrived at the two or three points in dispute, namely, the possession of Belfort, the amount of the indemnity, etc. Bismarck, although he already knew Thiers's powers, perceiving not only his ability and his *sang-froid* but his utter disregard of all fatigue, could not help expressing astonishment. The end was still more surprising. The discussion lasted a long time, and was drawing to a close when the dinner hour arrived. The other negotiators retired from the room one after another, until the two principal personages, Bismarck and Thiers,

---

* M. Fleury in the *Journal des Débats.*

were left alone to debate the contested points, and especially the cession of Belfort. The companions of Bismarck waited a long time for their chief, impatient to sit down to table. At length he appeared, very hungry, and declaring that Thiers had tried to conquer him by famine. After dinner, the cigars lighted, they returned to the chamber of the deliberations. Thiers was still there looking over documents. During that whole day he had only taken a cup of coffee. Bismarck was amazed. He did not intend to be forced by hunger to forget his diplomatic interests, but who knows whether a sentiment of respect, which he could not help feeling for the man who disregarded so completely his physical comforts, may not have contributed something towards a withdrawal of his demand for the cession of Belfort.

M. Henri Martin has recently furnished another example of Thiers's great patriotism, and which, at the same time, shows the tenderness of his feelings.

" I have seen him weep twice," says M. Martin in reference to Thiers; "this man whom so many events and so many years seemed to have hardened to all the blows of fate. It was when he brought to us at Bordeaux, the humiliating but necessary treaty, which he was forced to sign at Versailles, in order to save France from utter ruin; and it was when, during the civil war, he thought one morning that the Louvre was burning. I have seen him shed tears over the political grandeur and the intellectual grandeur of France, both given over to sword and fire." *

* Speech at Laon, August 27th, 1878.

His mental vigor and firm principles did not become weaker as he grew older. They remained the same to the last hour of his life. A perusal of the letter to his constituents * will show what strength his mind had retained under the weight of fourscore years. There is not a word in this document which suggests old age. It breathes the force and vivacity of the Protest of the Journalists under the Restoration, † tempered only by the gravity of a personal and individual situation. There is not less spirit, strength and common sense displayed in this arraignment of the Duke de Broglie, than in that of Prince Polignac; and Marshal MacMahon can find no more comfort in the last document, than did Charles X in the first. What mental energy and what logical precision in that passage, where, referring to the fall of the different governments that he had seen successively destroyed, he shows the cause to lie in their continual pretension of desiring to save the country by resisting its wishes.

But it was not only strength of mind and character that Thiers preserved to the last: he retained also his brilliancy, gaiety and freshness of imagination.

A few days before his death, which he did not expect so soon, though he often thought of it, he desired to read Æschylus, and had asked M. Bersot ‡ for a copy. M. Bersot sent him the volume, pretending that it was

---

* See Appendix D.   † See page 36.
‡ M. Bersot is the director of the Superior Normal School at Paris, and a member of the Institute of France.

a prize in French oratory, for the speech he had delivered to the citizens of Saint-Germain a short time before. The idea amused Thiers very much, and he acknowledged the book in the following letter, written a week before his death :

"Saint-Germain, *August 27th,* 1877.

"My Dear Master,who are a model for us all in talent, common sense and fine speech,—I thank you for the prize in French oratory which you have awarded me. I will put the little volume in my little library, which is not in my large room but in my bed chamber. I have there a hundred small volumes, handy, in clear type, plainly bound, clean and in good order; in a word, made to be read, and not to be looked at on finely polished shelves. When I am weary, out of sorts, sick of the opinions of our conservatives, I turn to these great minds, with whom alone I wish to live. There it is that you will come to bid me a last farewell, when I leave this world for the other, where we will find what we loved and esteemed. In the meanwhile, we must see each other, for the time that remains to me cannot be long ; so —before it is too late—I pray you to arrange with *Moussu Giraoud** to come and dine with us some day this week at St. Germain.

"Every day I admire more and more this beautiful region, much superior to Versailles as regards taste and

---

* The Marseilles pronunciation of *Monsieur Giraud.* M. Giraud, Dean of the Paris Law School, was a friend and compatriot of Thiers ; that is, he was a native of Marseilles.

true grandeur. I say this without any allusion to the Versailles of to-day, for I cannot think of the present with a volume of Æschylus in my hand.

"Farewell.

"Yours truly,

A. THIERS."

Thiers always had—to employ an image of his cousin, the poet André Chénier—"the wings of hope."* During his presidency, in the midst of the intrigues of the monarchical factions, whose object was the destruction of the Republic, he sometimes said in his fits of indignation, which were always intense: "They will kill me." But this was only a passing mood. He soon forgot it and was at work again, as full of hope as ever, saying, as he did one day in the presence of one of our friends: "My family was long-lived."

The day after his fall—May 25th, 1873—preparations for his departure from the presidential palace of the Elysée were actively going on, in order that Marshal MacMahon might enter forthwith. It was near eleven o'clock in the morning, when Thiers was told that the municipal council and the mayor of Versailles wished to see him. He was busy taking down, with his own hands, a picture from the wall, when the visitors were introduced into the cabinet. The visitors smiled as Thiers remarked: "You see I am moving." On all sides indeed was confusion: furni-

---

* L'illusion féconde habite dans mon sein ;
   J'ai les ailes de l'espérance.— *The Young Captive.*

ture disarranged, drawers open, piles of papers and books all about, trunks blocking up the passages, everything indicating that the hour of departure was near at hand. The mayor, M. Rameau,* spoke in the name of the council, and Thiers replied, thanking the people of Versailles, and praising their firm and moderate republicanism. Then, pointing to some pictures scattered about him, he continued : " There are some paintings that I mean to give to the Louvre, only I desire that Mme. Thiers may enjoy them until my death." " We hope then that this will be a long way off," said M. Charton,† then deputy from the Yonne and member of the council. " Don't fear," replied Thiers ; " I am more stubborn than Time."

The years advanced ; he was approaching his end without losing confidence, and, it is worthy of remark, that this obstinate faith in longevity, the sign of strong natures, associated itself not less with his ideas than with his plans. The defeat of the manœuvre of May 16th, 1877, when the Duke de Broglie aimed a last deadly blow at the Republic, was never doubted for an instant by Thiers, and awakened in him a belief of his early return to the presidency. On June 14th, 1877, in the midst of the crisis, he wrote the following note to one of his prefects, whom the conspirators had just driven from office.

---

* Rameau (1809—), who was mayor of Versailles during the critical period of the Prussian occupation, and risked his life more than once in the interests of the city, has been a republican deputy since 1871.

† Charton (1807—), author and republican politician ; deputy under the February Republic ; deputy since 1871 ; and now (1878) senator.

"My dear former and future prefect, I hope—I am responding very late to your letter of May 28th. Attribute it only to the difficulty of answering all that is written me, and always rely upon my perfect esteem and my sincere friendship. Those who have ousted you from office are fools, in the opinion of all France, and they will soon be disarmed by her. I hope this will be accomplished without great commotion, and I thoroughly believe it will be.

"Heartily yours,

A. THIERS."

Was it this feeling that made him so serene in the midst of the abuses heaped upon him by the reactionary newspapers, which favored the movement of May 16th? Among these lampoons, we instance the following, not that it is one of the severest, for in reality it was among the mildest, but because of the singular coincidence that belongs to it.

The *Grelot*, a caricaturing paper, published on September 2nd, 1877, the day before Thiers's death, a sketch representing Thiers holding a scythe and giving his arm to Time, who, broken down and bent, supported himself on a stick and hour-glass. Both advanced smiling, walking on reactionary newspapers, among others the *Soir*, the *Patrie*, the *Pays* and the *Ordre*. On the fragments of these newspapers were seen the following sentiments: "By this time, we are at length probably rid of the sinister old man who has been the author of so many crimes, and we * * * "—*Ordre*. " The sinister old man has at last given up his soul to the devil. He is dead, a just punishment for his crimes. May so perish those who * * * "—*Patrie*. " He is dead * * * "— *Pays*. " M. Thiers is very sick. The doctors promise to get rid of him for us * * * "—*Soir*. At the bottom of the page was printed the customary authorization demanded by the French press laws : " M. Thiers authorizes the publication of the present design.—August 20th, 1877." The caricature appeared on September 2nd, and on September 3d Thiers was dead !

Thiers liked humor. Caricatures afforded him great amusement. There was one which represented him as a cavalry-man, trailing behind him a long sabre, which was entangled in his short legs. He was delighted with this. He had a military temperament, and everything that smacked of the warrior found in his soul a ready response.

We have said that Thiers had a high sense of personal dignity. He ever kept it in view ; it was one of his sources of strength ; he even confounded it with his glory. In a speech delivered in 1866 in the Corps Législatif, he said : " My language is not inspired by any personal hostility, but by profound convictions with which, as a child of '89, I was born, with which, become a man, I have lived, for which I have sacrificed, when it was necessary, all personal ambition, and with which I will die ; for, throughout the long revolutions that I have experienced, there is but one interest that I have wished to guard, and that I wish always to guard, namely, my dignity."

There are several anecdotes that exhibit this feeling in Thiers. We give two. Marshal Mortier, Duke of Treviso, attached great importance to titles of nobility. With the intention doubtless of being agreeable to Thiers, he asked him one day: "How is the baroness?" "Thank you," was the simple reply, Thiers not wishing to show his contempt the first time. But a few days afterwards the marshal repeated the disagreeable greeting, whereupon Thiers remarked: "I am much obliged to you for the kind interest which you take in my wife's health, but I must inform you that I am not a baron, and that if the desire seized me to be ennobled, I would not have much trouble to be named a duke. But I like much better to be called simply Monsieur Thiers."

When Thiers learned that Disraeli had been elevated to the peerage, he said: "I cannot understand how when one has the good fortune to be named Benjamin Disraeli, he can be possessed with the desire to be called Lord Beaconsfield."

It is a singular fact, that he who living cared so little for the calumnies of party foes, was anxious about the time when he would no longer be able to hear them. The idea of being misjudged, especially by his contemporaries, was of course disagreeable to him, but it was doubly so when he thought that he might be misunderstood by posterity. Along with respect for his person, he had respect for his memory. Having learned in his latter years, that M. Taine was writing a book on the French Revolution, which belittled what he had adored, and that the icono-clast—this was the term Thiers used—aspired to his place in the French Academy, he selected a successor to his liking. It was Thiers who suggested M. Henri Martin, the distinguished historian, to his friends in the Academy. He wished to be sure of having a sympathetic and equitable interpreter, capable of presenting him in his true light as a representative of the French Revolution and of modern thought, in short, of "living France." *

---

* On the entrance of a new member into the French Academy, it is the custom that he deliver an eulogy on the academician whom he replaces. M. Martin was elected June 13th, 1878, to the seat made vacant by Thiers's death, and M. Taine, who has since been elected, was the candidate who opposed him. The work of M. Taine referred to by M. Thiers, is entitled the *Origin of Contemporary France*, (*Les origines de la France contemporaine*).

CHAPTER XI.

THE LAST DAYS OF THIERS.

In the afternoon of Monday, September 3d, 1878, it became known that Thiers had died at Saint-Germain-en-Laye, where he had been passing several days. He had left Dieppe, on the coast, a short time before, less to escape the too bracing air of the sea, than to be near Paris, in order to follow more closely the political struggle then in progress. At Saint-Germain he continued to work, write and receive visitors. Ten days previous, he had made a strong and spirited speech. The day before his death, he went to Poissy, a small town near Saint-Germain, to see Meissonier, the artist, who was going to paint his portrait. He returned early to Saint-Germain, where he spent the evening with some friends. He was in good spirits, and talked with his usual force and raciness. The conversation turned on the *fête des Loges.** One of those who had just returned from the festivities, was describing the amusements then in progress. Thiers listened with

---

* In the forest of Saint-Germain, at the end of a broad avenue, are the *Loges*, a number of buildings used as an educational establishment for the daughters of members of the Legion of Honor. On the broad green before this school, occurs the most popular public *fête-champêtre* of the environs of Paris.

enjoyment, interrupting the narrator from time to time, to relate some recollection of his younger days, suggested by the conversation. He passed an excellent night, and had even done some work. He arose at five in the morning. He intended going to Paris on that day, as M. Barthélemy-Saint-Hilaire had made an engagement for him, between three and four o'clock in the afternoon, to meet several persons, among others Gambetta, at the *hôtel* of the Place Saint-Georges.

After working until seven o'clock, he took a two hours' walk on the terrace of Saint-Germain, leaning on the arm of his servant. From the terrace, is a beautiful view of the broad valley of the Seine, with a portion of Paris, and a dim outline of the historic church of St. Denis, on the horizon. Thiers never wearied of this grand and suggestive panorama. On returning from this his last walk, he made a few turns in the pretty little garden of the hotel, stopping a moment at the stable to see his horses, for which he had a strong attachment, and entering his study, took up his work, which he continued until the hour of *déjeuner*. Very much occupied at this moment with his letter to his constituents,* and deprived of his first secretary, M. Aude, who was sick, he exerted his strength to a greater degree than ordinarily. This circumstance, perhaps, hastened his end. It can be said, however, to use the words of Montaigne, that "never did man live longer in death."

---

* See Appendix D.

At *déjeuner* he ate with relish until dessert, but then a sudden change in his face occurred. He placed his hand on his forehead, where he felt an intolerable heaviness; his mouth began to shrivel, and his eye grow dim; he could scarcely articulate some incoherent words, and sank unconsciously into an arm-chair. Dr. Le Piez, *fils*,*—who took the place of Dr. Barthe, the regular physician and friend of Thiers—was immediately called. Dr. Le Piez on arriving, saw that it was the beginning of serous apoplexy. He applied sinapisms to the patient's legs, and leeches to the nape of his neck. All was useless. Thiers had, in the meanwhile, been carried to a bed, and was unconscious. When Dr. Barthe—informed of the sad occurrence by telegraph—arrived at four o'clock, he had only to glance at the patient to see that all was lost. The eyes opening for an instant immediately closed; the pulse beat but feebly; the limbs were growing stiff. At six o'clock and five minutes Thiers was dead.

The following letter from M. G. Barbotte, the proprietor of the Hôtel du Pavillon Henri IV, where Thiers died, contains some interesting particulars of his last days at Saint-Germain :

---

* On Thiers's arrival at Saint-Germain, he sent for M. Le Piez, and said to him: "I have often heard you mentioned in Paris, sir. As Barthe is going away, you are to be my physician. Begin by making my acquaintance and feeling my pulse." This was said in a gay tone, and Dr. Le Piez little thought that the end of his distinguished patient was so near.

" *Hôtel du Pavillon Henri IV,*
                " *Saint-Germain, August* 31*st,* 1878.

"SIR:

" M. Thiers arrived from Dieppe, August 22nd, 1877, at 4.25. Mme. Thiers was with him. They had engaged the second floor of the hotel, charming apartments, whose windows looked out on the valley of the Seine. The suite was composed of a parlor and five bed-rooms. The two rooms near the parlor were occupied by Mlle. Dosne,* who joined the party a few days after their arrival. The others were occupied by the servants. It is a peculiarity worthy of remark, that the beds were not those of the hotel. Like Louis-Philippe, M. Thiers and his wife slept each in a little folding-bed, which they always carried with them when traveling.

" The life of the illustrious statesman was very regular. In the morning he arose at five o'clock. His *valet de chambre*, Louis, gave him a cup of *café noir* at six o'clock. Then he worked about two hours. Morel, his *valet de pied*, came at eight o'clock to take him to walk on the terrace, a promenade, by the way, that he liked very much. He returned about half past nine, slept two hours, and then took *déjeuner* with Mme. Thiers and Mlle. Dosne. He sometimes received visitors at this repast, but not very often. The meal was simple, they talked a little, and then work was resumed and continued until five o'clock, when he went out again for a walk. After this, he slept again until eight o'clock, at which hour he was awakened for dinner. After dinner he went to his desk, where he remained until one o'clock in the morning. He scarcely ever slept through the night, without waking

---

* Mme. Thiers's sister.

up several times, and calling the servant to bring him pen
and paper in order to make notes.

" M. Thiers often stopped to talk with us, and liked to
find out the names of the guests at the hotel at the same
time with himself. The wonderful facility with which M.
Thiers conversed on all subjects has frequently been
noticed. He often did me the honor to talk with me
about the supplying of our markets, and I must say that
he spoke with a perfect knowledge of the subject, even in
its smallest details.

"Three days after his arrival, a deputation of the principal republicans of Saint-Germain, came to welcome
him to our city. M. Thiers responded with a few affec-
tionate remarks, and finished his speech by repeating
these words that he had pronounced on a former occasion : ' Before separating, let me again say what I have
already said to you : the Republic will remain conservative
or it will cease to exist.'

" The night before his death, he was photographed on
the hotel stoop. * * * On September 2nd, he promised to meet Messrs. Gambetta, Calmon and Barthélemy-
Saint-Hilaire at the Place Saint-Georges, on the 4th.
On the morning of the 3d, he rang to have the hour of
déjeuner made earlier, that he might take the 12.55 train.
He sat down to table in fine spirits and with a good appe-
tite. The repast consisted of kidneys, cold chicken, *flag-
eolets* and pickles. He remarked that he never felt better.
But, in the midst of the meal, he became indisposed, asked
for air and requested Mme. Thiers to untie his cravat.
The physician was sent for, but all efforts were then too
late."

"Yours very respectfully,
BARBOTTE."

The news of the event spread immediately throughout Saint-Germain, and produced, at the same time, surprise and consternation. Silent and sad groups of people formed in front of the Pavillon Henri IV. Dispatches had been sent to Thiers's old friends: to M. Barthélemy-Saint-Hilaire at Paris, to Mignet and M. Calmon, the first at Aix, the second at Chatellerault. M. Barthélemy-Saint-Hilaire arrived at Saint-Germain at nine o'clock, bowed with sorrow. At about this same hour the fatal news was circulated at Paris, where it produced an indescribable impression. Since the death of Mirabeau, nothing similar had been known in this great city, so susceptible, however, to the emotions of public life, and which had seen so many celebrated men die.

The next morning, September 4th, by the first train, visitors began to arrive at Saint-Germain, and they made haste to express to the family of the illustrious deceased, the sorrow of the public and their own private sympathy.

Thiers was laid out on a a little folding bed, in a sombre and simple room, looking out on the valley of the Seine. All the blinds were shut, except one, by which entered an uncertain light, that added to the dolefulness of the apartment. The bed was placed directly in front of this open blind. The head, half lighted up, detached itself from the dark background. The features had preserved in death, during the first hours, their character so eminently personal. It was indeed Thiers as all Paris knew him, the Thiers of Bonnat's portrait,* only paler, more reposed and more severe. He was dressed in a long white robe, open at the throat, the hands lying outside the sheet, and on his feet was a tartan shawl, grey and red, which he was often accustomed to throw over himself when cold.

Among the first visitors, was Meissonier, the artist. He began immediately to trace the face of the dead, and worked nearly three hours at a portrait. At the same time, M. Breunt, the photographer, took a photograph, and M. Desuchez and M. Alfred Lenoir, sent by M. Gillaume, director of the School of Fine Arts at Paris, proceeded to make a mould of the face.

The next day, September 5th, the body was transported to Paris, arriving at the *hôtel* of the Place Saint-Georges at half-past five o'clock in the afternoon. A silent and sympathetic crowd,—in which all classes of society were represented, though workingmen in their blouses predominated—had collected in the square and in the neighboring streets. The body was carried to the second floor and placed in Thiers's study, which was transformed into a *chapelle ardente.* A great number of senators, deputies and persons of all ranks immediately filed by the body, as it lay there, surrounded with the burning wax candles. Early the next morning, the approaches to the *hôtel* were filled by a mass of people

* The portrait at the beginning of this volume is engraved from an *eau-forte* of Bonnat's celebrated picture.

come to insert their names in the register, placed in the garden for that purpose. A line over a hundred yards long and five or six persons broad was formed on the sidewalk of the rue Saint-Georges. The policemen detailed to keep order, allowed only about a dozen to approach the registers at once. After inserting the name, each visitor mounted the stairs to view the body and quietly retired. This silent grief touched everybody's heart. The spectacle continued up to the day of the funeral,—the same mute sorrow, the same vast concourse.

Public woe was seen on all sides, and was expressed in various ways. All the republican newspapers appeared in black, and filled with articles of regret and eulogy. The republican deputies met the first day and drew up an Address to the country to deplore the loss of the illustrious citizen, and to attest their attachment to the firm and prudent policy which he had marked out. The French Academy—convened as usual for its Thursday meeting—adjourned forthwith as a sign of respect. The Council-General of the department of the Seine, and the Municipal Council of Paris decided to participate officially in the funeral ceremonies. The students of the Paris Law School, Medical School, School of Fine Arts, and other educational institutions, likewise voted to take part in the funeral. The merchants of the principal commercial quarters of Paris resolved to close their stores on the day of interment, as a sign of "national mourning." From all parts of France, from many of her cities, from the French residents in foreign lands, came addresses of condolence to Mme. Thiers. The cities of Alsace and Lorraine were the first to pay their tribute of respect to the illustrious dead. The inhabitants of Belfort decided to send an immense crown of flowers to be laid on the coffin.

Foreign nations participated in this sorrow of France. " Europe has just lost its only great statesman," said Bismarck, and he ordered Prince Hohenlohe, who was at that moment in Germany, to return to his post as ambassador to France, and take part in the obsequies. Prince Gortchakoff wrote : " A great light has just been extinguished in Europe, at a moment when the political horizon is obscure." The President of the Chamber of Deputies of Vienna sent Mme. Thiers a telegram, expressing his regrets at the death of her husband, and recognizing the services he had rendered the cause of constitutional government. The Belgian Assembly decided to take part in the funeral ceremonies, in recognition of what the deceased had done for Belgium, especially in favoring the expedition against Antwerp.* The great families of Vienna, Rome, and of most of the capitals of Europe, sent Mme. Thiers messages of condolence. At Washington, the national flag was displayed at half-mast on all the public buildings, out of respect for Thiers's memory. This act of regard would not have touched his

* See page 65 and second foot-note.

heart the least, if that heart had still beat. His speech
of 1846—which we have already referred to *—shows
what a high opinion he had of the great trans-Atlantic
republic.

The expressions of eulogy and regret were unanimous,
except in governmental circles, and in the midst of the
reactionary parties, united at this moment to check the
great political work that Thiers had so powerfully aided.
The Ministry at first endeavored to cloak its real sentiments.   Marshal MacMahon, absent at this moment,
telegraphed that the death of Thiers ought to be made a
national manifestation and not a party affair.   This was
a wise and worthy idea, but it could not be realized, for
the Government was at this very hour—without the Marshal knowing it perhaps—the Government of a party, and
it was not able to dissemble the fact.   The Ministry
wished to regulate the ceremony, to strip it of its national
character, and to make it a simple official manifestation.
On September 4th, a decree announced that the obsequies
of Thiers would be conducted by the State, which would
have given the Duke de Broglie the right to regulate the
ceremony to suit his fancy.   Mme. Thiers refused her
consent, not being willing at this supreme moment to see
the friends of her husband relegated to the background,
while his enemies were brought forward to the front.
She, therefore, took the matter of the arrangement of the
procession into her own hands.   She desired that the

* See pages 121-2.

pall-bearers be two members of the Institute, the ex-
President of the Chamber of Deputies and Thiers's ex-
ministers; that only these speak at the tomb, and that
the members of the last Chamber, and of all the Chambers of which Thiers had been a member, should occupy
the place ordinarily given up to the Chamber of Deputies.
These conditions, and a few others not less reasonable,
were repelled by the Ministry, and a second decree annulled that of September 4th, and rendered Mme. Thiers
free to carry out her wishes.

The population of Paris keenly resented these paltry
proceedings, by giving to the funeral a character that
would have best satisfied the dead Thiers, and which
was very distasteful to his enemies. Never did the people
of Paris display greater calmness, better deportment and
more tact. Guibert, Archbishop of Paris,—which high
position he owed to Thiers—refused the use of the
Madeleine for the funeral service, and the smaller church
of Notre-Dame de Lorette had to be taken.

But the demonstration must be followed step by step,
to comprehend its imposing grandeur and its remarkable
significance. Its description pertains to history. It was
in fact, the whole of France, modern France, child of the
new civilization and of the free thought that it inspires,
which followed the coffin of "the little *bourgeois.*"

Rain fell in the morning, a cold heavy rain which threatened to continue all day, and which caused the *Français*—
the Duke de Broglie's newspaper—to say: "We count on

the inclemency of the weather to frustrate the republican demonstration." Nevertheless, at an early hour, large bodies of people began to direct their steps towards the Place Saint-Georges. From the Latin Quarter—the region of the great Paris schools—came delegations of students. The Faubourg Montmartre and the adjacent streets, the rue Notre-Dame de Lorette and the Place Saint-Georges, were the theatre of unusual commotion. Soon troops arrive, clear the square before Thiers's house, and only those are allowed to pass who have cards of invitation.

The front railing and the large vestibule of the house were heavily draped with black. Here had been erected a catafalque, covered with black velvet and besprinkled with silver stars. Behind it stood three large candelabra with twenty branches each, and with all the candles burning. On the catafalque lay the coffin, quite hidden under a mass of flowers and wreaths of *immortelles*. On either side of the coffin, were displayed the numerous decorations of the deceased, covered with a veil of crape. Senators, deputies, members of the Institute, and other distinguished people filled the adjoining rooms. The magnificent hearse, drawn by six horses, arrived at half past eleven o'clock. A half hour was occupied in the preparations of departure. On the hearse were heaped the wreaths and other floral offerings. Among these was an immense wreath made of white and blue daisies and red roses, and bearing the motto, "The Youth of Paris to M. Thiers." Another bore the inscription, "The Frenchmen of California;" a second, "The United States to M. Thiers;" a third, "The Legation of the United States, Messrs. Washburne and Noyes." The procession left the house at a few minutes past noon for the church. Behind the hearse walked a servant, carrying on a rich cushion the various insignia and decorations of the deceased. A mass of notabilities of all grades and nations accompanied the remains to the church.

At half past twelve the procession entered Notre-Dame de Lorette, which was hung with black both inside and outside. The pompous ceremonies of the Catholic church over the dead were performed, and at half-past one, to the sound of martial music, the procession turned towards the cemetery.

The rain had ceased to fall as the column, taking the course of the main boulevards, commenced its march to Père-Lachaise. The crowd followed, profound, grave and silent, loaded with *immortelles*. The side streets and the sidewalks of the boulevards, the windows, balconies roofs and chimneys of the houses, the seats of carriages and cabs, and the tops of omnibuses were packed with people. The stores alone were shut. Every opening was filled with faces. People sat on the edge of windows and balconies, in order to give those behind a chance to come nearer the passing procession.

Silence ruled along the whole route. When it was broken for an instant, it was admirable to see how quickly it was resumed again. Silence was the republican watchword for that day. The young men from the schools, common people, the workmen were the first to signify to the crowd the necessity of restraining its feelings. Some cries were heard at the sight of the Belfort banner, where the name of the city stood out plainly in large silver letters on a black background. It awakened genuine emotion. On a few other occasions spontaneous outbursts of deep feeling came from the impetuous mass. The republicans of Paris could not resist cheering their representatives so harshly treated by the conspirators of May 16th, 1877. Cries of "Long live Gambetta!" "Long live Victor Hugo!" "Long live Louis Blanc!" were heard at intervals, mingled with "Long live the Republic!" But the sentiment of the situation ruled: all was silence at the least sign from the leaders in the procession. This unanimity of feeling, that swayed the immense throng lining both sides of the course throughout its length, was very remarkable: it proved that republican Paris had learned self-control.

When the procession had arrived at Père-Lachaise, the speeches began in front of the family vault. M. Grévy, President of the last Chamber, spoke first. His oration—a true manifestation of lofty and firm reason, especially remarkable by its explanation of Thiers's belief in republicanism—was received with a hearty sympathy, which would have burst into applause, if it had not been delivered at an open grave. Admiral Pothuau followed in a few words, eulogistic of the patriotism and the military

knowledge of the historian of the Republic and the Empire. M. de Sacy * spoke in the name of the French
Academy, and dwelt upon the literary talents of his colleague, and M. Vuitry † on those which had gained him
his seat in the Academy of Moral and Political Sciences.
And, finally, M. Jules Simon, former minister of Thiers,
who had worked with him for the establishment of the
Republic from the time of the February election in 1871
up to May 24th, 1873, spoke of that memorable and last
period of the life of the former president, and acquitted
himself of the task with his usual talent.

Each of these orators developed one side of Thiers's
life and character, and united, their speeches form a *résumé*
of both. But they all failed, however, to touch upon one
trait, very essential to the entire truthfulness of the portrait, and for the complete exposition of that character of a
representative of the France of the nineteenth century,
that we wish to portray. M. Simon said that Thiers
showed what his nature was, when he started out in
1870 on his peace mission to the various Courts of
Europe, and that it might be summed up in these
words : *Patriam dilexit, veritatem coluit.* " He loved his
country and the truth." And M. Simon might have added, that this love of truth embraced everything ; that it

---

* Silvestre de Sacy, (1801—), son of the celebrated orientalist of the same
name ; member of the French Academy in 1854 ; senator in 1865 ; and an
assiduous and famous writer for the *Journal des Débats* since 1828.

† Vuitry, (1842—), has held many high places in the French civil service ;
governor of the Bank of France under the Empire ; and member of the
Academy of Moral and Political Sciences in 1862.

would interest itself in the most elevated problems not only of politics but of life, and that the statesman whom he was celebrating was, at the same time, a philosopher like himself.

This side of Thiers must not be neglected. He had an elevated as well as a comprehensive intelligence. Although, as a child of the eighteenth century, and imbued with its ideas, he adopted, instinctively and through affinity, the spirit of Voltaire's philosophy ; nevertheless, he wished to demonstrate for himself and by himself its principles and its legitimacy. If he were not harassed like a Pascal by the problem of the origin and the end of man, his accustomed serenity was not the effect of indifference ; for the great enigma, especially in the last years of his life, was often a subject of his deepest meditation. He searched for the answer in the chemical laboratory with M. Pasteur,* at the observatory with Le Verrier, in his wide readings, and in moments of earnest reflection, snatched from his busy days and nights.

The peculiar character of Thiers's mind never drew him towards dangerous hypotheses or seductive novelties. His nature, so variable in the vivacity of its impressions, presented an unchangeable constancy in the domain of ideas. We have seen this in politics ; the same is true in metaphysics. At twenty, he stands with Voltaire and Vauvenargues for the philosophy of common sense ; at

---

* M: Pasteur, (1822 ——), is a member of the Institute, a distinguished chemist, and a special authority on the germ theory.

eighty, we find him holding the same belief, only more deeply rooted. The theories of modern science were not repugnant to him in so far as they went, but he would not be held back by them, when his aspirations carried him beyond their limits. He accepted their facts, but not their conclusions. He held to the old doctrine, which could not comprehend motion without an author and a cause. Though creation appeared to him a mystery, the doctrine that motion arose from an impulse in the nature of things, from the spontaneous impulse of life, and that it had always existed, did not appear to him simply a mystery; it was an absurdity. Between two obscurities, he chose the least. Between an incomprehensible mystery and the reversing of the laws of the mind, he did not hesitate. He saw the doubt, although, as far as he himself was concerned, he would not resign himself to it. He disliked to believe in a nothing which produces matter and spirit, or in an eternal infinity, blind and deaf, assuming finally by the evolutions of a perpetual *becoming* (*das Werden*)—to use the word of Hegel—a conscience and a voice. He went still further, and, consistent with himself, he admitted final causes. "I am," he once said to Barthélemy-Saint-Hilaire, using parliamentary language, "and I shall always be, a blind partisan of Providence."*

It is to be regretted, that Thiers did not have the time to draw up a statement of his philosophical faith, as he did in the case of his political creed. But we hope that

---

* " Je suis et je serai toujours le *ministériel* de la Providence."

this blank will be filled.   He left among his posthumous
writings, a work begun in 1862, in which is treated the
History of Humanity in its Relations with the World,
and in which he affirms his belief in that philosophy of
common sense which was his own.   M. Barthélemy-Saint-
Hilaire, a very competent judge in matters of this kind,
intends soon to lay before the world these last meditations
of his distinguished friend,—" this final work in which
culminated all his scientific studies, all his experience of
life, and where, in this greatest of all subjects, that mind,
in which everything was clear and strong, will make itself
manifest."*

Let us hope also, that this work will tell us what Thiers
thought of friendship, and that it will show us, what there
was that the poet Béranger proclaimed good, in the depth
of the soul of this man, who was so often obliged to
lend himself to cruel acts of repression, and who, the
day that he signed the treaty of peace with Prussia, and
on another occasion at the end of the Commune, when
he thought that the Louvre was burning, could not keep
back the tears.   Then we would have a complete Thiers,
a sort of moral pendant to the portrait that Bonnat has
left of him.

The sketch that we have just presented, we know too
well, will appear incomplete.   It will be discovered imper-
fect in several respects.   It will be found, more than once, to

---

* M. Caro, professor of philosophy at the Sorbonne, in a recent meeting
of the French Institute.

deviate from the real likeness and from the truth. Contemporaries are not in the situation of equitable posterity. Enemies are too prone to censure ; friends, to admiration, and we may seem to have been of the last. This is a mistake. If we are far from accepting the views of the monarchists in regard to Thiers, we are also free from idolatry. We know all the reproaches that the republicans have cast upon Thiers, and some of them we consider just. Thiers was not infallible. It would have been strange if he had been, in a career filled with struggles and revolutions, for he would have had to combat the prejudices of others without having any himself, or to have had only just prejudices, a character which has not yet been given to a mortal.

But it is not by the stumbles on the way that the traveler is to be judged, but by the strength that he displays, by the obstacles that he surmounts, by the results that he attains. Posterity contemplates a man from this standpoint. Looked at in this way, the history of Thiers, such as we have endeavored to paint it, presents itself in a light in which its faults disappear, and leave only in view the grand character of a representative of the France of the nineteenth century, the mental qualities that he displayed in his various rôles, and the services that he rendered his country and the Revolution.

It was in this light also that the people of Paris viewed Thiers, in the homage that it paid him on the day of his funeral, and which it repeated recently on the anniversary

of his death.   Gambetta said one day in our hearing,
that if Thiers had not died a republican, Paris would
never have given him the funeral honors that we have
just described.   This is perfectly true.   But it is necessary to add, that Thiers would never have been the man
he was, filled with the spirit of the age, with the soul of
the French Revolution, always ready to yield to public
opinion when it made itself clearly known, if he had not
become a republican.   In closing his life as he did, he accomplished his destiny, and Paris performed its duty in
showering honors upon him.

APPENDIX A.

REGISTRY OF BIRTH.

In the year V (1797) of the French Republic one and indivisible, the 29th Germinal (April 18th), at five o'clock, appeared before us, clerk of the municipality of the Midy, canton of Marseilles, and in the office of the town clerk, the citizen Marie Siméon Rostan, health-officer and *accoucheur*, living in the rue latérale du Cours, block one hundred and fifty-four, number 6, who presented to us a boy, whose *accouchement* he said he had conducted, and whom he declared to have been born the twenty-sixth of this present month (April 15th, 1797), at two o'clock and ten minutes, of the citizen Marie Magdeleine Amic and the citizen Pierre Louis Marie Thiers, a freeholder, then absent from home, and in the house of the mother, situated number 15, rue des Petits-Pères, block five, to which boy has been given the names Marie Joseph Louis Adolphe. Done in the presence of the citizens Pierre Poussel, a freeholder, living in the rue des Petits-Pères, and Jeanne Imbert, living in the same street, principal witnesses, of whom the second cannot write, but which we have signed along with the first witness and the aforesaid health-officer.

P. POUSSEL,

J .JOURDAN,   Rostan,
Assistant Town Clerk.   *Health-Officer.*

APPENDIX B.

EXTRACT FROM THE DIARY OF THE PHYSICIAN WHO WAS PRESENT AT THIERS'S BIRTH.

" At five o'clock this morning I was present at the *accouchement* of the daughter of Amic. A severe travail lasting twenty hours. Bad presentation. Gestatory period nearly ten months. Child of masculine sex, turbulent and very viable, although his lower limbs are poorly developed. The young mother was a prey to great mental anguish, which explains these accidents. Her husband was not at home, and she does not know what has become of him. The mother, Santi-Lomaïca, was at her daughter's bedside."

APPENDIX C.

THIERS'S LITERARY HONESTY.

From the numerous proofs of Thiers's literary conscientiousness, we select the three following. To a gentleman offering him some documents he writes :

"SIR :—I received your letter and the note that accompanied it. It has always been my habit, to accept all the documents offered me, and to collect the truth wherever I could hope to find it. I am, furthermore, very thankful to whomsoever aids me in my search. I will be greatly obliged, therefore, to you and your father, if you will be so kind as to send me the new documents, and thus enlighten me in regard to the errors I may have made. I know that a great number have escaped me ; but I would not be blamed for this, if people were aware of the strenuous efforts I have made to examine carefully the mass of evidence that I have had to go over.

I remain, sir, most respectfully yours,

A. THIERS,

Jan. 2nd, 1829.   No. 6 rue Cadet.

Thiers's *Notice to the Reader*, in the *History of the Consulate and Empire*, begins with this paragraph :

" I have at last finished, after fifteen years of assiduous work, the *History of the Consulate and Empire* that I began in 1840. Of these fifteen years, I have not allowed one to pass, except that which political events forced me to spend outside of France, without giving all my time to the difficult work that I had undertaken. I know the task might have been performed quicker, but I have such a respect for the mission of history, that the fear of stating an inexact fact fills me with a sort of confusion. I can have no repose, until I have found the proof of the fact about which I have my doubts ; I look for this proof wherever I think it possible to find it, and I do not stop until I have discovered it, or until I am certain that it does not exist." * * * *

President White of Cornell University,—an eminent authority on French history — substantiates Thiers's own statements. Speaking of the *Consulate and Empire* he says :

" As to its fidelity in detail, I have no doubt. After reading it years ago in Paris, I went to the Hôtel des Invalides, made the acquaintance of intelligent old soldiers of the Grande Armée, and was able to verify various

See footnote on page 351

curious and interesting details in it. Indeed, I may also say, that I have verified some very interesting details in his *History of the French Revolu tion*, in conversation with an old republican of that time." * * * *

APPENDIX D.

THIERS'S LETTER TO THE VOTERS OF THE NINTH ARRON- DISSEMENT OF PARIS.*

[We have found in the papers of M. Thiers the following document. After having written the whole of it with his own hand, he had time to review the first part of it. The remainder needed revision, and he had reserved this task for the day that took him from us. We have not thought it best to make any change in these last views of M. Thiers, and, in publishing this document which he intended to publish himself, we only con- form to his wishes, which always had in view the truth and the public good.

MIGNET.]

MY DEAR CONSTITUENTS :
            The Chamber of Deputies elected in February, 1876, was in May, 1877, denounced before France by the Execu- tive, condemned by the Senate, and sent before the country, its unique and final judge. The Assembly has the legitimate right to defend itself, and I, in the name of my colleagues and my- self, am about to exercise this right, which no power can or will, doubtless, try to limit.

As for myself, I took so little part in the work of the Cham- ber recently dissolved, that I think I can consider myself an impartial witness of what it did, and I do not hesitate to say, with its distinguished president, M. Grévy, that it has not ceased for an instant to merit the thanks of France for its prudence, its moderation and its patriotism.

It is true that two ministries have fallen since the Assembly convened, but was this due to the Assembly or to the Execu- tive and his Cabinet ? The first of these ministries succumbed to the will of the Senate, as was stated by its able chief, M.

---

* The text that has been followed, is that of the *République Française*, (Gambetta's newspaper,) of September 25th, 1877.

Dufaure ; the second fell by the rupture between the Executive and the Assembly, a rupture which occurred very unex-
pectedly on May 16th of this year, and which has never yet
been completely explained.

Let us look for its explanation in the facts themselves, briefly
but sincerely stated. When this Chamber—the first elected
since the institution of the Republic—came together at Versailles, there was ground for some apprehension at the thought
of the multitude and gravity of the questions about to be submitted to deputies, for the most part new, and not very familiar
with public affairs.

There were five things to fear : 1, That, on account of the
enormous burdens bequeathed to the Republic by former governments, the difficulty of meeting these burdens would give
rise to projects of taxation, which would be contrary to true
financial principles ; 2, that the necessity of responding to the
simultaneous armament of all the European nations would give
birth to modes of recruitment, which would be detrimental to
the welfare of the army ; 3, that the political conduct of certain
prelates towards neighboring nations, certain pretensions of
the clergy irreconcilable with the ancient principles of the Gal-
lican Church, would provoke discussions that would endanger
the good relations between the Church and the State ;* 4, that,
in the midst of the general emotion produced in Europe by the
events in the East, the French tribune, so impetuous under the
Monarchy, would not be less so under the Republic, and that
thence would arise new difficulties for the maintenance of peace ;
5, and, finally, that the attitude of the majority of the Senate
towards the Chamber of Deputies, its disposition to oppose all
the views of the elective Chamber, its often-manifested preference for the monarchical form of government, and, in fine, its
pretension to participate actively in the vote of the budget,
would occasion dangerous conflicts between the two bodies.
The darkest forebodings were entertained everywhere on this
point. As for myself, if I was not so prompt to predict con-
tentions that I was far from desiring, I was not, nevertheless,
entirely free from fear.

---

* During the spring of 1877, some of the French bishops in their charges
declared that the Pope was a prisoner, berated the Italian Government very
severely, and called upon President MacMahon to re-instate him by force.
They also advocated vigorously the temporal power of the Pope.

In regard to the army, it was proposed to reduce the term of military service from five years to three years, and this Chamber, which was accused of favoring the abolition of standing armies, named a committee which rejected the proposal before it was scarcely presented.

As regards ecclesiastical affairs, the Church budget, by a singular coincidence of circumstances, was discussed at the very moment when public opinion was the most excited over the charges of certain bishops. But this budget left our hands increased by several hundred thousand francs ; no proposition threatening to the Concordat* was entertained, and the charges in question, deplored by all enlightened catholics, were only subjected to the mild censure of an order of the day.

But, some say, it would have been better not to have said anything about them. That is true ; but in order not to have had anything said, the charges should not have been written. And furthermore, if, after the first charge, the pen of our prelates had been laid aside, the matter would not have been so serious. But a second attack, still more violent, followed the first, a third was being prepared, and it was absolutely necessary to put a stop to this war of words, which was endangering the quiet of the public mind at home and peace abroad. In spite of these acts, the Church budget, we repeat, was not reduced but increased ; the Concordat remains untouched, and all unfortunate debate on this subject has been avoided or cut short.

Every tribune of Europe has, at the same moment, re-echoed with long discussions concerning foreign affairs. At Berlin, Vienna, Rome, London, Belgrade, Bucharest and Athens, the Eastern question has been debated. Everybody has spoken, even the diplomates who generally are quiet, and who have chosen the banks of the Bosphorus in order that their voices may be heard. Europe has been able to judge if it was in the interest of peace ! Paris alone was silent, and in our Chamber of Deputies, which, being young, might have been ambitious, there was but one opinion, and that was, to be silent. And this plan was followed, not that we might be thought skillful diplomates, but that no new sources of excitement might be added to the universal agitation.

---

* In July, 1801, Bonaparte, as first Consul, forced a Concordat out of Pope Pius VII, which was ratified in 1802, and which has ever since regulated the relations of the French Catholic Church with Rome. The Church became subordinate to the State in temporal matters, and the appointment to the bishoprics was retained by the Government.

There remained one more subject of a disagreeable nature which it was necessary to avoid : the relations between the two Chambers. When the Senate was seen to favor the election of candidates most notoriously hostile to the Republic, and eagerly entertained propositions directly opposed to the wishes of the Chamber of Deputies, it would not have been strange if this Chamber retaliated, especially on the occasion when the Senate made amendments to the budget.* But what really happened ? The Senate made seven amendments to the budget. Never in England has the House of Commons admitted the right of the House of Lords to interfere in financial matters, and if the latter suggest on this subject a good idea, it is not allowed to be made in the form of an amendment. In order that it be accepted, it must come through the House of Commons.

Everybody knew this. It was stated by eloquent voices. Nevertheless, on the motion of M. Jules Simon, the right of the Senate, though very questionable and strongly disputed, was admitted, and, of the seven amendments, five were accepted by the Chamber of Deputies ! Some will say that this was because the Senate was right. Perhaps so ; but, if this were so, the Chamber of Deputies deserves some praise for having condemned itself. And we ask of everybody who has in his breast a spark of the sentiment of justice, if the Senate, treated with so much deference by the Chamber, acted rightly in dissolving it.† But wait a few days. The Senate which has judged the Chamber will soon in its turn be judged by the country, the judge of us all, the highest and final judge.

Let us recapitulate these facts : The income-tax removed ; the term of military service preserved ; the church fund increased ; the Concordat untouched ; a simple order of the day opposed to dangerous charges ; absolute silence on foreign politics ; and, lastly, in regard to the relations between the great State bodies, marked deference on the part of the Chamber towards the Senate, and the very questionable financial pretensions of the latter conceded without contestation. Such are the facts as known to France and all Europe.

How explain then the onslaught made on this Chamber ?

---

* Towards the end of December, 1876.

† According to the present French Constitution, the President can dissolve the Chamber only when seconded by the Senate.

They say it was radical. Radical! What means this word, new at least in France, and now first introduced into our political language? Nobody speaks any more of socialism, and this is very natural. There was a time when it was proper in France to speak of socialism, for people were continually discussing property rights, the labor question, progressive taxation, the equality of wages, free and unlimited credit. These terms are now almost forgotten here, though they are being taken up in other quarters. Moral epidemics, like physical epidemics, rage for a while, and, when they have spent their force in one country, pass on to another.

Socialism has invaded neighboring lands, powerful and glorious, which have taken it in hand without showing any fear of it, for they know that real or affected alarm only renders epidemics more dangerous, and they are aware that with moral epidemics the only efficacious remedy is time, reason and liberty. It was in this way that we rid ourselves of socialism, and so will be delivered from it all the other countries that it has attacked.

But what is meant by radicalism, this word employed by the ministers of May 16th?* If by it is designated a certain conception of the democratic spirit, which threatens the civil administration, the finances, the army, the Church, and the good understanding that should exist between the different branches of the Government, if it mean the intervention of Parliament in foreign affairs, then, indeed, a Chamber should be energetically resisted which should allow itself to pursue such a policy.

But to call a Chamber radical which does not even discuss an income-tax ; which maintains intact the term of military service ; which votes the appropriations for all the religions recognized by the State, and augments notably that of the Catholic church ; which, in the presence of condemnable acts of certain bishops, restricts itself to a simple vote of censure, when all other citizens would run the risk of being severely punished for similar acts ; which, far from denying the just powers of the Senate, grants this body rights which England does not grant the House of Lords, and treats with scrupulous consideration an Upper House which does not reciprocate its courtesy ; should such a Chamber be called radical? No, the ministers may say so, but you will not think so.

---

* The republican cabinet of Jules Simon was dismissed by MacMahon,. and the Duke de Broglie, a moderate royalist, became President of the Council, with the notorious Fourtou, an old Bonapartist,. as Minister of the Interior, on May 16th, 1877.

And if, from these questions of principle, we pass to certain questions of an incidental nature that presented themselves, and which the enemies of the Republic hoped to make the occasion of attacks and trouble, such as amnesty and the law concerning university education, what happened?

For the last six years, permanent courts-martial have sat, daily pronouncing sentence on fresh victims of the Commune, who had returned to work or were ready to, and shutting them out from employment, rather than definitely establishing them in some occupation. It was high time to put an end to these prosecutions, and the Chamber did it. Other condemned Communists, transported to distant climes, displayed the best signs of repentance, by cultivating the soil and sending for their families. Those should be judiciously pardoned, and the Chamber left to the Executive the care of carrying this provision out, in meritorious cases and without harming the cause of justice. In the place of troubles resulting from this policy— troubles that had been predicted and perhaps desired—it had a pacifying effect.*

Many worthy people, liberal and religious, in the good accepta- tion of the word, regretted the creation of two systems of uni- versity education, one laic, the other Catholic, the two tending to perpetuate the existence of two nations within the nation, and, in the interest of national unity, they wished the law had never been made or carried out.† Others, more moderate, preferred that the matter be limited to the restitution to the State, of the rights which belonged to it in the conferring of degrees. The Chamber of Deputies—favoring the more moderate solution of the question—adopted the latter view. But the Senate refused to restore to the State its incontestable rights. The Chamber yielded, and the question was dropped.

When it is remembered that the Chamber was new; that every new Chamber has to be educated; that it is necessary to familiarize, with the enormous figures of the budget, men who have no idea of the expenses of a great State; to reconcile them with the central authority, which they have often com- bated in the Municipal Councils and the Councils-General;‡

---

* From December 1877 to June 1878, Marshal MacMahon pardoned or commuted the penalties of 890 Communists. The question of complete amnesty is now (1878) being agitated in the Chamber of Deputies.

† This law was passed in 1875.

‡ Each department has a Council-General (*conseil général,*) which may be likened to an American State Legislature.

that it is required to prove to them the utility, or at least the necessity of certain taxes which are the bane of their district ; that, all of them coming up with projects for internal improvements for the sea-ports, roads, canals and railways of their departments, have to be made to understand that, to carry out these improvements, useful without doubt, the State is powerless and time all-powerful ; that they are thus forced to undergo a series of disenchantments, which explains the fact that every vote of a new Legislature is a source of anxiety and danger to the Government ;—on considering these things, would it be surprising if the new Chamber—the first of the Republic—had met with the common fate and perhaps committed some blunder, passed some hasty vote, which would have to be reconsidered at the following sessions ? Far from this, the Chamber which was recently dissolved, has disappointed not our hopes, but our fears. To our great surprise, we found it pervaded by a spirit of good will not known in the last Chambers of the Empire, which were recruited from a democracy already republican, and unable to control a sort of feeling of bitterness towards a power which was not congenial to it. This Chamber, however, finding itself in harmony with the administration, desired the success of the Government and came to its aid. Discreet, moderate, intelligent, always ready to meet half way, without deception and without weakness, it knew how to avoid all dangers, except one, on which it did not fall of itself, but which seemed to be thrown in its way, like a rock suddenly rising from the waves.

But, I am told, you forget the shocking scenes that occurred there. No, not at all, I have not forgotten them. I saw them, and they are the worst, the most scandalous in which I have taken part for a half century. I have seen the rules violated, the President of the Chamber insulted, not being able to make his voice heard or his authority respected. Yes, I have witnessed all this. But can these scenes be laid at the door of the last Chamber? They were provoked not by it, but against its wishes ; by its enemies united for the overthrow of the Republic, and if, in its indignation, the Chamber did not instantly repress these disgraceful spectacles by an act of authority, it was not because the Chamber was weak, but because it had regard for the feelings of its enemies.

But let us leave this subject. The question is not concerning the faults of the Chamber, for it had none. Everything that has been said on this point is pure fabrication. Let us rather seek the truth in this matter, and the country, before whose eyes all has happened, will recognize it and proclaim it.

Here is the truth : In 1873, when the country saw administrative affairs, the army and the finances re-established, and the foreign enemy departed from our soil, a universal cry arose for the abandonment of the provisional form of government, and for the establishment of a permanent government, that is to say, to give to each party, weary of waiting, the government of its choice. But there were three monarchical parties,* and but one throne. The idea of gratifying them had, therefore, to be abandoned. As for myself, my mind was made up. In the presence of these three competitors, the Monarchy was impossible. The Republic was difficult without doubt, but possible if prudence and wisdom were exercised. Under the Republic France had just been revived. I would have preferred that the question had not been brought up, but it could no longer be evaded. A simple deputy, elected President of the Republic by my colleagues, I stated the question without allowing myself to solve it. I could do neither more nor less. The three monarchical parties, united in the common design of resisting the establishment of the Republic, proposed to the Assembly that it separate itself from me, and, as I was not less desirous of separating myself from it, I handed in my resignation, for which my successor did not have to wait ten minutes.

I might have remained in office as long as the Assembly itself : I was authorized so to do by a constitutional law ;† I could have done so on one condition : by dismissing a ministry in which I had confidence, and which had powerfully aided me in the work that I had accomplished. I was not willing to do this. A king, whom the monarchical principle obliges to remain at the head of the State, may employ this means of satisfying public opinion ; but an elective chief, chosen for the very reason that he always held that the Government ought to be in accord with the majority in the representative Chamber, from the moment that this accord ceases, is bound to resign. It is true that the country was with me, but not the Assembly which had elected me. I had a motive still loftier than my personal

---

* The legitimists, with the Count de Chambord at their head, the Orleanists, who allied around the Count de Paris, and the Bonapartists, led by the Prince Imperial.

† The Rivet Constitution. See pp. 229-232.

dignity, the most powerful and the most vital interest of the country. The question of the Monarchy or the Republic is the torment of France. To settle it is of prime importance for the nation's repose, well-being and future. As long as I remained in office, the question did not stand on its own merits ; it could be said that my ill-will was the only obstacle in the way of the re-establishment of the Monarchy. If I were out of the way, there would be the most astonishing and decisive evidence in favor of the Monarchy.

Well, through the action of the victorious majority, the Government was abandoned to the whole body of declared and well-known partisans of monarchy, who thenceforth had their own way. In defiance of the laws, and regardless of propriety, the crown of France has been hawked along the highways of Europe by men without authority ; and, after all these efforts, witnessed by all nations, it has been found necessary to admit that the Monarchy is impossible. One trial should have been enough. The first cost the country so dear, that it should not have been soon repeated. But everybody did not look at the question in this light ; and, a second time—on May 16th last—a final and signal demonstration was made.

On May 16th, 1877, as on May 24th, 1873,* the same sad spectacle was witnessed of three monarchical parties, united for the moment for the overthrow of the object of their common hatred, suddenly dissolving the union and loading each other with abuses and threats ; then, when they feel that it is dangerous to continue the rupture, coming together again, only to fall apart once more, and to fill France with disgust and Europe with commiseration for a grand and noble nation, given over to such deplorable distractions.

Then began that state of affairs, which could not last, of a republican constitution with an anti-republican administration : and herein lies the cause of the dissolution of the Chamber. In every branch of the civil service, and especially in those of a political nature, there have been—if we make a few exceptions—sub-prefects† governing in the name of the Republic, and not concealing either their aversion to it, or their conviction that it was impossible, or the hope that it would not last. In other divisions of the Government—where propriety

* The date of Thiers's resignation. See Chapter IX.
† A sub-prefect (*sous-préfet*) is the chief executive of an *arrondissement*, one of the divisions of a department.

imposed more reserve—the same sentiments existed, though kept in the background, and, descending from the great centres to the minor provincial offices, where people are under less restraint, the pettiest office-holders were found to entertain the same opinions. This state of things grew worse as the republican office-holders, or those converted to republicanism, who owed their places either to the Government of September 4th,* or to the Government of which I was the head, were successively eliminated, and, in a short time, we saw a government, republican in form, in the hands of an anti-republican administration.

This state of affairs, which always confuses the public mind, ended, after many changes, by becoming intolerable. When, after the elections of February, 1876, which went republican, the Chamber, which had been dissolved a short time before, came together again, it made known at Versailles the astonishment and disapprobation of the country. It acted discreetly, and the ministers chosen from its midst, obeying its wishes, made some modifications in this contradictory state of things, which put authority in the hands of men opposed to the nature of the government which they served. But, hampered in their efforts, they only partially satisfied a nation which expected a thorough change.

At each adjournment the Chamber remarked this spirit of discontent, and on re-assembling at Versailles it again called the attention of the ministers to the fact. It urged the subject upon them, not rashly but calmly, with regard for the feelings of the ministers whom it esteemed, and whose embarrassments it was aware of. It was impossible, in fact, that this lack of harmony should not soon become a subject of prime importance.

I declare before the country—certain of not being contradicted by it—that the situation is such as I have just described it.

From the force of necessity, the monarchical parties have conceded the Republic as a principle ; but they have seen fit to reserve the real power to themselves, and we have had, I repeat, a republican constitution with an anti-republican administration and anti-republican office-holders.

Every nation has a right to the form of government that pleases it, and when this government has been established, it has the right to require that this government be served loyally. Nobody is forced to serve a government that he does not like,

---

* See page 196, foot-note.

but if he accept it, and especially if he take office under it, he is bound to perform his duties faithfully, with a desire for the success, not for the overthrow of the form of government. Everybody, of course, has the right to aspire to office, whatever may be his party or his origin ; in fact, it is to be desired that men of experience—old public servants—continue to serve the State, but always on condition that they serve it loyally.*

It will be remembered that at Bordeaux† we, who served the Republic, were formerly monarchists. This, however, was not true of all. But we were demanded ; we did not step forward without being called, and we took office purely through good-will, because our presence re-assured the alarmed nation. And at last we were convinced of the necessity of the Republic. I wish the Republic many similar servitors, and from whatever quarter they may come, they will always be welcomed if they are honestly determined to help on the common cause, which, if it succeed, will be a blessing and not a detriment to France.

The question, therefore, raised by the proceeding of May 16th, may be summed up as follows : Is the Republic needed, and, if so, should it be firmly established by men who wish its success ? Herein lies the whole question at issue.

Now, I ask every honest man, to whatever party he may belong, if the Count de Chambord could be placed on the throne with the opinions that he professes and with the flag that he unfurls, or if it is hoped that he may some day be acceptable after he has modified his views? We respect him too much to believe it. I will say nothing of the Orleans princes, who wish to be mentioned only after the Count de Chambord, according to their hereditary rank ; but I ask if the country is ready to receive the Prince Imperial, who, though innocent of the misfortunes of France, suggests them so keenly, that the nation still shudders at the bare mention of his name? Nobody dare answer me yes ; and, in fact, all the friends of these candidates postpone, until a future time, the day when their claims

---

* Thiers must not be understood to advocate our pernicious American system of office-holding. He simply means, that office-holders should believe in the nature of the government they are serving, not in the infallibility of this or that party or chief, who all advocate the same form of government.

† The National Assembly, elected February 9th, 1871, first meet at Bordeaux, where it remained until March of the same year, when it removed to Versailles.

may be put forward. The truth of this statement is seen in
the fact that they make no move, though the greatest indulgence
has been shown all the monarchical parties.

Now, until this day—more or less distant—arrive, what will
France do ? France will wait until her future masters are
ready : until one is brought over to other ways of thinking,
until another has made an advance in his right of succession,
and until a third has finished his education. In the meanwhile everything will be in suspense, commerce, industry, finances, State affairs. How can business men be asked to engage
in great industrial enterprises, and financiers to negotiate loans,
when the future threatens fresh political troubles ? And how
can foreign Cabinets be expected to strengthen their relations
and form alliances with us, when French policy is liable to be
directed by new chiefs and influenced by new ideas? Dare
anybody ask such sacrifices of a great nation, that Europe has
admired in its prosperity and also in its misfortunes, on seeing
it restored once more, on seeing it revive again, displaying a
rare wisdom in the midst of provocations, which it endures
with such *sang-froid* and calm firmness ?

Some men who, because they call themselves monarchists,
believe that they know the secrets of the crowned heads, pretend that their reign is desired, and that then France will
regain its prestige and alliances. But we would say to these
men who think they understand Europe, but who, in reality,
know nothing about it, and attribute to it their own ignorance
and prejudices, that Europe looks with pity on their pretensions
and hopes, and blames them for having got their country into
the present trouble, instead of giving it the only form of government possible to-day. This Europe was formerly under absolute princes, but, recognizing the march of time, it is now ruled
by constitutional princes, and is satisfied with the change.
Europe understands that France, after the fall of three dynas-
ties,* has gone over to the Republic, which, during the last six
years, has lifted the country out of the abyss into which the
monarchists precipitated it. Europe has seen our military
prestige destroyed and a new prestige take its place, that of
the inexhaustible vitality of a prostrate country, suddenly rising
up and furnishing the world an unheard of example of re-

---

* The legitimist in 1793, and again in 1830; the Bonapartist in 1815,
and again in 1870 ; and the Orleanist in 1848.

sources of every kind, so that France, even after Wörth, Sedan and Metz, has shown herself to be great still. It was under the Monarchy that she fell, but under the Republic that she arose again. And once more on the road to prosperity, it was the monarchists again that threw obstacles in the way of her reconstruction. If it be the esteem of Europe that is sought, listen to Europe, hearken to its opinion !

For this it is, that we persistently ask if there be any other alternative than the following : Either the Monarchy, which is impossible, because there are three claimants and but one throne ; or the Republic, difficult to establish without doubt, not because of itself, but because of the opposition of the monarchical parties, and, nevertheless, possible, for it is supported by an immense majority of the people.

It is the duty, therefore, of this immense majority of the people to consult together, to unite and to vote against those who resist the establishment of the only government possible. The Monarchy to-day, after the three revolutions that have overthrown it, is immediate civil war, if it be established now ; and if put off for two years, or three years, the civil war is only postponed until that epoch. The Republic is an equitable participation of all the children of France in the government of their country, according to their abilities, their importance, and their callings,—a possible and practical participation, excluding nobody except those who announce that they will govern only by revolution. The Republic is absolutely necessary, for everybody who is not blind or deceitful must admit, that it alone is possible after all that happened in October, 1873,* and all that has occurred since May, 1877.

Our adversaries will retort, perhaps, that we calumniate them in saying that they do not want the Republic. No, we do not believe that they will call themselves calumniated. Can they pretend that they have rallied to the Republic, when their past speeches, their language of to-day, their confidential talk and their polemics in the newspapers which represent them, proclaim them legitimists, Orleanists, or Bonapartists ; when, consenting

---

* During this month, the legitimists made a strong effort in favor of the Count de Chambord, but failed utterly through the count's refusal to accept the crown, except as an advocate of anti-revolutionary principles. The Duke de Broglie was one of the prime movers in this " monarchical conspiracy." On October 12th, elections were held in four departments, and the republican candidates were chosen.

to serve the Republic, they do not deign to name it ; when a municipal magistrate, receiving the President with the respect that is due him, and telling him that the people will be charmed to show him their attachment for republican institutions, is removed from office for using this language, as was his predecessor for a similar sin ! No, we defy our adversaries to call themselves republicans. We wish we could believe that they were republicans, because they would then aid in the only solution of the difficulties with which we are surrounded. We wish it ; but they will expose themselves to contradiction from every quarter, if they dare to declare that they are republicans.

Others may say, perhaps, that they will accept in earnest a good Republic, but they do not want a bad one. And we agree with them : we favor the good and not the bad Republic, and no one of us asks for any other. But when did this question of a bad Republic appear ? What day did this bad Republic show itself ? Was it when at Bordeaux, Versailles, or Paris, in the midst of disasters without parallel, and in the midst of ruins, it re-established a government, an army, and the finances, stamped out anarchy, caused the laws to be respected, paid an enormous indemnity, freed our soil from the enemy's troops, and made France herself again ? Was that the bad Republic ? And again, when, in the midst of all sorts of difficulties created by its adversaries, this Republic, belied, harassed, directed however by republican ministries, calmed the people, and, without being able to satisfy all their wishes, secured them a tolerable existence from February, 1876, to May, 1877,—was this a bad Republic ? You can decide this, by comparing the year 1876 with the year 1877. Ask an answer from industry, from commerce, from all Europe, witness to the truth of our assertions ; and all will answer you, and will tell you what a difference there is between the good and the bad Republic, for they have been able to compare them.

Yes, you made the bad Republic known to us on May 16th ! Though, doubtless, in an embarrassed condition on the eve of this change, though disturbed by your menaces, the Republic was, nevertheless, still active, laborious, peaceable, protected, because its legality was respected, and acknowledged by all the political parties, because circumstances forced them to accept it. But what a spectacle does the proceeding of May 16th present ! Its authors say : We appeal to the country that it may make known its wish. It would be proper, then, to let the country speak freely, and especially to let it speak as soon as possible ; for such a state of critical suspense as the present cannot be made too short. While all our other governments have never taken more than twenty or thirty days to get a response, and on but one occasion sixty, this Government not only takes the three months authorized by law, but to these three months is added, by a manifestly illegal interpretation, a new delay ; and finally, instead of letting the country speak perfectly freely, since it is being consulted, the very contrary is done, by an outrageous violation of every observance. Not only are the essential principles of republican government ignored every day, but also the most incontestable principles of public right, observed among all free peoples, whether they live under a republic or a king.

In every free State the first care, when an election is to be held, is to obtain the untrammeled vote of the nation. With us, however, free discussion is interfered with on every hand ; the news-venders and the railroads are forced to surrender at discretion, without the Government giving a thought to the trials of those who are thus deprived of their daily bread ; and office-holders, who have nothing to do with politics, are struck down in order to intimidate rebellious voters.

Do they stop here ? No. Read what is written with impunity in the Government newspapers, with the Government's permission we may say, for the Government does not try to stop it. These newspapers speak out boldly, and declare that if the measures being taken do not defeat the return of the majority that was dissolved, the voice of the country must be disregarded. The Chamber should be again dissolved until the Government can have its way. The Constitution, in fact all constitutions hold that in case of a difference between the Chamber and the Government, the country is to be appealed to, and when it has spoken the difference is settled. Now, as it was not supposed that peoples or governments were fools, it was not laid down that, the country, having given its answer, should not be consulted a second or third time. Nothing was said on this point, because neither the governing body nor the governed were suspected of insanity. We should all use our common sense. The monarchists say that if the elections do not go as is wished, the Chamber will be again dissolved, and this will be repeated, as often as is necessary, until 1880.*

* This is the date fixed upon by the present (1878) Constitution of France,

But, though it takes time to bring about a dissolution, if December 31st arrive without the budget being voted, it will make no difference, the taxes will be levied without being voted. And, furthermore, there is the Senate. The Senate will vote the budget if there is no Chamber to do it, and then . . . and then . . . force remains, and force will be employed.

Such is their unblushing and audacious contempt of every law. I ask my contemporaries, those who recall the days of 1830, if, under M. de Polignac, anybody would have dared to say that, if the Chamber of Deputies did not vote the budget, the King and the Chamber of Peers could do so? No, evidently not; or the response would have been the same as that made to the famous Ordinances.*

Not only are the principles peculiar to a republic violated, but the simplest parliamentary principles observed by three constitutional monarchies† are disregarded. They would be guilty of an act that Napoleon III, in the height of his power, would never have dared to do : they would levy taxes that were not voted ! And, in fine, they write these criminal words, that if force be necessary, force will be used ! This is the bad Republic. It is the only one that has appeared since Bordeaux, and it is the production of the impetuous and audacious monarchical parties. Fellow citizens, here are the facts. You see them. It is not necessary to prove them. Have we ever had a more astounding example of the violation of every principle? Every means of circulation—the common property of all—usurped to profit an opinion ; every channel closed against the truth, when the nation needs and ought to know everything ; the insolent declaration that, if the country does not obey, does not vote as the Government orders, it will have to come to the polls again ; and that, if there is not time to vote the budget, the taxes will nevertheless be levied. This is published with impunity, this violation of every principle of a republic and a monarchy, of every principle no longer denied even at Constantinople. Personal violence is alone wanting ; and this will come if, as they have dared to propose, they add the crime—things must be given their right name—the crime of declaring the country in a state of siege ; that is, France called upon to vote under the jurisdiction of courts-martial. Such, I repeat,

when the Chamber and Senate are to unite in one body to decide what the future form of government will be, and to revise the Constitution.

* See page 35.

† The Restoration, the Orleans monarchy, and the second Empire.

is the Republic, not of the republicans, but of the anti-republicans. It belongs to them and to them alone.

What is the explanation of this misconduct? Here is the answer, which I have heard given for more than half a century: France is failing, is going to perish; she must be saved! Fatal idea, forerunner of all the faults of governments which go mad before falling to pieces. Alas! if this remark were true, how many times would not France have already perished! As often as she has been in trouble, as often as she has suffered, she has not perished; but those have perished who pretended to wish to save her. They have not been able to drag her down with them into the abyss; but she has risen up by the aid of honest men, who, after having in vain warned her of the peril with which she was being threatened, have done all in their power to protect her from it. And, in this connection, I pray the true conservatives, the honest men whom I do not confound with the sham conservatives who have the floor to-day,—I pray them to recall all the occasions on which they have exclaimed: France is in danger, let us save her, and to save her, let us resist, let us resist!

Resistance has been tried, and with what result? Under Charles X, under Louis-Philippe, and under Napoleon III the cry was: Let us resist. What was asked under Charles X? The recognition of the principle that the King could do nothing without the Chamber, that is to say, without the country. A resistance, culminating in the famous Ordinances, was kept up. But France did not perish; it was the throne of Charles X which was destroyed, and all parliamentary principles were, at the same time, consecrated by the Charter of 1830.* France suffered without doubt; but she soon revived, and it seemed as though her prosperity would continue a long time. One point, unfortunately, had been overlooked. The suffrage was too restricted. Two hundred thousand voters represented a population of thirty-seven million. It was evident to everybody that two hundred thousand citizens could not pretend to represent France entire. A modest reform, which would make thirty or forty thousand more voters, was demanded. Immediately was heard the cry: France is going to perish, if the revolution which is threatening be not resisted! Resistance was made: the revolution of 1848 broke out; and we had universal suffrage,

---

* See pages 48 and 49.

that is to say, from eight to nine million voters. France, however, did not perish, but constitutional monarchy, which might
have given us a judicious measure of liberty, did perish; and
France, after suffering—for every revolution occasions suffering
—became herself again and passed through the three years of
agitation and disorder, which brought her to Napoleon III.
He acted promptly, and, to save France, took away all our
liberties at one sweep. The Imperial Constitution of 1804 was
re-established. The press and Parliament were both muzzled.
Every year the budget could be discussed two weeks each session,
and then silence. The Emperor alone governed, the Emperor
alone! Every liberty was in his hands, which, in spite of himself, finally had to open. Every liberty escaped from him.
This would, perhaps, have saved him, if the old cry had not
been immediately sounded : France is going to perish! Then
he instinctively sought in war a refuge from regenerated liberty.
This time, indeed, France came near perishing. She was, however, only dismembered. She was obliged to yield to the victorious enemy an enormous portion of her riches. But finally
she recovered; and, after trying to re-establish the Absolute
Monarchy, she founded the Republic.

France has not perished; but three *régimes* have perished,
and France has been subjected to cruel trials, before she finally
attained, after three attempts, the modern democratic form of
government. She has made continual progress, presenting the
grandest spectacle of terror or admiration to the world, and
always showing herself worthy of the world's imitation.

I supplicate those honest men, those very honest and cultivated men, who are more cultivated than well-informed and
who are, unfortunately, very timid,—I supplicate them to look
at this picture of successive disasters and to reflect upon it.

The torrent—which they look upon as evil and before which
they cry each time, that France is going to perish, that resistance
must be employed, is it not this great century which is called
the nineteenth, and which sweeps all humanity along with it?
Who made this nineteenth century? Not we, no more than we
made the sixteenth, whence sprang Bacon and Descartes, that
is to say, modern philosophy; or the seventeenth century, the
age of Pascal, of Bossuet, of Newton and of Leibnitz; or the
eighteenth, which produced Montesquieu, Voltaire, Rousseau,
the great Frederick and that grand French philosophy, which,
applying the human mind to the study of the laws of society,

destroyed feudal monarchies, and which, applying science to the welfare of man, gave to Europe and the two worlds "the rights of man,—" not the equality of conditions but the equality of rights, the means of securing the equality of conditions in so far as possible ; which freed the serfs of Russia, the negroes of America, which gave steam to man, freedom of thought and freedom of conscience to all peoples ; which opened to the vision of men' the celestial spheres, and revealed to Laplace the secret of the world's system. And is not this resistance a veritable anachronism, this foolish resistance to that progress by which all humanity has so greatly profited, and of which France had the honor of giving the signal ? for she has marched, the torch of genius in her hand, at the head of humanity.

Would it not be well, therefore, after so many downfalls, to reflect, to ask one's self and to inquire, if it be not the march of humanity that is feared, if it be not this that is foolishly resisted ? France has not perished ; but three monarchies have perished. Their *débris* covers the ground ; their heirs, rising up again and threatening each other, wish to fight over the ruins. Let us stop them, let us compel them to support the Government of all, and to the profit of all, and let us repeat everywhere this truth :*

---

* The *fac-simile* of Thiers's handwriting, given at the commencement of this document, begins here and goes to the clause : " 2. The Republic is the form of government, etc,"

The French text of the *fac-simile* runs as follows :

" La monarchie n'est pas possible. Elle serait la guerre civile, ou différée ou immédiate.

" Faisons donc la République, la République honnête, sage, *dit* conservatrice, qui n'est pas impossible ; car elle commençait quand les héritiers intéressés des monarchies détruites sont venus la troubler et faire retentir à nos oreilles des menaces insensées et criminelles ; et vous, électeurs, à ces contempteurs de toute vérité, faites *leur* entendre une dernière fois, une fois décisive, les vérités suivantes, qui seront le résultat de votre vote :

" La nation seule est souveraine."

In the text, as published in the *République Française*, the first paragraph of the above extract reads as follows :

"La monarchie n'est pas possible ; elle aurait pour conséquence immédiate ou prochaine ia guerre civile."

In the second paragraph, the two words printed in italics do not occur.

We call attention to these little discrepances, because Mignet, in his introductory note, (see the beginning of Appendix D,) says, speaking of this letter of Thiers to his constituents : " —— he (Thiers) had time to review the first part of it. The remainder needed revision, and he had reserved this task for the day that took him from us. We have not thought it best to make any change in these last views of M. Thiers." (" Nous n'avons voulu faire aucune modification à la dernière pensée de M. Thiers.")

The reactionary newspapers of Paris pronounced this document apocryphal

The Monarchy is not possible ; it would have for its immediate or early result, civil war. Let us then found the Republic, the honest, wise, conservative Republic, which is not impossible ; for it began when the interested heirs of the fallen monarchies came to trouble it, and to make our ears ring with insane and criminal threats. And you, fellow citizens, by your votes, make these men who scorn the truth listen a last and decisive time to the following truths : 1. The nation alone is sovereign. 2. The Republic is the form of government by means of which the nation exercises its sovereignty. 3. The sovereignty is exercised by an elective chief executive, named the President of the Republic, and by two Chambers acting in accordance with the forms prescribed by the Constitution. 4. The elective chief executive can govern only with the co-operation of these two Chambers, and ministers approved by the majority. 5. The co-operation of one Chamber is not sufficient, and laws and subsidies voted by a single Chamber are absolutely null and void. 6. Taxes not voted by both Chambers can not be collected, and an attempt to levy them is an attack on the Constitution, on the property and liberty of the people. 7. In case of disagreement, attested by a vote, between the governing powers, and especially between the President and the elective Chamber, if this Chamber be dissolved, the executive power is bound to convoke a new one with the least possible delay. If the delay be protracted to a period longer than is absolutely necessary, the spirit of the law is violated ; if it be for more than ninety days, the text of the law is violated, and it should be looked upon as a defiance of the Constitution. 8. When the elections have been regularly held, the contest is at an end ; and resistance to the will of the nation is resistance to the Constitution itself. 9. A new dissolution can only occur after a session which gives rise to new questions, on which the country has not already voted. 10. Anything which violates the prescriptive rights rigorously deduced from our laws and Constitution, is an act of usurpation and a case of culpability provided for by Article 19 of the Constitution. 11. A free ballot is an essential principle. The expression of all opinions should be free, and every act which hinders this, by abusing the laws regulating the circulation of newspapers,

---

when it was about to be published, and said that it was a sharp dodge of the republicans to influence the elections then close at hand. This statement was even cabled to America. This *fac-simile*, however, gives the lie to the assertion and conclusively proves the authenticity of the document.

the hawking them on the streets, is an infringement on public rights. The daily press, the railroads, colportage, bill-posting, belong to the public. Nobody has a right to limit the freedom of the press beyond the regulations established in the interest of public morals. 12. As regards church matters, religious liberty is a principle of the French nation. Every sect recognized by the State should be protected, properly endowed, and profoundly respected, but should be strictly prohibited from interfering in State affairs. 13. French policy is a peace policy, except where the protection of national interests require a resort to force, and after the solemn decision of the public powers.

On these principles has been based the nation's policy since 1789. France wishes to continue to remain faithful to them, and it is important that you consecrate them decisively by your suffrages. It is the only wise and useful end that the nation ought to make to this crisis, and it may be briefly summed up as follows : National sovereignty, the Republic, liberty, scrupulous regard for the law, religious freedom, and peace.

Such are, my fellow citizens, the opinions of my whole life, and those of the nineteenth century, which will distinguish the history of France and of humanity, and which I trust you will support on this solemn occasion. A thousand calumnies will be cast upon me. You will reply to them by your votes, which have never been wanting for almost half a century.

A. THIERS.

G. P. PUTNAM'S SONS have in preparation a series of volumes, to be issued under the title of

CURRENT DISCUSSION,

A COLLECTION FROM THE CHIEF ENGLISH ESSAYS ON QUESTIONS

OF THE TIME.

The series will be edited by EDWARD L. BURLINGAME, and is designed to bring together, for the convenience of readers and for a lasting place in the library, those important and representative papers from recent English periodicals, which may fairly be said to form the best history of the thought and investigation of the last few years. It is characteristic of recent thought and science, that a much larger proportion than ever before of their most important work has appeared in the form of contributions to reviews and magazines ; the thinkers of the day submitting their results at once to the great public, which is easiest reached in this way, and holding their discussions before a large audience, rather than in the old form of monographs reaching the special student only. As a consequence there are subjects of the deepest present and permanent interest, almost all of whose literature exists only in the shape of detached papers, individually so famous that their topics and opinions are in everybody's mouth —yet collectively only accessible, for re-reading and comparison, to those who have carefully preserved them, or who are painstaking enough to study long files of periodicals.

In so collecting these separate papers as to give the reader a fair if not complete view of the discussions in which they form a part ; to make them convenient for reference in the future progress of those discussions ; and especially to enable them to be preserved as an important part of the history of modern thought,—it is believed that this series will do a service that will be widely appreciated.

Such papers naturally include three classes :—those which by their originality have recently led discussion into altogether new channels ; those which have attracted deserved attention as powerful special pleas upon one side or the other in great current questions ; and finally, purely critical and analytical dissertations. The series will aim to include the best representatives of each of these classes of expression.

It is designed to arrange the essays included in the Series under such general divisions as the following, to each of which one or more volumes will be devoted :—

INTERNATIONAL POLITICS,   NATURAL SCIENCE.

RECENT ARCHÆOLOGICAL DISCOVERY,

QUESTIONS OF BELIEF,

ECONOMICAL AND SOCIAL SCIENCE,

HISTORY AND BIOGRAPHY,   LITERARY TOPICS.

Among the material selected for the first volume (International Politics), which will be issued immediately, are the following papers :

ARCHIBALD FORBES'S Essay on "THE RUSSIANS, TURKS, AND BULGARIANS;" Vsct. STRATFORD DE REDCLIFFE'S "TURKEY;" Mr. GLADSTONE'S "MONTENEGRO;" Professor GOLDWIN SMITH'S Paper on "THE POLITICAL DESTINY OF CANADA," and his Essay called "THE SLAVEHOLDER AND THE TURK;" Professor BLACKIE'S "PRUSSIA IN THE NINETEENTH CENTURY;" EDWARD DICEY'S "FUTURE OF EGYPT;" LOUIS KOSSUTH'S "WHAT IS IN STORE FOR EUROPE;" and Professor FREEMAN'S "RELATION OF THE ENGLISH PEOPLE TO THE WAR."

Among the contents of the second volume (Questions of Belief), are :

The two well-known "MODERN SYMPOSIA;" the Discussion by Professor HUXLEY, Mr. HUTTON, Sir J. F. STEPHEN, Lord SELBORNE, JAMES MARTINEAU, FREDERIC HARRISON, the DEAN OF ST. PAUL'S, the DUKE OF ARGYLL, and others, on "THE INFLUENCE UPON MORALITY OF A DECLINE IN A RELIGIOUS BELIEF;" and the Discussion by HUXLEY, HUTTON, Lord BLATCHFORD, the Hon. RODEN NOEL, Lord SELBORNE, Canon BARRY, GREG, the Rev. BALDWIN BROWN, FREDERIC HARRISON, and others, on "THE SOUL AND FUTURE LIFE. Also, Professor CALDERWOOD'S "ETHICAL ASPECTS OF THE DEVELOPMENT THEORY;" Mr. G. H. LEWES'S Paper on "THE COURSE OF MODERN THOUGHT;" THOMAS HUGHES on "THE CONDITION AND PROSPECTS OF THE CHURCH OF ENGLAND;" W. H. MALLOCK'S "IS LIFE WORTH LIVING?" FREDERIC HARRISON'S "THE SOUL AND FUTURE LIFE;" and the Rev. R. F. LITTLEDALE'S "THE PANTHEISTIC FACTOR IN CHRISTIAN THOUGHT."

The volumes will be printed in a handsome crown octavo form, and wil sell for about $1 50 each.

G. P. PUTNAM'S SONS, 182 Fifth Avenue, New York.

www.ingramcontent.com/pod-product-compliance
Lightning Source LLC
Chambersburg PA
CBHW021711110726
47902CB00005B/1153